"A monumental work." —*Publishers Weekly*

Catherine Asaro has won numerous awards for her Saga of
the Skolian Empire novels, including the Nebula Award and
two *Romantic Times* Awards for Best SF Novel. Combining
cutting-edge scientific theory with grand romantic adventure,
this series represents space opera at its finest.

The Final Key is the second and concluding part of the story
arc known as Triad, which began in *Schism*. *Schism* ended
with the Skolian Empire torn asunder by personal conflict
within the royal family, as Sauscony defied her father and
joined the Skolian military.

Now in *The Final Key*, the Skolian Empire comes under
all-out assault from its nemesis, the Euban Concord, who
have undermined the Skolians via subterfuge and assassination, leaving them ripe for conquest. The war is devastating.
And the Skolian Empire's only hope is Sauscony, a young
woman barely out of her teens who hasn't even completed
her training as a cadet.

The fate of a vast interstellar empire rests in her untested
hands.

"Fans of this series will celebrate the return of these fantastic
characters. . . . This is an outstanding book."
—*Affaire de Coeur*

Tor Books by Catherine Asaro

THE SAGA OF THE SKOLIAN EMPIRE
Primary Inversion
Catch the Lightning
The Last Hawk
The Radiant Seas
Ascendant Sun
The Quantum Rose
Spherical Harmonic
The Moon's Shadow
Skyfall
Schism: Part One of Triad
The Final Key: Part Two of Triad

THE
FINAL
KEY

THE FINAL KEY

Part Two of Triad

Catherine Asaro

TOR®

A TOM DOHERTY ASSOCIATES BOOK
NEW YORK

This is a work of fiction. All the characters and events portrayed in this book are either products of the author's imagination or are used fictitiously.

THE FINAL KEY: PART TWO OF TRIAD

Copyright © 2005 by Catherine Asaro

A Tor Book
Published by Tom Doherty Associates, LLC
175 Fifth Avenue
New York, NY 10010

www.tor.com

Tor® is a registered trademark of Tom Doherty Associates, LLC.

ISBN 978-0-7653-3361-2

First Edition: December 2005
First Mass Market Edition: December 2006

Printed in the United States of America

P1

To Louis, James, and Gina,
with love

Contents

Acknowledgments

I would like to thank the following readers for their much appreciated input. Their comments have made this a better book. Any mistakes that remain are mine alone.

To Jeri Smith-Ready and Aly Parsons for their excellent reading and comments on the full manuscript; to Aly's Writing Group for insightful critiques of scenes: Aly Parsons, Simcha Kuritzky, Connie Warner, Al Carroll, J. G. Huckenpöhler, John Hemry, Ben Rosenbaum, and Bud Sparhawk.

A special thanks to my editors, Jim Minz and David Hartwell, for their support and suggestions; to my publisher, Tom Doherty; to Denis Wong for all his help; to art director Irene Gallo, publicist Jodi Rosoff, copyeditor Ed Chapman, production team Priscilla Flores, Jim Kapp, Meryl Gross, Milenda Lee, and Nathan Weaver; and to all the other good people at Tor and St. Martin's Press who did such a fine job making this book possible; to my excellent agent, Eleanor Wood, of Spectrum Literary Agency; and to Binnie Braunstein for her enthusiasm and hard work on my behalf.

A heartfelt thanks to the shining lights in my life, my husband, John Cannizzo, and my daughter, Cathy, for their love and support.

THE
FINAL
KEY

Prologue

"Make it stop, Hoshpa." Tears ran down the small boy's face, and his eyes were swollen from crying.

"It will get better." Eldrin murmured the words, agonized by the anguish of his six-year-old son, Taquinil. "It will get better." He sat on the floor cradling the boy in his arms, rocking him back and forth. He extended his telepathic reach as a shield against the pain that the boy couldn't block with his extraordinarily sensitive mind.

Gradually his mental shields muffled Taquinil's distress. The boy's sobs eased and his body relaxed. After several moments, Eldrin realized Taquinil had fallen asleep in his arms, his head against his father's shoulder. Eldrin breathed with relief. They had made it through another rough spell. He stood up, holding his son, and carried the boy to his room. After Eldrin tucked him in, he sat watching Taquinil sleep. Black hair was tousled about his son's face. Eldrin brushed back the disheveled bangs, and wished he could as easily brush away the boy's night terrors.

Footsteps sounded in the living room of the royal apartments. Startled, Eldrin straightened up. He glanced one last time to make sure Taquinil was peaceful. Then he went out to the hallway. Low voices were coming from the living room at the end of the hall.

Eldrin found Dehya, his wife, sitting on the sofa with one of her doctors. She had slouched down with her head thrown back, her eyes closed, and her long hair disarrayed like black silk. The doctor, Alaj Rajindia, was a dark-haired nobleman. The House of Rajindia provided the military with the neurological specialists who treated psions. Alaj was an expert in the medical treatment of telops, the telepathic operators who used the vast mesh of information that stretched across the Skolian Imperialate, tying the interstellar civilization together into a coherent whole. The existence of that mesh depended on the unique abilities of telops, and Dehya was the ultimate telop, the most versatile operator alive.

Alaj was checking her with a scanner. Eldrin hesitated, unsure if he should interrupt. Dehya had been in the webs for two days straight, working, and also chasing down clues about Vitarex Raziquon, the sadistic monster who kept appearing in Eldrin's nightmares. Eldrin hated that her concern about his dreams added to her exhaustion. In his nightmares, Raziquon was torturing him, blinding him, crippling him, leaving him in unbearable pain, except he had to bear it. But it wasn't *him;* he always awoke in the royal suite here on the Orbiter space station where he lived with his family.

Alaj was speaking to Dehya. "I'm going to prescribe it anyway. Take it. Exactly the dose I give. No more."

She sat up wearily. "I won't take it."

The doctor scowled at her. "You've tied your mind into knots. If you keep this up, you will injure your brain."

"Neural relaxants are dangerous."

"I'll monitor you." He set down his scanner and took an air syringe off his belt. As he programmed it, he said, "The molecules will form complexes with the neural structures and transmitters in your brain that interpret telepathic or empathic input. It will block the process enough to relax your mind."

"Relax." Dehya exhaled. "I've forgotten what that is like." She leaned back and closed her eyes. "All right. Do it."

Alaj injected her with the syringe. "It doesn't need long to take effect."

"And tomorrow?" she asked. "When I want more?"

"You'll be fine." Alaj slid the syringe into its case on his belt. "I've given you just enough to release your neurological knots. You may be edgy tomorrow, but you'll think more clearly."

"All right." She already sounded calmer.

"Contact me if you have any problems," Alaj added.

"Hmmmm . . ."

"You shouldn't stay alone. Is your husband here?"

Eldrin walked over to them. "Yes, I'm here." He pushed down the tugs of suspicion he felt any time another man came near his wife. "Is she all right?"

"I'm fine." Dehya opened her eyes dreamily. "Just fine."

Alaj looked up at him. "You'll need to tend her. Can you do that? Perhaps I should call in help for you."

Eldrin stiffened. Even though he had been married to Dehya for seven years, her people still patronized him. "Of course I can look after her." He hesitated, reluctant to reveal his ignorance but fearing a lack of knowledge on his part could endanger his wife. "What did you give her?"

"It's a Kyle relaxant," Alaj said.

Eldrin had no idea what he meant. "I see."

Alaj was watching him closely. "It's analogous to a muscle relaxant. If you push yourself too hard and too long, physically, your muscles can spasm. Keep pushing after that, and you could do serious damage. You need something to relax the spasm. I gave her the neural analog of that medicine."

Eldrin had never reached his physical limitations. In that sense, he didn't know what Alaj meant. But he had seen his father's epileptic seizures. Although his father had been in treatment for years, in his youth he had apparently almost died from the severity of his attacks. Several times Eldrin had suffered similar episodes—not epilepsy, but still an overload to his densely packed, overdeveloped neural structures. For him, it had happened in combat. Battle lust, they called it, but it was actually a convulsion. He couldn't control it. Dehya obviously had no desire to cause harm, nor did she suffer epilepsy, but he could see how the tremendous neurological strain could cause her mind to tie itself into knots in a manner similar to a muscle spasm. At his request, the Skolian doctors had treated him so he would never again experience those rages.

"I understand," he told Alaj.

"Good. Just stay with her." He turned to Dehya, who smiled at them both, her black lashes shading her eyes in a lush fringe. Alaj squinted at her, then turned back to Eldrin. "Make sure she doesn't wander off or hurt herself."

"You worry too much, Doctor Alaj." Dehya languorously

rose to her feet and shooed him toward the door. "Go on. Go treat my nephew's bodyguards. They always look stressed. Just imagine their lives, guarding him."

Although Alaj smiled, he seemed more alarmed than amused at the mention of her nephew, Kurj Skolia, the Imperator—military dictator of an empire. Eldrin had never seen the Imperator in that negative light; in many ways, Kurj was like a father to him.

"Call me if you have any trouble," Alaj told her.

"I will." Dehya pushed him out the door. "Go on."

Eldrin watched her, intrigued. She was far more relaxed this evening than was usual for his restrained, aloof wife. He thought of how she had looked up at him through her dark lashes. As he considered her, she turned and smiled slowly. Then she came over and put her arms around his neck.

"My greetings, gorgeous," she murmured.

He grinned and slid his arms around her waist. "You should take this medicine more often."

A shudder went through her. "I hope not."

He didn't want her mood to darken. Bending his head, he kissed her cheek. "It's certainly put you in good spirits."

She relaxed, pliant against him. "Doctor Alaj thinks I need to sleep more," she said softly. "What do you say? Bedtime?"

Eldrin laughed, his lips against her ear. "I think he is a wise doctor."

"Is Taquinil all right for the night?"

His good mood faded. "I hope so." He lifted his head so he could look down at her. "He had another attack. I got him to sleep just before you came home."

"Ah, no. I knew I felt something." She took his hand and headed down the hall. "It's no wonder my mind was in such terrible knots, if he was hurting."

As they reached Taquinil's room, Eldrin heard the boy mumbling in his sleep. Light from the living room filtered into the bedroom. Taquinil was a mound under the quilt, his cheek against the pillow. Even with his son sleeping, Eldrin felt the boy's mental strain.

And yet, as they approached the bed, Taquinil breathed out, long and slow, his body losing its rigid tension under the quilt. He sighed and settled deeper into the covers. Even in the dim light, Eldrin saw the dramatic change as the drawn lines of the boy's face smoothed out.

Dehya sat on the bed, taking care not to jostle her son. When she took his hand, he turned toward her, and his shoulders released their clenched posture. His fists uncurled and his breathing deepened.

"That's amazing," Eldrin said.

Dehya pressed her lips against Taquinil's forehead. Then she carefully let go of his hand and stood up so she and Eldrin were standing side by side. "He's so peaceful."

"He's a treasure." Eldrin drew her out of the room so they could talk without waking Taquinil. "How did you do that? It's the first time in days I've seen him at peace."

She walked down the hall with him. "I didn't do anything."

"Maybe it's the Kyle relaxant. It affects Taquinil, too."

She came to a stop in the entrance of the living room. "Gods, I hope not. It's nothing Taquinil should ever take."

"Not the drug. He has none of its chemicals in his body. But he's such a sensitive empath. He senses your relief and it eases him." It wouldn't be that unusual; among the three of them, they often affected one another with their moods and health. This was a more dramatic effect than usual, but not unreasonable.

"If that helps, I'm glad." She pulled him close, and her body curved against him. Her voice turned throaty. "We were discussing our own bedtime, if I remember correctly."

Eldrin's pulse surged. This wasn't his reserved wife, the restrained and distant Ruby Pharaoh of the Skolian Imperialate. In the darkness of their bedroom, the ice queen often melted in his arms, but tonight she was heating up before they came near their bed. He pulled her into a kiss, hungry, and he was still kissing her when they stumbled into their room. They fell onto the floater together, and the pillows bounced around them. Out of habit, he and Dehya shielded their minds, giving them privacy from everyone but each other.

Eldrin ran his hands over her slight curves and scraped at the fastenings of her jumpsuit. The cloth crinkled as he dragged the outfit off her body. Then he held her breasts, kneading them, probably too hard, but she didn't object. As her breathing quickened, she tugged at his clothes. Soon they were bare skin to bare skin, and he knew only his hunger. He rolled her onto her back and settled on her body, trying to restrain himself so he wouldn't bruise her. She was pulling him to herself with an urgency that matched his own.

Later, they lay tangled together in the covers, sated and quiet. Dehya was sleeping on her side, her body pressed against him. Eldrin slid his hand over her hip. He hadn't felt this content in a long time. He closed his eyes and finally let go, unafraid of his dreams. Her neural relaxant had done wonders, her euphoric mood affecting him, too. For the first time in days he fell asleep without fear . . .

Asleep . . .

Dreaming . . .

Mind relaxing . . .

PAIN. Blindness. Such pain! Vitarex hungered for his agony, his grief, his torment. The monster sat on his stool, brutal in his transcendence, and the agony went on and on, inside his body, inside his soul . . .

A scream yanked Eldrin awake. He bolted upright, reaching for a sword he hadn't carried in years. Bleary and dazed, he scrambled out of bed and yanked on his sleep trousers. As he strode for the archway, shrugging into his shirt, another terrified cry broke the night. He ran through the dark, down the hall.

"Lights on!" he called. The hallway lit up as he entered his son's room. Taquinil was sitting up in bed, his terrified face stained with tears.

"It's all right," Eldrin said as he strode to the bed. "It's all right." He lifted the boy and cradled him against his chest. "I'm here, Taqui. You're all right. It'll be all right."

Taquinil buried his head in his father's shoulder and wept, his small body shaking with silent sobs. Eldrin walked from the room, gently bouncing his son in his arms, pacing down the hall to the darkened living room. He searched the silent, darkened suite. No Dehya. It was probably why Taquinil's distress had returned; the ameliorating effects of her relaxed mental state were gone.

"Where is your mother?" Eldrin said, more to himself than his son. Alaj had warned him to look out for her. "Laplace," he said, addressing the Evolving Intelligence, or EI, that served the royal apartments. "Where is my wife?"

A well-modulated voice answered. "Pharaoh Dyhianna left about four hours ago."

Eldrin continued to walk, his head leaning against his son's head. "Where did she go?"

"I don't know," Laplace said. "However, she received a message. Do you wish to view the log of your mesh-mail?"

He stopped by a console in the living room. "Yes." If the mail had come on Dehya's private account, Laplace wouldn't show it to him. But most of her correspondence came over the account she and Eldrin shared.

Taquinil was shaking in his arms with silent sobs, unable even to cry aloud. Eldrin held him close. He didn't want Laplace to read aloud and disturb the boy, so he had the EI scroll through the mail, pausing each one long enough for Eldrin to struggle through the message. He could read well enough now to decipher most of them. Alaj's medical report had come in with specifics of Dehya's treatment and advice that she rest. So why wasn't she resting? Where the hell was she?

Taquinil cried out and his small fists clenched in Eldrin's collar-length hair. "Hoshpa! The man with the bad name!"

Eldrin knew he meant Vitarex, the Aristo in his nightmares, which had spilled into Taquinil's painfully sensitive mind. Eldrin swayed back and forth, murmuring. "I won't let him get you. You're safe, Taqui." On the console, mail continued to scroll by.

"Laplace, stop." He saw the message to Dehya: a major space station had lost many of its primary systems due to a crisis in the Kyle web beyond the ability of their telops to fix. Millions of people lived on that station, and they were losing environmental systems, defenses, even port controls. They couldn't evacuate without launch bays. Dehya had been called in to fix the web before the station died.

Eldrin swore under his breath. He knew she had a duty to help, but when would she ever get to rest? This happened all too often, that she would disappear while he slept, dragged back to her work by her endless responsibilities as pharaoh. He knew she didn't want to disturb his sleep, but it unsettled him even more to awake alone.

"Was she all right when she left?" he asked.

"She seemed fine," Laplace said.

Eldrin hoped so. He headed down the hall to Taquinil's room.

Make it stop! Taquinil cried in his mind. *Please, Hoshpa.*

I will, Taqui. I'll make it better. Guilt saturated Eldrin. His nightmare had done this. If only he could take his son's torments into himself and free the boy. Dehya had helped; tonight was the first time in days Taquinil had relaxed. But she was gone now, and so was the effect of her medicine. Every time Eldrin fell asleep, he made it worse. He could handle the nightmares; he had mental defenses to mute their effect. Taquinil didn't. When he shielded the boy with his mind, his son was all right, but in sleep, Eldrin lost his ability to provide that protection. He didn't know why he was suffering these nightmares, but he feared someone he loved was in trouble, someone in his family, for they were the only ones whose minds linked strongly enough to his to affect him this way. When he slept, his barriers eased and the connection could intensify. As far as he knew, everyone in his family was fine, yet the dreams continued. Taquinil continued to tremble, his tears soaking into Eldrin's hair, and Eldrin couldn't bear his misery.

He knew what he had to do.

Eldrin returned to the living room and brought up Alaj's medical report. He memorized the details he needed, then carried Taquinil through the master bedroom and into a refresher chamber beyond. Holding his son in one arm, Eldrin took Dehya's personal air syringe out of a cabinet. Normally, someone who wasn't a doctor couldn't have a medical-grade pharmaceutical supply in her possession. But as pharaoh, Dehya had a full dispensary, all in a slender syringe that wasn't even the length of her forearm.

Eldrin could have asked Alaj to help Taquinil, but it had never worked in the past, and he had lost faith that the doctors could do anything but disappoint his son. It took a Rhon psion to protect a Rhon psion, and the only Rhon in existence were Eldrin's family. He also knew Alaj would never approve this solution. Too bad. Alaj wasn't the one whose son was in agony.

Eldrin entered the prescription Alaj had given Dehya and was relieved to find the syringe had the components needed to prepare the medicine. He wasn't certain about the dose he should use on himself; he was larger than his wife, but she had been in difficulty and he was fine. He settled on the same dose Alaj had given her and injected himself in the neck. He winced as the syringe hissed, not from any pain but because it reminded him of the doctors and their advice against using medicine without supervision. This would be all right. He had watched Alaj treat Dehya, read the doctor's report, and followed it with care.

He put away the syringe and shifted Taquinil to both arms. The small boy shivered in his embrace. Eldrin paced through the royal apartments, walking his son, murmuring comfort.

So far, no effect.

He kept walking, singing now, soft and low, a verse he had written when Taquinil was two years old:

> Marvelous bright boy,
> Wonder of all years,
> Precarious joy,
> Miracle from tears.

He sang it over and over. The night took on a trance-like quality and his voice rolled like waves on a shore, the endless ocean of waves, lapping, lapping, rocking, soft and smooth.

Waves murmuring.

Waves rocking.

Rocking.

Eldrin sighed and settled Taquinil more comfortably in his arms. He could carry his son forever, his beloved son. If only he could heal the pain, if only he could make Taquinil's life as serene as his own . . .

Serene?

Not likely. Many words described his life: confusing, lonely, painfully beautiful—but "serene" wasn't one of them.

It was true, though. He felt remarkably calm.

Taquinil sighed and sagged against Eldrin. Tension drained out of his body. Immensely grateful, Eldrin closed his eyes. He wandered through the suite, less focused, aware of little more than his relief that Taquinil's attack had passed. It surprised him that the relaxant had acted so fast; usually this soon after taking medicine, he felt only preliminary effects. He rarely needed any, though; he had top-of-the-line nanomeds in his body to maintain his health, and he almost never fell ill. He was only twenty-three and he rarely thought about growing old, but someday, when it became an issue, the meds would even delay his aging.

Taquinil began to breathe with the steady rhythm of sleep. After a few more minutes, Eldrin took him to his room and tucked him into bed. The boy settled under his covers, his face peaceful.

Joy filled Eldrin in seeing his son content. Tranquillity spread through him. He hadn't felt this good since—well, never. No wonder Alaj had prescribed this medicine for Dehya. His wife deserved peace in her life.

Peace.

Weese.

Geese.

Fly.

Fly away.

The living room swirled in a rainbow of colors. Eldrin didn't remember coming back here. With a satisfied grunt, he dropped onto the couch and stretched out his legs. His body seemed to float. A thought came dreamily to him: he could go outside to the balcony, jump off, and fly over the city. Except he didn't want to move. He felt so incredibly *good*. He hadn't been this happy in ages, maybe never, surely never, nothing compared to this. It was almost too much, too much, too much happiness. *His mind swirled, unraveling in ecstasy, lost to the lovely, glorious night . . .*

Wake up! Father, wake up!

The words in his mind went on, such a dear sound . . .

"Please." The young voice pleaded. "Father, what's wrong? Wake up! Please!"

Eldrin blearily opened his eyes. Taquinil was standing next to him, dressed in pajamas, his eyes wide as he anxiously shook Eldrin's arm. As soon as Eldrin met his gaze, Taquinil made a choked sound and climbed up next to him. Confused and groggy, Eldrin put his arm around his son's shoulders and peered around. He was sprawled on the couch, his body slumped against the white cushions. Light from the Sun Lamp streamed through a window at an angle that suggested it was early morning in the thirty-hour cycle of the space habitat's day.

Eldrin sighed. So beautiful a day. He squeezed Taquinil's shoulders. "Don't be scared. I took some medicine last night, that's all. It made me sleepy."

Taquinil curled against his side. "I thought you were sick."

"I'm fine. Really." Eldrin leaned his head back and closed his eyes. The world flowed around him . . .

"—time to eat," Taquinil prodded. "Come on, Hoshpa."

Eldrin lifted his head, blinking and unfocused. Taquinil wasn't snuggled against him anymore. In fact, the boy was standing in front of him, dressed in dark blue trousers and a lighter blue pullover. His shoes peeked out from beneath his trousers.

Eldrin tried to focus. "How are you feeling?"

"Fine, Hoshpa." Taquinil looked much calmer.

"Good." Eldrin rubbed his eyes. "Have you had breakfast?"

"An hour ago." Taquinil's forehead furrowed. "You should eat. That medicine makes you too sleepy."

Eldrin sat up and rested his elbows on his knees. He grinned at his son. "You're a delightful sight for your hoshpa's eyes."

Taquinil blushed and smiled. "Come on." He took Eldrin's hand. "I'll make you breakfast."

Eldrin wondered if other people's six-year-olds spoke this way. He had no formal education in childhood development, but he was the oldest of ten children, and none of his siblings had been like this. Taquinil had a boy's voice, but sometimes he sounded more like an adult than some adults. From the effusive comments of the boy's tutors, Eldrin gathered that most children didn't learn to read before they were two. Lyshrioli natives didn't read at all. He didn't know many Skolian children, and Taquinil's handful of friends were older than him, which made it hard to judge. Besides, royal tutors always praised royal children. That had certainly been true for Eldrin, even when he didn't deserve it. He did know that Taquinil could read and write much better than he, and that the boy understood more math than Eldrin would probably ever know. He didn't have a good sense of how far above the norm Taquinil was, but it made him proud to have a smart son.

"My thanks, young man," Eldrin said. As he stood up, the room swirled around him. It had settled down from last night, though, and from his dreams, which had floated in a blissful fog. He let out a satisfied breath. "I feel good."

Holding his son's hand, he went to the kitchen. He walked by the wine cabinet with barely a thought for a drink. And if his head was beginning to ache and his pulse to stutter in odd ways as the medicine wore off, well, that would go away soon, he felt certain.

Surely he had nothing to worry about.

1

Reunion

S tarship engines.

Soz considered them the sexiest subject at DMA, the Dieshan Military Academy. Full-color holos of an inversion engine rotated above the media table. She highlighted the fuel selector in purple, the cooling coils in green, and the engine column in white. Her course in Jag engineering was sheer pleasure. It almost let her forget the threat of war that loomed over her people.

Almost.

"Look at you," Soz crooned. "Beautiful engine."

A laugh rumbled nearby. "Maybe if you treated your dates that way, you'd have more success with men."

She looked up with a jerk. Jazar Orand was leaning against a console with his muscular arms crossed and his dark hair sleek against his head. At nineteen, he was a year older than Soz. Last year they had entered the Dieshan Military Academy together, but since then she had skipped more than a year ahead. With him giving her such a cocky look, she was tempted to tell him that he had to salute her now that she was an upper-class cadet. But, of course, they were in the library. The DMA powers-that-be had ruled the library exempt from that regulation because it interfered with the ability of the younger students to study.

"My dates aren't as sexy as this engine," Soz said. Or as sexy as Jazar, but she was trying not to think about that. At the academy, fraternization was grounds for expulsion.

Jazar laughed amiably. "You know, I've always wondered why someone as good-looking and well-connected as you has so much trouble with men. It's no wonder, if you go around telling your dates they aren't as desirable as a bunch of machinery."

She crossed her arms. "Did you come here to analyze my love life?"

His grin flashed. "No, but it wouldn't take long."

"Jaz, I *swear*—"

He held out his hands in surrender. "Don't attack."

Soz glared at him.

"You have a visitor," he added. "A girl."

She couldn't think of any girls who would visit her. "Where?"

"In one of the common rooms. I asked around. People said she came to see you. I offered to let you know."

She considered him warily. "Jazar Orand, I am sensing ulterior motives here."

"Well—" He scratched his ear. "I was hoping you would introduce me."

"Whatever for?"

"Oh for flaming sakes, Soz, you really are dense sometimes."

"Yes, well, I'm densely not going to introduce you to my visitor." Apparently this "girl" was older than she had thought. She told herself she wasn't bothered by his interest. At least arguing with Jazar was better than dwelling on the bigger reason for her loneliness, the unwanted isolation she had endured since her father had disowned her. In such a close-knit family, it was like having a part of herself cut away. She feared she would never again see her home or the members of her family that lived there.

"Come on," he coaxed. "Tell her I'm your great friend."

"Why? Who is this person?"

"I've no idea. She's star-jazzing gorgeous, though."

"Oh, well, that tells me a lot." Soz had never been a judge of beauty in women. Men were another matter. A frustrating matter, but that had nothing to do with Jazar's request, which was annoying her far more than it should. So what if he thought this woman was gorgeous. Pah.

"She's gold," he added. "Hair. Eyes. Everything."

That got her attention. Could it be who she thought? Her hope surged. To cover it, she grinned at Jazar. "You want me to introduce you? Why, Jaz? Going to ask her out?"

He squinted. "Why is that funny?"

Soz just shook her head. She couldn't be certain who had come to see her. She feared to hope too much. So she just went with him out of the library.

Cadets were everywhere on the pathways outside, mostly quiet. A subdued atmosphere had settled over the academy since the attack on Onyx Platform, a military base that supported millions of people in a cluster of space stations. Soz's brother, Althor, had flown one of the Jag starfighters that rebuffed the attackers. His bravery had saved uncounted people at Onyx—and cost him his life. Although his ship had resuscitated him, his brain activity had stopped by that time. He lay in a hospital now, brain dead. Even if some technological miracle could have healed his cortex, the result wouldn't be her brother. His personality, his intellect, his memories: all were gone. Now the Imperialate teetered on the edge of war, and every cadet here knew they could end up in combat within a few years.

Lower-class cadets saluted Soz as they approached, extending their arms straight out at chest height, fists clenched, wrists crossed. They always passed on her left, as per regulations. Soz returned the salutes, but she didn't stop or greet anyone. She had spamoozala duty later today, cleaning AI sewers full of the interminable flood of junk holomail that swamped the meshes.

Soz grimaced. She was going to be in spamoozala hell for the rest of her life. She had achieved two distinctions at DMA: she was going through her studies faster than any other student, and she had more demerits than anyone else at the academy. She might be one of the smartest cadets at DMA, but she was also, apparently, the worst behaved.

"You're quiet tonight," Jazar said.

Soz tried to smile. "Just tired."

"I'm not surprised." He hesitated. "Is it true what I heard, that you've got a tour of duty on a Fleet battle cruiser?"

Soz squinted at him. "Where did you hear that?"

"It's all over."

"How? I only told my roommates."

Jaz cocked an eyebrow at her. "Guess your new ones aren't as discreet as your old ones."

"Guess not." She and Jazar had roomed together their first

year, along with Grell, another female cadet, and Obsidian, the top cadet in the second-year class now that Soz had moved up. Although Soz had known male and female cadets might be in the same quarters, it had flustered her back then. In combat, Jagernauts worked in squadrons of four. They lived, fought, and survived together, and they had to get used to it now, when their lives didn't depend on whether or not they could deal with the situation.

Soz wondered what her father would do if he knew she had bunked in the same room as two men. Probably have heart failure. He wouldn't believe the truth, that they had neither the time nor the energy to look cross-eyed at one another, let alone misbehave. Sure, some cadets had liaisons, but it was a lot rarer than most outsiders believed. Soz tried not to think of her father. He had disowned her when she came here after he forbade it. It had been over a year since she had seen him. He hadn't written, answered her letters, or even acknowledged her existence.

That wasn't the worst of it. Eubian Space Command, the Trader military, had breached the supposedly impregnable defenses of her home world, and an Aristo called Lord Vitarex Raziquon had captured her father. They had rescued him, but not before he nearly died from the torture. The monster Raziquon had left him blind and crippled. Although the doctors saved her father's life, his body couldn't incorporate the new eyes or legs they gave him. He would never walk or see again.

After that, he refused to see anyone. Soz knew he turned away from his family because he didn't want the people he loved to see him in such a condition. She even knew why he had disowned her: he couldn't bear to think of her going to war and suffering at the hands of someone like Raziquon. Instead, the Traders had caught *him,* and now he thought he had nothing left to give his family. He was wrong, so very wrong, and she missed him more than she could say.

Eventually she and Jazar reached the dormitory. They entered through dichromesh-glass doors polarized to mute the sunlight and through a lobby that displayed historical objects such as Jumbler guns used by early starfighter pilots. The common room beyond had blue couches and white walls with holomurals of the Dieshan sky, sometimes pale blue, sometimes hazy red. Soz's visitor was standing across the room, gazing out a window, a rose-hued dress clinging to her dancer's body.

Soz's pulse leapt. She hadn't been wrong. It truly was who she had hoped.

Jazar elbowed her. "Introduce me."

Soz slanted him a look. "You want to get to know her, eh?"

"That's right."

"She's already spoken for."

His disappointment showed. "She's married?"

"To my father."

His mouth fell open. "That's your *mother*?"

"Yep."

Red flushed his cheeks. "Oh."

She smiled. "It's all right, Jaz. You aren't the first to react that way." Her mother, Roca Skolia, looked as if she were barely in her twenties, her youth preserved by nanomeds within her body, but she had actually lived for more than eight decades.

"Uh, hmmm." Jazar cleared his throat.

Roca turned around and her face lit up. "Soz!"

At that moment Soz forgot her probation, her appalling social life, and this odd business about a tour on a battle cruiser. Suddenly she was home in rural Dalvador on the world Lyshriol. Her mother brought memories of suns and warmth, laughter and love. Soz wished she were small again and could run to her for comfort. She couldn't, but seeing Roca meant more than she knew how to say.

"My greetings, Mother." Soz heard how formal she sounded, as if she were thirteen again, that year she had hardly spoken to her parents, using grunts or one-word sentences—not for rudeness, but because she had needed to stop depending on them when she felt so uncertain about her life. She went forward—and then she and Roca were hugging. She hadn't realized until this moment that she had questioned whether she would see her mother again.

Finally they let each other go. Soz smiled awkwardly,

aware of Jazar a few paces back. Roca appraised her with a firm gaze. "You aren't eating enough. And are you going to bed on time? You look tired."

Soz laughed shakily. "Mother, I'm eighteen. Not ten."

A rosy blush stained Roca's gilded cheeks. "I know that."

Soz beckoned to Jazar. "This is my friend, Jaz."

He came forward and bowed deeply. "My honor at your company, Your Majesty."

Soz almost groaned. She had convinced her friends to treat her like everyone else, and usually they forgot her royal heritage. The glamour fast disappeared when you woke up every morning with bleary eyes or stumbled off the training fields covered in sweat. Soz appreciated that Jazar offered her mother honors; Roca descended from the dynasty that had ruled the ancient Ruby Empire and she was the second heir to the Ruby Pharaoh. She had also won election as a Councilor in the modern Assembly that governed Skolia. But Soz hoped no one saw Jaz bowing. At DMA Soz was just another cadet, and she wanted it to stay that way.

Roca smiled. "A friend of my daughter's is a friend of mine."

"Thank you, ma'am." He regarded Soz with a question in his gaze. She felt what he didn't ask. Did she want him to leave?

Soz glanced at her mother, but Roca had guarded her mind. After living in a family of empaths, they all knew how to keep their emotions private, and her mother was showing courtesy by holding back her preferences. Although Soz enjoyed Jazar's company, she wanted to catch up with her mother in private, especially on news of her father. Realizing how much she missed her mother made her father's absence that much more painful.

Jazar was watching Soz's face. Then he spoke to Roca. "It was a pleasure to have met you, Councilor."

Roca inclined her head. "A pleasure shared."

"I better go study," he told Soz. "I've a test in Kyle space theory."

"Yes, of course." She sent him a mental glyph of gratitude. "I'll talk to you later."

"Sounds good." He bowed to Roca and withdrew.

Roca was watching Soz with veiled amusement. "He's charming."

Soz scowled. "He's a rogue."

"A handsome one."

"Don't tell him that," Soz said, alarmed. "I'll never hear the end of it."

Roca's smile seemed strained. "Ah, well."

Soz's mood dimmed. "Did you see Althor?"

"Yes." That one word, full of sorrow, told Soz more than any description of her brother's condition. He hadn't improved.

Roca spoke in a low voice. "Althor's doctors want to know if we wish to keep him on the machines."

"Don't take him off." Soz's voice caught and betraying moisture threatened her eyes. "Please don't."

"Don't cry." Roca looked as if she wanted to shelter Soz the same way she had years ago, when scraped knees or night terrors had darkened her child's life. She hugged Soz again, and somehow it seemed a little better. To Soz, her mother's beauty had nothing to do with her face or form. It came from within, from a woman whose heart held boundless warmth for her family.

But Soz couldn't run to her the way she had as a small child. Those days had passed. She pulled back, unable to reveal her emotions for long, and spoke more formally. "It's good to see you."

"And you, Soshoni." Her mother paused. "I'm not alone."

"Did Denric come?" Of all her siblings, he was the only one Soz could imagine leaving their home. Next year he would go to the university on the world Parthonia. Her sister Aniece or her brother Kelric might have come, but they were probably too young.

"Not Denric." Roca hesitated. "He's in the other common room. He wasn't sure if you wanted another visitor."

Soz suddenly realized who she meant. Her brother *Eldrin.* He was eldest of her nine siblings, twenty-four, a father with a young son, her nephew Taquinil. She was a terrible sister! Normally he lived on the Orbiter with his wife, the Ruby

Pharaoh, but he had been here for the past year, since the attack on their father had ripped apart their lives.

Soz wasn't certain what had happened to Eldrin; he kept it to himself. But she knew his mind had been unusually sensitive to the torture their father had experienced, perhaps because Eldrin was the most like him of all the children. Taquinil was an even more sensitive psion, and Eldrin hadn't been able to stop him from experiencing his nightmares. To protect his son, Eldrin had come here, which meant he had been living by himself for the past year at the Ruby Palace high in the Red Mountains.

It was only a short ride by flyer to the palace. Soz had little free time, but DMA did grant the cadets leave. She could have visited Eldrin. With all her demerit duty, she lost track of things. He hadn't contacted her much, either, but he knew their father had disowned her, and he might think she was angry or uncomfortable about seeing any of the family.

"Yes, of course," Soz said. "I'd love to see him."

Roca looked relieved and a little confused. The doorway to a second common room was across from where Soz had entered this one. As she and her mother walked to its archway, Soz thought about how she would apologize to Eldrin. She should confess she had demerit duty. It would be mortifying, since he would ask why, but better he knew the truth than he thought she had been ignoring him.

They entered a wood-paneled room. Eldrin was standing on the other side, dressed in a white shirt and blue pants, with dark knee-boots. He was studying a portrait of their grandfather. Soz hesitated. Had he lost weight? He seemed . . . odd. She recalled his shoulders as broader and his legs as longer. It worried her how tired he looked. His wine red hair was longer, almost to his shoulders. It had a streak of gray she didn't remember. And why was he wearing spectacles—

Soz drew in a sharp breath. It wasn't her brother.

It was her father.

Lord Valdoria, the Bard, a leader among his people and the consort of a Ruby Dynasty heir, turned around—and froze.

Soz felt as if her world stopped.

His voice caught. "My greetings, Soshoni."

She wanted to answer, but the words caught in her throat. He leaned forward as if to take a step, but then hesitated and looked from her to her mother, his forehead furrowed.

The dam within Soz broke open. "Father! You're—you're *standing.*"

He didn't answer. Instead he leaned on his cane, a staff of blue glasswood with an animal head at the top. Then he stepped toward her. Soz held her breath. He walked with such care, she feared he might fall. But he was walking.

"Hoshpa." For the second time this afternoon, she wanted to cry. "You can see, too."

Still he made no response. His concentration seemed absorbed in his walk, and he leaned heavily on his cane. She waited while he took step after resolute step, resting between each with his weight on the staff. Finally he reached her and regarded her with an uncertain expression. She wanted to throw her arms around him, but she wasn't certain how he would respond.

He took an audible breath. "I practiced what I would say to you for many hours during the trip here. Now it seems I have forgotten everything." He hesitated. "If you will forgive my clumsy words, which lurch and stumble as much as my legs—I—I hope—you will always want to come home." He reached out his free hand to her. "You are always welcome, Soshoni."

Soz felt as if a wind blew through her heart, cleaning out the debris of the last year. She took his hand and he pulled her into a hug, dropping his cane. A sob caught in her throat.

"Always welcome," he whispered.

It was a while before she drew back, slowly, so he wouldn't fall. She picked up his cane and handed it to him. "How?" she asked. "The last I heard, you would never walk or see again."

"Ah, well." He shifted his grip on the cane from hand to hand. "It seems my mind is rather strange. It doesn't respond the way these ISC healers expect. Their healing didn't work. Not at first. Or at second or third, either." He smiled ruefully. "But I'm a stubborn old barbarian. Eventually it worked."

"I'm so glad." Soz rubbed tears off her cheek. "And you aren't a barbarian."

Roca spoke to Soz. "You look as if you've had a long day. Perhaps we should sit down."

Soz knew her mother wanted her father to rest. But Roca wouldn't hurt his pride by suggesting he was too tired to stand.

"I've been cleaning robots," Soz admitted.

Her father frowned. "What for? You came here to be a warrior."

Embarrassed, she said, "Ah, Hoshpa, they think I misbehave. Can you imagine such a thing? Me, misbehave."

"Quite a concept, eh?" He laughed, a deep sound with a musical quality. "Cleaning robots is good for the character, I've heard."

"Then I must have great character," Soz grumbled. For some reason, that made him smile. She would have glared at him, as she had often done as a child, except she was so glad to see him that she simply couldn't.

They went to a sofa against the wall, taking it slow. As they settled on the couch, it adjusted its cushions beneath them, easing tension it detected in their muscles. Her father sagged against the cushions with obvious relief.

"Eldri?" Roca asked. "Are you all right?"

"Just a little tired." He considered Soz, who sat between him and Roca. "After I've rested, you must show us around this school that has so many robots to clean."

"I'll do that." Right now, Soz would have shown him the spamoozala grottos if he had wanted to see them.

They spent a wonderful few hours together, and she rejoiced that they had found their way back to each other. But a cloud dimmed their reunion. Her father had also disowned Althor, for agreeing to take Soz away from home and for refusing to marry. For all that her father didn't understand his massive, cyber-warrior of a son, Soz knew he loved Althor. She mourned that they could never reconcile.

Soon she would receive her own commission as a Jagernaut. When that happened, she would go out and avenge her brother and her father. She would fight for the people of the Skolian Imperialate, the civilization named after her family, the Skolias. She would protect them all against the relentless onslaught of the Traders who sought to enslave an empire.

2

The Dyad Chair

E ldrin returned home after the harsh Dieshan sun had set.
His flyer settled onto the roof of the Ruby Palace, where
onion towers were silhouetted against the sky in the afterglow
of dusk. The sunset turned the world a rose color, deep and
shadowed on the Red Mountains that surrounded the palace
and stood high in the distance.

The cabin of the flyer resembled an elegant hotel suite
with carpet and wood paneling. Eldrin had taken the craft out
to combat his boredom, but he had done little more than sit in
the cushioned pilot's seat while the flyer's EI brain guided it
through the mountains. Although for six years he had been a
"modern" man, he had never felt at ease with all that it
meant. After his rural childhood on the world Lyshriol, his
life these days seemed a hard-edged universe of components
and chrome. He had yet to make peace with the contrast between his rustic youth and his role now as consort to an interstellar sovereign.

The Imperialate was a strange mix of advanced and primitive cultures. Six millennia ago, an unknown race of beings
had taken humans from Earth and abandoned them on the
world Raylicon. Some scholars believed calamity had be-
fallen the abductors before they could complete their plans.
Whatever the reason, they had vanished, leaving behind their
empty starships. Over the centuries, from the records on
those ships, the humans had gleaned enough knowledge to
develop star travel. Then they had gone in search of their lost
home. They never found Earth, but they built the Ruby Empire and scattered colonies across the stars. Lyshriol had been
home to one such settlement.

The Ruby Empire collapsed after only a few centuries.
During the four millennia of Dark Ages that followed, many

of the stranded colonies failed. Those that survived, including Lyshriol, backslid into primitive conditions. When the Raylicans finally regained the stars, they split into two civilizations: the Eubian Concord, also called the Trader Empire, which based its economy on the sale of human beings; and the Skolian Imperialate, ruled primarily by an elected Assembly that considered freedom a right of all humans. The Ruby Dynasty also survived, and wielded power behind the scenes. Earth's people eventually developed space travel—and found their siblings already out among the stars, two thriving but irreconcilable civilizations. The Allied Worlds of Earth became a third, and the three powers maintained an uneasy coexistence.

Eldrin's father was a native of Lyshriol and descended from the ancient colonists. His mother was an offworld technocrat. She had brought advanced technology to her husband's home, with caution. The Lyshrioli continued their agrarian lives, but they now had access to the advantages of an interstellar civilization. Like many of his people, Eldrin had never felt easy with his mother's universe. It hadn't mattered when his tutors said he had a good mind: he knew he was slow. A barbarian. It gave him a certain pride that he had ridden to war at sixteen and distinguished himself in combat, but remorse haunted him. What did he have to offer a star-spanning empire—that he could kill with a sword, even his bare hands, but he couldn't read or write? At home he had been a hero; anywhere else, his life would have marked him as a juvenile criminal.

After his combat experiences, his confusion had surged. He hadn't known how to deal with the vastly different cultures of his mother and father's universes. Guilt and self-doubt plagued him, and frustration with his inability to learn. He had grown angrier each day. Finally he lost control and went on a rampage in the school his parents insisted he attend—he who had fought as a warrior. His tutor had stood flattened against the wall, his face terrified, while Eldrin hacked apart the desk console with the same sword he had used to kill two men.

His parents had sent him offworld then. At first he hadn't understood. If he couldn't manage his life at home, how would he deal with the Orbiter, a space station, a center of Imperialate civilization? But instead of the heartless ship he had expected, he found a paradise of rolling hills and wildflowers that existed within a gigantic sphere. The habitat had only one sun, a lamp actually, but it was extraordinarily beautiful. Its one city was all gossamer towers and pastel hues. His tutors at the school there specialized in "learning disabilities." They said he had many talents.

Then they taught him to read.

It was one of the greatest gifts anyone had ever given Eldrin. They linked it to his music. He had sung all his life, as heir to his father, the Dalvador Bard. First Eldrin had learned to read music. The day he wrote the words of a ballad he had composed, he cried, in private where no one could see. He learned to read what other musicians wrote. Then he read about the musicians. One day, he realized he could read and write about other subjects. It was one of the most gratifying moments in his life.

He and his son Taquinil had studied together. Initially his tutors wanted to separate them, afraid it would discourage Eldrin to learn with a toddler who was less than two years old. Eldrin insisted they stay together. It gave him no end of joy that his miraculous son was a genius.

Eldrin's abilities with a sword bemused the people on the Orbiter, who seemed both fascinated and bewildered by his antediluvian talents. But they lauded his voice without reserve. In his first concert, when he had been seventeen, millions had tuned into the virtual mesh-cast. *Millions.* The Parthonia Choral Society had paid an exorbitant fee to provide listeners with verification that his voice, including his five-octave range, was genuine, untouched by technological improvements. Reviewers used heady words like "spectacular" and "unparalleled." Doctors studied his vocal cords. Skolians championed his art. It changed his life, giving it exquisite textures he had never imagined.

He was less sure of Dehya, his wife, this enigmatic pharaoh of an empire. They had been strangers when the Assembly arranged their marriage, forcing the union despite their objections. Dehya was much older, though she didn't look it, and related to him through his mother's side.

Legally, their contract was on shaky ground. The Assembly demanded it anyway, in desperation. They called on an ancient law that decreed a Ruby Pharaoh must choose her consort from among her own kin, supposedly because only they were exalted enough for such a union. It was ludicrous and the Assembly knew it, but the law had never been repealed.

The Assembly wanted them to have children. Skolia couldn't exist without the meshes that tied it into a coherent civilization, and fast communication across interstellar distances was possible only through the Kyle web, which existed outside of spacetime. Humans could enter Kyle space mentally but not physically. Any telop could use the Kyle web, but only a Dyad could sustain it. Without the Dyad, the web would collapse. Only the Rhon, the most powerful known psions, had the mental strength to create a Dyad. And the only known Rhon psions were the Ruby Dynasty. Eldrin's family. It was why they had such power even in this age of elected government.

The Kyle genes, a set of genetic mutations, created a psion. The Rhon had every one of the recessive genes. However, children couldn't be Rhon unless they received the Kyle mutations from *both* parents. It took two Rhon psions to make a third. Unfortunately, in vitro methods of reproduction became unreliable for people with the Kyle mutations. The more Kyle genes they carried, the greater the problems. For Rhon psions, who had two copies of every gene, it was almost impossible to reproduce by artificial means. The doctors had explained it to Eldrin, about embryos and failed cloning techniques, but as with so much else about their universe, he hadn't understood.

What Eldrin did know was that both of his parents were Rhon psions, which meant their ten children were as well. They provided the Dyad with many heirs and spares. The Assembly still wanted to ensure a supply, especially given that the training for military heirs included combat experience. Eldrin's mother had struggled with her pregnancies, and the doctors advised against her having any more. The solution was obvious, at least to the Assembly: make the Ruby Dynasty interbreed. They picked Dehya because she had less genetic connection to the Valdoria branch of the family, and they chose Eldrin because he and Dehya had the fewest deleterious matches among their genes.

It had dismayed Dehya and Eldrin. They fought the Assembly—and lost. So they married. As husband and wife, they remained formal, two strangers forced into a union neither wanted. And yet . . . as time passed, Eldrin acknowledged his affinity for his wife. They were Rhon. Like sought like. Even with his being a psion, it had been a year before he could believe the incredible truth, that he loved his wife—and she loved him.

He still felt out of his depth with her, a forbidden stranger in her royal apartments. He cared for their son, Taquinil, composed music, trained his voice, and gave concerts. It was a good life. He really did believe that—and if he drank too much at night when his son slept and he hadn't seen his wife in days, well, everyone needed a release.

A pleasant voice broke his reverie. "We have arrived, Your Majesty." It came from a comm near his chair. The engines of the flyer were fading into silence.

"Thank you." Eldrin felt odd thanking a machine, but it seemed appropriate. "Release pilot."

"Released." The control panels around his seat swiveled away.

Eldrin stood up slowly. Although he weighed less here than on Lyshriol, it was more than on the Orbiter space station where he normally lived. As he crossed the cabin, he had to retime his steps and modulate how high he lifted his foot. So strange, to analyze a process he usually took for granted. It was better now than a year ago, though, when he had first come here. Although the gravity felt awkward, he could handle the difference. He did exercises every day so he wouldn't lose his ability to handle heavier gravity. He wanted to ensure he could always go home to Lyshriol and to his family, no matter where they lived.

He paused, disheartened. He had come here to protect Taquinil from his nightmares. Eldrin loved his son more than his own life, but he knew he and Dehya should never have had a child. Their boy, so beautiful and brilliant, might never survive on his own. Born of two people on the extreme end of empathic sensitivity, he couldn't block emotions with his mind. He had no barriers against the onslaught. It took another Rhon psion to provide the mental shields he lacked, which meant only the Ruby Dynasty could protect him. His doctors were searching for a treatment that wouldn't destroy the boy's magnificent neural structures, but unless they succeeded, Taquinil could never leave the protection of his family. It wasn't a problem for a seven-year-old boy, but that would change as he grew older. His independence could cost him his sanity.

Eldrin was also an unusually sensitive psion. If anything powerful happened to his family, he sensed it. He had taken easily to fatherhood because of his role model, his father, the Dalvador Bard, a man he loved and admired above all others. A link as strong as theirs could extend into Kyle space and reach Eldrin light-years away. But their closeness meant Eldrin endured any intense experiences his father suffered—including the agony inflicted by Vitarex Raziquon. Although over a year had passed since it happened, the memory continued to haunt Eldrin's dreams.

The violence of Althor's combat death had impacted Eldrin almost as much as his father's suffering. Of the ten Valdoria children, Eldrin was closest in age to Althor. Although Eldrin managed his grief during the day, nightmares haunted his sleep. It should have stopped: his father had escaped Raziquon—and Althor had died. But he continued to dream horrors.

It tore him apart to know that his dreams hurt his son. Only distance muted the effect; the greater his separation from Taquinil, the less his nightmares affected the boy. So he had left Taquinil with Dehya and come here, to Diesha.

At least he could visit them through the webs. Buoyed by that thought, he disembarked from the flyer. Outside, the crenellations that edged the roof curved gracefully in the twilight, interspersed by small totems sculpted from balls. It was beautiful, created more for art than defense; no archers would ever hide behind these scalloped edges. Far deadlier defenses guarded this palace: EI-controlled security, mountain installations, and one of the most advanced orbital defense systems ever designed by humans.

Eldrin jumped down into a night of dark red hues. He misjudged the gravity and didn't bend his knees enough when he landed. The impact jarred through him, and he winced as he straightened. No one had come to greet him, which probably meant his half-brother Kurj wasn't here. Although this palace served as the Imperator's residence, Kurj often stayed down in HQ City, where he worked.

Although many people called Kurj a military dictator. Eldrin had never seen him that way. He had known Kurj all his life, and their bond had strengthened through the years. Eldrin would have liked to see him now, but it seemed he was alone in this huge, echoing palace. Kurj preferred mechanized staff to humans. It seemed lonely to Eldrin, but he respected his brother's wishes and brought no human personnel here. The only person he knew well enough to invite for a visit was Soz, and she had school to worry about. He didn't want to distract her from her studies. Even if he had known other people here, they would have to pass endless security checks before they could visit the palace.

As he crossed the roof, warm gusts ruffled his clothes. A tower rose nearby, its rounded top and spire sharp against the darkening sky. He stopped in front of its gilt-edged door, which analyzed him and opened without challenge. Inside, he descended a staircase that spiraled around the tower. He could have taken a lift, but he preferred to walk. Ruby and diamond tiles patterned the goldstone steps in geometric designs. Around and around. He submerged into a trance so he wouldn't think about the emptiness.

He surfaced from his daze when he reached the bottom, where an archway opened into a large hall. Rose-quartz columns filled it, row after row, tiled with mosaics that matched the tower. He crossed the hall, his tread muted. Far overhead, the columns met in graceful arches, and red crystal lamps hung from their topmost points on gold chains. The floor was inlaid with a dramatic sunburst mosaic, the insignia of the Imperialate.

He wandered through the palace until he reached the pharaoh's suite. In the Red Mountains on sparsely settled Diesha, they had no worries about space. Dehya's entire apartment on the Orbiter would fit in this living room. Originally the jeweled mosaics on the walls had been abstract, but she arranged to have them redone when Eldrin came to live with her. Now they evoked the plains and spindled peaks of his home. Although he had never told her how much he missed Lyshriol, she knew. In the beginning, when it had been even harder for them to talk than now, she had showed affection with such unspoken gifts. It had taken him years to believe they were offerings of love from a pharaoh who had little ease with words.

Eldrin roamed the suite, through alcoves shaped like flowers, bathrooms with tiled pools, and the bedroom with its tapestries and velvet-covered bed. He missed Dehya. Then again, he always missed her, even when he was on the Orbiter. She spent hours, sometimes days, working in the web. Their times together were too short, with too long between.

His head throbbed. He needed his medicine to deal with the neurological knots that tangled his empath's mind. Hell, a good, stiff drink would help. He paced, agitated. Although the medicine eased his discomfort, he didn't like to depend on it. He wanted to deal with this himself.

Finally he went to the console room. White Luminex stations glowed in the dim light. He settled into a chair within a circular console, and its exoskeleton folded around him. Prongs clicked into sockets in his ankles, wrists, lower spine, and neck. When the Assembly had first suggested putting biomech in his body, it had horrified him. They wanted him to become a telop, preparing for the day he might join the Dyad. Initially he had refused. Gradually, though, he had realized it would let him "meet" with Dehya in Kyle space. Finally he agreed. After a time, his fears that it would make him less human abated. He remained Eldrin. He hadn't become a machine.

A visor lowered over his eyes and darkness surrounded him. The console accessed his brain directly; the visor was only to ensure that no view of his surroundings interfered with the virtual reality created in his mind.

A "thought" came to him from the console, routed through his biomech web to the node in his spine. Welcome back to the palace, Your Majesty. What can I do for you this evening?

My greetings, Etude, Eldrin answered, directing his thought to his personal EI. **I would like to see my wife.**

A simple request—and it required the most advanced communications ever created by humanity. The console would access the Kyle mesh, and telops operating in the mesh would route his signal through Kyle space to the Orbiter. Eldrin needed no other protocols. His direct line to Dehya on the Orbiter would be more secure, better, and faster, than other lines. Being the Ruby Consort had advantages.

Gradually the darkness eased. He was standing in a graceful room with high ceilings. Holoart swirled on the walls, behind a white sofa. The tables at either end of the couch were wood, a valuable material on a space habitat. His wife sat on the sofa, her black hair cascading over her shoulders, arms, and hips, making Eldrin want to fill his hands with it. Her green eyes tilted upward, fringed with black lashes. She had the face of a waif, heart-shaped. Her slender figure appeared delicate, as if she might break, but he knew a will of steel ran through her.

Taquinil was sitting cross-legged on the sofa, his bangs tousled over his forehead, his black hair brushing his collar. His eyes shimmered gold. He had grown since Eldrin had been home last year. People said he had Eldrin's features, but it was hard for Eldrin to tell. It just amazed him that he had sired such an incredible young man.

The boy's face lit up. "Hoshpa!" He jumped to his feet, then remembered himself and spoke with impeccable manners. "My greetings, Father."

Dehya smiled at Eldrin, and her voice came like dusk in the Dalvador Plains. "And mine, Husband."

"My greetings." A deep relief settled over him. They were a balm to his eyes. "You both look well."

"Come sit with us." Taquinil flopped back on the couch.

"I wish I could." But he couldn't leave the holopad that was projecting his image to the Orbiter. "What did you do today?"

"We went to City again!" Taquinil's gaze was radiant, as if he glowed from within. "The bridges float. They came to the ground and we got on them and they went up."

"I always liked that." Eldrin's reaction to City during his first years on the Orbiter had been much like his son's. The airy towers and spires, the drifting paths, the ethereal colors—it all had a luminous beauty. They should have let someone other than Kurj name the place, though. His half-brother had many good qualities, but subtlety wasn't one of them. Kurj had christened the city "City" and the valley where they lived "Valley." Eldrin suspected that if Kurj ever sired an heir, he would name his child Son or Daughter.

"How is your stay on Diesha going?" Dehya asked him.

"Uneventful." Eldrin paused. "I've been practicing."

"I miss your singing," Taquinil said. "Every night."

Eldrin's voice caught. "I miss singing to you." Although he had continued training his voice, he was having trouble composing songs. His muse seemed to have left him, and he had lost the will to give concerts this past year.

"We will be glad when you can come home," Dehya murmured.

"It won't be long." Gods, how he hoped that was true.

"How are you doing?" she asked.

"All right." It wasn't true, but he didn't want to burden them with his loneliness. "I saw Althor today."

Her voice quieted. "How is he?"

What could he say? *He's dead.* "No change."

Taquinil watched him with concern. "Did your bad dreams go away, Hoshpa?"

"They're much better," Eldrin assured him. In truth, he had no idea when they would stop. Medicine helped, and it had helped Taquinil during the boy's attack, but Eldrin wasn't certain it was good to expose his son to its effects too often, especially now that Taquinil was fine.

"Come to the Dyad Chair with us," Taquinil invited.

Eldrin glanced at Dehya. "Are you going into the web?"

She nodded. "Taquinil wanted to come. Major Faryl said he would look after him while I worked."

Eldrin wondered how many majors had babysitting the pharaoh's heir as part of their job description. It bothered him a great deal, but what could he say? He wasn't there to look after his child. "I can meet you in the Dyad Chamber."

"All right, love." Her face gentled. "Ten minutes?"

"Ten minutes, yes." It warmed him when she called him that. He signed off and darkness cloaked him again.

Etude, attend, he thought.

Attending, the EI answered. Would you like me to establish a link to the Dyad Chamber in ten minutes?

Yes. That would be good.

While he waited, Eldrin tried to relax. It did little good. The Dyad Chamber always unsettled him, even when he was there only as a virtual simulation. It had an eerie intelligence unlike anything else he had encountered.

After a while, Etude thought, Your transmission is open.

Thank you. Eldrin opened his eyes. He stood within a forest of gleaming struts. They supported a geodesic chamber that shone with synthetic starlight from a holodome far overhead. He had never understood why struts circled this chamber and propped up the walls. Simpler means of support existed. He doubted anyone knew the reason. Imperial Space Command had found the Orbiter derelict in space, a giant sphere that had been adrift for five thousand years. They had yet to fully understand what they had found, but they had learned to use it. This room's ancient apparatus waited in the center of the chamber.

The Dyad Chair.

Information meshes networked the Imperialate. Some were tiny; many were of moderate size; some encompassed billions of users. Anyone could access the meshes, even with just a chip in their jewelry. For more involved work, they could find a console. Control chairs were more advanced consoles and allowed a person to act as an operator in the mesh. They were the goal coveted by those who desired influence within whatever hierarchies of power defined their lives. Command chairs were even rarer, and only the most highly placed operators had access to them. Such chairs allowed their user to command vital resources, such as a battle cruiser or Assembly communications. They offered great power.

They were nothing compared to the Dyad Chairs.

The Dyad Chairs came from the Ruby Empire. Only seven had survived, all built with ancient technology that modern scientists had yet to reproduce. They dwarfed even the massive command chairs such as the one where Kurj sat in the War Room. To use them required a mental power greater than most humans possessed. Only a Rhon psion could operate one, and in practice, only the Dyad could survive the immense force of its mind.

Dehya had already settled into the technological throne. Robot arms and conduits surrounded her, and panels enclosed her in a maze of chrome and composites. The exoskeleton sheathed her body with a silvery mesh. As techs fastened her into it all, the equipment adjusted around her body. The Chair was the terminus of a robot arm that could carry it anywhere within the chamber. The holodome glowed above them with holostars: sapphire and topaz, ruby and diamond. It produced the only light, and cast pale luminance over Dehya and the techs.

Whenever Eldrin entered this room, he sensed its banked power, which extended into Kyle space as well as the real universe. Fear made him edgy when he saw Dehya in the Chair. She seemed fragile, her face dominated by large green eyes, her body caught in a machine with a mind too strange to comprehend. It responded only in this chamber, when it was lifted up to the holodome, though *why,* no one knew. Nor did anyone know why the Chairs allowed the Dyad members to operate their functions. Every time Dehya sat in one, Eldrin feared she risked igniting its unfathomable mind. His apprehension was all the more intense because he couldn't imagine what it might do to her. Chairs were too different, their intelligence too alien. They had almost no intersection with human thought.

Taquinil stood near the Chair, watching with concern while the techs strapped his mother in. Eldrin felt a pang, seeing his son, so bright and vibrant, but also so vulnerable. He stood with a lanky man in the uniform of the Pharaoh's Army. Major Faryl. Eldrin gritted his teeth.

Dehya smiled at Taquinil and lifted her hand. He waved at her with a small child's trust that all would be well. As Eldrin thought of his wife, she looked across the room. When she saw him, her smile took on a sultry hint of what waited when he came home. He flushed, hoping no one else noticed the change.

My greetings, husband. Her thought came into his mind like dusk and wine. *You look handsome there.*

Eldrin smiled. **Dehya, behave.**

Her lips curved. *Never.*

Seeing her focus shift, several techs glanced in his direction. As soon as Taquinil caught sight of him, his face filled with relief. Eldrin knew how much it unsettled the boy to see his mother in that mammoth Chair, even if he had a child's naïve belief that his parents actually knew what they were doing.

Taquinil ran across the room. "My greetings, Hoshpa." He stopped at the holopad and motioned excitedly at the Chair. "Can you feel? It is alive! It talks to us."

"Yes. It does." Eldrin doubted anyone in the room besides Dehya and Taquinil could feel the intelligence of the Chair. To most people it was just a big piece of equipment. He stretched his arm out to his son, but they couldn't touch. He was no more than a projection of light. As his hand went beyond the boundary of the holopad, it vanished. He drew it back, making it reappear, and Taquinil laughed. The boy's smile was strained, though. Eldrin felt the same way. He had been away from his family for too long. It hurt like hell. He needed them.

Taquinil reached across the pad's boundary, and his hand passed through Eldrin's arm. "Look!" He laughed, a full, contagious sound Eldrin had always loved. "You're a ghost."

"I hope not," Eldrin said. He wanted to hug his son.

"Will you go into Kyle space with Mother?"

"I'm already there."

The boy paused. "I'll go watch closer. Is that all right?"

"Yes, go ahead." Although Eldrin knew it unsettled Taquinil to see his mother caged by machinery, he had long ago realized his son loved technology. So Eldrin tried to adapt, learning to accept the dreams of the boy's universe.

Taquinil ran across the chamber, the only child allowed to visit this strategic command center of an empire. It grated on Eldrin to see his son left with a soldier while his mother was bound to a soulless mesh and his father exiled on another world. Dehya's upward-tilted eyes were closing, the long lashes covering her exotic sunrise gaze, a film of rose and gold pastels overlaid on her pupils. The techs were running tests on her much as a ship's crew ran preflight checks on a spacecraft. They calibrated the feeds that provided nutrients and kept her hydrated, and checked the med lines that monitored her health, making it possible for her to stay in the Chair for days, if necessary.

Finally they stepped back, and one of them spoke into his wrist comm. With a deep hum, the robot arm rose from the floor and carried the Chair up into the holodome. Eldrin felt Dehya submerge into the Kyle web. Her mind spread out in ripples, and she *became* the mesh that held a universe created by human thought. She almost seemed translucent, as if part of her had transferred into the ghostly web that spanned Kyle space.

Come, she thought.

The Chair answered without words, only an implicit sense that it understood her request. Dehya went to work then, creating and re-creating the web. She built new nodes, made repairs, and established real-space gates into Kyle space. She tended the fluxes and flows of data and thought, tracing patterns, spanning a star-flung empire. She was always watching, always moving, the Shadow Pharaoh who went everywhere, including places no one else could access, probably some that no one else even knew existed.

Always, as she worked, she also searched for clues about how Vitarex Raziquon had infiltrated Lyshriol and captured Eldrin's father. They could never ask Vitarex. One of Eldrin's younger brothers, gentle Shannon, had rescued their father. Only fourteen at the time, Shannon was the dreamer of the family, smallest and least warlike of the Valdoria sons—and yet he was the one who had murdered Vitarex to avenge their father.

The Aristo had taken his secrets to his grave. Now Dehya's mind flowed around the edges of secured Trader meshes, looking for anything that might unravel the knot of how Vitarex had trespassed on Lyshriol. The same thought drove her that hung like a specter over all of them; if the Traders could violate the Imperialate stronghold of Lyshriol, no place was safe.

Eldrin felt her fatigue. She was responsible for a system

that served trillions of people. Any telop could monitor the web, but her job went much deeper. She created it—and ensured it survived.

Kurj also worked the web as a Dyad member. With it, he built the Imperialate military into a sleek, deadly machine that even the Traders, with their greater military resources, couldn't defeat. Dehya was the Assembly Key, linking the web to the government: Kurj was the Military Key, linking it to ISC. Dehya had nuance: Kurj had blunt power. Dehya was the Mind of the Web: Kurj was its Fist. Together, they held together the meshes that made Skolia an interstellar power.

It wasn't enough.

They were exhausted. Two people, no matter how driven, couldn't keep up with the ever-changing demands of that voracious mesh, which added billions of networks per hour. Eldrin knew the truth no one admitted, that the Assembly kept quiet, that ISC buried. No one spoke it, but it terrified them all. The web was growing out of control. If the Dyad didn't find a solution, the mesh would collapse under the sheer weight of its success—and kill the Dyad.

3

Bliss

The hospital viewing room looked the same today as every other day Soz had visited. The sofa was along the wall to the right of the entrance, with an armchair beyond and another to the left of the door. The furniture was upholstered in subdued forest hues, and abstract holoart swirled on the walls. The lamps gave enough light to see by, but nothing bright or jarring. It was all very calming, but Soz didn't feel the least bit soothed. Every time she saw what the Traders had done to her brother, she wanted to kill someone. Aristos, specifically.

She went to the window that filled the top half of the wall

opposite the door. In the room beyond, Althor lay on his back, on a floater, a bed with a rudimentary intelligence. It could react to tension in his body, ease muscle strain, massage him, anything.

None of it helped.

He was a huge man, over two meters tall, seven-foot-seven, with a muscular physique and metallic gold skin. He had been a force to reckon with, a powerhouse. Now he lay unmoving, his body gaunt and wasted, his face sallow. She had spent hours watching the rise and fall of his chest. It killed her to know he would never awake. Surely someone could discover a new technology that could return his life, his brain, his memories.

Soz thought of her brother Kelric, nine years old. He looked so much like Althor, and he, too, longed to become a pilot. How many brothers would the war take from her? She thought of her sisters, Chaniece and Aniece, her closest friends, though they constantly challenged her view of the universe. They had never fathomed her fascination with all things military. And what of Kurj? Fighting the Traders all his life had hardened him beyond healing. How many people she loved would have their lives demolished by the Aristos, the arrogant sadists who never suffered themselves?

The door hummed behind her. Soz jumped and turned around as a man entered. He was Althor's age, in his early twenties. Well-tended blond hair brushed his shoulders. He had blue eyes and chiseled features, extraordinarily handsome. Soz always felt like a mess in his presence, drab in her cadet's jumpsuit, with her hair curling haphazardly around her face.

He hesitated when he saw her. Then he came to the window and bowed. "My greetings, Your Highness."

Soz inclined her head stiffly. "Chad." She hesitated. "Call me Soz, please." She had little desire to offer him that familiarity, but she didn't want anyone treating her like royalty. At the academy, she was a cadet like everyone else.

Surprise sparked in his mind, strong enough that she felt it despite his carefully constructed mental barriers. He nodded formally. "Soz."

They stood together at the window watching Althor. After a moment Chad said, "He's always the same. Every day I come."

She couldn't hide her bitterness. "Maybe if you had come back to him sooner, you could have seen him alive."

Chad exhaled, and Soz immediately regretted the words, but it was too late to take them back. Her anger at Chad still simmered.

So they stood, neither speaking.

Finally Chad turned to her. "We should talk."

Soz faced him and crossed her arms. "Why?"

"We're both grieving for him. We shouldn't hurt each other, too."

Soz wished she could let her anger go. But if she weakened, if she let down her defenses even a bit, the grief would overwhelm her. "You gave up my brother for drugs. How can I forgive you for that?"

He stared at her. "Do you have any idea how addictive phorine is for an empath?"

"It doesn't matter." Yes, she knew. *Addictive* was a massive understatement. The stronger the psion, the worse the dependence. They called it node-bliss. She sensed Chad's mind even through his mental shields; he was a powerful empath, probably also a telepath, able to pick up unusually intense thoughts from another psion when neither of them was guarding his mind. Soz knew Chad couldn't have quit on his own, but her emotions rejected that logic. Althor had given Chad an ultimatum—him or phorine—and Chad had chosen the drug.

Her brother had never taken bliss. The doctors had checked him thoroughly. It wasn't because of Chad's addiction; they hadn't known Chad existed. The hospital had tested Althor for a wide range of drugs to ensure they would encounter no problems with any medicines they gave him. Soz would have known even without that, though. Althor would never touch phorine. He just wasn't the type. The DMA honor code and his sense of duty as a cadet meant too much to him. It was a good thing, because if he had tried phorine, based on what she knew about the drug, he wouldn't have survived. He was a

Rhon psion, brutally susceptible to any dose. The withdrawal could kill even a man as strong as Althor.

"Couldn't you get help?" Soz asked Chad.

"I thought I could quit on my own." Strain flattened his usually rich voice. "I couldn't. But when Althor turned me in, it felt like a betrayal." His voice quieted. "I'm grateful now. If the bliss hadn't killed me, I would probably be rotting in some hellhole. At the time, though, I couldn't handle it."

"Have you ever wanted it again?"

He regarded her steadily. "Every day. But I won't take it. I hate it even more than I crave it."

Soz hesitated. "I guess I don't understand why you never tried to contact Althor after you got out of treatment."

Chad spoke tightly. "He left me."

"He loved you."

He made an incredulous noise. "Do you honestly think he wanted to see me again after what I did?"

She could understand why he would feel that way, but he didn't know her brother as well as he thought. She saw no use in stirring rancor, though. "I am glad you came to see him." It was true. He had helped her understand Althor better.

They turned back to the window, and stood vigil for the pilot who would never greet them again.

Twilight was deepening across the academy grounds as Soz headed to the engineering labs. Cadets were walking along the pathways, some in conversation, others working on their mesh gloves, with tiny holos floating around their hands, menus for mesh-mail, schedules, or schoolwork. A primed tension pervaded the scene, everyone aware of who surrounded them, saluting where required, passing upperclass cadets on the right, following the stratified protocols of the academy.

Jazar Orand came up alongside her and saluted. "Orand, *ma'am!*"

Soz returned the salute. "At ease, Cadet."

He lowered his arms and grinned wickedly. "Heya, Soz."

She had to smile. Really, he ought to get demerits for being so distracting. "Heya, Jaz."

His hair clung damply to his forehead. She remembered how he used the cleanser unit in the evening before he went to study. She missed rooming with him, Grell, and Obsidian. Although they had come in with her as first-year students, they were second-year now and she had advanced to senior level. She already had the biomech in her body that enhanced her strength and speed, as well as a node that augmented her brain. She had been assigned to a room with similarly augmented seniors. Her new roommates were fine, but she missed her friends.

"Where you headed?" Jazar asked.

Soz glared at him.

He laughed softly. "Demerit duty, right? Is it maintenance? Engineering? I know. Mesh Sciences, to work in the spam gutters."

"Pah."

"I swear, Soz, you get in more trouble than the rest of the cadets combined."

"I do not." Then she relented and added, "I have droid duty." She didn't know why they called it that; she would be cleaning mechbots, not droids. No matter what its name, the job was vile.

"What did you do this time?" Jazar asked. "Tell one of your instructors your idea was better than hers? Talk during formation? Come late? Misplace a book in the museum?"

"I do not misplace books," Soz said with dignity. "I was showing it to Grell. She had never seen one with paper pages. I was going to put it back where it belonged."

He smirked. "All right. You borrow any more books?"

"No." She paused, suddenly tired. "I went to Commandant Blackmoor's office and confessed to cracking the field mesh so I could learn the new patterns on the Echo obstacle course."

His smile faded. "Cracking meshes is a serious offense."

"Yes." It had been her way of dealing with the grief, to push herself through the obstacle course at breakneck speed so she could finish her training sooner and avenge her brother's death. "Commandant Blackmoor asked why he shouldn't expel me."

"Gods," Jazar said under his breath.

"Yeah." She exhaled. "He didn't, but they took me off the

honor roll and put me on probation. It'll take me a year to work off all those demerits."

Jazar drew her to a stop, an unusual act for a cadet, not quite breaking regulations, but close because he touched her. In the growing darkness, his eyes were hardly more than shadows. "Are you all right?"

She knew he was asking about Althor. "I'm okay." She wasn't, she was dying inside, but she couldn't say that.

He reached for her hand, then stopped. She knew why; someone could all too easily report their touching as inappropriate.

"If you need to talk," he said, "I'm here."

"Thanks." Then she remembered. "But I won't be here! The brass is sending me for that tour on the Fleet cruiser. If I'm going to command ISC someday, I have to get experience in all four branches." She and Althor had been the Imperator's two heirs, both expected to prove themselves over the years. Then suddenly it had changed. Now Kurj had one heir. Her. She would have gladly given up the title to have Althor back again.

Jazar blanched, less relaxed with her now even than when he had to salute. "Sometimes I forget who you are."

"Jaz, don't." Soz didn't think she could bear it if he put that distance between them. So many people felt it with her. "It's just me."

His grin reasserted itself. "Soz, condemned to rule the universe. Come on, Your Majesticioso Empress. I'll walk you to Engineering."

She grimaced. "Majesticioso? Was that a word or noise from your eating too many beans?"

Jazar laughed. "Ah, Soz, you are unique."

She walked with him, glad of his friendship.

Eldrin paced the bedroom of the royal suite, unable to stay still. It was beautiful here, the mosaics sparkling and tall vases standing in the corners. Diamond chandeliers hung from the ceiling. But he felt suffocated. The heavy drapes closed in on him, and his head ached. He loathed the thought of calling a doctor. Leaving Taquinil and Dehya because his mind endangered his son was torment enough; having to seek help for his extreme empathic sensitivity would be humiliating.

Gods, his head hurt. He strode to the cabinet against one wall and clicked open the crystal doors. The bottles inside were gorgeous, especially the carafe shaped like a flying dragon with wings spread. The deep blue glass and iridescent highlights pleased his sense of aesthetics, at least as much as he could feel pleasure when he was so uncomfortable.

His hand shook as he pulled out the decanter. Red wine sloshed within the bottle, too loud, grating on his nerves. He shook his head, trying to clear it, then winced as pain stabbed his temples. He grabbed a crystal tumbler, a smaller version of the dragon, and poured a drink. Too agitated to put away the wine, he set the decanter on the counter and paced away, across the room, to a wing chair upholstered in dark red brocade. When he sat down, the cushions shifted, trying to ease his rigid posture. He had only meant to sip his drink, to savor its quality, but he finished it so fast he barely tasted the wine.

He set his glass on a table by the chair and thought of getting more. Then he steeled himself. He wouldn't drink tonight. None of his medicine, either. Nor would he call for help. He was a fighter and a bard. He would get through this.

Eldrin closed his eyes, trying to ease the ache behind them. It had spread throughout his head. Sleep. He needed sleep. His augmentations could help. They included nanomeds that patrolled his body, repaired his cells, tended his health, and delayed his aging. The tiny molecular laboratories could release chemicals that would help him rest. He concentrated, using biofeedback techniques to enhance the response of the meds much in the way an empath could use biofeedback to heal himself, or others, if he turned his empathic abilities outward. Gradually he nodded off, dozing in fits and starts . . .

"Make it stop, Hoshpa." Tears ran down Taquinil's face, and his eyes were swollen from crying . . .

Eldrin jerked awake. His headache raged and sweat soaked his clothes. He would have lost his dinner, except he hadn't eaten. He rose out of his chair, but then he fell, landing on his hands and knees, unbalanced by the Dieshan gravity. *Diesha.* He wasn't at home, caring for Taquinil. That had all happened over a year ago.

He remembered little of that first night after he had taken Dehya's medicine. The relaxant had drenched his mind. He had collapsed on the couch, and he hadn't come back to consciousness until the next morning, when he awoke to find Taquinil shaking his arm. Eldrin had spent the day in a haze of tranquillity, but the effects had faded over the next few days. Headaches had plagued him, and his hands had shaken so much he had trouble holding a glass. His condition affected Taquinil, not as much as Eldrin's horrendous dreams, but enough that the boy felt his distress. Then Eldrin's nightmares had started up again, for that had been during the time Vitarex Raziquon had been torturing his father.

Finally he had given in, unable to bear the headaches or the dreams. He had taken Dehya's medicine again, cutting the dose by 80 percent. That solved his problems, replacing his pain with serenity. With the dosage so much lower, he didn't lose touch with the world, either. It had still been too much. He had trouble caring for Taquinil when he so easily became distracted, but when he didn't take the medicine, his distress made it impossible for him to function and his nightmares tormented his son.

If Dehya had spent more time with him, he could have injured her, too. She had noticed his erratic moods, and she had bothered him about what she called "his drinking." If she had realized the extent of his nightmares, she probably would have pressured him to see a specialist. He couldn't bear the thought of a therapist poking into his private life, and he feared Dehya would turn from him if she knew the truth, that he was sick, using her syringe without her permission. He had known then he had to leave before he hurt his son and ruined his marriage. He hated being away from his family, but at least they were safe from him. When he recovered from these humiliating problems, he could go home.

In the year since he had left the Orbiter, he had suffered attacks in which his head seemed to splinter and his body shook with uncontrolled tremors. Only the medicine helped.

At a dosage equal to 10 percent of what Alaj Rajindia had given Dehya, it alleviated Eldrin's symptoms without incapacitating him. He wanted to stop using it. The medicine had taken over his life. Just this morning he had vowed, yet again, that he would take no more. Only now he was desperate. He tried to get up from the floor, but he was barely off his knees when his body went rigid.

Eldrin's father had told him once that he was never aware of his seizures, but for Eldrin it was excruciatingly different. He fell to his side, convulsing, and he felt every terrifying moment. The attack seemed to go on forever, a waking nightmare.

Mercifully, it finally stopped. Eldrin went limp on the floor, gasping. For a moment he just lay there. Then, clutching the armchair, he dragged himself to his feet. He stumbled into the bedroom where he had stored his travel bag, which he had never unpacked even though he used its contents, because he kept hoping he could go home.

His medicine was inside the bag.

With shaking fingers, he pulled out the syringe he had taken from Dehya's suite and programmed in the relaxant. He had just managed to inject himself when he collapsed on the bed and began to convulse again. He wanted to scream, but he couldn't make a sound. His throat closed up while his body arched and seized.

When his muscles finally released, Eldrin groaned with relief. The drug was taking effect. His body slowly relaxed, muscle by muscle, and his nausea receded. The pain in his head eased. For a long time he lay on his back. He didn't understand what was wrong with him. Only Dehya's syringe could be programmed to dispense this medicine he so needed with such urgency; others he had tried didn't even recognize the drug Alaj had prescribed her.

Eldrin would never forget its name.

Phorine.

4

The Claret Suite

Soz was almost ready to go to the starport. A shuttle there would take her to a transport ship in orbit, and the transport would carry her to her new assignment, a tour onboard the Imperial Fleet battle cruiser, *Roca's Pride*. Good name, that. She approved.

But first she had two stops to make.

After seeing her parents a few days ago, her mood had lifted. Her father hadn't been able to walk much, so she had kept the tour of the academy brief and spent most of the time talking to them. Even after they had left, her spirits had remained high. But now they dimmed.

She rode a mag-lev train into HQ City. It didn't take long to reach the hospital. Today she went inside Althor's room instead of staying in the viewing chamber. She walked quietly to the bed, though only she could hear her footsteps. He lay on his back, his face gaunt, his body kept alive by lines and machines.

Soz sat in a chair by the bed and spoke softly. "I came to say goodbye, but just for now." Her voice caught. "Althor, you must get better. You have to carry your half of this Imperial Heir business."

Only machines whispered in the room. Soz couldn't believe he had been dead for over two months. **Althor, come back,** she thought.

His eyes opened. She almost jumped out of her chair and shouted for the doctors. Then she saw his blank gaze. The monitors around his bed confirmed the truth: his condition hadn't changed. His brainstem had partially survived, and it continued to control his heart rate, breathing, reflexes, the contraction of his pupils, his swallowing reflexes. It even regulated his sleep cycles. Yesterday he had moved his fingers. If a sharp edge touched his skin, he jerked. But he was conscious of nothing. His cerebral cortex had died. He had lost the functions that gave him personality, intelligence, memory. Modern medicine could do a great deal, but it couldn't repair his mind. The essence of Althor, her brother, was gone.

"I don't want to say goodbye." A tear ran down her face. "I'll see you again. I promise."

Soz walked out onto the training fields. She had one hour left, just enough time to complete one last task.

In a distant quadrangle, Lt. Colonel Dayamar Stone was working with a group of novices. Sunrays slanted across the fields, gilding athletes with antiqued light as if they were figures out of a legend rather than real people. They were doing calisthenics, led by a cadet in their class. Soz jogged over and walked around their formation, hanging back. Stone stood several meters to one side, peering at a holoboard. As she approached him, he glanced at her.

Soz stopped a few paces away and snapped a salute. "Sir!"

He returned her salute. "At ease, Valdoria."

Soz relaxed an infinitesimal amount.

"What brings you out here?" Stone asked.

"I leave tonight for *Roca's Pride,* sir."

"Yes. I heard."

"I was wondering—"

He waited. "Yes?"

"Sir, I'd like to run the Echo."

Stone visibly tensed. He was the one who had suspected her of cracking the meshes so she could cheat on the obstacle course. He hadn't had any evidence; Soz knew how to cover her tracks. If she hadn't confessed, they probably couldn't have proved anything. But she would have known. Her grief was no excuse. Confessing had been one of her hardest moments, and she regretted losing her honors status, but she couldn't have lived with herself otherwise. The cadets thought her clever for cracking the system, but to Soz, an accomplishment gained by unfair advantage meant nothing.

"You know the course has been reprogrammed." Stone made it a statement rather than a question.

"Yes, sir. That's why I want to run it."

He considered her. "Very well."

Stone gave his holoboard to the cadet leading the exercises. Then he and Soz walked across the fields. She halted at the Echo and narrowed her eyes. This course had been her bane. Her half-brother Kurj, the Imperator, had ordered her to run it on one of her first days at the academy. But to do well on the Echo, a cadet needed the physical augmentation they received their third year. Although she had never run the course, she hadn't wanted to lose face in front of Kurj or her classmates. Then he had added one last command: beat the record of nine minutes, forty-three seconds. Soz had gritted her teeth, tried the impossible, and failed. Her time had been appalling. Only later did she learn that she had been the first novice in ten years to finish the course on her first try. Kurj had neglected to mention that fact. He was too busy giving her hell because she was his heir and his cocky sister and who the blazes knew why else.

Since then, she had tried the Echo numerous times but never beat the record. Often she limped off the course covered in mud and bruises, humiliated by her time.

Then the Traders had killed her brother.

Soz had gone a little crazy then, obsessed with revenge. She had sworn to rip through her training and graduate so she could go out and destroy the Traders who had ended her brother's life. She cracked the field webs, memorized the Echo files, and pulverized the previous record. But it hadn't been real, and it hadn't helped her grief.

Today she again faced her nemesis, this time the honest way.

Stone held his timer and said, simply, "Go."

Soz took off.

The entrance to the Echo looked like a dirt path, but it was actually perplex, a material saturated with sensors. It evaluated her stride, weight, brain waves, and any other data it could use to analyze and predict her actions. So she didn't go down the path. Instead she ran along a narrow bar at its border. Although the bar could also gather data about her, the information wouldn't be as accurate. Any advantage she gained, no matter how small, could help. She sped along the bar, her speed and reflexes enhanced. It shuddered, trying to knock her back onto the perplex, but she outwitted its attempts.

A vaulting horse blocked the end of the path. Soz jumped in front of it, never breaking stride, and hurtled over the horse in a flip. She nailed her landing and sprinted forward, carried by her momentum. The scaffolding loomed ahead, a structure of metal struts that vibrated, bent, and snapped with rudimentary intelligence. When she jumped up and grabbed a bar, it almost succeeded in throwing her off. The techs had added odd nuances to its vibrations. She grabbed new bars as the ones she held sagged and jerked. She swung through the crazily shaking struts, letting go of each just *before* she grabbed the next, so that for an instant she was airborne with no handhold. She had discovered it confused the program that controlled the structure. The bars responded to her touch, and if she broke contact, they couldn't react as well.

She made it through the framework, but her unfamiliarity with the changes in its behavior slowed her down. At the other side, she let go from high up and dropped. The impact of her landing could have broken her knees before ISC had enhanced her body. Now they bent at exactly the amount necessary to cushion her landing, and her augmented legs absorbed the force. She took off and ran hard, her feet drumming the ground. The perplex surface bucked, trying to throw her off balance, but she had evaded enough of the Echo sensors that it had trouble judging her stride. It failed to toss her to the ground.

The pool lay before her, serene, reflecting the pale sky like a visual echo. Its mirror quality came from oil that coated its surface. The first times she had done the course, she had tried running around the stone rim, but keeping her balance had proved impossible. She always slipped into the oil and ended up covered with crud. Today she jumped. The pool was too large to clear even with her enhanced muscles, so she leapt to the rim, touched down, and leapt again. A third jump and she cleared the pool.

Next she faced the aural labyrinth, an enclosed maze of tunnels that echoed, making it hard to judge direction. The walls rose higher than her head. Inside, she lost her way twice and had to backtrack. She kept running, pushing to the limit, and exited the maze on the far side.

Rebounders crashed and bounced ahead of her, a series of gates that operated in complex rhythms, snapping open and slamming closed. She dodged through the clanging portals, but they managed to crash into her body anyway. She didn't fall because they struck from both sides and held her up, but it felt like hell. Gritting her teeth, she kept going. By the time she lurched through the last gate, she was gasping. She stumbled into a white sand trap and leaned over, her hands braced on her knees while she heaved in air.

As her pulse calmed, she straightened up and looked around. Stone was a few paces away, studying his timer. As Soz walked over to him, he glanced up.

"Nine minutes, fifty-two seconds," he said. "Almost the record."

Oh, well. "Almost isn't good enough."

"It is when it's honest." He spoke quietly. "It's a good time, Soz. Be proud of it."

She had to admit, this result felt far better than when she had shattered the record last time. "Thank you, sir."

For the first time in ages he smiled at her. "Good luck on *Roca's Pride.*"

Soz grinned. "Good name for a ship, eh, sir?"

He chuckled. "That it is."

They headed back then, he to the first-year cadets and she to the dorms. She was almost there when someone fell into step beside her. She glanced up to see a tall fellow with dark hair and eyes, broad shoulders, and devilish good looks, one of the cadets who had been doing calisthenics with Stone's class. He saluted her with a powerful slap of his crossed wrists.

Soz returned the salute. "At ease."

"Thanks." He looked her over.

"Who are you?" Soz asked.

"Rex. Rex Blackstone."

"Well, Rex Blackstone, what do you want?"

He wasn't the least intimidated by her bluntness. "I saw you run the Echo."

Soz shrugged. "It wasn't much."

"Looked like much to me."

Soz was tired, not to mention jittery about leaving Diesha. "You want something, Blackstone?"

"Maybe." He considered her with that appraising gaze of his. "I want to get a look at the wildcat they call the toughest, smartest, worst-behaved cadet at DMA."

Soz gave a startled laugh. "Well, you got your look."

His eyes flashed with a wicked glint. "Remember me, Valdoria. When you're in command of the toughest, smartest, most notorious squadron of the J-Force, I'll be flying with you."

"Is that a challenge?"

"Hell, yes."

"All right, you got it," Soz said. "You graduate top of your class and when I'm in command of that squad, I'll tell HQ you're one of mine."

"Deal." He held out his arm, his fist clenched. Soz laid her wrist on top of his, her fist also clenched, sealing the pact as Jagernauts had done since the first pilots took to space.

Rex jogged off then, headed to the first-year dorms. Watching him, Soz felt a chill run up her back. She suddenly had a vision of him jogging with her out to a tarmac where four Jag fighters waited. Gray streaked his hair and he wore the gauntlets of a Secondary, the second-highest rank in the J-Force.

She wore those of a Primary.

Soz shook her head. Her imagination was getting ahead of her. She had yet even to graduate.

Eldrin was reading a novel when he heard the noise. He had been struggling with the words, looking them up in the dictionary that came with the holobook. Although he was no longer illiterate, he read slowly. Glyphs for the same words never looked the same to him, though he had come to understand that certain arrangements referred to the same word even when they showed up in different places, in different fonts, even different colors. It had taken him a long time to learn to process those differences. Reading was no longer an exercise in teeth-gritting frustration for him. It was even fun.

He gradually became aware of the rattling. Nothing in the sitting room looked out of place, though. Just empty. The Ruby Palace always seemed that way to him even when he wasn't the only one here. He wished someone would visit. Not that anyone could come without his invitation; so many installations protected the palace, he could live here in peace and quiet even if a horde of maniacs was storming the mountains.

Eldrin glanced at his holobook. He was reading about ISC. The Assembly wanted him to learn about the military in case he ever became a Key, a member of the Dyad. As pharaoh, Dehya was the Assembly Key: as Imperator, Kurj was the Military Key. Eldrin wasn't first in line for either title; Soz was Kurj's heir, and Taquinil was Dehya's. The Assembly wanted to name Eldrin as the second heir to the Assembly Key, though, after Taquinil. The title went according to ability as well as heredity. Although he didn't understand the technology of Kyle meshes, he apparently had the mental sensitivity required to create and manipulate them. He was much farther down the line of succession for Imperator, but he was in there somewhere, probably eighth or ninth.

The Assembly Key didn't have to be the Ruby Pharaoh, but Dehya held both titles. The pharaoh's consort didn't assume her royal title on her death; traditionally it went to her oldest daughter. Dehya had defied tradition and made her son her heir, so Taquinil was also first in line for the Ruby Throne. Dehya's second heir was her sister Roca. That did put Eldrin in the line of succession, through his mother rather than his wife, making him third in line for the throne after Taquinil and Roca.

Eldrin felt painfully unqualified for all three titles. He had been a good warrior on Lyshriol, with a sword and bow, but he didn't have the mind for modern warfare. He wasn't a politician, either, though he did attend Assembly sessions. It intrigued him to watch Dehya in that theater of power. The title of Pharaoh was supposedly titular, but she had forged it into an immense, shadowy power he could barely fathom.

He could work the web, though. For him, more even than for Dehya and Kurj, it came as naturally.

A rattle disturbed the silence.

"What is that?" Eldrin muttered. He put down his book and went to the console across the room. When he touched a fingertip panel, his personal EI spoke in a mellow voice.

"Good evening, Your Majesty."

"My greetings, Etude," Eldrin said. "Did you hear a noise?"

"I detect many noises."

"This one was out of place, like a rattle in the walls."

"Ah. Yes, I heard it." Etude paused. "It came from the system that heats these rooms. A conduit is loose. I have sent a mechbot to fix it."

"Good." The problem surprised Eldrin; the bots were obsessive about maintenance, if one could ascribe human attributes to machines. He supposed it was more accurate to say that whoever had designed them was dedicated to ensuring the palace stayed clean and well-organized.

He went to the liquor cabinet and took out the dragon carafe. "Will it take long to fix?"

"About ten minutes." Then Etude said, "Your Majesty, in the past few days you have consumed an amount of alcohol large enough to register as a concern on my medical scanners."

Eldrin picked up a crystal tumbler. "Don't start again."

"Again?"

"Bothering me about a drink." He wondered if the same person who programmed the cleaning bots had coded Etude. "Don't you have anything else to do?"

"One of my functions is to protect your health. You consume too much alcohol and take too much medication."

Eldrin tensed. How could it know about the phorine? He used only the syringe he had brought, which had no connection to any mesh in the palace. The syringe belonged to Dehya, which meant if she needed more of the medicine, she wouldn't have it. Alaj could issue her another one, though. She apparently hadn't used the phorine since then, anyway. He doubted she had even noticed the syringe was missing. Sometimes he wondered if she knew he was missing from her life.

"What medications?" he asked warily.

"I don't know. However, judging from your behavior before and after you inject this drug, it has a strong effect."

Eldrin poured himself a glass of whiskey, which he now kept in the carafe instead of wine. "Yes, well, that's why I have to take it."

"Your symptoms indicate either a neurological disease or an addiction. I have no record of any disease."

Eldrin's hand jerked and gold liquid sloshed over his fingers. "Are you calling me an alcoholic?"

"No. Are you?"

"No. I can stop drinking any time I want."

"This may be. However, your situation has triggered alarms in my systems. I should contact the medical authorities, but I have been unable to do so. I'm blocked by a security protocol called Epsilon."

"I know." Eldrin didn't actually understand Epsilon. Taquinil had found it on Dehya's console and said it gave people privacy. Eldrin had the impression the files were games Dehya had left for the boy. He had asked Epsilon to prevent Etude from sending out warnings about his use of the medicine. He didn't know why it worked, but apparently Taquinil was right, this Epsilon game did protect his privacy.

He returned the dragon flask to the cabinet. "I have reason to want a drink."

"Perhaps you would tell me this reason?" it said.

Eldrin didn't want to tell it anything. He had developed a taste for alcohol after his marriage. He had been sixteen, well below the legal drinking age among Skolians. But Dehya was gone so much, and she never locked her wine cabinet. Confused, angry, and lonely, he had found that alcohol helped.

They married him to Deyha, literally at gunpoint, and then left him on his own to deal with the impossible.

So he drank.

When he had first come to the Orbiter, Eldrin had seen a specialist, a military doctor who helped him deal with his "post-traumatic stress" from combat. Those sessions had been an oasis in the midst of his confusion. On Lyshriol, people treated him as a hero, but he knew the truth. He had committed murder. He killed two men with his sword and another in hand-to-hand combat. His people called him a man of courage and honor, but he felt like slime. Going to a counselor had helped. But after the Assembly forced him to marry Dehya, he stopped seeing the specialist. He hadn't wanted to talk to anyone. He had just plain hated himself.

Somehow, incredibly, he and Dehya had found their way to each other. They formed the bonds only Rhon psions could know. They were alike far more than he could have imagined. She understood his painful sensitivity to emotions because she was the same way. She and Taquinil became gems in a life that otherwise bewildered him.

Eldrin hadn't drunk as much then, but since coming here, he often sought the solace of alcohol. He felt ripped in two by this separation from his family. He took a swallow of whiskey, and it spread warmth through his body. He didn't need phorine yet; although the euphoria had faded, he felt no symptoms of his illness. Whenever he stopped taking it, his head ached, worse and worse, until he went into convulsions. He knew he should go to a doctor, but he hated to admit his weakness, and the doctors would reprimand him for using medicine without supervision. They might even take it away. No. He was strong enough to deal with this on his own. He would manage. Somehow.

To Etude, he said only, "I'm lonely." It was easier to admit that to an EI than to a living person.

"I may be able to help," it said.

"Really?" Eldrin doubted it, but he thought it charming the EI offered assistance. "How?"

"Imperator Skolia is en route to the palace. He should be landing here soon."

"Kurj is coming home?"

"It appears so. Will that help your loneliness?"

"Yes, actually, it will." Kurj had been staying down in the city, in the skyscraper where he had his office, in daily strategy sessions with his top officers. Eldrin hadn't expected to see him at the palace at all.

"When will he arrive?" Eldrin asked.

"Within the hour," Etude said.

"I'm glad." He finished his whiskey, savoring the haze of

warmth it created. But he poured no more. Perhaps Etude was right, he depended on it too much. He made a resolution: he would stop the alcohol and phorine both.

He would manage.

Somehow.

5

The Ruby Palace

"They're claiming the attack came from pirates," Kurj said. "Rogue marauders." Even in the spacious living room where he and Eldrin had retired, he looked huge. He sat on a brocaded couch, his booted legs stretched across the gold carpet, creasing the pile. His hands were folded around a steaming mug of kava laced with rum.

Eldrin sat across from him in an armchair, one with those annoying cushions that kept trying to make him relax. He was glad to see Kurj, but his brother's news disquieted him. "The emperor claims the ships that attacked Onyx acted without authorization?"

"It seems so." Sarcasm saturated Kurj's voice.

The steam from Eldrin's drink wafted over his face. He didn't take a swallow. The kava had rum in it and he meant to keep his pledge. No more alcohol. It would be mortifying to tell Kurj why he had made such a resolution, though, so he kept holding the mug.

"It's absurd," Eldrin said. "First they expect us to believe a hard-line emperor with years of experience didn't know one of his top people had infiltrated a major ISC system and attacked my family? Now we're supposed to accept that eleven ESComm ships went rogue and committed an act of war? How stupid does he think we are?"

Kurj took a swallow of kava. "Qox is playing a game—a vicious, calculated game. If we attack in response to the Onyx affair, he will claim we started the war."

"It's obviously a false claim."

"False, yes. Obvious? To us, yes. To the Allied Worlds of Earth? Maybe not." Kurj rubbed his eyes with no attempt to hide his fatigue. He rarely relaxed his defenses and let anyone sense his emotions. Eldrin was one of the few people who saw the human side of his daunting half-brother. It had taken Eldrin years to realize how the rest of humanity viewed Kurj, because the Imperator tended to ease up with him.

"It wouldn't take much to put off the Allieds," Kurj said.

"They already don't trust us."

"It's disheartening."

"Yes." Kurj's inner lids slid up, revealing his gold eyes. "Tell me something more cheerful, heh? That's why I came home." He let his body sink into the sofa and made a visible effort to relax his tensed muscles. "How are Dehya and Taquinil?"

"Beautiful," Eldrin said. "Dehya's tired, though. The Kyle web takes a lot out of her. Both of you."

"That it does. It's like a quicksand, an endless pit." Kurj shook his head. "It takes everything we have and wants more. I don't know how much longer Dehya and I can maintain it."

Eldrin hadn't expected that. "But the two of you can find a solution, can't you?"

"Just between you and me," Kurj said, "no. I don't see how."

Eldrin stared at him. What Kurj had just revealed went against every public portrayal he had seen of the Dyad. Although Dehya shielded her mind, he had picked up hints from her. He knew she was exhausted. But he hadn't realized it was that bad. "What will happen to the Kyle web?"

"As long as Dehya and I can keep going, we'll be all right." Kurj downed the rest of his kava and set his mug on the table. "Just pray nothing happens to either of us."

Eldrin felt cold. "And if it does?"

"Your son is too young to join the Dyad." Kurj spoke quietly. "Mother is the next in line. Or you."

"You know I'm not ready," Eldrin said. Putting him in the Dyad was a surefire way to ensure the fall of the Imperialate.

Kurj smiled. "Don't look so alarmed. I'm not planning on dying any time soon, and I'm sure Dehya feels the same way."

"Gods, I hope so." Eldrin couldn't bear to think of losing his wife. So much responsibility for the survival of the Imperialate rested on her fragile shoulders. Alaj had prescribed a phorine dose for her *ten times* what Eldrin took and it barely affected her. That told him volumes about how much her work tied her mind into knots, yet even with that, she had shielded him and Taquinil from the worst.

"She is going to Parthonia," Kurj added.

"Parthonia?" Eldrin tried to reorient his thoughts. "She didn't mention it to me." He shouldn't be surprised; Parthonia was the Imperialate capital, after all. Dehya attended Assembly sessions there, either in person or as a simulation through the meshes. He could see why she would go in person for the upcoming session; after the lapses in ISC web security that had allowed the ESComm attack, no one trusted the web. But it bothered him that Kurj had known her plans first.

Kurj was watching him. "I talked to her before I came here."

"Oh," Eldrin said. Nothing required his wife tell him first. He should stop being so insecure. "Is she taking Taquinil?"

"She wants to," Kurj said. "I don't think it's a good idea. No other Rhon psions are on Parthonia to protect him, which means he will have to go to the Assembly sessions with her."

Eldrin took a swallow of kava, then remembered his resolution and set the mug on the table. "I can take care of him."

"Have your nightmares stopped?" Kurj asked.

Eldrin wished he could say yes. But he dreamed of Althor's death often. "No."

Kurj had the kindness to say nothing more. If Eldrin had thought he could protect his son from himself, he would have gone home in a moment. But he couldn't.

"At least Althor isn't in pain," Kurj said.

No, he wasn't in pain. He was dead. "I don't understand why I have nightmares about him," Eldrin said. "Is it possible I'm picking up his dreams?"

"You couldn't. He has no higher brain functions." Kurj spoke quietly. "I'm sorry."

Eldrin struggled with his grief. "Maybe my mind can't

accept that." He truly could use a strong drink. He glanced at the steaming kava, but left it on the table.

A chime came from across the room, originating with an artfully rounded console that matched the gold and red wall mosaics, like part of the décor.

"Jason, what is it?" Kurj said.

Eldrin blinked. "Who is Jason?"

"Earth mythology," Kurj said absently. "He had Argonauts."

A deep voice came from the console. "A flyer is arriving at the palace."

"Jason is your EI?" Eldrin asked. It hadn't occurred to him to ask the palace if Kurj had a personal EI here. Perhaps he should have, as a courtesy. Could you be rude to an EI? After so many years, he should know what etiquette applied to created intelligences, but none of it felt natural.

"Yes," the EI said. "I am Jason."

"My greetings," Eldrin answered, feeling awkward.

"Who is on the flyer?" Kurj asked.

"Councilor Roca and her consort," Jason said.

Eldrin sat forward with a jerk. "My *father?*"

"Both of your parents are in the flyer," Jason told him.

Kurj wasn't smiling. "My stepfather never comes here."

"He is tonight," Jason said.

Eldrin couldn't believe it. His father, who had refused to see any of his family for over a year, was *here?* He had come, even blind and unable to walk? Eldrin flushed, uncertain whether to rejoice or worry about the unexpected visit from this man he always thought of as the Bard, in honor of his glorious voice and the love of singing he had imparted to Eldrin.

Kurj, however, didn't look surprised. Eldrin's anger sparked. Had Kurj known Eldrin's parents were on Diesha and never told him? Gods, Eldrin hadn't seen his father in two years. Kurj had no right to keep this from him.

Enough, Eldrin thought. He took a slow, calming breath. Kurj could have forgotten. He had other matters to consider, after all—like an interstellar war.

The Imperator was watching him, his mind shielded.

Eldrin suspected his own emotions were far more obvious to Kurj than the reverse. He had never been good at hiding them.

"I've been in conference with Dehya and my commanders," Kurj said. "I haven't had time for personal matters."

"Of course." Eldrin had to accept that explanation. But his parents didn't know he was here. If they had stayed somewhere else instead of the palace, he might never have known they had come to Diesha.

At night, the temperature in the Red Mountains dropped sharply. Eldrin pulled his climate-controlled jacket tighter around his body. He was standing outside the circle of light shed by lamps around a landing pad on the palace roof. The flyer had just finished setting down. Its engines died, and an oval-shaped airlock snicked open in its side.

Eldrin's mother jumped down onto the tarmac. Her skin and hair glimmered in the lamp light. Eldrin started toward her, his mood lifting, but when she turned back to the hatchway, he froze. He had forgotten the medtechs would need to carry out his father. He stepped back and waited with Kurj, in the darkness beyond the light. A lump seemed to have lodged in his throat. After more than a year of worrying, he would see his father. Roca waited on the tarmac, looking up at the flyer.

A figure appeared in the hatchway.

Eldrin's breath caught. His father was *standing*, gripping the edges of the hatch, silhouetted against the light inside. Standing—and seeing. He wore a pair of wire-rimmed spectacles. He smiled at Roca, then looked out beyond the circle of light. It didn't surprise Eldrin that his father had chosen to wear glasses; the Bard had always avoided more advanced technology if he could manage on his own.

He knew the moment his father saw Kurj. The Bard's posture went rigid and his expression shuttered. His mind became closed. At Eldrin's side, Kurj seemed to turn into stone. He had raised so many mental barriers against his stepfather, his mood became opaque, even to an empath of Eldrin's strength. But he needed no empathy to know that

Kurj was no happier to see his stepfather than the Bard was to see him.

Suddenly the Bard's mood lightened. With a start, Eldrin realized his father was looking at him. Serenity flowed to Eldrin from his father, real this time, nothing induced by phorine or alcohol.

Eldrin walked forward. Roca turned to him, and welcome filled her mind. Eldrin reached her first, and he hugged her tightly, his eyes closed, his head bent next to hers. When they separated, he looked up at the flyer and offered his hand. As soon as he saw his father stiffen, Eldrin regretted the gesture. He should have remembered his father's pride, which among Roca's people was sometimes all he had to buttress himself against their disdain.

Then the Bard reached out and grasped Eldrin's wrist in a hold they had often used when climbing in the Backbone Mountains, two fingers on each side of his wrist. Eldrin closed his four-fingered hand around his father's wrist and braced his feet so the Bard could use him for support.

His father let himself down from the hatchway. Straightening up, he dropped Eldrin's arm and stood on his own. He regarded Eldrin steadily, and the lenses of his glasses caught a glint from the light in the flyer. Eldrin experienced the same odd disorientation that he had felt since he was fourteen. It came to him every time he stood next to the Bard and realized he had grown taller than his sire. He grinned and his father's face warmed with affection. Then his father clapped him on the shoulder.

Kurj stood back, watching them, his mind shadowed.

Roca selected rum from the well-stocked cabinet in the living room where Kurj and Eldrin had relaxed earlier. Kurj dropped onto the brocaded couch. A robot trundled in with a tray of steaming kava in mugs shaped like the bells of sunset-dragotus blossoms.

"We arrived on Diesha this morning," Roca said. "We came straight from Lyshriol." She leaned against the cabinet. "It took three days, ship's time."

"It seemed longer." Eldrin's father lowered himself into

an armchair and exhaled as the cushions eased his body. It told Eldrin a great deal about his father's exhaustion that he so obviously appreciated the chair's ability to deduce his needs and provide comfort. Normally the Bard abhorred technology.

"Space travel feels long to me, too," Eldrin said as he settled into his own armchair. They had pulled the seats into a semicircle facing the couch. Even with everyone guarding their minds, Eldrin sensed how much his father's legs ached. Sometimes he and his father seemed like two parts of one mind. But Eldrin had come to the Orbiter as a teenager, apparently during a surge of neural development in his brain. Whether or not that had made it possible for him to learn to read and write, he couldn't have said, but he did know he had become less like his father then.

Right now, something felt odd in their connection. Wrong. He sensed . . . static. The Bard was staring blankly ahead.

"Father?" Eldrin asked. "Are you all right?"

The Bard continued to stare, looking at no one.

Roca turned from the cabinet where she was putting away the rum. "Eldri?" As soon as she saw her husband's face, she went over and knelt on a footstool by his chair, bringing her eyes level with his. She touched his cheek. Then she lowered her hand and simply waited.

"What's wrong with him?" Kurj demanded.

"It's a seizure," Roca said.

The Bard suddenly blinked. He rubbed his eyes, then let out a long breath and lowered his arm. For a moment he just looked at Roca. Then he said, "I think I need to lie down."

Lines of worry creased her forehead. "Are you all right?"

"Just tired. It was a long day, eh, with Althor and Soz?"

"Quite a day." Roca stood and offered her arm. He even let her help him to his feet. He seemed confused, his motions slowed. Eldrin also stood, intending to offer support, but his mother shook her head slightly at him. He understood. His father disliked revealing his vulnerability, especially in front of Kurj.

The Bard nodded good-night to both Eldrin and Kurj. With Roca at his side, he limped out of the semicircle of chairs toward an archway that exited the room.

Kurj rose to his feet, towering. "I'll go wake his doctors."

With a slow pause and turn, the Bard looked back, his face strained. "That isn't necessary."

"We can't take chances with your life," Kurj said.

The Bard's voice tightened. "The doctors will tell you what I already know. I need to lie down. If you must have your EI monitor my room, go ahead."

Roca turned to her oldest son. "He will be fine."

"You are certain?" Kurj asked.

"As certain as is possible," she said.

Eldrin knew why Kurj was asking. As Imperator, he was charged with the protection of the Ruby Dynasty, and that included his stepfather whether he liked it or not. Eldrin shielded his mind from Kurj and directed a private thought to his father. *You look tired.*

I am fine, his father answered.

Roca frowned at her husband. *This has happened every day for the past ten days.*

Every day? Eldrin had never known his father to have such frequent seizures.

Kurj's thought rumbled. **Every day hardly sounds like "fine."**

Eldrin winced. Apparently he hadn't hidden his thoughts as well as he believed. The Bard recoiled from Kurj's force, taking an uneven step backward. Eldrin felt his father *shut* his mind, locking them all out so he could escape the mental power of his formidable stepson.

Kurj exhaled, his face drawn, his inner lids down. He jerked his chin at the archway. "Go ahead," he told his stepfather. "Rest. Let us know if you need anything."

Roca inclined her head to her son. The Bard gave the barest nod, just enough so he didn't ignore the Imperator. He left then, leaning on Roca's arm. That he accepted her help, even with Kurj watching, told Eldrin a great deal about the severity of his condition. Eldrin wanted to go with his parents, but he held back, knowing his father would prefer privacy.

When Kurj and Eldrin were alone, Kurj asked, "Are you sure he will be all right?"

"I think so." Eldrin wasn't certain, but his mother would see that his father had whatever he needed. She had been doing it for twenty-five years. He was in good care. The last thing he needed was Kurj's hostile attention.

The two of them sat down, awkward. Eldrin didn't know what to say. He could sense a bit of his brother's mood even through Kurj's barriers; whatever the Imperator thought of his stepfather, he was genuinely concerned for his health. The Bard's epilepsy was growing worse despite his treatments.

None of this boded well. They had to keep his father's condition private. Over the past eight years, Eldrin had seen how factions within the Assembly considered his father inferior, little better than breeding stock. It had so angered Eldrin, he had taken his Assembly seat to spite those who considered his bloodline tainted and unwelcome in their halls of power. He looked like his father, thought like him, sounded like him. He had a "civilized" veneer, but he was very much his father's son. Let the power-mongers choke on that resemblance.

As a member of the Ruby Dynasty, Eldrin had the right to vote in Skolia's governing body; a few nonelected seats existed, most of them held by his family. Except for those of the Ruby Pharaoh and Imperator, the hereditary seats carried few votes. Eldrin's siblings usually let Roca cast theirs by proxy, but Eldrin voted his own. Although he didn't yet understand the nuances in the flows of power, he was learning. To his surprise, it intrigued him.

Skolia had five political parties. Royalists particularly disliked his father. They harkened back to the days of the Ruby Empire, when the Ruby Dynasty ruled and heredity meant everything. No commoner could have wed a Ruby heir then. They found it appalling that Roca had taken an untitled "barbarian" as her consort. They knew perfectly well that if the Bard carried the Rhon genes, he probably descended from the ancient dynasty. They chose to ignore that fact. As far as Eldrin could see, their attitude was prejudice, pure and simple, because his father was uneducated and came from a world they considered beneath them.

The Traditional Party was even worse. Eldrin loathed them most, for they also wanted to deny Taquinil the title of Ruby Heir. In their view, only women should inherit property or power. Eldrin would fight them from here to another galaxy to ensure his son's right to the throne. They knew damn well

Taquinil wouldn't be the first male pharaoh. Two were famous in history: one had been a pharaoh's consort until she died in battle, after which he assumed her title through savvy politics and leadership; the other had been the son of a pharaoh who had no daughters, like Dehya. If the Traditionalists had their way, they would confine all princes in seclusion, hiding them in robes that covered their bodies. Hell, they probably wanted Eldrin to live that way.

The Progressives had no complaints about Eldrin's father, but they were too proactive, always proposing this and that, major changes in the political, cultural, and social landscape. It gave Eldrin hives. He never understood the ramifications of their suggested changes well enough to judge the potential effects. He often wondered if even the Progressives understood them. In the end, Eldrin had registered with the Moderates, the largest and least polarizing of the parties.

He glanced at Kurj, who was sipping kava, lost in his own thoughts. His half-brother had registered with the fifth party, the Technologists. Kurj eschewed the Traditional Party for obvious reasons. Eldrin suspected he chose the Technology Party over the Royalists only to avoid the appearance of bias, given Kurj's royal title. It was hard to know, though; Kurj certainly fit his idea of a technocrat. The Imperator had so much augmentation to his body that in some ways he seemed more machine than human.

With a start, Eldrin realized Kurj was smiling at him. He flushed. "What's funny?"

"You're so somber," Kurj said. "You are thinking of politics?"

"Unfortunately." He should learn to shield his moods better. At least it helped distract him from worrying about his father. He glanced at the archway where his parents had disappeared. Were he in a similar situation, he wouldn't want his wife or son to see his infirmity, either, but knowing that made it no easier to sit here. "I'm concerned about Father."

Kurj spoke carefully. "He has good care on Lyshriol. But the time may have come when he needs a facility that can provide more specialized treatment."

Eldrin had wondered it himself. "Corey Majda could bring more specialists to Lyshriol." Corey commanded the orbital defense system, or ODS, that protected Lyshriol. She also provided the military doctors who treated his father.

Kurj took another swallow of kava, his second mug of the night. "It would make more sense if he went to the treatment facility rather than attempting to reconstruct one at Lyshriol."

"I suppose." It made perfect sense, except of course the Bard hated being away from home.

"Roca can take him to the Orbiter," Kurj said. "They have one of the best medical research centers in the Imperialate."

Eldrin sat up straighter. "Taquinil could see him!" His son had been terribly worried about his grandfather. The Bard doted on Taquinil, and spending time with his grandson could make the rest of his visit to the Orbiter more palatable. "He and Taqui could stay together while Dehya is on Parthonia."

"Do you think your father would agree?" Kurj asked.

"I don't know," Eldrin admitted. "He won't like leaving my younger siblings alone on Lyshriol."

An odd look came over Kurj's face, and Eldrin caught a hint of his mood. Loneliness.

"You are always welcome to visit Lyshriol," Eldrin added. "I think the family would like to know you better."

"I'm too heavy there," Kurj said curtly.

"Even so." Eldrin knew the real reason Kurj didn't visit. It wasn't the heavy gravity. He felt uncomfortable in his stepfather's territory. "You are always welcome."

Kurj's voice quieted. "Thank you."

Then the Imperator finished his kava.

The Claret Suite muffled the Bard as if it could hush his voice. The brocade walls, dark red drapes, the red and gold vases, the domed ceiling with mosaics in red and amber, the dark red carpet with a pile so lush it covered the toes of his boots—it all made the place too quiet and heavy. The canopied bed had blackwood posters and dark red drapes, red velvet covers, and dark gold sheets. He wished someone would open a window and let in some light and air.

He lay on the bed and closed his eyes. This visit had drained him: the pain of seeing Althor, his joy in reconciling with Soz, the tension of Kurj, and then another damnable seizure. It amazed him that Roca had stayed with him throughout the last miserable year, even when he had threatened to divorce her if she didn't get out of his bedroom, which had been truly stupid.

The bed shifted as Roca sat next to him. When she brushed his hair off his face, he opened his eyes. "Why do you put up with me? Kurj is right. You need a husband worthy of you."

"Oh, stop." She didn't sound as if she took him any more seriously now than the hundred other times he made that statement. He smiled. Perhaps he said it so she would tell him to stop.

"Eldrin looked so worried," Roca said. "I should go downstairs and let him know you're all right."

"In a bit." He liked just lying here, looking at her face. Her gold skin glimmered.

"Eldri, are you truly feeling all right?" Roca asked, concerned.

"Now I am." Only she could get away with calling him Eldri; to everyone else, he was Eldrinson. It bemused Roca's people, who couldn't understand why the father was Eldrinson and the son Eldrin. Well, he hardly intended to saddle his firstborn with the name Eldrinsonson. In the tradition of his people, they alternated generations with the word "son." His father had been Eldrin, he was Eldrinson, and his son was Eldrin. He had hoped Eldrin would continue the tradition, but having two Eldrinsons alive at the same time was just too confusing.

He brushed his finger over her lips. He had gone for a year without touching his wife, during that time he had refused to see his family. Since then, they had been making up for the lost nights. Even knowing she would come right back tonight, it disquieted him when she left. He had been without her for too long.

"Kurj's EI will let him know I am fine." He tugged on her arm and murmured, "You should stay here."

"I thought you were tired." She was smiling, though. She lay down next to him.

He pulled her into an embrace. "I need my medicine. You."

The Skolian doctors could have their hospitals and machines. Roca did more for him than they had ever managed.

She smoothed his hair back from his face, her hands gentle but sensuous. They undressed in the dim light from a lamp on the nightstand. She was a balm in his arms, then a temptress, then fire. They made love as they had the first night they spent at Castle Windward, twenty-five years ago, while a blizzard whirled outside and the only other heat came from a fire in the hearth.

Tonight, in the Ruby Palace, they barely noticed the rattle in the walls.

6

Firestorm

*R*oca's Pride* rotated in space, huge and massive, a Firestorm battle cruiser, flagship of the Imperial Fleet. It was a cylinder ten kilometers long and one in diameter, capped by a half-sphere at one end and open to space at the other. A docking tube extended down the center, circled at intervals by huge rings. Spokes extended from the rings out to the cylinder's rim, allowing the ship to turn while its docking tube remained stationary. Gigantic thrusters circled the perimeter of the cylinder at its open end. Lights flashed across the hull, from the antennae, pods, cranes, flanges, and crawlers on its myriad surfaces.

As Soz's transport approached the *Pride,* she floated in its viewing bay and gazed at the gargantuan cruiser. A flotilla of smaller ships accompanied it: bristling destroyers and frigates; Starslammers and Thunderbolts; stinging Wasps and Scorpions; razor-edged Scythes; ram stealth tanks that appeared and then vanished; unfolding Jack-knives; Leos, Asps, and Cobras as deadly as their namesakes; bolts, masts, rafts, tugs, booms, blades, fists. Jag starfighters shot through the fleet, luminous and brilliant, the flotilla vanguard. It all gleamed against the dazzling backdrop of interstellar space, the spumes of nebulae and stars in red, blue, gold, and white. The sight made Soz feel alive in a way she had never known before. She was part of this great universe, a tiny speck against its unbearable grandeur.

Roca's Pride grew on her view screen until the open end loomed before them, each of its thrusters many times the size of the transport ship. The end of the docking tube opened like a bud unfurling its petals. Soz could imagine power thrumming through the tube, the cruiser, the entire flotilla. The transport sailed into the pod, tiny against its immense doors. They closed around the ship and cut off her view of the stars.

A voice came from behind her. "Ready?"

Soz drifted around to see Secondary Tapperhaven floating in the hatchway. The older woman's short, dark hair stirred around her face. The sight of her DMA instructor relieved Soz. Tapperhaven was as tough as case-hardened steel, but she was also fair. She would continue Soz's training as the Imperial Heir during this tour.

"Ma'am! Yes, ma'am." Soz saluted while hanging on to a grip in the wall.

A smile tugged Tapperhaven's face, a change for the taciturn Jagernaut. "You look as if you're lit inside by a thousand lights."

Soz tilted her head toward the view screen. "It's hard to believe humans created all that."

"The first time I boarded a Firestorm, I felt that way, too." Regret flickered in Tapperhaven's eyes. "I forgot why it exists. We've fashioned incredible wonders, but we've created them for combat. It is a terrible beauty, and if you forget, the truth will break your heart."

Soz had never heard Tapperhaven speak with such feeling. "I'll remember."

"Well, so." Tapperhaven grinned. "Let's board."

"Aye, aye, ma'am!" Technically, that wasn't the response for a J-Force cadet, but since they were boarding a naval vessel, she figured she would get used to the naval protocols.

They exited the transport into a spherical decon chamber with Luminex walls. As they floated, a message came from her node. Intruding meds detected.

Those are decon meds, Soz thought. It probably already knew but they were still learning each other, she and her node, becoming two parts of one mind.

Their picoweb is linking to the picoweb for your health meds, it thought.

Good. The decon species would verify she carried only meds to maintain her health and repair cells. Although her meds attacked unwanted molecules, they should recognize and accept the decon species.

Soz had studied decon chambers as she studied every aspect of the ISC ships. Her advisors wanted her to major in military strategy, which she apparently had talent for, but she preferred ship design, what cadets called star-rigging. Decon meds had one goal: search and destroy. Like nano-thugs cruising the body, they sought out molecules that could endanger the ship. When they found invaders, they attacked until they disposed of the intruder or disintegrated. When the decontamination process finished, any decon meds left intact would fall into pieces the body could use or flush out of its system.

Are my health meds getting along with the decon meds? she asked.

They seem to like each other, her node answered. Its ability to converse was improving. At first, it hadn't even understood slang, let alone known how to respond. Decon had detected intruders, however. Then it thought, That's odd.

What?

You carry a peculiar med species that doesn't appear in their databases.

That was indeed odd. Surely ISC would have noticed anomalous meds drifting around in her body. **What does it do?**

Apparently it neutralizes blue food coloring.

Soz laughed, evoking a puzzled look from Tapperhaven, who was floating at her side. Soz reddened. Nothing like acting strange in front of her CO.

"My node said something funny," Soz said.

Tapperhaven smiled. "They can do that at inconvenient times."

"I guess so." To her node, Soz thought, **Those meds come from my father. They were engineered five thousand years ago when colonists settled Lyshriol. They deal with impurities that make water blue on Lyshriol.**

Ah. That would explain their nonstandard structure.

"What was funny?" Tapperhaven asked.

"Decon doesn't recognize my Lyshriol meds." She tensed as a thought came to her. "It better not get rid of them."

"It won't. We forwarded the specifications here. It will just take longer for it to verify their status."

You may keep them, her node informed her. Without them, your urine will turn green on Lyshriol.

Thank you, Soz thought dryly. **I needed to know that.**

Decon meds are now friendly with your Lyshriol meds.

Good.

"Decon complete," a voice said. "Permission to board."

"Acknowledged," Tapperhaven said.

A portal opened across the sphere, and they squeezed into a tube with glowing white walls. Blue Luminex rails ran along its sides, "above" Soz's head and "below" her feet, though without gravity she had no real sense of up and down. A magcar waited on the side of the tunnel, its entrance at right angles to her body. She reoriented and followed Tapperhaven inside. After they strapped into seats, the door clanged shut.

The car raced through the tunnel like a projectile hurtling down the bore of a gun. Soz thought maybe she had spent too much time studying, if she saw even magcars in terms of artillery.

They traveled the length of the ship, ten kilometers, to the hemisphere that capped the end of the cylinder. She and Tapperhaven disembarked and cycled through another airlock. They floated into the hemisphere, an area more than half a kilometer across—the bridge of *Roca's Pride*.

Robot arms crusted with mechanical paraphernalia shifted aside as they squeezed through the jungle of equipment surrounding the airlock. As per regulations, Soz went first, which meant she would hit any obstructions, nuisances, or dangers ahead of her CO. It was great policy for higher-ranked officers, but annoying or even deadly for the minions.

No matter what her civilian titles, when it came to ISC, she was at the bottom of the hierarchy.

The bridge was essentially a hollow shell. Its rotation could provide pseudo-gravity, if desired. Unlike habitats designed for beauty rather than efficiency, here they used all available space. Robot arms and independent units moved within the hemisphere in every direction. The center was more open, but the inner hull bristled with equipment, glinting silver and black. The officers' stations looked as small as metal studs from here, half a kilometer away, but they had to be full-sized consoles. Sparks of light flickered everywhere from screens, holos, and panels.

Holding a grip by the airlock, Soz peered at the command chair in the center of the bridge, curious to see her new CO. The chair formed the terminus of a mobile robot arm. Right now it faced forward, giving a sense of the captain looking in the direction of the cruiser's travel. It also meant Soz couldn't see who sat there. She wasn't the only one sent here to learn; Kurj expected all his top commanders to be familiar with more than one branch of ISC. During this training run, an officer from the Pharaoh's Army would be in command, coming up to speed on naval procedures. Although spacecraft differed in the various branches of ISC, the Imperial Fleet and Pharaoh's Army both utilized Firestorm battle cruisers, which meant an officer who had commanded one for the army could in theory do so for the navy as well.

Kurj hadn't yet chosen who to send when Soz left Diesha. The chair rotated to the side, revealing her new CO—

Ah, hell. It was Devon Majda.

Soz knew she shouldn't have been surprised it was a Majda. Their House had long supplied top officers to ISC. Jazida Majda, Devon's aunt, commanded the Pharaoh's Army and served as Kurj's second-in-command at ISC. Jazida wasn't the Matriarch of the House of Majda; that title had gone to her niece, Corey Majda, who commanded the orbital defense system at Lyshriol. However, Corey had an older sister.

Devon.

Brigadier General Devon Majda had once been the Matriarch of her House, a queen in her own right. The Assembly had betrothed her to Soz's brother, Vyrl, when he was fourteen. Or almost betrothed. Vyrl had run off and married his childhood sweetheart. It caused an interstellar crisis, given the grave insult done by the Ruby Dynasty to the most powerful noble House. Soz had been twelve at the time, a wayward adolescent. *She* could have told them the betrothal was a bad idea, if anyone had asked her. Vyrl would have been miserable married to a Majda warrior queen; he just wanted to farm and dance and have babies with his sweet-natured wife.

Then Devon had shocked everyone by abdicating her throne so she could marry the man she really loved, a commoner her own age, a clerk in the Assembly. Personally, Soz found it delightful that they had all broken so many rules. Given how upset everyone else had been, though, she kept her amusement to herself.

Unfortunately, Devon Majda now commanded *Roca's Pride.*

Just her luck to serve under the brigadier general her teenage brother had jilted. She couldn't see much from here except that the general was a tall woman with short, dark hair, which Soz already knew.

With no warning, the holoscreens in the hull came on, the entire hemisphere activating at once. Suddenly Soz was floating in space, surrounded by a spectacular vista of stars. Her hold on the grip tightened convulsively. It took a moment for her pulse to settle and her mind to reinterpret the scene. She wasn't in airless space; the screens were showing what was outside the ship.

"Whoa," Soz said.

Tapperhaven was holding onto a grip at Soz's side, surveying the bridge. "Impressive, yes?"

"Oh, yes." Consoles that had been "above" when she entered the bridge were now to the side. "We're moving, too."

"General Majda is rotating the bridge."

"Ultra," Soz said.

Tapperhaven blinked. "Ultra?"

"Radiant, ma'am," Soz explained. "Jagged to the max. Supernova sizzled."

The toughened Secondary actually smiled. "Does that

translate into a language your aging, decrepit instructor knows?"

"It's amazing, ma'am." The bridge was turning separately from the main cruiser, and Soz's hand-grip was on the cylinder cap. So the bridge turned around her. She knew most captains spun it for a portion of each shift, to give the crew a break from microgravity, but knowing that and seeing it happen were two different things. The equipment on the hull rotated with the bridge; the robot arms, cables, and mechbots needed rudimentary intelligence to readjust their relative positions as they moved about. Far above her, a man was walking across the hull upside down relative to Soz.

Tapperhaven nodded to Soz, giving her leave to proceed. With a shove, Soz pushed away from her hand-grip, flying toward a cable. She misjudged her force and rammed into it, smacking her nose. Swearing, she managed to grab the cable before she bounced away. Tapperhaven sailed past and caught the line farther down its length. Soz glared, but fortunately her instructor didn't see. So much for Soz leading the way. She followed Tapperhaven, pulling herself hand over hand along the line, skimming along. Soz had caught her hair in a regulation knot at her neck, but one curl had worked free and bedeviled her face, bouncing across her nose. Although some officers cut their hair, she liked knowing she could let hers go free when she was off duty.

The cable stretched beside the robot arm, along the rotation axis of the hemisphere, leaving Soz and Tapperhaven in microgravity. As Soz propelled herself forward, she trailed her hand across the ridged conduits in the arm. Tapperhaven was speaking into the comm of her wrist gauntlet, probably to Devon. The general looked back at them from her command chair at the end of the arm. Starlight lit her face, those high cheekbones and straight nose, chiseled and aristocratic, a true Majda. Her eyes slanted upward, as black as space.

Soz slowed to a stop when she and Tapperhaven reached the chair. The Secondary saluted General Majda. "Request permission to come onboard, ma'am."

"Permission granted, Secondary Tapperhaven." Devon glanced at Soz, her face impassive.

"Request permission to come aboard, Captain," Soz said.

She thought it odd to request permission for what they had already done, but Imperial Fleet protocol dictated they weren't onboard the ship until the captain said so.

Devon nodded to her. "Granted, Cadet Valdoria." She glanced at Tapperhaven. "You can go see the Exec. She'll check you both in."

"Aye, aye, ma'am," Tapperhaven said. It intrigued Soz to hear her instructor respond to Devon much as Soz responded to Tapperhaven, except here they used Fleet protocols.

After the general dismissed them, Soz and Tapperhaven turned to leave. Then Devon said, "Cadet Valdoria, stay a moment."

"Yes, ma'am," Soz said. They were all shielding their minds, but Tapperhaven's pause made Soz suspect she hadn't expected this. Tapperhaven couldn't say anything, though. She gave Soz a warning glance, undoubtedly cautioning her to behave. Then she headed to the airlock, leaving Soz alone with Brigadier General Devon Majda.

"At ease, Cadet," Devon said. She was like the ship, exuding an aura of contained power.

Soz endeavored to look at ease. "Aye, aye, ma'am." It felt strange for a J-Force cadet to give a naval response to an army officer, but what the hell.

"How have you been?" Devon asked.

That caught Soz off guard. "Uh, well, ma'am." She couldn't tell the truth, that she was exhausted from demerit duty.

"How is your family?"

Was Devon asking about Vyrl? Maybe she wanted to know about Althor or Soz's father, or even Soz's brother Shannon, who had killed the Aristo that tortured their father. Then again, given Devon's high rank and the fact that her sister Corey commanded the Lyshriol ODS, Devon probably knew more about them than Soz did herself.

"We're getting along," Soz said. She was worried about Shannon, but she couldn't say that to her CO.

"I'm sorry about Althor. His courage will be remembered."

Soz felt a hollowness within herself. She would rather have Althor alive than remember his courage. "Thank you, ma'am."

Devon spoke carefully. "And Vyrl?" She pronounced his

name *Vahrielle,* with a proper Iotic accent. Soz always drawled *Verle* like all the other farmers in Dalvador. Although Devon's expression remained neutral, her fingers tightened on the arm of her chair.

"He's fine," Soz said. "He has four children."

Devon didn't look surprised. "His psychological profile suggested he would want such. It's one reason I offered for him."

Well, that was romantic. But Soz supposed worse methods of matchmaking existed than using psychological profiles. When the Assembly had decided the Majda Matriarch should marry a Ruby prince, they had sent a dossier on Devon to Soz's parents and dossiers about the Valdoria princes to Devon. It didn't surprise Soz that Devon had chosen Vyrl; he was the most domestically inclined of her brothers, ideal for an aristocratic matriarch. Soz had to admit he could be charming when he wasn't annoying. And even she could see he was gorgeous.

An alarming thought came to Soz: what did *her* dossier say? Gods forbid. She doubted "domestic" was even on the horizon. She wanted an arranged marriage about as much as she wanted a case of Prolarian heat-hives, but she was almost lonely enough to consider it. If the Assembly arranged matters, she could quit worrying about her nonexistent love life.

Devon smiled with unexpected warmth. "Your moods cross your face like clouds over the sun."

Soz flushed. "My apologies, ma'am."

Devon laughed softly. "Relax, Soz."

It wasn't possible. She was nervous, exhilarated, and as tight as a coil, hanging in space, surrounded by stars and nebulae. She motioned to the bridge around them, holding herself in place with one hand. "I don't think I could ever relax with a view like this. It's glorious."

"Aye, that it is." Devon's dark eyes reflected the starlight. "Learn it well. Someday you will inherit this."

Gazing at the panorama of interstellar space, Soz wondered if she would ever be ready for the role demanded of her by the serendipity of genetics.

Submerged in a trance, Shannon lost his identity to the night. For this timeless moment, he wasn't a Ruby Dynasty prince, sixth son of the Dalvador Bard, heir to an interstellar empire. He was a Blue Dale Archer, no more, no less, lost in the moment, his mind floating.

Blue on blue, leather on stone, down and around, down and around. Shannon descended the tower in a trance, his boots padding on each step, muffled, down and around. At the bottom, he walked out into the castle where he had lived all of his life, his footsteps keeping pace with his thoughts:

moonglaze, moonglaze,
lyrine of power, lyrine of night,
lyrine of beauty, lyrine of sight.

Moonglaze's vague acknowledgment brushed Shannon's thoughts.

moonglaze, moonglaze, moonglaze. Deep in his trance, Shannon became one with each moment, with the bluestone castle, the scented night, and especially with the lyrine he had come to love.

moonglaze, moonglaze . . .

Outside, he crossed the courtyard under the starry black sky. The stable hunkered in the dark, its blue glasswood walls and roof visible in light that spilled out of windows in the castle. When he entered the stable, Moonglaze whistled. As Shannon let himself into Moonglaze's stall, the lyrine butted his shoulder. He felt the animal's great strength. Light filtered over them from a gold sphere-lamp that had lit up and drifted to the stall when Shannon entered.

He put his arms around Moonglaze's neck. "I can't bear it. Althor is never coming back."

The animal snuffled against him.

"I want to go," Shannon whispered. Images of the Blue Dales haunted him, dreams of blue fog and hidden valleys in high northern peaks, places of blue stone and blue storms. And Varielle. His memories of her beset him the most, waking and sleeping. It was useless, he knew. Such a woman would never want him, especially after he had been gone for over a year. But he couldn't leave here, not yet. Varielle probably had a man by now anyway, one far more suitable than a boy his age; Shannon was still one year shy of two octets. Yet his mind and body tormented him with yearning, and nothing he did helped.

Shannon hadn't returned to the ethereal fogs and ghost-trees of the Blue Dales because his parents hadn't come home yet with conclusive news of Althor. They sent messages, but it wasn't the same. He had struggled to interpret their complicated moods before they left, their sorrow for their children who chose paths that led to such pain. It was another reason Shannon hadn't left. He wanted to tell them good-bye in person, let them know he loved them even if he couldn't stay.

So he held Moonglaze, grieving, waiting for the final words of Althor's death.

Devon Majda accompanied Soz to the observation bay, which curved out from the hull of the cylinder in a transparent bubble of dichromesh glass. The gravity from the ship's rotation put the bubble "below" them, and Soz climbed down into it on a transparent ladder. They could have taken a lift, but she preferred using her muscles. It helped keep her in shape in the ship's low gravity. The spherical bubble was twenty meters in diameter, but seen from out in space it was no more than a tiny spark of light on the hull of the cruiser.

Interstellar space surrounded Soz, its jeweled stars and galactic dust visible through the transparent walls of the bay. A huge chair at the end of a robot arm occupied the center.

Dyad Chair.

Devon was above her on the ladder. Soz glanced up at her. "Does anyone use this Chair?" Only seven such Chairs existed, and only Rhon psions could survive their power.

"Not recently," Devon said. "You're the only Rhon psion who has been onboard for months."

"Why is it on the cruiser?" As far as Soz knew, neither Kurj nor Dehya came here with any regularity. If some other Rhon psion attempted to access a Dyad Chair, they probably wouldn't succeed. Kurj had tried with several before he became Imperator. The Chairs hadn't harmed him, but neither had they responded to his presence.

"Imperator Skolia needs a backup," Devon said. "We can

take this Chair anywhere, if something happens to the ones he and Pharaoh Dyhianna use."

Soz reached the bottom of the ladder and stepped onto a clear platform. The Chair was ten meters above her, huge and silent. An odd sensation tugged at her mind, hard to define . . . familiarity? The Chair recognized her. But surely that was fancy. It was an inanimate object.

Devon joined her and they stood considering the Chair. Then Devon said, "Hard to believe its power can kill."

Soz extended her arm toward it, her fingers curved as if she would touch the great throne, though it was far out of reach. And yet . . .

She lowered her arm. "It knows I'm here."

"Why do you say that?" Devon asked.

"Right now it's quiescent, but only in our universe." She turned to Devon. "It isn't certain about me."

Devon stood against the backdrop of stars, her hair as dark as space, a star queen in a star field. "No one else has reported feeling life within it."

Soz didn't know if "life" was the right word. Sentience maybe. "It wants a member of the Dyad. Not me."

"I've always wondered what the Chairs think about the Dyad," Devon said. "Does it consider them part of itself? Colleagues? Children? Something else entirely?"

"It watches over them." Soz hesitated. That wasn't right. "They are part of its universe. It knows. It watches." She stopped, frustrated, aware she was repeating herself but unable to find better words. "It wants their existence to continue."

Devon regarded her curiously. "Why?"

"I've no idea," Soz said. The chair dated from the Ruby Empire, a civilization that had fallen thousands of years ago, and with such a thorough collapse, modern peoples might never recover its lost sciences. This Chair had spent five millennia in space, untouched by humans, adrift in a derelict space station. Maybe that was why it watched over Kurj and Dehya; they and Soz's grandparents were the only humans it had known during all those thousands of years.

But it wasn't ready to accept Soz. It might never be. And if it didn't accept her—it might kill her.

7

A Leviathan Fallen

Although Roca had lived on Lyshriol for twenty-five years, the Orbiter was central in her memories. When she thought of her family, she recalled this space station where her parents had spent so much of their lives; where Dehya and Eldrin lived with Taquinil; where Kurj stayed when he wasn't on Diesha; where members of the Ruby Dynasty came in retreat, to the glades and slopes of Valley, forever spring, basking in the light of the Sun Lamp as it moved across Sky. Conflicted emotions surged within her, the bittersweet joy of returning home.

As a former dancer in the Parthonia Royal Ballet, and now as an Assembly Councilor, Roca spent a great deal of time on the world Parthonia, in Selei City, capital of the Imperialate. She knew well the Amphitheater of Memories where the Assembly met, the Hall of Memories that housed state functions, and the Hall of Chambers, a vaulted cathedral where the Assembly recorded news broadcasts. Her mother had declared the birth of the Imperialate there. Selei City spoke to both the artist and politician within Roca, facets of her personality that were more alike than most people realized. She performed in the Assembly, seeking to sway other councilors to her view. But when she came here, to the Orbiter, it was for family, not politics.

In the fertile Valley, Roca and the Bard strolled across a meadow, and the velvety silver-grass sprang back up after they passed. Flower cups, rosy and round, grew in scattered bursts of color among the green. The magrail station lay behind them, its rustic platform blending with the landscape. Ahead, the land sloped upward, lush as it climbed into the mountains. Groves of trees imported from terraformed worlds clustered on the hills and shaded several houses.

Eldrinson leaned on his cane as he walked, his hand hinged around the lyrine head at its top. His doctors had offered him mechanized braces for his legs, assuring him that he would barely notice the mesh covering. He would have none of it. He limped so much, Roca worried he wouldn't reach the house. Yet he seemed content, much more so than on Diesha. The rural surroundings here soothed him even if it wasn't the Dalvador countryside he longed to see.

Roca would have given him anything, anything at all, to make him happy. She wished he would let her lavish him with gifts, as Ruby queens had done for their consorts throughout the history of the Ruby Empire. But he didn't want presents. He just wanted to go home to his family and his work as the Dalvador Bard. He never truly understood his status as her consort, what it meant that he had the right to an Assembly seat. Politics alternately bored and annoyed him. Her attempts to stir his interest put him to sleep. He couldn't care less about her power; he had married her for love.

The scent of bell-cones on the trees tickled Roca's nose and she sneezed. It stirred her memories from early childhood: her father, laughing as she gathered armfuls of bells and brought him the sticky mass like a present.

About a kilometer distant, the valley cut steeply upward. The house where she had lived as a child with her parents stood up there, a stone mansion with spare, clean architecture. Its windows were open to the air and its wide entrance had no door, only a polished stone border. It never rained on the Orbiter, the breezes were always gentle, and the sky never clouded. On a world where they could have perfect weather every day, they needed no windowpanes or doors.

Kurj lived there when he was on the Orbiter, which meant right now it was empty. Roca and Eldrinson were headed to a different house at the base of the slope. Spiral-leaved trees shaded it and dappled its walls. This home did have a door, and it glowed with holoart, a swirl of blue, a wash of blossoms, a hint of gold tessellations around the edges, all subtle, all lovely. Mirrored tiles paneled the roof and reflected the sky—blue sky, the color humans tended to choose. Its McCarthy-wellstone surfaces adapted to temperature changes, reflective to cool the house or dark to absorb heat, whatever the inhabitants desired. The tiles glistened in the light of the Sun Lamp.

Eldrinson spoke for the first time since they had left the magrail station. "I like it, too."

She smiled, and his eyes crinkled with affection. When they reached the house, she touched a gold circle by the door. Chimes rang within and the scent of bell-cones wafted about them. After a few moments the sounds and the fragrance faded. They continued to wait, but nothing more happened.

Eldrinson adjusted his spectacles. "Perhaps no one is home."

Roca frowned. "I thought Dehya was going to be here."

"Our ship was early," he reminded her.

"I sent a message." She studied the door, trying to find some hint in its swirling patterns that it knew they had arrived.

"Greetings?" she asked.

"Are you talking to me?" Eldrinson asked.

"To the door."

"Greetings," the door said in a mellow voice.

Eldrinson jerked, his hand reflexively tightening on his cane. "The house is talking to us."

She smiled at his alarmed expression. "You see me talk to windows and walls all the time."

"That doesn't make it any less bizarre." He eyed the door warily. "House, are you going to let us in?"

"You may enter if you wish," the house answered.

He rested his hands on the head of his cane. "Won't it annoy the Ruby Pharaoh if you admit people when she isn't home?"

"You and Councilor Roca are on the list of those allowed automatic entry."

"Oh." Eldrinson blinked. "Well. Good."

The door shimmered and vanished.

"Ah!" He backed up with a fast step. "What is this?"

"That's new," Roca said. "It must be a molecular airlock." She walked into an airy foyer inside and turned back to him. "ISC passed funding a while back for the naval research labs to develop better airlocks, but I didn't realize they had done a model for houses."

"Gods forbid the door should just open," Eldrinson muttered. He limped inside, glowering, which reminded her of Soz. She held back her smile, though. Neither father nor daughter appreciated that others found their vexation charming. Both considered it an affront to their dignity.

"It's improved technology," Roca said.

"Then it should go away." Eldrinson scowled at the space where the door had stood. "So what is it?"

"A molecular airlock is a membrane," Roca said. "A modified lipid bilayer. It contains enzymes. They're like keys. They fit other molecules in the membrane. Locks."

He limped cautiously back to the entrance and squinted at the door frame. "How did it vanish like that?"

"The house applies a potential to the membrane."

He regarded her dubiously. "A what?"

"Potential," she said. "It's a field you can't see. Different potentials activate different keys. The key fits the lock, and that changes the permeability of the membrane." She motioned at the entrance. "Right now it looks empty, but really the membrane is in a new state, one permeable to air and light. And us."

He blanched. "What if it changes while we are in it?"

Roca thought about it. "It would be like slamming a door on your body, I'd guess. But the EI should be smart enough to avoid that. When we want to 'close' the entrance, it applies the previous key and the door reappears."

"Like Dehya and Kurj."

Roca went over to him. "Dehya and Kurj are lipid bilayers?"

He laughed softly. "Judging from the look on your face, I take it that would be an odd comment."

"I don't know. I'm not sure what you mean."

"Neither am I." He motioned at the door. "All this about keys and locks sounds like the Dyad. Dehya and Kurj joined the Dyad by entering Locks. Now they are Keys. Valdor only knows how that all works."

Roca smiled, thinking it unlikely that Valdor, the larger of the two Lyshriol suns, knew how it worked. It was true, though, that the lost technology which had set Lyshriol in its unlikely orbit around a double star had also produced the

Locks. The people of modern Raylicon had yet to figure out the ancient technology they had rediscovered when they regained the stars. Only three Locks existed: the Orbiter, or First Lock, found derelict in space; the Second Lock on the world Raylicon; and the Third Lock, a station currently orbiting Parthonia, but which ISC intended to move to Onyx Platform.

Perhaps ESComm had learned of the plan to move the Lock and attacked Onyx to steal it. Until her people unraveled the technology that had created these ancient machines, no one could build more Locks. However, Rhon psions could use them to create the Kyle web, with the Dyad as Keys. The Traders had neither Locks nor Keys: hence, no Kyle web. They deplored the disadvantage that gave them in comparison to the Imperialate.

"That's clever," Roca said. "I would never have thought to compare Dyad Keys and Locks to a molecular airlock."

He grinned at her. "Of course it's clever. I thought of it."

"Such modesty."

He smirked. "That is why you love me so much."

A snort came from the doorway. "For your humility? I think not, Eldri."

Roca looked around. Dehya stood in the entrance, one hand on her hip. She wore a white jumpsuit, the type used by travelers because its cloth was intelligent enough to clean itself and stay free of wrinkles.

"My greetings," Dehya said.

"Of course for my humility," the Bard told her. He lifted his cane and pointed it at her. "You must not be intimidated by my intellect, Dehya."

She raised her eyebrows, which gave her waif-like face a fey quality. "Now I know you must be feeling better. You are as annoying as ever."

He glared at her, but Roca knew he was enjoying himself. "I am not the one who cavorts around the Assembly instead of meeting her in-laws."

"Well, I am the pharaoh, you know. Governing is what we pharaoh types do."

"Yes, well, you should be a man."

Dehya laughed. "Good gods, Eldri, I hope not."

"A man should be the ruler," he said patiently.

Dehya strolled into her house. "Men, my dear brother-in-law, should be secluded in harems."

He shook his cane at her. "You are deluded."

"You would look very nice in those long robes."

What he looked was unimpressed. "I shall send my army to take over this Orbiter and put a proper Bard on your throne."

Her eyes danced. "If you would like to send handsome fellows here to sing, I'm sure our women wouldn't protest."

"I will send some genuine men," Eldrinson offered. "Not like the ones here who let women tell them what to do."

"Oh stop, you two," Roca said, laughing. In truth, it relieved her to hear them argue. Even a month ago Eldrinson would have had no spirit for such bantering.

"Grandfather!" The boyish voice burst out behind them.

Roca turned with a start. Eldrinson maneuvered around more awkwardly, but faster than she had seen him move since he started to walk again. A seven-year-old boy was running up a hallway deeper within the house, his black hair disheveled over his shirt collar, his gold eyes fringed by black lashes.

A smile creased Eldrinson's face. He braced himself against the wall with one hand as the boy barreled into him and threw his arms around Eldrinson's waist. The Bard put his free arm around the boy and hugged him back.

"Taqui!" Dehya hurried over and caught Eldrinson's arm as he staggered under the boy's onslaught. "You mustn't knock over your grandfather."

Taquinil let go of Eldrinson and looked up, brimming full of excitement, as if he were lit from inside. "I was reading cosmology. I didn't even know you were here!"

"Cosmology?" Eldrinson asked.

"Are you going to stay with me?" Taquinil's words tumbled out like balls bouncing everywhere. "Is it really true?"

The Bard's face gentled. "It really is true."

"I'm so glad!" Taquinil grabbed his hand and tugged him forward. "We can play games. I'll show you my Bessel function generator. And you can see where I swim! It has a waterfall."

Eldrinson laughed as he struggled to keep his balance. Dehya nudged Taquinil back so he didn't send his grandfather toppling. The boy suddenly realized who else was standing nearby. He hurled himself into Roca's arms. "Grandmother, you're gold."

Roca held him close. "I've always been this color."

He stepped back. "I just forget the way you're like metal instead of normal."

"Taquinil!" Dehya turned red, an unusual state for the normally unruffled pharaoh. She gave Roca an apologetic look. "He didn't mean that the way it sounded."

"But it's true," Taquinil said.

"It's all right," Roca said, laughing. "Look at your eyes, Taqui. They're like mine."

He regarded her somberly. "Like Uncle Kurj's."

Eldrinson grunted. "No need to insult yourself, young man."

Roca frowned at her husband. "Eldri."

"Well, it's true." He winked at Taquinil. "We will have great times together, eh?"

"Yes! I'm so glad you came." Taquinil's smile faded. "But are you really sick? You don't look sick."

Dehya glanced at Roca. *Did you tell him Eldrinson was sick?*

Roca shook her head. She could speak mentally only with people she trusted enough so that she and the other person were willing to drop their mental barriers. Even then, it only worked if the sender focused the thought. They both shielded their thoughts from the boy.

I didn't tell him, Roca thought. **Did you?**

Only that you and Eldrinson were coming. I wasn't sure about Eldri's condition or how much he wanted your son to know.

Taquinil was watching them. His thoughts sparkled as clear as rain water. Grandfather is here to heal his epilepsy.

Roca winced. She should have known they couldn't hide their thoughts from the boy, at least in such close quarters.

Eldrinson gave Taquinil a reassuring smile. **Maybe the doctors here can help.**

I hope so. Taquinil could have spoken, since they were all in the conversation now, but telepathy with his family came so easily to him, he often didn't seem to distinguish between speech and thought. *Your neurons fire too much.*

Dehya put her hand on her son's shoulder. *Have you felt your grandfather's seizures?*

Like an echo. His gaze took on an otherworldly quality. *It's a storm that flares, wild and mad. It jumps until his mind aches.* He regarded his grandfather. *It is not demons, Grandhoshpa. Really.*

Eldrinson tilted his head as if he were seeing Taquinil for the first time. In some sense he was; Roca traveled more often than her husband or grandson, so she had experienced far more of the boy's remarkable mind. For all that Taquinil paid a price in his extreme mental sensitivity, his gifts of the intellect and his empathic kindness made him a marvel.

Eldrinson put his arm around the boy's shoulder. **You and I will chase those demons down.**

We will! Taquinil tugged his hand. *Come see the holo palace I built.*

Eldrinson chuckled, and winked at Roca. Then he went off with Taquinil, down a blue hallway with holosunsets on the walls.

Roca turned to Dehya. "Your son is good for Eldri." She spoke aloud; unlike Taquinil, most of them had trouble maintaining telepathic conversation for long.

"Taquinil loves him so much." She walked with Roca outside, into the dappled shade of the trees. Dehya was twenty-five years her senior; as a child, Roca had admired her genius sister, and as adults, they often turned to each other for support. But Dehya's marriage had nearly destroyed their bond. Roca knew her anger should have been directed at the Assembly rather than the victims of its machinations, but her heart couldn't hear that logic. The situation had created a rift between her and Dehya that took years to heal. Roca was only able to accept it when she saw how much Eldrin thrived with his family.

Lately he even seemed euphoric, so much that it didn't seem normal. It troubled Roca; she wondered if he had "help" for his mood. Since his separation from his family, he was drinking more. But perhaps she was overreacting. The last time she had seen him, at the Ruby Palace, he hadn't touched the rum-laced kava that Kurj had enjoyed.

"How are things with you and Eldrin?" Roca asked.

Dehya was quiet for a moment, her gaze downcast as they walked under the trees. Then she said, "I miss him terribly." She looked up at Roca. "I don't understand why he can't come home. I've been afraid . . ."

Roca waited. "Yes?"

"That he doesn't want to come back."

"He does." Roca had no doubt on that score. "He's worried he'll hurt Taquinil. Or you."

"He would never harm us."

"Intentionally, no." Roca hesitated. "Does Eldrin still see the therapist?"

Dehya frowned at her. "Of course not. He isn't sick, and I don't want people making him think something is wrong with him. He gets enough of that rubbish from the Assembly."

"No, he's not sick." Roca drew her to a stop in a cluster of spiral trees. "Dehya, he can be healthy and still be troubled in his life. He *needed* that counseling. It was one of the reasons his father and I arranged for him to come here eight years ago."

Dehya's delicate fist clenched at her side. "If you mean he was traumatized by going into that barbaric war with your husband when he was sixteen, then hell yes. But that's *over* now."

"It's not over." It frustrated Roca that Dehya could be so brilliant in so much, yet so blind in this. "It isn't just the war. It's everything, the differences in his father's culture and mine, his feelings of inadequacy compared to Althor, and now Althor is *dead*—"

"Inadequacy?" Dehya stared at her. "He has no reason to feel he is less than his brother. They are completely different." A shadow crossed her face as breezes shifted the trees. In a subdued voice, she added, "Were completely different."

Were. Roca spoke past her grief. "We know that. But see it from his view. Althor is two years younger than Eldrin, but they hit puberty together. By that time, Althor was bigger, stronger, faster, better in school, and at ease with modern culture. Althor qualified for the Dieshan Military Academy when Eldrin could barely learn to read and write."

Dehya crossed her arms. "Eldrin isn't stupid."

"I didn't say he was stupid!" Roca wanted to shake her. "You've seen the records. His father isn't stupid, either, he's neurologically incapable of written language. Eldrin inherited whatever causes it. Eldrin learned to read because we caught it earlier, but he may have lost something valuable in the process. We just don't *know*. Althor learned to read when he was three; Eldrin when he was seventeen." Her voice quieted. "Althor was, to everyone on Lyshriol, the epitome of the warrior, the golden prince, the star warrior who rode the skies in a glowing ship."

"Eldrin is an artist," Dehya said. "His voice is an unmatched gift."

"I agree. But Lyshriol culture values warriors." Roca pushed back the tendrils of hair blowing over her face. "The girls in Dalvador wanted Althor, including the girl Eldrin liked. Even if Althor never said anything, Eldrin knew his brother had no interest in those girls. That, in a culture that considers heterosexual marriage the only valid expression of sensual love. Eldrin couldn't deal with all the contradictions and comparisons."

Dehya crossed her arms. "Eldrin isn't responsible for the prejudices of Lyshriol and your husband."

Roca stiffened. "We weren't talking about my husband."

"He's the one who disowned Althor."

"He disowned Althor for taking Soz to DMA." Roca knew it was more complicated, but she felt how much her husband mourned that he had never reconciled with Althor. He would live the rest of his life grieving that his last words to his son were spoken in anger.

Dehya scowled. "Soz would have gone crazy if he had made her stay home and get married."

Roca crossed her arms, mirroring her sister. "I do not wish to discuss your problems with my husband."

"I don't have problems with your husband. I like him. My problems are with his attitudes."

"Yes, well, he says the same about you."

"Eldrin is changing." Dehya lowered her arms, making an obvious effort to relax. "You've seen him in Assembly. He comes to almost every session."

There was that. It impressed Roca. She had never expected her son to take an interest in politics. His first appearance in the Assembly had shocked everyone. She knew he believed it was because they considered him inferior. And it was true, some of the more foolish delegates felt that way. But his age caused the greatest consternation. Among the thousands of representatives, Eldrin was by far the youngest.

Most members of Skolia's governing body won their hard-fought seats after decades of political maneuvering. The few hereditary seats held by the noble Houses went to senior members of those families. Everyone in the Ruby Dynasty had a seat, but most of Roca's children were too young and none had shown an interest. Almost none. The day seventeen-year-old Eldrin had walked into the amphitheater and settled regally into his chair, Roca's jaw had dropped along with everyone else's. It pleased her no end that he chose to participate.

"I'm proud of him." Roca made herself lower her arms as well. She could guess why Dehya resisted hearing about Eldrin's problems. "Everyone, at some time or another, needs help. It doesn't mean the people who love them have failed them."

Dehya watched her for a long moment. Then she stared at the hills beyond the glade where they stood. "I will miss this place while I'm gone."

Roca understood her well enough to recognize the topic was closed. But she knew Dehya. The pharaoh was thinking about what she had said.

"When do you leave for Parthonia?" Roca asked.

"In a few hours." Dehya glanced at the house. "I wish I didn't have to go."

"I, too. But I need to get home." Although she trusted her older children to look after the younger ones, she didn't like leaving them. "I'll attend this Assembly session through the web."

"I worry about security." Dehya began walking with her

again. "When I'm extended through the meshes, I absorb so much data, it's hard to define individual pieces. But the web seems jagged lately. Less stable."

"Do you think it would be safer if I went to Parthonia?"

Dehya hesitated. "I would say yes, but Kurj wants the Rhon dispersed as widely as possible. He isn't happy with you going to Lyshriol, either, with so many of your children there, but I don't think he will forbid it. He knows they need you, even if he has a hard time saying that."

It exhausted Roca dealing with Kurj's conflicted emotions toward his half-siblings. He obviously loved them but he refused to admit it. "What do you think? Is our family in danger?"

Dehya gathered up her hip-length hair and began twisting it into a braid. "Yes. Everyone is. Certainly we should minimize our vulnerability. That doesn't mean we should hide and tremble. It does no good to have the power of Rhon psions if we're too afraid to use it."

Roca thought of her husband. He should have been protected on Lyshriol. "No place is safe."

Shadows shifted on Dehya's face. "I will be glad to be with Eldrin in Selei City."

"I thought he was on Diesha."

"He is." Dehya paused in braiding her hair. "I have been thinking it would be good if he and I could spend more time together." She spoke awkwardly. "The medical staff at the Sunrise Palace above Selei City has an excellent counselor he can talk to. If he wishes."

A tightness within Roca loosened, and she felt a sense of lightening. Perhaps Dehya and Eldrin would work out their difficulties. "Do you think Kurj will allow Eldrin to travel there?"

"I think so. Eldrin is as safe with me on Parthonia as with Kurj on Diesha. Kurj already sent Soz to your cruiser."

"My what?"

"Roca's Pride."

Roca winced. "I can't believe Kurj named that battle cruiser after me."

A smile quirked the pharaoh's lips. "Be flattered. He meant it that way."

"Yes, well, you might feel differently if he had called one of those big cans *Pharaoh's Pride.*"

Dehya laughed. "He did. *Pharaoh's Shield*, actually."

"Oh." Roca squinted at her. "I fear ISC will start naming warships after our children."

"Perhaps we could distract them with other suggestions." Dehya smirked. "How about *Kurj's Calamity*? Or *Majda Madness?*"

"Majda nobles are the epitome of perfection," Roca said dryly. She thought of her son Vyrl, who had run off with his child sweetheart instead of marrying Devon Majda. Then Devon had abdicated to her sister Corey. "Did you know Corey Majda commands the Lyshriol defense system?"

"I doubt that's coincidence." Dehya finished braiding her hair. "The Assembly still wants the Majda Matriarch to marry one of your sons. They're just being more subtle this time."

Roca smiled. "I better get home fast, before Corey rides off with Denric or Shannon." Ideals of beauty among the nobility came in two varieties: the powerful dark aristocrat, like Dehya or Devon; and the slender blond youth, like her younger sons. If either Shannon or Denric ever spent time in the Imperial court on Parthonia, they would find themselves pursued and feted by noblewomen from every House.

"It is hard to believe so many of your children are adults," Dehya said.

"They certainly think they are." Roca grimaced. "There ought to be a law that prohibits unsuspecting parents from having so many teenagers at once."

Dehya's face gentled. "I've never seen you so happy as you are with them."

It was true, as much as Roca liked to grumble. "Yes, well, perhaps I should happily get home before they do something dire to the house." Her smile faded. "We still haven't figured out how Vitarex broke through the Lyshriol defenses. ISC has fortified and upgraded them until they're convinced nothing could breach them."

Dehya just looked at her. Roca needed no telepathy to know her thought; ISC had believed those defenses were impregnable before. "I'm leaving this evening," Roca added.

"Do you have any time before you go?"

"About three hours."

Dehya spoke more formally. "I would ask for your help then."

Her tone puzzled Roca. "Yes?"

"I need to work in the web. But I must leave for Parthonia." Roca couldn't tell what she was about, and Dehya had shielded her thoughts more than usual. Curious, Roca said, "What can I do?"

"Complete some work for me." Dehya sighed and rubbed the small of her back, arching a bit as she worked the muscles. "I've been developing some new meshes. I need to link them from Kyle space into our spacetime."

Roca stared at her. "Good gods, Dehya, that's Dyad work."

"Not exactly." She regarded Roca steadily. "It's true, you will need to operate in Kyle space at a level you haven't done before. And you must use the Dyad Chair; no other node can join structures in two universes."

"Kurj can't do it?"

"Kurj is planning a war." More quietly she said, "Should anything happen to me, you would take my position in the Dyad. Taqui is too young."

Roca understood then. Just as Kurj had sent Soz to the battle cruiser to learn ISC, so Roca needed to learn the Dyad. It shook her. Whatever her difficulties with Dehya, Roca didn't want to acknowledge the possibility of her death. But regardless of how she felt, she had to know this work.

"Yes," Roca said. "I will help."

Kurj accompanied Eldrin to the starport and saw him off on that star yacht bound to Parthonia. Then Kurj headed back to his office in HQ City. Halfway there, he decided to go home instead. He felt unaccountably tired. It made no sense: he had so much augmentation to his body, he could turn off portions of his systems to "rest," which recharged him enough that he required only about two hours of sleep per twenty-hour cycle. Apparently he needed more today, though. His head felt odd. So did his stomach.

Node A, he thought.

Attending, his spinal node answered.
Why do I feel strange?
You have the flu.
What is the flu?
A minor illness common prior to the advent of nanomed technology.

Kurj scowled. With his exercise regime, strength, and health meds, he rarely experienced illness. **Then why do I have it?**
No medical system is 100 percent perfect.
Delete it.
It is not possible to delete the flu.
How do I remove it?
Sleep. Plenty of liquids. Ibuprofen can help.
Ibru-what?
Medicine. I can prescribe it.
I don't have time to be sick. Reprogram my meds to eliminate flu.

His node responded with its limitless patience. If that were possible, I would have done so. However, you can check yourself into the Pharaoh's Hospital in HQC and ask them to design new nanomeds for you.

For flaming sakes. **That would take more time than being sick.**
If you allow yourself to be sick and recover, your body will create its own specialized form of nanomed to defeat this flu.
I thought you couldn't reprogram my nanomeds.
I can't. Your body, however, can make antibodies.

The whole business sorely tried Kurj's patience. However, he felt less robust every moment. **Very well. I will go home, sleep, and consume liquids. Let me know when I have completed enough of these actions.**
I will do so.

Kurj had his flyer take him to the Ruby Palace, where he could be sick in peace.

Eldrin threw up in the medical bay of the yacht. Then he fell back on his side, on the bed, exhausted, and lay still while medbots cleaned him up. The ship's dark-haired doctor hovered over him. He didn't recognize the name on her white jumpsuit and he doubted he could pronounce it. He felt too sick to ask.

After the bots had scrubbed him clean, Eldrin rolled onto his back. The pastel holoart on the Luminex walls was supposed to soothe him, but it only made his nausea worse. He was dimly aware of his bodyguards hulking around the bay, and of the doctor with the unpronounceable name working nearby. He just stared at the ceiling. When he had gathered enough strength, he rolled his head toward the doctor. She was studying one of the monitors by his bed.

"Do you know what's wrong with me?" Eldrin asked.

She rubbed her chin. "Initially it looked like the flu, of all things. Then it got worse." She indicated holos rotating above one screen with views of various chemicals. "A foreign med species in your body made you sick. You have defense nanomeds that are disposing of the invader. It's odd."

"Odd how?" He hadn't been aware of any anomalies.

"I've never seen anything like the defense meds. But they're documented in your files." She glanced at him with a puzzled look. "Why ever would you carry meds to remove blue food coloring?"

"Oh, those." Eldrin smiled wanly. "It's for an impurity in the water and air on the world where I grew up."

"Well, you're lucky for that."

He appreciated her manner; she neither condescended to him nor had the ingratiating manner some people assumed because of his titles. She treated him like any other patient.

"Are the blue-dye meds causing my illness?" he asked.

"Not at all." She indicated the holo of a complicated chemical structure turning above her console. "An unidentified species caused your illness. The dye species neutralized it." She studied glyphs scrolling across the screen below the holo. "Fortunately you took in few enough of the invader meds that your dye meds could destroy them all."

"How did I get the invader species?" His dizziness surged and receded like a wave rippling through the Dalvador Plains.

"I'm not sure. I'll need a list of everything you ate and drank in the past few days."

"All right." What Eldrin really wanted to do was sleep.

"Huh." She was scrutinizing a new display of molecules with atoms highlighted in different colors. "That's strange, too. This compound doesn't match anything in your records." Eldrin's nausea had returned. "What is it?"

"Some sort of neurotransmitter . . ." She rubbed her chin. "You've a chemical in your brain I don't recognize. It's forming complexes with your neurons."

He didn't like the sound of that. "Is it dangerous?"

"I don't know. I've never treated a Rhon psion before." She turned to him. "According to your records, you're undergoing treatment to control seizures."

Eldrin tensed. How could she know that he had convulsions when he didn't take the phorine? He had told no one. He tried to sound natural. "What seizures?"

She indicated another display of hologlyphs. "Those."

Eldrin could read two-dimensional text, but three dimensions was too much, especially now. "What does it say?"

"That you requested this treatment when you were sixteen."

"Oh." She meant his battle-rages. "Those attacks only happened a few times."

She studied the molecules rotating over another screen. "Probably these anomalous neurotransmitters relate to that treatment. I'll send an inquiry with the report on your illness."

Eldrin wondered if the transmitters came from the phorine. He knew he should tell her about it, but he feared she would confiscate the syringe. Someone would figure it out, though, if she sent a report. The Epsilon files on his home nodes could keep his personal EI in check, but he doubted they could block her medical system. "You don't need to put that in my file," he said. "My doctors already know."

"I have to put in everything." She frowned at him. "Including one other thing."

"What?"

"You drink too much."

How could they tell so much? He had no privacy. "I quit."

She indicated her holos. "These say otherwise."

"It's only been a day."

She seemed uncertain whether or not to believe him. "I can give you something to cut down the craving."

Eldrin almost said no. He could take care of himself. But that was hard to remember when he needed a drink. He was having more trouble cutting back than he expected. When he was sober, he couldn't forget what had happened to Althor. He remembered when he had been seven and Althor five, how close they had been, playing and running and laughing. Althor had looked up to him and Eldrin had sworn he would always protect his brother. Those memories were full of sunlight.

Then one day he had let himself see the truth; his "little" brother had grown stronger and smarter than him. The girl Eldrin dreamed about every night had wanted Althor, who had no interest in any girl. It enraged Eldrin, and he often ended up fighting his brother. He knew his behavior bewildered Althor. Eldrin hadn't understood how Althor could be everything their people defined as powerful and masculine, more so than Eldrin himself, and yet not be a man according to their customs.

Eldrin had been living on the Orbiter when he heard about the Battle of Tyroll back home. Sixteen-year-old Althor had also ridden into battle with their father—except Althor had taken a laser carbine and slaughtered three hundred men in five minutes. It ended warfare on Lyshriol. How could swords and bows compete with interstellar weapons? Eldrin knew his brother had struggled with remorse, but Althor *dealt* with it. Eldrin had refused to use offworld weapons; it had seemed morally wrong against men with only swords and bows. Althor had no qualms—and he had stopped the war. No one else would die. Which was right?

Eldrin doubted he would ever have answers. But he had gradually come to terms with the differences between Althor and himself. He would regret all his life that he had never put right the strain between them, for now he would never have the chance.

"Your Majesty?" the doctor asked.

Eldrin spoke with difficulty. "Yes. If you could—help with the craving, I would appreciate it."

"Certainly." She clicked an air syringe out of the console and dialed in a prescription. As she injected him, she said, "For now, sleep as much as possible and drink water to flush out the detritus of the dismantled meds."

He nodded, glad to oblige, because he felt like hell.

"Jason, answer," Kurj whispered. He lay sprawled on his bed, unable to move. The whir of bots cleaning him up had stopped. Nothing remained for them to clean. He had nothing left to throw up.

"Jason." His voice rasped. "Contact the hospital."

The EI remained silent. No alarms activated.

Emergency systems networked the Ruby Palace, the best ISC could design, all with one purpose: to protect the Imperator. The moment he had collapsed on his bed, alarms should have gone off. By now, medtechs should be swarming over the palace.

Nothing happened.

Kurj managed to pull himself another few inches across the bed. If he could reach the edge . . .

When he became aware again, the room had gone dark. Dimly he thought, **Node A.**

Attending.

Light . . . where?

It is night.

He must have passed out. **When . . . flu end?**

I no longer believe you have the flu. Your condition is life-threatening. You must have medical help.

Hospital.

I have been trying to notify them. No palace systems will answer.

Kurj thought of dragging himself farther, but he couldn't move. He lay among the cushions he had scattered when he toppled onto the bed. The illness had hit with such speed, he hadn't had time to remove his boots, which had hit a bed post, damaging it . . .

His boots . . .

Damage.

Fighting to stay aware, Kurj moved just enough to jam his boots against the footboard of the bed. **Extend spikes.**

Extending gear designed for climbing in rough terrain will damage the footboard.

Extend . . . the damn spikes.

Extended.

Kurj's grip on life dissolved and the night closed in.

8

Pico Assassins

The Dyad Chair enclosed Roca. Panels folded around her, glowing with multicolored displays. The silver exoskeleton fit her body snugly and plugged psiphon prongs into her neck, wrists, back, and ankles. Intravenous lines fed her nutrients and water. The armrests were blocks, half a meter wide and a meter long, packed with webtech. More tech embedded the massive backrest. The chair's visor reflected the holostars that glowed in the dome above her. Their radiance edged the techs as they fastened Roca into the Chair. The visor lowered over her head, cutting out light that might distract her concentration. Her pulse sped up and she could feel blood pumping through her body. A part of her wanted to tear away the constraints of this alien throne; another part waited with anticipation. She couldn't see the robot arm as it lifted the Chair into the dome, but the growl of its engines thrummed through her.

A sentience stirred. **WHO?**

Even having trained for decades to make this contact, Roca was unprepared for the power that coursed through her mind. No simulation could evoke the sheer force of this intelligence. Her trial runs had included a sense of the Chair's power, but never sentience.

I am Roca Skolia, she thought.

NOT DYAD.

I am a Dyad heir. I come to complete the meshes designed by Pharaoh Dyhianna.

YOU FASHIONED THE IMPERATOR.

I am his mother, if that is what you mean.

THE IMPERATOR MUST CONTINUE.

Yes. He must. She paused, uncertain what it wanted. *Is he involved with these meshes?*

BOOTS.

Boots?

The visor retracted. Roca tensed; nothing in her training had included the Chair disengaging itself during a session. The starlight from the holodome had vanished, leaving her in darkness. As her eyes adjusted, she had another jolt. She no longer sat in the Chair. She was standing in a shadowed bedroom. The scene was hazy and rippled the way simulations became when viewed through the mesh with poor connections.

This looks like the Ruby Palace on Diesha, Roca thought.

YES.

Roca peered into the shadows. The Kyle web had many links to the palace, and she would have expected better resolution in a connection. A man lay sprawled on the bed, his body twisted at an odd angle as if he had dragged himself diagonally across the mattress. One of his legs had caught the footboard.

Kurj.

Roca couldn't understand why the Chair would show her Kurj sleeping in a strange position. *His foot is caught.*

IT DAMAGED THE BED. A REPAIR BOT RESPONDED.

Roca could see the bot. It had lodged itself near Kurj's foot. *It isn't doing anything.*

IT CANNOT REMOVE THE SPIKE. NO SYSTEMS HAVE RESPONDED TO ITS SUMMONS FOR HELP.

Roca went cold. Housekeeping, maintenance, and repair bots saturated the Ruby Palace. They were designed to pursue their duties with single-minded diligence. It was impossible that the bot couldn't find help in fixing the damage.

Bring the Chair down! Roca's mental shout echoed.

DESCENDING.

A hum intensified. The image faded and she realized the visor had never retracted. Frantic, she pushed it up and found herself in the Chair, lowering to the floor in the Dyad Chamber. She had to make a concentrated effort not to tear away the meshes and lines holding her to the throne. Approval came from the Chair; it had achieved its purpose.

Now she had to achieve hers: help her son.

If it wasn't too late.

Soz finished her shift on the bridge. Her console was similar to the one used by Weapons and only a few paces away from the Weapons station. Holoscreens on the hull showed space outside the ship, an eerie sensation, as if she and the weapons officer were actually hanging out in the starred cosmos.

Soz extended her arms and saluted Weapons, a stocky woman from the world Sandstorm. Weapons returned her salute, wrists crossed and fists clenched. Then she spoke into the comm on her console. "Weapons One here. I have the console, Cadet Valdoria." The comm transmitted her voice to the other stations and the distant captain's chair occupied by Devon Majda.

"Valdoria here," Soz said. "I stand relieved." She wasn't really being relieved; Weapons had been here the entire time, guiding Soz. But they followed the protocol.

Soz headed across the bridge. She still had a good two or three hours of studying before she could sleep. She might have resented the double load, except her course work was easy. Besides, she adored being in space. A few more days working with Weapons and she would move on to Navigation.

The rotation of the bridge created an odd pseudogravity. It bewildered some spacers, but Soz enjoyed it. The point where the rotation axis pierced the forward hull was a pole, just as a planet had north and south poles. Unlike on a planet, the crew here could walk on the inside of the sphere. Gravity pointed at right angles to the axis and depended on the distance from the axis to the hull, which meant the deck under her feet became steeper and gravity weakened as she approached the pole. The Weapons stations sat nearly on top of it, so Soz weighed next to nothing and the hull was almost vertical. Her station jutted out like a terrace.

She walked "downhill," her steps long, her weight increasing as the incline leveled out. Above her, a cable stretched through the air. Her muscles had developed on Lyshriol, with its heavier gravity, and she easily jumped the several feet to grab the cable. She hauled herself along, hand-over-hand toward the base of the hemisphere, which capped the cylinder. Right now the cylindrical part of the ship was turning with the bridge. Near her goal, she launched off the cable and sailed through the air, weightless. As soon as she grabbed a handhold on the rotating cap, she was dragged toward its outer edge. She hung on, her arms and body stretched out, and grinned for the sheer fun of it.

When she smacked her palm against a panel, a hatch in the cap opened. She climbed up and maneuvered into an airlock tube that connected the bridge to the main ship. At the other end, she came out into a hub where she was weightless again. Tunnels extended outward from the hub in spokes, and ladders went down each spoke. A duty officer was climbing out of one tunnel into the hub. Soz hooked her arm through a grip and saluted. He returned her salute as he floated past and made his way into another spoke.

Soz located the spoke she wanted by lights around its edge; three blue and one violet, for β–β–β–α deck, also called Midshipmen's Purgatory. As she drifted into the spoke and grasped the ladder, a tug of gravity returned and her perception shifted. Suddenly she was climbing down the ladder. By the time she reached the bottom, she weighed about half what she would on Lyshriol. She came out into a corridor studded with equipment in haphazard patterns, depending on how it had been added. She nodded or saluted other crew members as they squeezed past each other. At the end, she exited—into a city.

Silver and bronze towers gleamed, magrails curved among them, and blue Luminex "sky" glowed overhead. Soz jogged along a white casecrete path that glinted with the flecks of sensors that tracked pedestrians. This place of bright metal was completely unlike the silvery green hills of Dalvador where she had grown up.

She felt at home here.

Lying on her bed, Soz closed her eyes. The walls dimmed, leaving only faint light from a holoscape above her bunk. The holo shifted to a night scene she had programmed, the Blue and Lavender Moons in Dalvador. It shed just enough light to reveal her console against one bulkhead. Her quarters were barely big enough for the bunk and console, and she shared her cleanser unit with three other midshipmen. She would have preferred to share larger quarters rather than have this coffin-like solo, but they hadn't had enough of the roomier units.

Soz had only needed two hours to catch up in her courses. She had spent another hour downloading and studying specs on the navigation systems in preparation for her next apprenticeship. With all that done, she could sleep. Except her mind refused to rest. Filled with equations, facts, and worries about her family, her thoughts spun around.

After a while she said, "Sigma Three?"

The ship's EI answered. "Attending."

"Any messages from my family?"

"Nothing this evening. You have a letter from DMA, though."

DMA? Grell must have sent it. She was keeping Soz apprised of Althor's condition. Every message was the same: no change. As much as Soz knew she had to accept the truth, she didn't feel as if her brother had died. Surely she would sense a hollow place within herself. She knew only that she was grateful her parents left him on life support.

Grell remained matter-of-fact in her audio-letters, but Soz knew how much she cared for Althor. Nor did Soz miss the stiffness in Grell's voice when she mentioned Chad. Grell had realized that if Althor married her, it would only be because Soz's father and the Assembly wanted him to sire heirs. When her father disowned Althor, Soz knew the Bard's bewildered anger had gone beyond his anguish over losing his children to a war he couldn't comprehend. They were a family of psions, mentally guarded, yes, but still empaths. Although their father didn't know about Chad, he had realized he could wait forever for Althor to marry. So he had given his son an ultimatum: don't come home without a wife. It told Soz just how much that break had devastated Althor, that he had courted Grell even though he would never see her as more than a friend.

Apparently Chad often visited the hospital. Although Soz respected his loyalty to her brother, she also resented it. Chad should have given Althor that fidelity when it could have made a difference.

"Shall I play the message?" Sigma Three asked.

Soz rubbed her eyes. "Yes, please."

A man's voice floated up from the console. "Heya, Soz. Whooz me a whoozola. It's dull without you raising hell."

"That's Jaz!" Soz laughed. Whooz him a whoozola? "What time is it at DMA?"

"One-twelve in the morning."

Jazar might be sleeping. Or maybe not. When they had roomed together, he often stayed up late to study. She missed her verbal parries with him. Sending personal messages from a battle cruiser through Kyle space was hardly routine, but no regulations prohibited it if she wasn't on duty.

"Sigma," she asked, "what's left of my personal comm time?"

"Six minutes and two seconds."

"Put me through to DMA, then. Personal web, Jazar Orand, second-year dorm, code four-three-alpha-gamma-six."

"Connecting."

"Thanks." Soz closed her eyes. It would take a while for her call to clear security, given her low priority.

She was drowsing when Sigma said, "I have Diesha."

Soz stirred herself awake. "On audio." Visual was too costly on her meager account.

A man's voice floated into the air. "Soz? You there?"

"Heya, Jaz. Did I wake you up?"

"I never sleep. I'm cybernetic, remember?"

"Hah! You aren't cybernetic. Not until your third year."

"Well, in spirit," he amended.

It was good to hear his voice. She grinned. "They must not be working you hard enough, if you have time to take messages."

"Funny, Soz." His voice turned smug. "You have to come back. We're drowning in spamoozala. No one cleans it up anymore."

"I'm never cleaning that gunk again."

"A likely claim."

"What, you think I can't keep my record clean?"

He was laughing now. "Since you ask, no."

"You wait until I get back. We'll see who gets demerits."

"Ah, Soz, I miss you."

Soz smiled. "You better."

"Or else what?" He sounded intrigued.

"I'll think of something."

"Sounds like fun." He stopped as a voice spoke in the background. "That's odd."

"What happened?" Soz asked.

"My roommate says there was a spike in our transmission. It registered on his console."

"What kind of spike?"

"The energy that supplies your console? I don't know. Anyway, it's fine now." He sighed. "I better go. If I don't sleep tonight, I'll crash in class tomorrow."

"All right. Have fun."

"You, too." After a pause, he added, "I'm glad you called."

That made her feel strange inside. Good strange. "Me, too."

After they signed off, she lay thinking about Jazar. Sexy Jazar. As she drifted to sleep, she wondered what had caused the energy spike.

"We're in the palace!" The colonel spoke into his wrist comm and he and his medical team ran across the hall of columns. "We're picking up signs from his suite upstairs."

The voice on his comm said, "A racer is landing on the roof. The crew will meet you at the Imperator's suite."

"Got it." The medical team sped up the staircase that curved up from the hall. They couldn't use any lifts; no mechanical, electro-optic, biosynthetic, nanotech, or picotech worked in the entire palace. Only the cleaning bots that acted without the meshes were operational, either too crude or too autonomous to experience whatever killed the other systems.

They found the Imperator sprawled on his bed. The doctors immediately went to work. One fact was blazingly obvious: Kurj Skolia was dying.

"His biomech shut off." That came from the doctor monitoring him with her hand-held console. Another medic inserted a line into Kurj's body, flushing him with kamikaze nanomeds that would obliterate invaders even if they had to destroy themselves in the process. A third doctor injected him with meds to keep his heart beating while others set up nutrient lines to replenish his dehydrated body.

"He needs the hospital," the colonel said.

The doctor with the hand-held suddenly swore. She flicked through holos so fast, they blurred over her console. "If we don't stabilize him, he won't make it that far."

They worked faster, injecting Kurj with med serums. Another team ran into the suite with an air stretcher. It took only moments to carry the Imperator to the racer on the roof, and within seconds they were airborne, streaking through the night.

That was when his heart stopped.

9

Spikes

"You cannot go to Diesha." Jazida Majda, General of the Pharaoh's Army, regarded Roca implacably from the holoscreen.

Roca was sitting in the copilot's seat on a racer, one of the fastest spacecrafts in ISC. She had headed to Diesha the moment she realized Kurj was in trouble, but now Jazida insisted her pilot change his flight plan. Roca was acutely aware of the exoskeleton that sheathed her body, on order of the general. It was monitoring her health to ensure she didn't succumb to whatever had attacked Kurj.

"He is my son!" Roca clenched the armrests of her chair. "The second one who lies in some gods-forsaken hospital." It was all she could do to keep from shouting. "Damn it, I will not go into hiding while my children are dying."

"The answer is no." Majda's face was like granite. "We've identified the meds that invaded Imperator Skolia's body. They match the signature of a species designed by ESComm. This was an assassination attempt, Councilor, and it may yet be successful. The doctors barely revived him after his heart stopped. We *cannot* risk your life. If your son dies, you will have to join the Dyad. None of your children have anything resembling your preparation. We are sending you to Safelanding."

"I can't join the Dyad at Safelanding," Roca said. "It has no Lock." A Dyad Chair allowed her to use the Kyle meshes at a high level, but she needed a Lock to become a member of the Dyad.

"None of the three Locks are currently secure," Jazida said. "I intend to keep you safe."

"You have no authority over me."

The general regarded her with the iron gaze she had inherited from the ancient line of Majda warriors who had served the Ruby Dynasty for five thousand years. "With Imperator Skolia incapacitated, I am in command of ISC."

"I'm a civilian," Roca said. "Not military. As a member of the royal family, I outrank you. And you answer to First Councilor Meson." The First Councilor was the head of the government, elected by the Assembly, whose representatives were elected by the citizens of Skolia. Meson had authority over even the Imperator.

"In peacetime, yes." Majda waited a beat. "That condition may no longer apply."

"You've declared war?" Roca asked, incredulous. Even the Imperator couldn't do it without the First Councilor's assent.

"I am in contact with First Councilor Meson," Majda said.

"She concurs with my decision. We are taking you to Safe-landing."

Roca wanted to rage against the decision. Her dying sons were on Diesha and many of her children were alone on Lyshriol, the oldest barely into their twenties, her youngest, Kelric, not even ten yet. She had to go to them.

She also knew, however, that if she was assassinated, it would endanger her family far more than her absence. She could do nothing for Kurj or Althor, nor could she protect her children on Lyshriol better than the military. She would help them best by cooperating with ISC. But her logic and her parental instincts warred, and she barely managed to bite back her protests.

Roca spoke tightly. "Very well."

"We will take care of them." Majda's voice quieted. "Councilor, you visited Imperator Skolia at the palace not long ago. Have you suffered any ill effects?"

"Nothing." Roca leaned forward, and the monitors around her beeped in protest. "My husband came with me, and our son Eldrin was there when we arrived."

"Your consort shows no problems. Your son was ill, but he's fine now."

"Eldrin was sick?"

"He ingested a number of the assassin meds, but far less than Imperator Skolia. Also, a med species that neutralizes blue-dye impurities in his body counteracted the attacking species." Majda glanced to the side at something on her desk Roca couldn't see, possibly a display. "The dye meds rely on an ancient design we no longer use but that the Trader scientists took with them when they separated from our ancestors."

"You think the Traders are using a pattern we haven't seen for centuries?" Roca asked.

Majda nodded. "More than centuries. The dye meds descend from colonists who settled Lyshriol five thousand years ago. The Trader meds could derive from a similar stock."

Roca had never thought she would be so grateful about a treatment for food coloring. "Can the blue-dye meds help Kurj?"

"Perhaps if we had caught the damage earlier. But it has gone too far." Her gaze never wavered. "The Traders will pay for these crimes against the Ruby Dynasty, Your Highness."

"Yes," Roca said grimly. "They will."

She didn't add what they both knew: that if Kurj died, it would be a blow that ISC and the Imperialate might not recover from in time to survive a war.

The blare of a level-two alarm yanked Soz out of a nightmare about Vitarex Raziquon and her mother. Even as she scrambled out of her bunk, remnants of the dream nagged her mind. It was too vivid, what she called a bonecrusher, a nightmare that came with inescapable intensity and told her something she didn't want to know. Bonecrushers made her feel deadened, futile, because they often turned out to be premonitions. She couldn't pretend such an intense dream meant nothing, but she was certain the Traders didn't have her mother. And Vitarex was *dead*. It had to be wrong.

Soz pulled on her blue jumpsuit, groggy but moving fast. "What's the emergency?"

"I don't know," Sigma answered. "You're to report to General Majda on the bridge."

"Got it." Soz strode out of her quarters, her steps long and high in the low gravity. She ran to the nearest mag station and caught a car. Four Fleet officers were onboard, men and women who looked like they had been pulled out of sleep, too. No one knew what had happened. They soon disembarked, but she stayed on, riding to the end of the ship.

When Soz entered the bridge, it was in full view-mode, the holoscreens activated to show space. Soz had become so accustomed to the microgravity, she needed little help as she launched herself forward. At Devon's command chair, Soz grabbed a cable and braked to a stop.

"Cadet Valdoria, reporting for duty," she said, saluting Devon with one arm hooked around the cable.

Devon nodded. "At ease."

Soz lowered her arms, bursting with curiosity. She

couldn't see why Devon would call a cadet to the bridge during an emergency. They needed seasoned officers up here.

Devon spoke in a low voice. "It's your brother."

Soz froze. Her mother had sworn they wouldn't take Althor off life support. "What happened, ma'am?"

The general's eyes seemed darker than usual. "Someone sent assassins against him."

"Althor?" Why assassinate a man who was already dead?

"No. Imperator Skolia."

Soz felt as if her stomach dropped. She couldn't have heard right. Kurj was a constant they all depended on, the rock, the strength, the fist of ISC. He couldn't have died. Soz would know. She would *know*.

Then she remembered her dream. Bonecrushers were rarely exact. Had it been about *Kurj*?

"Did he survive?" Soz asked.

"Yes." Devon hesitated only one moment, but that pause revealed a world of information, none of it good. "His biomech web went into failure. Many of his organs stopped. The doctors started regeneration as soon as they found him, but great damage had been done. They had to replace his biomech and some of his organs." Her voice quieted. "They don't know if he will live."

Soz's mind whirled. First her father. Then Althor. Then Kurj. Her dismay shifted into hatred. No wonder the decades had hardened Kurj. "The Traders think they can kill us off." She clenched the cable hard. "They're wrong."

"Yes, they are." Fatigue showed in Devon's gaze. "If I were a Traditionalist instead of a Royalist, this is the time I would bemoan the practice of sending men into battle. But that is nonsense and it changes nothing."

Soz felt a strange disorientation, hearing the roles reversed after living in a culture where only men fought. This much she knew: if ISC proved the assassination attempt originated with ESComm, they would wage war *now*. This ship would go into battle.

With her on it.

The Bard couldn't remember enjoying technology so much. In years past, the games his children played had intrigued him, their tech-mech puzzles, the glittering robots Kelric adored, the holo armies Soz had created. They also perplexed him. He was never sure how they worked. He had tried to hide his confusion; it would be too embarrassing to tell his children he couldn't understand their games. He suspected they knew anyway, but they never said anything.

Perhaps age had mellowed him, or maybe almost losing his life had made his pride matter less. Sitting here with his grandson on the floor of the pharaoh's living room with sunlight slanting across them, he felt content.

"See this one, Grandfather." Taquinil unrolled an iridescent film on the carpet. "You'll like it." He touched a corner of the film and a menu of little holos formed, all plants and animals. The boy flicked his finger through one that resembled a stalk of grain. The menu vanished and a rippling field of holo-plants appeared, golden and top heavy.

"You can go first," Taquinil offered.

Bemused, Eldrinson peered at the field. Although pleasant to see, it didn't seem to have a purpose. "What do I do?"

"You have to figure that out." In a more confidential tone, Taquinil added, "Usually you find treasures and defeat monsters."

"Ah." For want of any other idea, Eldrinson waved his finger through the nearest stalk of grain. A small animal with blue fur and floppy ears poked its head out of the field. With a squeak, it ran off into the swaying grain.

Eldrinson laughed. "What does that mean?"

"I'll bet we're supposed to follow him." Taquinil waved his hand through the place where the animal had disappeared. It poked its head up and ran off again. "The little figures mostly match terms in a series. If you figure out the next term, it reveals a code that tells you what it will do. This first level is easy, just linear or geometric progressions. The hole it hopped out of is a term in the Fibonacci series."

"Oh," Eldrinson said. Taquinil didn't sound like any seven-year-old he had ever known, but the boy seemed happy. "Fibonacci tells you something?"

"Sure." Taquinil beamed at him. "You can figure things out

about the field. Like how many tricks a grain plant can do. My favorites are hidden doorways." He indicated a waving stalk. "See this one? You use calculus to integrate its shape in three dimensions. It gives you an exact number. Four. That's how many doorways it hides. Then you figure out how to open the doors."

Eldrinson had no clue what his grandson had said. No matter. He loved how the boy's mood sparkled.

Taquinil talked as they played, describing how to create holos using equations Eldrinson didn't think a child that age should know. Together, they chased all manner of odd creatures. Often when animals dropped down holes, the scene changed, rippling into an underground grotto, a mountain retreat, a dark castle. He and Taquinil defeated monsters and found baubles that earned them points. Eldrinson enjoyed the sword fights most, though whoever had designed this game knew next to nothing about true swordplay.

Eventually, he figured out patterns that helped him predict the behavior of the creatures. Taquinil saw the patterns faster and could have easily won, but he had no wish to compete. The boy wanted them to play as a team, cooperating to increase their combined score. It was odd to Eldrinson; he thought in terms of fighting and victory. But this seemed more suited to Taquinil's gentle personality. It didn't surprise him, given Taquinil's parents. For all that the boy's father, Eldrin, was a gifted swordsman, it had devastated him to go into battle. Eldrin had distinguished himself in combat and come home a hero, but it had taken a soul-parching toll on him.

When the Bard's two oldest sons had dropped the fetters of cultural expectations and truly pursued their dreams, Althor had gone to war and Eldrin had become a singer. Eldrin he understood; he was a singer, like his father. Although combat hadn't scarred the Bard as deeply as it had his son, he much preferred farming to leading an army. It was Althor who confused him. How could his towering warlord of a son not have wanted a wife? An alarming thought came to him. Would Althor have taken a *husband*? No, he couldn't think about that. All he knew was that he had told Althor not to come home, and he could never take back those words.

This past year, the Bard had rethought many assumptions he had taken for granted, including the idea that all youths should train as warriors. A military education would be a disaster for Taquinil. If the scholarly boy preferred to chase floppy-eared animals instead of staging battles, it seemed best to let him. In acknowledging that, Eldrinson faced a more difficult truth; Soz had also chosen the path best suited to her. He needed to accept that, somehow. It was too late with Althor, but he had another chance with Soz. He would endeavor this time to make a better job of matters.

Nor was it only Soz. When he returned home, he would do his best to put things right with Shannon. At least he understood his Blue Dale son better than his children who wanted to go offworld. Shannon's trances and longing for the mountains made sense to Eldrinson. It was in Eldrinson's blood, too, even if he didn't feel the pull of the Blue Dales with the same intensity.

The front door chimed, the notes trilling like the musical equivalent of a stream burbling over rocks. Eldrinson's pulse jumped; perhaps Roca had returned from Diesha. She hadn't known exactly what the Chair wanted to tell her, but she was convinced Kurj was in trouble. For all that Eldrinson feared and resented his stepson, he hoped for Roca's sake that Kurj was all right.

He stood slowly, awkward with his biomech joints. He could ask the house who had come to call, but technology stole all the surprises out of life. Some he could have done without, like Vitarex Raziquon, but the house wouldn't let anyone visit who posed a danger.

"Wait, Grandhoshpa." Taquinil scooped up Eldrinson's cane and jumped to his feet. "I'll go with you." He hooked his arm with his grandfather's and looked up at him with large gold eyes.

Eldrinson patted the boy's hand. "Thank you."

"Here." Taquinil offered him the cane. When Eldrinson took it, the boy straightened, very grown up, though he just came to Eldrinson's elbow.

They crossed to the entrance foyer. Despite his intent to surprise himself, Eldrinson hesitated. How did he know he wanted to greet whoever had come to visit?

Taquinil glanced at him, then said, "Laplace, who is outside?"

The house EI answered. "Officers from the Pharaoh's Army."

"Why have they come?" Eldrinson asked.

"I don't know," Laplace said. "Shall I inquire?"

"Yes." Eldrinson shifted his feet apart for balance. He planted his cane in front of his body and put both hands on its lyrine head, bracing himself. ·

"They wish to guard the two of you," Laplace said. "I must open the door. They have orders from First Councilor Meson and Jazida Majda, the General of the Pharaoh's Army."

Eldrinson would have liked to refuse, but he had been around his wife's people enough to know they would persist. He sighed. "Very well."

Part of the wall shimmered and vanished in an archway. A cluster of military types stood outside, men and women in army green or fleet blue, and two in the black leathers of Jagernauts.

A dark-haired woman bowed to Eldrinson. She had far too many muscles and towered over him. Her face looked female, but more ascetic than the lush women of his world. Although she had curves, their muscular sculpting would put Dalvador warriors to shame. No doubt she could throw him over her shoulder without working up a sweat. It was most disconcerting. He wished Roca were here.

"My honor at your presence, Your Majesty," she said. "I am Colonel Starjack Tahota."

Tahota! He knew that name. Eldrinson scowled at her. "You came to Lyshriol over a year ago and took away my daughter."

She had the decency to look uncomfortable. "I regret any difficulties that caused."

At least she didn't make excuses. With reluctance, he stood aside so his unwanted visitors could enter. Taquinil stayed close to his side and watched with a concerned gaze.

The colonel bowed to Taquinil. "My honor at your presence, Your Highness." Kindness toward the boy showed in her face, which made Eldrinson warm to her a bit.

Taquinil inclined his head as his parents did when addressed by their titles, except he seemed uncertain he was doing it right, which made the gesture charming rather than formal. Eldrinson held back his smile.

As the officers spread through the house, the colonel walked with Eldrinson to the living room. "How are you feeling?"

"Well enough." He couldn't stop limping, but he did his best not to lean on his cane.

Taquinil walked next to him, hovering. Eldrinson winked at him. **I'm fine, Taquinilli.**

The boy laughed at the nickname, a play on Nilli, his favorite character in the hologame. Tahota glanced at them, but she didn't intrude.

The colonel's gauntlet buzzed. She lifted her arm and spoke into a mesh. "Tahota here."

"The house is secure, Colonel," a man said.

"Good work," Tahota said. "Keep monitoring the area."

"Is there a problem?" Eldrinson asked.

Roca's people often avoided his questions, assuming his background made him stupid, but to her credit, Tahota answered immediately. "We know what the Chair was trying to tell your wife. Someone attempted to assassinate Imperator Skolia."

Eldrinson stared at her. "How?"

"Poison meds."

"Will he live?"

Tahota exhaled. "We don't know. He's in a coma."

Eldrinson thought of Althor. If Kurj died, too, what would happen to ISC? For the military to lose its highest commander on the eve of war could be disaster. "Gods pray that he recovers."

"For all of you," Tahota said quietly.

Her underlying concern came through to him despite the mental barriers they both had raised. She made him self-conscious. This warrior had no reason to care what happened to him, yet she did. They sat on a couch in the living room, she on one end and he on the other, and Taquinil flopped down between them.

"Have you heard from my wife?" Eldrinson asked Tahota, looking at her over Taquinil's head.

"She's spoken with General Majda," Tahota said.

He squinted at her. "Which one?" ISC seemed to have a plethora of Majda generals.

Whatever his expression, it made Tahota smile. "Jazida Majda."

The General. Eldrinson found Jazida even more alarming than this Starjack. At least his present visitor didn't seem to think he should be locked up in seclusion and never allowed out unless robes and a cowl covered him from head to toe. Pah.

"Your Majesty?" Tahota asked. "What is wrong?"

Eldrinson flushed, realizing his annoyance must have shown on his face. He composed his expression. "I was wondering when my wife would arrive on Diesha."

"Councilor Roca is en route to Safelanding."

"Where?"

"It's a secret place," Taquinil said. "ISC hid it in an asteroid belt. Almost no one knows about it."

Tahota stiffened. "Then how did you know?"

"From mother's mesh accounts," Taquinil said.

"You should know better than to play with your mother's console," Eldrinson admonished. He would have scolded the boy more, except he caught sight of Tahota's expression. She was staring at Taquinil and her face had gone pale.

"That information is secured," Tahota told the boy. "How could you find it?"

"It was easy," Taquinil said. "I followed the tangles."

"Tangles?" Tahota asked.

"In the mesh. I untangled them. I found the Epsilon Files."

"Saints almighty," the colonel muttered.

"What are the Epsilon Files?" Eldrinson asked.

"It's secured," Tahota said. She spoke sternly to Taquinil. "You must never mention what you found to anyone."

The boy looked a bit startled. "Yes, ma'am." He hesitated. "Is my Hoshma going to Safelanding, too?"

"The pharoah is on Parthonia," Tahota said. In a reassuring voice, she added, "It already has the best defenses in the Imperialate, and we've upgraded them since what happened on Lyshriol."

"Then why take Roca to this Safelanding?" Eldrinson asked, uneasy. "If Taquinil can find it, so might the Traders."

"They won't find it," Taquinil assured him. "They can't break the codes."

"Then how did you?" Eldrinson asked.

"It was already on Mother's console."

"So you found the information there," Tahota asked. "In her private files?"

"No. I just rewrote her Epsilon spy codes."

Eldrinson wasn't sure what Taquinil was talking about, but the boy had clearly been misbehaving. Before he could ask whether or not his mother knew what he was about, Colonel Tahota made a rather odd sound, like a choked gasp.

"You *rewrote* the Assembly Key's spy codes?" Tahota asked. "I'm almost afraid to ask how."

"You know," Taquinil said. "The underworld."

"No, I don't know," the colonel said.

"The world under the meshes. Shadow places. Wavefunctions that haven't collapsed."

Eldrinson scowled at him. "Taqui, are you making this up?"

The boy flushed. "No, really I'm not."

Tahota pushed her hand through her hair. "I think he is talking about the underlying structure of the web, the quantum processes that make it work."

"Is that wrong?" Taquinil asked.

The colonel spoke with a kindness that surprised Eldrinson, given her imposing presence and the boy's mischief. "You shouldn't play with ISC security. But I think our intelligence people will want to talk with you. You could probably tell them a lot."

Taquinil looked a bit wary. "All right."

"Why can't my wife stay here for protection?" Eldrinson asked.

"General Majda doesn't want too many members of your family in one place." Tahota leaned against the couch, her elbow resting on its back. She crossed her booted legs with one ankle on her other knee, the way a man would. Eldrinson was growing more accustomed to her, though. She wasn't as cold as he had expected. It occurred to him that he wouldn't have automatically attributed those qualities to a male colonel.

"My children are alone on Lyshriol," Eldrinson said.

"Our understanding is that most are adults according to your culture," Tahota said.

Eldrinson scowled. "They're teenagers." He used the Skolian decimal number, since the Lyshrioli octal count of years tended to confuse his wife's people. Del and Chaniece were a little older and Vyrl was married, but "teenager" would do. "Kelric is nine and Aniece is twelve," he added. "The older ones can take care of the younger, but it isn't the same as having their mother or me there."

"Please be assured," Tahota said. "We will make sure no one in your family goes without protection or supervision."

He felt far from assured. He had been under ISC protection when Raziquon captured him. "How long will this last?"

"We aren't certain. As long as we have reason to believe your family is in danger."

Taquinil paled. "It's my father, isn't it? He's sick."

The Bard tensed and turned to Tahota. "Something happened to my son?"

She answered quickly. "Prince Eldrin ingested some of the assassination meds. But they had almost no effect on him."

Panic edged his thoughts. *Another* of his sons? " 'Almost?' Is he sick, too?"

Taquinil was listening with an expression Eldrinson recognized, as if every word was a spinning ball he had to catch. "Will he be all right?" the boy asked.

Tahota gentled her voice. "He's fine."

"How did the bad meds get inside of him?" Taquinil asked.

"From a drink. Kava." Tahota glanced at Eldrinson. "You and Councilor Roca were there, also. We're fortunate that neither of you drank the kava."

Well, that explained why ISC doctors had practically dissected him these past few days, supposedly "verifying his health" before they began his epilepsy treatments. He hadn't believed them; the doctors treating his epilepsy hadn't even been present.

"How did the meds get into the kava?" Eldrinson asked.

"From the auto-kitchen. As to how they ended up in the machinery—" Tahota shook her head. "We don't know yet."

"Will Uncle Kurj get better?" Taquinil asked.

The colonel hesitated. "We hope so." She controlled her expressions well, but Eldrinson sensed her disquiet, that the ISC commander lay dying on the brink of a war.

If Roca lost Kurj, too, Eldrinson knew it would tear her apart. And what would happen to the Kyle web? Together, Dehya and Kurj barely kept it alive. If one of them had to do it alone, the work could kill them or the meshes might unravel, negating Skolia's advantage over the Traders.

"What if Kurj never recovers?" he asked Tahota.

She met his gaze, her own stark. "Hope that he does."

He understood now why they were hiding Roca. They might soon need her in the Dyad. Given the threat of war, that could make her the single most valuable human being in the Skolian Imperialate at this moment in history.

"Could you put Roca in the Dyad link now?" Eldrinson asked.

Tahota shook her head. "If a third person tries to join while Imperator Skolia lives, it will probably kill the Imperator."

Eldrinson saw then the enormity of the decision they faced. When Kurj had joined the Dyad decades ago, it had killed his grandfather. Kurj's mind had been too much like his. The link couldn't support them both. His grandfather had relinquished his hold on life so that his grandson could live.

Now the Assembly and ISC had to choose. They needed the Dyad. If they put in Roca, making it a Triad, Kurj could die. Her mind wasn't as close to Kurj's as his had been to his grandfather's, but they were similar. The Traders had gambled with their assassin meds and hit a jackpot. No matter how the Ruby Dynasty responded, they would suffer. If Roca didn't join the Dyad, the weight of supporting the entire Kyle web alone could destroy Dehya. If the pharaoh survived, the web would probably still collapse, leaving Skolia vulnerable.

Taquinil's thoughts hovered at the edges of Eldrinson's mind. The adults around him tried to shield their minds, but Eldrinson had already realized his grandson picked up far more than anyone told him. He knew his parents were in danger.

The Bard put his hand on the boy's shoulder. "I will be here for you. Remember that. No matter what happens, I am here."

Taquinil spoke shakily. "And me for you, Grandfather."

Tahota watched them with compassion in her expression— and great sadness.

The energy spike registered in six different power stations that orbited the planet Parthonia. Techs at four of the stations recorded it in their logs. Two of them alerted ISC security on the planet. One even sent notification to Diesha. After the Dieshan report cycled through many layers of security, it was forwarded to a team investigating the attack on the Imperator. The officer in charge had assigned a battery of EIs to look for patterns in the behavior of every system that served the palace. It was an exhaustive search which had so far yielded nothing useful, but they were nothing if not thorough.

A match came up: energy spikes similar to the one at Parthonia had been observed three times on Diesha in power grids, all late at night when energy usage was low enough that it didn't swamp out the spikes.

The major in charge of the investigation widened the search. Two hours later, another match came up: such spikes had also been observed roughly two years ago at the starport on the planet Lyshriol, home to the Valdoria branch of the Ruby Dynasty.

The major sent a priority message to Jazida Majda, the acting Imperator, who was currently on the Orbiter. It arrived in the middle of the night. The EI secretary at her residence in City noted that the message was tagged with a Priority One flag and routed it to the private console in her bedroom, where she was sleeping. The console hummed, buzzed more loudly when Majda didn't awake, and then sounded a siren. Majda sat up fast, still half asleep, and smacked the receive panel on the console by her bed. She came awake immediately when she heard the major's report. Its concluding recommendation consisted of one sentence:

We must get the Ruby Pharaoh and Assembly off Parthonia NOW.

10

Starliner Drop

On a cool, windy morning, the yacht carrying Eldrin landed in the Admiral Starport, a military facility in Selei City. Dehya met him on the tarmac, guarded by eight Jagernauts, all members of the Abaj Takalique, the elite bodyguards who had served the Ruby Dynasty since before the Ruby Empire. Seven feet tall with black hair and eyes, hooked noses, and black uniforms, they had the timeless quality of a race that had called Raylicon home for six thousand years.

An attendant rolled a morph-stair up to the yacht. Eldrin could have requested it change into a lift that would ferry him to the ground, but he preferred to walk down the stairs and stretch his legs, which felt shaky after his sickness. He had disliked the way his bodyguards hovered over him on the ship and how the doctors insisted he stay in bed after he felt better. From their minds, even through their shields and his own, he had picked up their worry about him being a Ruby heir. Eldrin knew they had to protect him, but they were going overboard about this whole business. It was only a minor illness.

His need to drink bothered him far more. The medicine that the ship's doctor had given him eased his craving, but it didn't fill the hollow spaces he had to face when he was sober. Only phorine helped. He hadn't taken it on the yacht, but he would need another dose soon. Without it he felt as if he were dying. Several times the doctor had asked about the treatment for the seizures Eldrin had suffered as a youth, and he was almost certain she was mistaking evidence of the phorine for a medicine he hadn't taken in several years. Perhaps the chemicals were related. But surely phorine wasn't so rare that they couldn't recognize its properties. Although he had never heard of it before, he wasn't a doctor. Regardless, he kept his use a secret.

Eldrin descended the stairs with four Jagernauts. Dehya waited at the bottom, a welcome sight, smiling, fragile in the midst of her Abaj warriors. Machine men. Had his own brother not been a Jagernaut, Eldrin would have wondered if they were human. But all that augmentation hadn't saved Althor.

He recognized the lights flickering on the gauntlets of his bodyguards; they were communicating with Dehya's guards. If a Jagernaut focused his thoughts in a certain manner, bioelectrodes fired his neurons and let him "think" to his node. It sent his messages along threads in his body to his wrist sockets, which linked to his gauntlets. They transmitted the data to the gauntlets of the Abaj Jagernauts, which relayed it to the Abaj's brain by the reverse process. For people close together, it essentially gave them technology-produced telepathy.

Eldrin and Dehya also had internal systems that monitored their surroundings. If either of them needed help, transmitters within their bodies notified their bodyguards and the nearest ISC receiver. Systems within the port were undoubtedly watching them as well, and within the yacht. Eldrin chafed at the surveillance, but it was actually easier to deal with the machines than with the Jagernauts. He could ignore machines. The Jagernauts made it impossible to forget he and Dehya were guarded everywhere, even in their own home, and would be for the rest of their lives.

Eldrin relaxed his mental barriers and concentrated on Dehya. By the time he reached the bottom of the stairs, he knew two things: she was upset and he was about to be angry. Empaths didn't always pick up exact moods or interpret what they sensed correctly, but it was obvious something bothered his wife.

Her silky tunic and trousers were rippling in the breezes.

After so many days apart, he wanted to embrace her. But he held back, aware of their audience. In public they rarely showed affection. It wasn't necessary. They didn't even need a formal greeting. They had been in a mental link since he disembarked from the yacht.

"I'm all right," he said.

The wind blew hair across her face. "Kurj isn't."

Kurj? "What happened?"

She spoke bluntly. "Someone tried to assassinate him. And you. They almost succeeded."

"Good gods. Is Kurj all right?"

She spoke in a subdued voice. "He might not make it."

His stomach clenched. Not Kurj, too. Although nothing changed in the bluish sunlight, the day seemed to dim, as if clouds had covered the sun. The behavior of the people on the yacht suddenly made sense. "My doctor knew. That's why she hovered over me so much." Eldrin scowled at the Jagernaut captain by his side. "You knew, too."

The captain spoke awkwardly. "Yes, Your Majesty."

"Gods forbid anyone should tell me," Eldrin said.

"Why didn't they?" Dehya asked the captain.

"Orders from Imperator Majda," he said. "It was on a need-to-know basis only."

"Well, of course," Eldrin said. "Why would I need to know? It's only my *life*." He led a fractured existence, guarded as if he were more valuable than the rarest transition metals, yet treated as if he couldn't be trusted to know about threats to his own life. And he was perceived as more "civilized" than his father. If it was this bad for him, it was no wonder his father hated spending time among the Skolians.

Dehya laid her hand on his arm. "It's not their fault."

He pushed off her hand. "ISC thinks I'm your goddamned pet."

"Dryni," she murmured.

He shook his head. "Let's go home."

"All right."

They walked across the tarmac, and he strove to ignore the guards surrounding them. The faintest shimmer in the air was the only indication that a sensor shroud protected them out here.

After several moments, when Eldrin's anger had calmed, he asked, "Why was Kurj affected more than me?"

"He drank several mugs of the kava." A shudder went through her slender body. "He was almost dead when the medics found him."

The words felt like a punch. "Help should have arrived immediately."

"Yes." Her face was drawn. "The assassin meds replicated like mad. They were all over. They sabotaged machinery. In Kurj's body, they destroyed his biomech. The kava dispenser was hit early, probably because it was next to the first conduits they reached in the auto-kitchen. By the time our people got there, they were in every system."

He stared at her, incredulous. "How could they attack the palace that way? It can't be that vulnerable."

"That's what we thought," Dehya said. "All we know so far is that the more isolated systems weren't affected. The simple ones were the hardest to sabotage. Like the repair bots. Kurj figured that out in time."

They had reached the dichromesh-glass gate into the terminal. Lights flickered on the gauntlets of one Abaj, and the polarized door slid open. They entered a spacious room where a woman sat behind an artistically rounded Luminex table. White carpet covered the floor, and holoart on the walls showed graceful streets shaded by droop-willows.

One of the Abaj spoke with the woman at the console. Although technically security had to clear Eldrin's arrival with the port authority, it was only a formality. They were hardly going to deny the pharaoh's consort entrance into the capital of her empire.

Within moments, he and Dehya were walking down a concourse lined with food stations, cafes, and shops—all empty. The Jagernauts surrounded them, but the only other people in the area were security officers from the port. It flustered him that ISC emptied out an entire terminal just for his arrival. That paled, though, next to his dismay over the news about Kurj.

"Thank the saints, the repair bots could help him," Eldrin

said. "Saints" referred to some of the lesser gods in Lyshriol mythology; when he was upset, he tended to revert to idioms from his own language.

Dehya nodded, her face drawn. "The bot was supposed to fix damaged furniture, but it couldn't repair the footboard Kurj had cracked. That flummoxed the signals from its pico-chip. The palace is saturated with links to the Kyle meshes, enough so that even without a direct connection, the bot's signals caused a slight perturbation in a local mesh. It wasn't much; to pick up something that faint, you needed a telop in a Dyad Chair. Kurj was counting on me. We would have—" She took a shaky breath, then tried again, her voice low and strained. "We would have figured it out in time if I had been in the web. But I wasn't."

Eldrin drew her to a halt. "It's *not* your fault." She was shielding her mind, but it didn't work as well with him. He felt the guilt that was eating her hollow. "You can't be in the web all day, every day of your life! It's impossible. You would die."

"I should have been there." Her face was as pale as alabaster. "If not for Roca, we would never have found him in time."

His mother had been on Diesha? "I thought she went to the Orbiter with my father."

"She did." Dehya started walking again, her gait slowed with fatigue. "She used the Dyad Chair there. It showed her Kurj." She lifted her hand, then dropped it. "We know so little about the Chairs. They allow the Dyad to use their functions. Sometimes they do other things, like this. But why? Their intelligence exists in Kyle space, not here. They are too different from us."

"Well, they seem to like you and Kurj." Maybe the Chairs didn't want the Traders in charge of the Kyle meshes, either.

"I don't think they have emotions, at least not the way we do." Dehya smiled wanly. "Maybe we interest them."

"Just as long as they don't turn on you."

"Why would they?"

"Because you're trespassing in Kyle space."

The gauntlet worn by the captain of Dehya's Abaj buzzed. He lifted his arm to speak into the comm. Or at least Eldrin thought he meant to speak. The man's face furrowed and he lowered his arm again, slowly. Static buzzed at the edges of Eldrin's mind.

Dehya was watching the captain. "What is it?"

"I thought I received a page," he said. "But it wasn't."

She regarded him uneasily. "Check it out."

He nodded, and his face took on the inwardly-directed quality of a Jagernaut communicating with his internal node.

A hum came from behind Eldrin. As he turned, a teardrop car floated alongside him. It was open to the air, shaped like its name, and just large enough for two people to sit. Several other cars whirred around them, enough for their bodyguards.

Eldrin smiled, intrigued. "Where did these come from?"

"I called them." Dehya lifted her hand toward the car as if offering an invitation. "Care to ride?"

He bowed to his wife. "My pleasure, lady."

They all boarded the cars. As Eldrin and Dehya whirred off, the Abaj captain pulled up alongside them in his car. He said, "I've tracked down the page, Your Majesty. It was a spike in the energy output of a system here in the port."

Dehya frowned as their cars sped down the concourse. "Send a report to ISC."

They continued on, headed for Selei City, where a new session of the Assembly would soon open, gathering hundreds of leaders from all over Skolia in one place—including the First Councilor, Skolia's elected leader, and the Ruby Pharaoh, its hereditary sovereign.

Soz sat at the end of a robot arm with a terminus just big enough for her console, which formed a cup, curving under her feet and around her lower body. She had become so used to the psiphon prongs that clicked into her sockets, she barely noticed them. Transparent panels positioned themselves around her and holomaps rotated above them while the iridescent ripples of holograms shifted on their surface like rainbows on an oil slick.

Today Soz was in the main body of the ship rather than on the bridge. From out in space, the cruiser resembled a tubular shell, but that "shell" was hundreds of meters thick, with many decks where crews lived and worked. Soz tended to think of bays in terms of the observation bubbles where a person could look out at the stars, or else medical bays, which she avoided. This bay was a cramped chamber, spherical in shape, with featureless walls. The robot arm held her in the center. Known as a telop bay, it provided an environment where a telop could more easily detach her attention from spacetime and submerge her mind into Kyle space.

Sigma Pride respond, Soz thought.

Attending. The thought came from one of many subshells created by the EI brain of the battle cruiser *Roca's Pride.*

Visor, Soz thought.

The visor lowered and plunged her into darkness. A display of psicons formed like the icons that floated above mesh screens, except these were in her mind, created when her node accessed her brain. She concentrated on the icon of an old-fashioned horn, the type a town crier might have used to announce news.

Communications, Soz thought.

The horn grew until it filled her mindscape. Then it blinked out and left her in darkness.

Soz scowled. Well, flat damn. That wasn't supposed to happen.

Return psicon display, she thought. The icons reappeared as before, except the horn was pulsating red. **Sigma, what is wrong with my link to your communications systems?**

Sigma rumbled. **The error appears to be in your spinal node.**

Soz directed a thought to her node. **Why can't you link to the comm systems of this ship?**

Her node's "voice" was quiet compared to Sigma. Your wet-codes are incompatible.

You mean my thoughts?

Not thoughts. The commands encoded into the bioelectrodes in your neurons are incompatible with the commands Sigma expects you to send so that you can communicate with the ship.

Soz didn't like the sound of it. **They have to be compatible. ISC designed Jagernaut biomech specifically for use with ISC systems such as this.**

Yes. However, your bioelectrodes have been altered.

Soz went rigid. Altering her bioelectrodes required access to her brain. **Do you know how it happened? Because I sure as blazes don't.**

Checking. After a pause, it thought, the alteration took place during a communication you had with Diesha several days ago.

You mean when I talked to Jazar?

Yes.

I don't recall anything unusual.

I recorded an energy fluctuation toward the end of the transmission.

Now that Soz thought about it, she did recall Jazar mentioning an energy spike. **A fluctuation that just "happened" to reprogram my bioelectrodes?**

The electrodes aren't reprogrammed. Just disrupted.

Why did it happen when I talked to Jazar?

I don't know.

Did it affect any other Jagernauts onboard this cruiser?

I don't know. You must ask the ship.

She redirected her thought. **Sigma, what do you know about it?**

Nothing, the ship answered. I have no public records of other Jagernauts reporting such an effect.

What about private records? Soz asked.

Private records are private.

Well, yes. **All right. What is the procedure for dealing with alterations like those in my bioelectrodes?**

I have no established procedure.

Interesting. If this was a known problem, medical would have a means of dealing with it, especially since so many systems on the ship required access to the Kyle web. **We need to establish one. I can't do my training if I can't link to your comm systems.**

Checking. Then Sigma thought, **It should be possible for one of my nodes to reprogram your bioelectrodes.**

That sounds straightforward.

Yes. Shall I proceed?

Is there any danger to me?

It does not appear so.

All right. Proceed.

While Sigma worked, Soz pondered. If the problem was this easy to fix, the solution should have been readily available, assuming someone had reported the difficulty. Either it was classified for some reason or no one had experienced the effect. ̶

Reconfiguration of your bioelectrodes complete, Sigma thought. **I am connecting to communications nodes.**

Does everything work?

Yes. You are connected. Its "voice" took on a new layer of richness.

Good. Now disconnect me.

You haven't completed your training session.

I will. I want to ask you some private questions first, though.

Disconnected. Sigma's voice lost its extra layer.

Sigma, does my spinal node have any differences compared to those of other people who have nodes on this ship?

Yes.

Soz waited. When it didn't continue, she sighed. Sigma reminded her of the ever-literal Kurj. **What are the differences?**

Your node has more memory.

Soz thought of her first experiences with the node, in the hospital on Diesha. **Because I'm a Ruby psion. So I have more neural structures it can utilize.**

Yes.

Soz rubbed her temple, wondering what secrets hid within the ephemeral flashes of her neurons. Had her increased memory caused her biomech web to malfunction?

Sigma, send a report about my biomech anomalies to Medical.
Done.
Good. Now disconnect your prongs from my body.
You haven't completed your training session.
I will. Later. She wanted to study the record of her biomech problems without Sigma eavesdropping.
Disconnected. Its response had a disapproving quality. For flaming sakes. A battle cruiser was scolding her. Well, they had named it after her mother. Even so. For Sigma's benefit, she scowled at the monitors set around the bay.

Then Soz directed a private thought to her own node. **Do you remember when I cracked all those field training systems at DMA?**
I have full records of your infractions.
Soz winced. Even her node was disapproving. She thought back to her unauthorized explorations at DMA. **When I tampered with the security mods, it caused an energy surge in the system. I had to disguise it. Do you still have a record of that?**
Yes, I do. Shall I compare it with the spike that disrupted your bioelectrodes?
Yes. She wondered if Jazar had played a trick on her. It would be out of character; he tended to go by the book, which was one reason she liked spending time with him. He moderated her urge to bend rules. It also made him a delectable target for her teasing. She could never be sure about Jazar, though. He had a streak of mischief. If he had perpetrated some prank on her, she would figure it out and reverse the process.

Soz paused. How would he manage a trick through Kyle space? She doubted she could have done it, and she knew the meshes better than most cadets. He might have had help, but that would take someone relatively high in ISC security, hardly a person likely to abet such shenanigans.

Soz rubbed her chin. Perhaps the problem originated here.
I've finished my comparison, her node thought. **The spike that scrambled your bioelectrodes is similar to the one you created when you cracked the DMA meshes. However, the two spikes have different signatures.**

I don't understand what you mean by signature.
A waveform modulates signals in Kyle space. The envelope for the spike you created differed from the one that affected your talk with Jazar Orand. ISC signals have characteristic envelopes. I don't recognize the one in your communication with Orand.

Her unease was growing. **Reconnect to Sigma. Send Security the record of the problem with my bioelectrodes, and include the analysis you just gave me.**

Connecting, her node thought.

Sigma's voice growled in her mind. **Records forwarded.**

Good. Soz released a breath, trying to center herself. She wanted to pursue this anomaly herself, but she had a long shift ahead of her. She made herself return her focus to Sigma. **You can commence my training session.**

Commenced, Sigma thought.

Probably Security would recognize the signature. She sure as hell hoped so. Otherwise, someone had figured out how to sabotage Jagernauts.

Roca was sleeping when the alarms went off. She sat up in bed, groggy, peering into the dim light. When she set her palm against the wall, the comm panel glowed blue.

"What's going on?" Roca asked.

"This ship is being boarded," her AI answered.

"That's impossible!" She climbed out of bed. Unused to the low gravity from the ship's rotation, she stumbled and fell, her descent languid until she landed on her hands and knees. In standard gravity, she would have hurt her legs when she hit the deck, but now she hardly banged them.

"Councilor," the AI said. "Your bodyguards need to enter."

Roca swore under her breath. She yanked her nightgown over her breasts and pulled down the knee-length shift. Before she could do anything else to cover up, the door shimmered and vanished in a molecular airlock. She knew the airlock provided protection for her, but it flustered her to have one in her cabin so deep inside the starship. It highlighted how much ISC feared for her safety.

The entrance framed two Jagernauts. As she sat up grog-gily, they strode inside, two warriors in black, a looming con-trast to the Luminex walls. The man put his arm under Roca's elbow and drew her to her feet. The other Jagernaut, a large woman with a braid of black hair, scanned the cabin with a monitor in her gauntlet. The ship's alarm continued to blare.

"Are you all right, Councilor?" the man asked.

"Yes, fine." Roca pushed her hair out of her face. "What's going on?"

"We dropped out of inversion for routine verification of our position and time," he said. "We sent a Kyle message to HQ. We were almost immediately surrounded by ESComm ships."

Roca went cold. "We aren't in their territory."

"Not even close," he said grimly.

Hell and damnation. Interstellar space was vast, limitless on human scales. The probability was infinitesimal that the Traders would just happen upon her ship. ESComm must have stolen intelligence about the route. But that would mean they had broken ISC security at its highest levels. She felt ill: first an Aristo had infiltrated Lyshriol, then ESComm infil-trated Diesha, now they intercepted her ship. Where would they hit next? The only major Imperialate center they hadn't yet—

"Gods, no!" Roca jerked away from her bodyguard and lunged toward the comm in the wall.

The Jagernaut grabbed her with enhanced speed. "Coun-cilor, you must come with us."

She struggled to pull out of his grip. "They're going to hit Parthonia!"

The female guard grasped Roca's other arm. "We have to get you off this ship."

"Don't you understand?" Roca resisted as they hauled her out of the cabin. "The Assembly is on Parthonia *right now*."

"Councilor, we can't do anything for them," the woman said. "Our responsibility is to get you to safety."

They pulled Roca down a corridor of the ship, and she had to run to keep up, steps long and high, flying. Her feet barely skimmed the floor and her nightgown whipped around her knees. They had more experience in this gravity, and she let them pull her along, sailing through the air in leaps that devoured distance. Their gauntlets glittered. At the edges of her mind, she caught whispers of their interaction with the ship's EI.

Suddenly they jolted to a stop, so abruptly that she ran into the woman. With a heave, they spun her around and took off in the opposite direction. She asked no questions; she couldn't risk interrupting whatever communications they were receiving. Her upper arms ached where they were gripping her.

Just as fast as they had turned, the Jagernauts stopped again, looking back the way they had come, then down the corridor ahead. The woman slapped her gauntlet and the bulkhead before them vanished. They shoved Roca forward and sailed through the opening into a tube crammed with repair bots and coils. Craning her head to look back, Roca saw the bulkhead solidify behind them.

They followed the tube to a branching point and squeezed down a new tube, this one even more confined. Several times Roca hit her head on the overhead curve or caught her limbs on projections. The neck of her nightgown snagged a sharp edge and ripped. Airlocks on bulkheads opened before them and shimmered into place behind. These changeable corridors seemed to riddle the interior of the starliner. The Jagernauts made and remade them, apparently with commands from their internal nodes.

Finally they stopped at the junction of two tubes, grabbing handholds to halt their motion, each with a hand gripped around one of Roca's upper arms. Her momentum made her body swing forward, her feet flying out in front of her. As her bodyguards twisted around in the small space, the entrance of a new tube shimmered in the wall next to them. Gray smudges flickered in her side vision. Looking right and then left, she saw soldiers approaching from both directions.

They wore ESComm uniforms.

"Ah, Gods." Roca grunted as the Jagernauts shoved her into a new tube that had just opened.

"Run!" the female Jagernaut hissed. The ESComm officers were only a few meters away. The bulkhead shimmered into place behind Roca and cut her off from both her bodyguards and the invaders.

Roca gulped in air as she pushed down the cramped tunnel. She prayed the Jagernauts survived. Then she thought of the hells they would suffer if ESComm took them prisoner, and she prayed they either escaped or died. She propelled herself along faster—

ESComm soldiers stepped into view ahead.

"No!" Roca tried to turn back. She didn't have the facility of the Jagernauts in this gravity and her nightgown wound around her thighs, hampering her movements. In the seconds it took her to maneuver around, the soldiers caught up. One grabbed her from behind, clamping his arm around her waist and pulling her against him. She felt his arm through the flimsy cloth of her nightgown; his limb was metal embedded with conduits.

Roca rammed her elbow into his stomach, causing them both to swing around. Instead of hitting flesh, her elbow jarred a hard surface. Body armor. She twisted in his grip and swung at his head, but her knuckles only glanced off his helmet. As he caught her fist, their struggle knocked them down the tube and their feet left the ground in the slight gravity. Her hip-length hair caught on projections and hindered her movements.

Someone else grabbed her arm and pressed a syringe against her neck, delivering gods only knew what drug. Frantic, Roca fought harder. The hem of her nightgown caught on a strut and a strip of cloth ripped off. The ESComm soldier behind her hooked his leg around both of hers, keeping her in place with her back to his front. As they reeled into a bulkhead, she hit her head and spots danced in her vision.

Roca's vision was dimming. Whatever drug they had given her worked fast. One of the soldiers wrenched her arms behind her back and crossed them, one forearm on top the other. Pain shot through her muscles. As they bound her arms together, she kicked the soldier in front of her. They all lurched to the side, into a robot sweeper hooked in the wall. She was having trouble focusing and her motions felt sluggish.

The soldier behind Roca yanked her around to face him. She could see nothing of his head, only his silver helmet. He reached out, his motions seeming slowed to her drugged mind, and drew his fingertip along her lips. She tried to jerk back, but she could barely move. He wore a silver glove as part of a metal gauntlet. It probably had sensors that could feel her skin. The thought made her nauseous.

Fog filled her mind. Someone behind her dragged down the shoulder of her nightgown. The tip of a syringe pressed her neck again. As her sight went dark, the soldier holding her from behind slid one hand across her chest and fondled her breast. Dimly she heard another man speak in Highton: *Leave her alone. She isn't ours.*

No, Roca thought. But she could no longer speak, and they would never hear the thought.

Someone was tying her ankles. He jerked the bonds tight and she groaned as they cut her skin. Or she tried to groan. No sound came out. She thought they were moving, but she could no longer see. Her arms ached behind her back and her ankles throbbed. She felt the cavity in their minds, emptiness, threatening to swallow her. Her captors were anti-empaths. They had Aristo blood. When she suffered pain, they transcended . . .

Mercifully, her mind faded into blackness.

11

Aristos

Shannon noticed the distant rider when he saw a drifting cloud of bubbles in the plains. He was standing on top of the wall that surrounded Castle Dalvador, and his hands rested on cool bluestone at the low point of a crenellation. He watched the rider, knowing it was a woman, knowing she came to change his life, but he couldn't let her, not yet, not until he understood the foreboding that plagued him.

So he watched, in a trance.

Sometime later he realized she was nearing the castle. He could wait here or go to meet her. He followed the walkway on top of the wall until it intersected a tower with a blue turreted roof. Submerged in trance, he opened the blue glasswood door and entered a chamber of polished bluestone, only stone, no furniture, nothing but a stone bench circling the wall. He went through it and down the spiral stairs, around and around, his soft boots silent. At the bottom, he walked out into the courtyard, his mind drifting, no definite thoughts, only impressions: the distant calls of stable hands working with lyrine; a solitary gold bubble floating over the wall; packed dirt under his feet.

The gate out of the courtyard was open. A plaza lay outside, and beyond it, the cobbled lanes of Dalvador sloped downhill to the northwest and uphill to the east. Round white houses jumbled together, each capped with a turreted blue or purple roof. Bubbles floated in the air, disturbed from plants. A blue one popped and sprinkled glitter over the lane.

Shannon went downhill, vaguely aware of other people walking. His mind hummed. When he left the village, the reeds of the plains were stubbly under his feet; then they were poking his calves with hard, stubborn bubbles; then they were brushing his thighs, supple now, with bubbles that detached from their stalks and bobbed around him in a glistening cloud. He gazed toward the Backbone Mountains, where gaunt peaks jutted up like bones into the lavender sky.

The rider approached.

They met out in the waving reeds, out in a sea of silvery stalks. Shimmerflies glided around the woman as she brought her lyrine to a stop. Her white-gold hair drifted across her face and shoulders, covering her eyes, then uncovering them. Silver eyes. Here in Dalvador, away from the high reaches of the Blue Dale Mountains, she seemed delicate, small, vulnerable.

Shannon spoke in the Blue Dale dialect, his words chiming more than normal Trillian. "My greetings, Varielle."

She slid off her lyrine and landed with a thump. The reeds brushed her blue boots and leggings, and reached up to her hips. Her tunic was blue, the color of clouds. It clung to her slender body, revealing hints of her small high breasts and slender waist. She hinged her hand around her lyrine's bridle, twining her four fingers in the braided hemp-leather.

"My greetings, Shannon." Her voice chimed like crystal bells.

"You have ridden a long way," he said.

She came forward, bringing her lyrine with her, and stopped in front of him. She spoke without preamble. "You have made my life difficult. I go about my business, but you always and ever come into my thoughts. I have no peace."

His mood soared. "You disquiet me also."

"So." She seemed satisfied with his answer. "Come back."

"This is my home."

She looked past him to Dalvador. "It stays in one place."

"It does," Shannon admitted.

She hesitated, an unusual expression on her heart-shaped face. "I cannot stay here. Archers must wander."

"You would stay with me?"

"You are a fine, strong man, Shannon of Dalvador." She looked him over with approval. "I would have you for my companion."

He stood up straighter, feeling tall. "I would think on this suggestion."

She blinked at his answer. "If you think too long, we shall be old and decrepit before you decide."

He held back his smile. "You are blunt."

Varielle twisted the bridle around in her grip. "I have come a long way, to country that doesn't suit me, in search of you."

Her declarations might not be the most romantic ever uttered by a woman to a man, but they pleased him greatly. "You make compelling arguments."

"Perhaps you would make a compelling answer."

His good mood faded. "My family is in trouble. I cannot leave until I know how my parents fared in their journey."

She inclined her head with respect. "Family is important."

"I would ask that you wait for me."

A smile curved on her face, transforming it into silvered, fey beauty. "Is that your answer?"

Shannon hesitated. He wasn't sure what she was asking. Some youths his age took wives. His brother Eldrin had married at two octets of age, only one year older than Shannon was now. Vyrl had been even younger, just one octet plus six years. None of his other brothers had shown any inclination to marry, though, and he had never even kissed a girl. He wasn't sure he was ready for Varielle.

"What do you mean by companion?" he asked.

She wound the reins around her four fingers. Her lyrine snuffled with annoyance and tried to tug the braided lines away. "What would you like it to mean?"

Shannon traced his boot in the dirt, which was saturated with glitter. "I would live with you, Varielle." As soon as he spoke, he wanted to vanish into the reeds. He had just asked her to be his lover. What if he had misunderstood her intent? She might say no.

Her smile returned. "I would like this." She tilted her head toward the mountains. "In the Blue Dales."

"Can you wait?" Shannon asked. "I mustn't leave until I know about my family."

"What do you wish to know?"

"If they are safe." He didn't have words to describe the Skolian Imperialate to her. "They have traveled very far to deal with people who tried to kill my father and my brothers." Unease washed over him more and more lately. Other members of his family had also suffered, he was certain. But they were too far away; his sense of them was diffuse, hazy, impossible to pin down.

"We have a ceremony." Varielle's upturned eyes took on a distant quality. "A ceremony of calling."

"Calling?" He tried to orient on her words. "What is that?"

"Calling to the Otherplace."

"I have never heard of this place."

"It is where thoughts hum."

"Whose thoughts?"

"Archers." She shook her head, and silver hair drifted about her shoulders. "It is hard to explain, Shannon of Dalvador. A place where we have always gone. Our legends say the Memories of your people helped us many eons ago, and your Bards sang us into the Otherplace, a part of our two suns, two moons, two twos of fingers on two hands, two twos of toes on two feet. Twos. Octets."

"Binary and octal?" Shannon asked. "Some types of mesh use those numbers. Do you mean a web? A living mesh of Archers?"

"I understand not these words," she said. "The Otherplace is the Otherplace. The Blue. The place of trance. Of thought."

His pulse jumped. "You can't mean Kyle space."

"I can't, that is true," she said dryly. "I have never heard of it."

This time Shannon did smile. She reminded him of Soz. "My kin go there. You reach this Otherplace during trance?"

"By myself, no. With my tribe, possibly."

Could their tribal trance connect to Kyle space? It seemed unlikely, nothing more than a forlorn hope born from his longing to help his family. Yet it made an eerie sort of sense. The Ruby Empire builders who engineered Lyshriol and its colonists must have had a purpose; why create a people with such unusual minds? Perhaps many reasons. He could be indulging in wishful thinking. But he couldn't ignore this.

"I will go with you," Shannon decided.

Varielle stopped twisting the reins of her vexed lyrine. She touched Shannon's cheek, and her slim fingers lingered. "I am glad."

That night, under the Blue and Lavender Moons, they rode across the Dalvador Plains, headed for the Blue Dale Mountains.

The Skolian Assembly met in the Amphitheater of Memories in Selei City on the world Parthonia. Councilors, delegates, and aides from a thousand worlds and habitats attended, filling the cavernous theater. Tier after tier of seats ringed the central area, and balconies stacked up above them. Robot arms with console cups gave speakers motion throughout the amphitheater. People filled every seat. In VR benches, delegates flickered into view, attending via the Kyle web that made virtual transmission possible across light-years. It all ringed a dais that could rise or descend according to where a speaker wished to address the audience. Controlled pandemonium reigned; consoles glittered as people conferred, bargained, debated, and otherwise conducted business before the session opened.

The dais was currently halfway up the amphitheater. At a large console there, the Councilor of Protocol was queuing up questions and comments from the delegates so discussions could proceed in an orderly fashion once the session began. Dehya stood nearby, with one hand resting on a translucent podium while she gazed around the amphitheater.

Lyra Meson, First Councilor of the Assembly, stood at Dehya's side. As the civilian leader of the Imperialate, Meson had been in office less then two years. She wore white trousers and a pale blue tunic with an elegant cut. Short, dark hair framed her head. The tattoos adopted by her mercantile family curved along her jaw in a line of blue circles. She had served for twelve years in the Pharaoh's Army and retired as a lieutenant colonel. Then she turned to politics and won election as an Assembly delegate from Metropoli, the most heavily populated world in the Imperialate. She had risen within the ranks until she became the Councilor of Industry within the Inner Circle, which consisted of the eleven most powerful Assembly Councilors. From there, she won election as First Councilor.

Meson was more than a head taller than the pharaoh. Standing next to her, Dehya was acutely aware of how slight she felt in comparison. No matter. It didn't change their unwritten status. Their civilization was called an "Imperialate" for a reason; its people had yet to fully accept their elected government. They remained tied in many ways to the dynastic roots of their heritage.

Eight Abaj bodyguards stood on the dais. They weren't the only defense for Dehya and Meson, not by far; systems throughout the amphitheater, city, and planet also kept surveillance. But the Abaj were the most visible. Dehya looked up at the giant at her side. He regarded her from a height of two meters and inclined his head, a gesture of honor given by the Abaj to their pharaoh since before the Ruby Empire, six thousand years ago. His black hair was caught in a warrior's knot at his neck and hung down his back in a queue. His hooked nose, strong features, and deep-set eyes evoked the ancient statues in the ruins above the City of Cries on Raylicon. The warriors who had inspired those statues came from a barbaric era; these Abaj were cybernetic marvels.

Meson glanced at Dehya and smiled slightly, indicating the amphitheater. "They are noisy today."

"That they are," Dehya said. In a moment she and Meson would open the session. She looked for Eldrin, but his seat was empty. It worried her. He had always taken pride in his Assembly attendance, but this past year it had fallen off.

Protocol rose from her console, her dark gaze intent on Dehya and Meson. "We have a delay. I'm receiving a message from the War Room on the Orbiter. They want us to cancel the session."

"Why?" Dehya asked. "Who is it from?" As they joined Protocol at her console, Dehya was aware of people watching them, the thousands in the amphitheater turning from their deliberations, expecting the session to open.

Protocol indicated her comm. A light glowed to indicate someone was on the line, but its holoscreen remained dark. Whoever had contacted them declined to use visual. Dehya's unease increased. ISC streamlined procedures when they wished to conserve resources or increase confidentiality. It didn't take much to transmit a holo of one's face; the military only went to that level of caution in extreme emergencies.

Protocol spoke into the comm. "General Majda, I have the First Councilor and Ruby Pharaoh here."

A dusky voice answered. "Have they started the session?"

The hair on Dehya's neck prickled. That was Jazida Majda, General of the Pharaoh's Army, the acting Imperator.

Meson leaned over the console. "General, this is the First Councilor. We haven't yet opened. Is there a problem?"

Jazida wasted no time. "Councilor, I am invoking the Imperator's right of wartime command."

Dehya went rigid. In wartime, the Imperator had authority to act without approval from the First Councilor. It had to be that way; in conflicts that could span many star systems, the Imperator might not have time to wait for a response from the First Councilor. But asking for that transfer of authority was no simple matter.

"We aren't at war," the First Councilor said.

"Respectfully suggest you change that," Majda said. "Then evacuate the amphitheater. We have reason to believe the Traders are about to attack Parthonia."

Dehya spoke sharply into the comm. "On what evidence?"

"We have detected five spikes in the energy grid," Majda said. "Perhaps six."

"That's it?" Meson demanded. "On that basis, you want me to declare war?"

"That is correct," Majda said. "We have linked the spikes to the assassination attempt against Kurj Skolia and the abduction of Lord Valdoria on Skyfall."

Meson glanced at Dehya. "What say you?"

Dehya straightened up, regarding Meson and Protocol. The delegates in the amphitheatre had gone quiet, and she felt their unusual quality of *waiting*. This session offered the perfect time for ESComm to hit Parthonia. To do so, they would have to break through the best defenses ISC had to offer, which was impossible—but it had been impossible on Lyshriol, too.

Dehya spoke quietly. "Declare war."

Meson turned to Protocol. "What say you, Councilor?"

Sweat sheened Protocol's forehead. She was a member of the Inner Circle that advised Meson: Judiciary, Finance, Stars, Industry, Nature, Domestic Affairs, Foreign Affairs, Life, Planetary Development, Protocol—but she held the least influence of them all. However, she was the only one here on the dais.

Protocol took a deep breath. "If the Imperator says we must declare war, I say do it."

Meson nodded, her gaze hooded. Then she strode to the podium. Her voice rang out, carried through the amphitheater via comm, console, wireless, and the phenomenal acoustics of the great hall. "I have an announcement." She paused as the hum of discussion stopped. Then she said, "The Skolian Imperialate is in a state of war with the Eubian Concord. We must evacuate immediately."

Silence followed her words. Then consoles lit up all over the amphitheater and Protocol's comm buzzed madly. Protocol started to turn back to her console, but Meson held up her hand, stopping her. Then she spoke in a voice only those on the dais could hear. "Activate emergency procedure alpha-two-niner-omega."

Protocol nodded, her face pale. She sat at her console and went to work, her hands flying over panels.

Meson spoke to the Assembly again. "Evacuation procedures are being sent to your consoles. Stations set up here and in the city will facilitate the process." She lifted her chin. "Gods' speed, my friends."

People were rising from their seats, their voices a low roar of agitation. Robot arms growled as they ferried people to exits, as specified in the evacuation protocol. Many of the procedures were automated, with tall mechbots and movable tracks in the floor guiding the disorganized Assembly delegates.

Three robot arms came to the dais. The army major in the open cup at the terminus of the first opened a gate and motioned to Protocol. The first Councilor bowed to Dehya, nodded to Meson, and then went forward. They would all be taken to different places, to decrease the probability of a strike taking out those who formed the core of the government.

Dehya and Meson moved forward as the other two robot arms docked. Their Abaj bodyguards had taken up formation around them, their cybernetic arms glittering as they monitored the evacuation. The captain at Dehya's side spoke in a low voice. "Please board, Your Majesty."

Four Abaj came with Dehya as she stepped into one of the console cups; the other four accompanied the First Councilor into the other console cup. The Jagernauts towered even over Meson, their black uniforms a contrast to her pale clothes. The gate closed, encircling Meson's group in a white Luminex cup with just enough room for the five of them to stand.

The First Councilor nodded to Dehya, her chiseled features composed but her face drawn. "Good luck, Your Majesty."

"And to you, Councilor," Dehya said.

Their robot arms moved toward different exits, separating the Ruby Pharaoh and First Councilor. Dehya raised her hand in a universal gesture to wish a traveler well, and Meson responded with the same.

Dehya hoped it wouldn't be for the last time.

Secondary Tapperhaven, Soz's instructor from DMA, stood next to Soz in the medical bay on *Roca's Pride,* studying a report on her holopad. "Cadet Valdoria, you're the only person who reported anything unusual. But we checked everyone onboard who has a biomech web." She looked up. "They all had damaged bioelectrodes."

Gods. *All* of them? "Didn't they have trouble linking into Sigma's comm system?"

"You were the only one," Tapperhaven said.

Rajindia, the adept who had trained Soz to use her biomech web, was leaning against a console. ISC had sent her to monitor how the Imperial Heir integrated her biomech systems while serving on the battle cruiser. Her dark hair gleamed and the light caught glints in her upward-tilted eyes. She had focused on Soz with that sense of *presence* created by a strong empath. Kyle genes appeared more frequently in the noble houses than in the rest of the population, and a biomech-adept had to be an empath to monitor her patients. Soz felt Rajindia's mind questing as the older woman studied her.

"Your biomech has unique properties," Rajindia said. "Most psions don't have such a dense pattern of neural structures. Imperator Skolia has more, but with less intricacy. The same was true for your brother, Althor. Your aunt, the Ruby Pharaoh, has structures even more intricate than yours, but less robust."

"So my biomech did something no one else's can?" Soz asked.

"Apparently so." The adept rubbed her chin. "Do you recall how your node jumped into an accelerated mode the first time you used it?" When Soz nodded, Rajindia said, "It utilized the bioelectrodes in your neurons in an attempt to affect the speed of ion transfer across the cell membrane."

"I remember." They had taken out the extra memory until she learned to control the effect. "But we dealt with it. I haven't had trouble since you put back my extended capability." Although it sometimes strained her, she no longer had problems with control.

"That matches the records we've downloaded from your system," Rajindia said. "Your node interacts with your bio-electrodes more than in other Jagernauts. When the energy spike disrupted them, your node detected the problem and tried to fix it. In the process, it interfered with your ability to access Sigma."

"Why didn't my node inform me?" Soz asked.

"It couldn't," Rajindia said grimly. "The tampering wipes out the section of code that gives the warning. You have extra memory, so the deletion partially failed."

It suddenly made sense. "My node warned me by damaging my biomech even more than the spike. Then I *had* to notice."

"It appears so," Rajindia said.

Soz jumped down from the table. "We have to tell HQ the Jagernauts on this ship have been compromised!"

Tapperhaven put up her hand, stopping her. "We've sent the report. ISC knows." She spoke firmly. "You need to stay here so we can run more tests."

Soz loathed sick bay. She wanted to take action. She didn't know what expression she had, but it made Tapperhaven smile. "Be assured, Cadet, your tests provide an invaluable service to ISC."

"Yes, ma'am." Soz knew arguing would do no good. She resisted the urge to grumble and sat back down. "Ma'am, I was wondering if you had heard anything about my mother." She glanced at Rajindia. "Either of you?"

"Councilor Skolia?" Tapperhaven said. "No, I don't think so."

"Nor I," Rajindia said. "Should we?"

Soz shifted her weight uneasily. "I keep dreaming she's been captured by the Traders."

"Where is your mother now?" Tapperhaven asked.

"On the Orbiter, I think."

"It should be impossible for you to detect her brain waves from so far away," Rajindia said. "But it's hard to tell with psions as strong as your family. When your father was hurt, you knew." She spoke thoughtfully. "DMA has many gateways into Kyle space. So does this ship. Could a strong enough psion interact with them and not realize it? If even a small portion of the wavefunction for your brain overlaps with the gateway when you aren't linked into it, you might sample part of Kyle space. Distance has no meaning there. Your mother could be light-years away in spacetime but close to you in the web."

"I tried contacting her through long-distance comm," Soz said. "But I've only limited privileges. I couldn't get through to the Orbiter."

"I've more seniority," Tapperhaven said. "I'll check for you."

"I can as well," Rajindia offered.

Relief flooded Soz. She had slept very little last night, plagued by nightmares about her mother. "Thank you. Both of you."

Rajindia inclined her head. "It is my pleasure to aid the House of Skolia."

Her choice of words startled Soz. She thought of herself as Ruby Dynasty rather than the House of Skolia, but both references to her family were equally valid. The Skolian Imperialate took its name from her family—the Skolias.

ESComm could destroy both.

Roca was drowning in a sea of blurred sensations. She hurt. Gradually she comprehended that she was kneeling on a cold surface. Diffuse light surrounded her, but she couldn't focus. Her arms were twisted behind her back and her forearms bound together, one on top the other. Her ankles were tied. Someone had stuffed a cloth into her mouth and taped her lips shut. She had on the remains of her nightgown, with one shoulder pushed down, and her hair had fallen forward around her face.

Slowly her vision focused. She was kneeling on a Luminex floor. It provided the only light; shadows collected on the walls and ceiling. The cylindrical room had no adornment, no furniture, nothing. Her hair was having a hard time settling around her body, which suggested she was in low gravity, either on an asteroid or a ship. Her knees, arms, and shoulders burned. How long had she been here, her muscles stiffening and her strained joints aching, she had no idea.

"Awake, I see," a woman said behind her.

Roca froze. The speaker used Highton, the language of the Aristos. Roca looked around. A woman stood a few paces away, lit from below by the floor, dressed in a black jumpsuit. Her black hair glittered, shifting over her shoulders. Her red eyes were as hard and cold as rubies. She had alabaster skin and flawless features, from her smooth forehead to her straight nose and high cheekbones, all icy perfection.

"It is exquisite, the suffering of a Ruby psion," the Aristo murmured. "In providing me transcendence, you exalt yourself."

Go exalt yourself. Roca sent the thought with Rhon focus. The Aristo couldn't receive it, but she might sense the defiance. Roca maneuvered around so she didn't have to twist her head to see her captor. Pain blazed in her knees every time she moved.

The Trader sat down, cross-legged in front of Roca. "My brother wishes to question you." Her blissed-out look of "transcendence" hardened into something much colder. "Your son killed our father. It is only fitting my brother have a go at you, hmm?"

Hell and damnation. They had sent Vitarex's heirs after her.

A line appeared in the wall behind the woman. A section slid to the side, leaving an entrance in the shape of a tall octagon. Another Aristo stood in the archway, a tall and powerfully built man in a black uniform, his glittering hair cut short. He had the same arrogant features as the woman.

"My brother." The woman didn't turn around. "Kryx."

Kryx walked forward, his eyes glazed. "My greetings, Councilor Roca."

His sister stood up. "She is yours for now. Just remember that ESComm wants her alive and coherent."

"So do I." Hatred edged his unnaturally deep voice.

His sister glanced at Roca, pity in her gaze. Then she left the chamber. The door slid into place behind her, closing Roca in with Kryx Raziquon.

"So." Kryx knelt on one knee. "Welcome to our ship."

Go to hell, Roca thought.

"They say you are the most beautiful woman alive." He spent several moments looking her over. "Such hyperbole. You aren't. Any of my providers is better. But you will do."

Roca tried to scoot back from him, but he grabbed her arm and yanked her forward. She groaned as pain stabbed her limbs. For a moment she thought she would pass out, mercifully, but then she recovered. She was too damn healthy.

Kryx touched her cheek, and she jerked her head away.

"You don't like me," he said.

Well, that was brilliant.

"Why aren't you afraid?" he asked, curious.

She was terrified. She had no intention of letting him know.

"You know your mother was created to serve us," he murmured. "The ultimate provider. It is what you were made for."

Roca gritted her teeth on the gag. She had always balked at accepting that the Aristos had created her mother. They had wanted a Rhon psion, not because they knew anything then about the Kyle web, but because the Rhon were powerful providers, stronger than any other psions. Her mother had escaped and built the Skolian Imperialate to defy them.

Roca met his gaze steadily. He frowned and pushed her shoulder until she fell backward. It was excruciating for her already over-taxed knees, so painful that this time she did start to black out. Spots filled her vision . . .

A syringe hissed against her neck. Roca floated on the edge of consciousness. Gradually she revived. She was lying curled on her side with the Luminex floor cold under her cheek. She would have groaned except she didn't want to give him the satisfaction of hearing her dismay.

"That's better." Kryx fumbled with her ankles, untying them. He moved over her, pulling apart her legs—and she jammed her knees into his stomach.

Kryx doubled up, his face contorting. She felt his outrage: providers never fought back.

When Kryx raised his fist, Roca rolled away from him. He yanked her back, so she clenched her teeth and used her momentum to keep rolling until she crashed into him. With a grunt, he fell onto his back. Roca rolled up to her knees, and her hair flew forward, wrapping around her body in metallic tangles.

Kryx sat up, his face contorted. "You will pay for that."

Roca sent a message to Arabesque, the node in her spine. *Turn me off.*

Turn you off how? Arabesque asked.

Anything! Cease my brain activity. Scorch my brain cells if you have to. Do something! This bastard is going to torture me until I scream for mercy.

Are you certain you want me to put you out? Arabesque asked. It will probably kill you.

Yes. He can't transcend unless I experience pain. Make me end.

Understood. It paused. I am sorry, Councilor. Ending.

Her world went black.

"... no response." Kryx's voice cut through the darkness.

"You had better hope she hasn't died," his sister said.

Roca inwardly swore.. She was lying on her side with her arms still bound behind her. She felt numb and her thoughts were oddly muffled, but she hadn't expected to survive Arabesque tampering with her neural processes.

I didn't affect them enough to kill you, Arabesque thought.

Why not? Roca feared death as much as the next person, but she feared becoming a Trader provider more.

Making you unconscious achieved the same result.

Yes, well, it isn't permanent. She hesitated. *Something is wrong. I feel strange.*

There was brain damage.

Brain damage. Two simple words with so much destructive power. *If you do it again, will the damage get worse?*

Yes. I am also damping your pain receptors, which is why the Aristos haven't sensed you are conscious, but this injures your brain, too. They will soon realize you are awake, but if I increase your protection, it will injure you more.

Roca thought of her husband, his body crippled by the

Traders. If by some miracle she escaped this nightmare alive, he would get his wife back with her mind crippled.

I have a suggestion, Arabesque said. *If I put you in a coma, the Aristos can't transcend. It will then serve no purpose to hurt you. If the danger passes, I can remove you from the coma.*

That sounded too easy. *What condition will I be in when you wake me up?*

A long pause followed. *You might relearn how to live.*

In other words, I'll be a mental vegetable.

I am sorry. It is the best I have to offer.

Roca knew she couldn't keep this up much longer. The node couldn't damp all her pain; sooner or later she would groan or otherwise slip up. *Can you map the neural structures in my brain and their firing patterns?*

Yes, it is within my abilities.

What if you make a map and store it in your memory? Then put me in a coma. She almost started her next sentence with "if," then decided to be more positive. *When you bring me out of the coma, could you reestablish my mental patterns?*

It might be possible. I would need you to do exercises now to help me make the map. We must hurry, before they realize you are conscious. Do the multiplication tables from one to twelve, in base ten and base eight.

Roca multiplied as fast as she could. Arabesque put her through memory, logic, analysis, recall, and reasoning drills. She was in the middle of balancing a chemical reaction when Kryx said, "I think she's awake."

"Her neural activity has increased," his sister said.

"Are you awake, Councilor?" Kryx asked.

Roca kept her eyes closed.

His sister spoke. "My scanner says she is."

Kryx laughed softly. "Good."

Roca opened her eyes to see Kryx leaning over her. "We have many drugs for you," he murmured. "Designer chemicals." A smile spread across his face. "We can make you feel anything we want."

Roca felt sick. *Arabesque, are you ready?*

Yes.

You're sure they won't hurt me while I'm out?

I cannot make that guarantee. However, it appears unlikely.

Then turn off my brain.

Done—

12

Code One

Shannon rode with Varielle through the mist. They had gone ever higher since leaving the Dalvador Plains, first crossing the Backbone Mountains that separated Dalvador from the lush western province of the Rillian Vales, then heading north into the huge range known as Ryder's Lost Memory. From Ryder's they traveled higher and farther north into the Blue Dale Mountains.

They were traveling in a forest, where the trunks were hollow tubes of jewel-like glasswood, all translucent, glistening in the fog. Smaller tubes branched out from the trunks and filmy disks hung from them, some a handspan in diameter, others smaller. Each tree was one color, but the forest had many hues: ruby, sapphire, emerald, gold, and a violet as pure as the eyes of a Rillian. They ducked their heads under dusty clusters of bubbles. Shannon's arm brushed a blue disk and it inflated into a sphere. It floated into the air, detaching from the tree, then hit another branch and popped. Sparkling blue glitter dusted across Shannon and Moonglaze, his lyrine now, gifted to him by his father. Multicolored glitter already covered both him and Varielle, and also their lyrine.

The forest went on in every direction, endless it seemed. The air had turned chill, and they wore heavy tunics and sweaters with double leggings. They kept their bows and quivers lashed to their travel bags so neither would stab bubbles on the trees and inundate them with more glitter.

They finally reached a high valley submerged in blue fog. This was the land of the legendary Blue Dale Archers that the people of Rillia and Dalvador no longer believed existed. Mist veiled the tents on either side. Sentries came out to meet them, eerily beautiful Archers with silvery hair flowing like moonlight and silver eyes that slanted upward.

That night, Shannon sat with Varielle's tribe around a fire that flickered in blue and gold flames. The scent of burning glasswood permeated the air, fragrant and pungent. The mist felt damp against his cheeks, mixed with ashes and glitter. The senior members of the tribe had all come, and Varielle sat at his side.

They drank wine together, a rare vintage distilled from bubbles that grew only here in the Blue Dales. When the wine had saturated their senses, Shannon joined the Archers in a trance. One by one they revealed their names. He knew most of them from the many octets of days he had spent with this tribe last year. But speaking their name was a ritual as old as the millennia they had roamed these mountains. To unveil one's name was to offer acceptance, something the elusive Archers hadn't done with an outsider for centuries.

In the late hours of the night, with the moons hidden by blue fog, they gave him a final gift: the name of their tribe.

Eloria.

The word came from an ancient form of Trillian no one had spoken in the Plains for thousands of years. Eloria. It meant The Misted Ones. Shannon recognized the word because, as a son of the Valdoria Bard, he had learned the ancient tongues. If ever he became Bard, he would need to sing and interpret songs handed down over the millennia.

In giving him the name of their tribe, the Eloria offered him a place as one of them. All his life Shannon had known he differed from the people of Dalvador. His Blue Dale heritage had come down from one of his father's ancestors and manifested in Shannon after many generations of dormancy. He looked like the Archers, went into trance like them, blended his emotions like them. He, too, needed to wander the mountains. He had craved the Blue Dales even before he visited them.

Tonight the Eloria offered their name.

So it was that Shannon Eirlie Valdoria Skolia, formerly of the Dalvador Plains, became a Blue Dale Archer.

The Bard held Taquinil's hand as they crossed a slope carpeted with grass. They had climbed a hill above the house where the boy lived with his parents in Valley on the Orbiter. Their Abaj bodyguards ranged across the countryside around them, though at enough distance that Eldrinson didn't feel suffocated. But he couldn't escape the agitation that had plagued him all day.

"Me, too," Taquinil said softly.

Startled, he glanced down at the boy. "What do you mean?"

Taquinil regarded him with a haunted gaze, his gold eyes large in his face. "I'm afraid for them. For Hoshpa and Hoshma, for Grandmother and Uncle Kurj and Uncle Althor." His young voice cracked. "I want to help, Grandfather. But I don't know how."

Eldrinson pulled the boy into his arms and hugged him. "It will be all right." He had to believe that. "Come on. We will try again to reach them." He would settle for talking with anyone: Roca, Eldrin, Dehya, any person who had even seen a member of his family.

They returned to the house and went to the console room where they could connect to the offworld meshes. They had the same result as every other time they had tried: communications to the interstellar meshes was down and nothing could go out or in. Telops continued to assure users there was no need to worry, just maintenance work, life was proceeding as normal.

Eldrinson didn't believe them.

Callie Irzon was the top biomech surgeon in HQ City on Diesha. She had implanted the biomech webs carried by

Althor and Soz Valdoria, the two Imperial Heirs. Tine Loriez had assisted her. Now she and Tine entered a viewing chamber in the ISC hospital, both of them in white jumpsuits with silver medical insignia on their shoulders. At the window across from the entrance, they paused. A man lay motionless in the room beyond, his wasted body quiescent in the hospital bed. The only light came from monitors and screens around him, their lights glowing amber or red. A second man sat sprawled in a chair by the bed, asleep, his head back, his legs stretched out.

"The order said *every* Jagernaut," Tine said.

Irzon set her palm against the window, a sheet of programmable matter that was transparent on this side and a mirror on the other. Their orders from HQ had no ambiguity; all living Jagernauts must have their bioelectrodes analyzed. Technically, Althor lived. His node no longer communicated with his brain, but it wasn't inoperative, only dormant. It couldn't do anything given that he was brain dead, but even that minuscule risk had to be addressed.

They entered the room quietly, but the man in the chair by the bed woke up anyway. Lifting his head, he rubbed his eyes, his blond hair falling back from his face.

"I'm sorry to disturb you," Irzon said. She didn't recognize him, and she doubted she would have forgotten such a distinctive person. He reminded her of the artists in a colony on the outskirts of HQ City, a group of theater types. The graceful quality of his movements made her wonder if he were an actor, a successful one given his expensive clothes. Judged by his tousled hair, he must have been here for hours, even days.

He stood up and pulled down his sweater, a blue pullover that set off his well-toned physique. He lifted his hand and turned it palm upward in a civilian salutation. "My greetings. I'm Chad." He sounded older than he looked. And tired.

"My greetings," Irzon said. She gave him an apologetic look. "We need to run some tests. It won't take long."

"Do you want me to leave?" The way he had one palm resting on Althor's arm made her reconsider her assumption that he and Althor were only friends.

Loriez said, "It would be better if you waited out—" He stopped when Irzon raised her hand.

To Chad, Irzon indicated a chair with soft cushions across the room. "You can wait there if you like. We won't be long."

"Thank you." Chad nodded, his motions slowed with fatigue. He went across the room and settled into the chair.

Loriez raised his eyebrows at her. Normally they only let a spouse or family member stay. She was uncertain about the young man's relationship with Althor, though. She shrugged at Loriez and tilted her head toward Althor, hoping the doctor would understand. He nodded slightly and made no protest.

The equipment they needed for their tests was already in place, including the medical EIs that monitored Althor's body and biomech. Soon the two doctors were deep in their tests of Althor's biomech systems.

"That's odd," Loriez muttered.

Irzon looked up from the screen she was studying. "Problem?"

"Not exactly." He was frowning at a cluster of graphs floating above his console. Data glowed beneath them, symbols flowing across the screen in a river of golden, three-dimensional holos.

"Did you find tampering?" Irzon asked.

"No, it's fine. It's just—" He indicated a graph. "His node is quiet, but I don't think it is dormant. It's . . . well, it seems to be *waiting*." He looked up at her. "I don't know what for. Maybe it thinks he'll call on it again."

"Can't it tell he's—" She stopped before she said *dead*, aware of the man across the room.

Loriez motioned at the lines, machines, and aids that surrounded the bed. "His body lives. His brain has no activity, but the tissue is healthy."

"We can keep his brain cells alive for years." She didn't add that it did little good if the cells no longer functioned.

"I think his node is waiting for his brain to start again."

"Start how?" Irzon asked.

Loriez shook his head. They both knew it waited in vain. He glanced at the youth across the room, then looked away. Irzon could see the man in her peripheral vision. He was like the node, waiting futilely for Althor to resume a life that was over.

Loriez tapped a panel, and the graphs vanished. "I've sent our test results to HQ. They'll continue monitoring his node to see if anything comes up."

"That should do it, then," Irzon said. Sorrow weighed on her. As they were leaving, she spoke gently to Chad. "You can go on back."

He nodded as he stood up. His expression seemed hollow, as if he had exhausted his emotional resources. He returned to his chair by the bed and resumed his vigil.

Soz and several midshipmen ran along the corridor, their long strides devouring distance. They jogged into their destination, a cavernous area that resembled a docking bay. It was overflowing with crew members, officers and noncoms alike, most in Fleet uniforms. Devon Majda stood on a platform at one end of the bay, ramrod straight in her uniform, surrounded by her top officers, her hands resting on a Luminex rail.

A nearby woman spoke in a low voice. "Why do we have to come here? They could have transmitted any announcement over ship's comm."

Soz looked around at the people in the bay. "Maybe for moral support."

A man next to them spoke tightly. "For what?"

"Gods only know," another man said.

Just a fraction of the crew fit in here; a Firestorm carried tens of thousands of people. They would be meeting in similar bays throughout the ship, gathering before a holo stage that projected an image of Devon Majda live from here.

Devon raised her hand and the rumble of talk stopped. Comm spheres floating throughout the bay amplified her voice. "I have a message from Imperator Majda."

The silence was so complete, Soz could hear people breathing.

"Forty-three minutes ago," Devon said, "First Councilor Meson declared war against the Eubian Concord."

"No," someone said.

Soz suddenly felt as if she couldn't breathe. War? Now?

"As you know," Devon continued, "we have been on a training run. That has changed. As of this moment, we are on active duty." She looked out over them. "I have every confidence in the ability of our fine crew and vessel to meet this challenge."

Soz's thoughts whirled. She had spent only a few weeks on this ship. A flotilla accompanied it, including a contingent of Jags, but she couldn't fly someone else's fighter. Although she had begun working with the EIs of several Jags, she was nowhere near ready. She hadn't even been commissioned yet. She would have to serve aboard this cruiser, the antithesis of the one-pilot fighters she was training to fly.

War. The prospect had never seemed real. It had been remote all those years she imagined attending DMA.

It was remote no longer.

Dehya and her bodyguards sprinted to a sleek gold and black shuttle that crouched on a tarmac of the Admiral Starport. It would whisk her to an armored racer in orbit, which would take her away from Parthonia. *Fast.*

They scrambled into the shuttle and the airlock snapped closed behind them. Dehya dropped into the copilot's seat while her bodyguards strapped into passenger seats. The pilot was doing preflight checks. Dressed in the dark green of an army colonel, he was ensconced in his chair and surrounded by panels. Dehya's exoskeleton folded around her and clicked psiphons into her sockets. They linked her to the EI brain of the shuttle, through the shuttle to the racer in orbit, and from the racer into Kyle space.

She didn't need access to Kyle space, however, to reach the person she had been trying, desperately, to contact. Again she tapped the code into her wrist comm that should have linked her to Eldrin—and again it came back with the message: *no response.*

"Communication from Imperator Majda, Your Majesty," the pilot said. "On Kyle."

"Got it," Dehya said. *Relay message,* she thought to the shuttle EI.

Incoming, the EI answered. *The Orbiter Kyle systems are also linking with your Abaj Jagernauts.*

Jazida Majda's thought came into her mind. *Your Majesty, the energy spikes can sabotage Jagernauts. We're checking your Abaj now.*

Dehya looked back at her bodyguards. They regarded her with black eyes, secure in their seats, installed in their exoskeletons. *Are they affected?*

They're clean, Majda thought. *It's the webs! That's how the Traders are infiltrating our defenses. It has some connection to your family's use of Kyle space, but we don't know how. We're cutting ALL Kyle space links with you. Until this is over, you will be in a communications blackout.*

Understood. If the Traders had found a way to reach her family through Kyle space, Skolia was in even worse trouble than she had feared. She tried to get Eldrin again on her comm and received another *no response.* Sweat ran down her neck. If she didn't get him now, he would have no way to know she had gone offworld.

Dehya spoke to the pilot. "Can you raise Prince Eldrin at the palace?"

"Checking." He took on the inward expression of someone accessing his biomech web. It would link to the shuttle EI, which would contact her home on Parthonia.

A voice came out of the comm. "This is the EI Secretary at the palace. Prince Eldrin went to the Amphitheater to meet his wife."

Dehya leaned forward. "Who is with him?"

"His bodyguards, Your Majesty," the EI said.

General Majda's thought crackled in her mind. *His bodyguards have received the evacuation order. They will see that he gets offworld—*

"What the holy blazes?" the pilot shouted.

Majda's thought thundered. *GET THE PHARAOH OUT OF THERE.* Then her presence in Dehya's mind vanished like a doused flame.

With no warning, no clearance, nothing at all, the pilot cold-started his engines. The craft leapt off the tarmac with a roar, blasting the ground with exhaust, its acceleration slamming Dehya into her seat. The pilot's hands blurred as they flashed over his controls. His node had to be controlling his motion; no one could move that fast on his own.

"Prepare to invert," the pilot said.

Dehya stared at him. "What the hell is happening?" Within moments they would be high in the atmosphere and going at a good clip, but inverting this close to a planet could damage them and possibly Selei City below. She focused her mind on the pilot, but his interactions with the ship were too fast to distinguish. Although her own EI could operate faster, during emergency she couldn't risk interfering with the link between the pilot and the shuttle.

When the ship tried to invert, nausea surged over Dehya. They twisted out of real space, hurtling into a complex universe where their mass, energy, and momentum had imaginary as well as real parts. She groaned and her body felt as if it turned inside out. They weren't going fast enough—

And the cabin melted around them.

Eldrin threw clothes and personal items out of his travel bag, frantic. He had put it in here, he knew he had, he couldn't have lost it—

There! He grabbed the syringe and stabbed his finger against its miniaturized panel, entering his prescription. An unfamiliar red light glowed at its tip, and glyphs appeared on the tiny screen wrapped around the tube. He ignored them, too agitated to read. With jerking hands, he pressed the syringe against his jugular vein and injected the phorine.

Alone in the royal suite of the Sunrise Palace, Eldrin sank to his knees and bowed his head. His entire body was shaking. He couldn't hide from the truth any longer. He had tried to quit, tried many times, determined to succeed. He had failed. His hunger for the phorine was killing him. He needed help, and if he didn't admit it now, the obsessive craving would wreck his life. The nightmares that had separated him from his family all this miserable, lonely year weren't due to illness or grief. It was the phorine. His compulsion for it was taking away the family he loved, ruining his music, turning his life into a single-minded nightmare, and he couldn't bear it any longer.

It also gave him a window into the gruesome toll Dehya's work exacted from her, that to survive with her mind intact she needed a dosage of this medicine ten times greater than what he had been taking. What knots did the Kyle web inflict, that such a gargantuan dose barely affected her? Lost in his confusion and loneliness, he hadn't seen the magnitude of what she faced, every godsforsaken day of their lives, year in and year out, with no reprieve.

Gradually his pulse calmed. He lifted his head and breathed in deeply, his hands on his thighs. Although his symptoms had decreased, he was edgy and distracted. Usually by now he felt traces of euphoria. Uneasy, he peered at the syringe, studying its glyphs with the painstaking care he needed to read. It was hard, for they were smaller and on a curved surface, different enough from how they would look in a holobook that his mind wanted to interpret them as different words. But he doggedly deciphered their message. The syringe had used up several ingredients it needed to synthesize phorine. It could make no more.

"No." Eldrin struggled to his feet and stumbled to a console against the wall. "Etude?"

"Here, Your Majesty." This Etude was a copy of his EI at the Ruby Palace on Diesha. "Prince Eldrin," it said urgently. "You must allow your bodyguards to obey the order they received from ISC."

"The what?" Eldrin's fist clenched on the syringe.

"The order for them to report to the hospital this morning to have their bioelectrodes tested."

He braced his hand on the console. "Didn't they go?"

"No, sir. You asked them to wait."

He shook his head, trying to clear it. Just before he had come upstairs, frantically searching for his syringe, the captain of his Abaj had said something about ISC and the hospital. Eldrin vaguely remembered telling them to wait until he finished here. His EI couldn't override his orders because it carried a copy of the Epsilon code that gave Eldrin privacy.

"Etude, I need you to do two things." With trembling hands, he clicked the syringe into a slot on the console.

"First, have the palace medical system replenish this syringe. Then tell the hospital that I'm coming in with my Abaj. I have to see an expert in treating psions. Tell them it's an emergency."

"Understood." After a pause, Etude said, "Medical can't restock two ingredients in the syringe. They're used to make phorine, which it doesn't have the authority to dispense."

Gods, no. Eldrin dropped into the seat and put his forehead in his hands. "Then get me a doctor," he whispered. "Tell them the Ruby Consort is going into phorine withdrawal."

"Message sent."

Eldrin didn't know how long this reprieve would last. The syringe had given him a lower dosage than usual. Nor was it likely that any but his personal physicians could help. Only those who treated psions would have expertise with phorine, and only a few of those had dealt with the Rhon. Empaths were rare, one in a thousand even for the lowest ratings, scarcer as the rating increased. The weakest telepaths were one in a million. He had heard it estimated that if the Rhon hadn't been deliberately bred by the Assembly, they would occur no more frequently than one in a trillion.

Etude suddenly spoke again. "Prince Eldrin, the Assembly is evacuating the Amphitheater."

"What?" Eldrin lifted his head. "Why?"

"I don't know. You're expected at the starport."

"No! Put me through to Dehya."

"I can't. Pharaoh Dyhianna is under a security blanket."

He rose unsteadily to his feet. "That shouldn't cut out me."

The door to the royal suite snapped open, revealing his four bodyguards. As they entered, their captain said, "I'm sorry to intrude, Your Majesty. We have orders to take you to the port."

"Can you reach my wife?" Eldrin asked. Even if she was under a shroud, these Abaj should have clearance through its security.

The captain's face took on the distant expression of a psibernaut linking to a mesh. Then he said, "I can't get a response."

What the hell? "Take me to the Assembly hall," Eldrin said. "I'll find her there."

"I'm sorry, Your Majesty, but we can't." As the captain spoke, all four of the Abaj were moving around Eldrin, taking up a protective formation, one in front, one in back, one to each side.

"We must go to the Admiral Starport," the captain said. "We will take the flyer from the roof."

Eldrin knew arguing would do no good. He had already pushed them too far, insisting they wait to report to the hospital while he found his syringe. If he didn't come now, they would force him. He spoke stiffly. "Very well." He turned to the console. "Etude, let the hospital know we're going to the port."

"Not the Assembly hall?" Etude asked.

Flustered, Eldrin said, "No, apparently not."

"Understood." Then Etude added, "Good luck, sir."

"Thank you." Eldrin didn't doubt they would need that luck.

Eldrin's bodyguards couldn't operate the flyer on the roof of the palace. For some reason they couldn't link to its EI. The flyer's responses were scrambled and nonfunctional, and it refused orders. They finally gave up and took Eldrin down through the palace to an underground level where a black hover limousine waited.

Inside the limo, Eldrin sat in the back, in a seat that faced forward. One of his bodyguards took the end of the seat, and the captain and another Abaj settled into a seat facing him across a wide space. The fourth Abaj "drove" up front, though the limo's AI actually did the work. The seats were a plush black material that felt like velvet but seemed far more durable. A blue carpet covered the floor, with the emblem of the House of Skolia in gold and white. It resembled the insignia for the Skolian Imperialate: a golden sunburst exploding past a white circle. The Imperialate symbol, however, also had a silver line slashed through it to represent the Dyad.

It didn't matter how posh the limo, Eldrin was as stiff

as casecrete. He could have watched the news on a screen that swung to wherever he wanted it, he could have rested by reclining his seat into a bed, or he could have had the cover retract on the small pool in the back so he could bathe. But he was too agitated to concentrate, let alone indulge in activities that even after eight years as the Pharaoh's consort felt decadent to him.

The limo hummed through the landscaped gardens of the palace. Droop-willows shaded blue stone sculptures that reminded him of Dalvador. But nothing on Lyshriol had such perfection. Everything here was elegant and restrained, from the immaculately tended gardens to the blue gravel paths with no stone out of place. It confined his mind. He was relieved when they left the grounds through the vine-draped archway of a wrought-iron gate. But nothing eased the tension, neither his nor that of his bodyguards.

The palace was high in the hills above Selei City. They drove down a winding road with no traffic or houses, just willows lush with silvery bells. At the bottom, they encountered a few other vehicles. By the time they reached the outskirts of Selei City, the scatter of hovercraft had turned into a steady flow. The evacuation seemed to be proceeding smoothly, but his Abaj couldn't get any information beyond their preliminary orders. It disquieted Eldrin that they were having so much trouble, first with the flyer and now with the meshes.

Municipal EIs monitored the traffic. The limo was taking him to the Admiral Starport, a facility used by military and government officials. Most vehicles were headed in other directions, probably to the huge Selei Interstellar Starport across the city, to underground bunkers, or out of the city. ISC couldn't evacuate the entire city into space; even Selei Interstellar couldn't handle an influx that large in such a short time.

Eldrin clenched a polished handle in the door. "I'd like to go to the Assembly hall first."

The captain answered quietly. "I'm sorry, Your Majesty. Our orders are to take you to the Admiral Port." Then he added, "I'm sure your wife is already there."

"Do you know yet why we're evacuating?" Eldrin asked.

"General Majda asked the First Councilor to give the order. We have no other details."

"Do you—"

"Sir!" The Abaj next to the captain went rigid. "I'm getting a priority red message."

"Got it!" The captain swung around and spoke to the limo driver. "Override evacuation protocol! Get Prince Eldrin to the closest port *now.*"

The limo braked so fast Eldrin was thrown out of his seat. He fell onto his knees on the carpeted floor, catching himself on his hands. Then he was knocked sideways as the car made a tight swerve, one the traffic grid would never have allowed. It was illegal and supposedly impossible to take a vehicle off the grids during an emergency, but the Abaj up front was driving on his own, without grid control. The limo jolted over a curb and accelerated down a street in the opposite direction from the Admiral's Port.

As Eldrin sat up on his knees, the Jagernaut who had been sitting next to him reached to help—and froze with his arm outstretched. His eyes glazed. The captain and other Abaj in the seat facing Eldrin went rigid—and the Abaj next to Eldrin toppled onto the floor.

The captain's face paled, and he made a strangled sound. He rasped into his gauntlet, "Put the car back on the grid!" Then he collapsed and fell into Eldrin, knocking him to the floor.

"No!" Eldrin struggled out from under the giant Abaj. He could no longer see the driver at all. The limo kept going.

Eldrin shook the captain. "What's wrong? What happened?"

No response.

Dismayed, Eldrin pulled himself to his feet and braced his hand against the top of the limo. The driver was sprawled across the front seat. Eldrin started to call out—

The words died in his throat.

Looking through the front windshield, he could see the city spread out below. The limo was careening down a hill with tall houses on either side. About a kilometer distant, a column of light stabbed out of the sky and hit the Admiral Starport. Even through the heavy shielding of the limo, he felt the violent explosions as the beam hit the ground. Flames and smoke mushroomed into the air. Nor did it stop there; the beam slashed across the city, leaving a path of billowing smoke and devastation in its wake.

13

The Snarled Mesh

E SComm didn't sneak into Parthonia—they slammed into the star system, blasting at its defenses. Two battle cruisers led the force, mammoths as versatile as any Firestorm. With them came a massive fleet, including Solo starfighters, the ESComm equivalent of Jags, but without the mind links formed by a Jag squadron.

Then ESComm activated the sabotaged Jagernauts.

The Traders flooded Parthonia with signals targeted against the faulty bioelectrodes. A substantial portion of the Jagernauts would have malfunctioned if ISC hadn't already repaired them, and that made the difference between defeat and hope. Some Jagernauts still had problems: an inability to engage EIs, difficulty in communicating, glitches in input. But every biomech-adept in Selei City was on alert and ready to give treatment. Even with so little warning before the attack, the evacuation went off with relatively few hitches.

It was still a nightmare.

For the first time in recorded history, an interstellar force attacked a major civilian center. Chaos didn't immediately erupt. EI-controlled vehicles, walkways, flyers, and buildings conducted the evacuation. Their purpose: clear Selei City without a panic. To some extent they succeeded. But nothing could lessen the brutal impact of laser fire cutting through the capital, leaving flames and ashes and death; and nothing could prepare the people for antimatter beams that annihilated all matter, including air molecules, and created fireballs so intense, it was as if tiny suns blazed above the city.

People flooded every shelter available, seeking protection, however ephemeral. The Annihilators ate away the surface of the planet, but only if they made it through the atmosphere, which attenuated their power in brilliant displays of energy and showered the land with killer radiation and particle cascades. Lasers burned into the earth, and the attacks cut great swaths through the city.

The first strike destroyed Admiral Starport. Thousands of people poured into every other transport facility: flyer pads on roofs; minor ports that served planetary traffic; military bases; but most of all, Selei Interstellar, the primary starport for the city, a major Imperialate hub for space traffic. It was so large, it formed its own city. Refugees flooded its terminals and gates. They crowded every available ship, of every size and class, and spacecraft took to the skies in unprecedented numbers.

Space law required a ship to be out of orbit and well into space, moving at relativistic speed, before it inverted, but now frantic pilots were trying to make the jump into superluminal space while they were still in orbit. Some succeeded, though it left their passengers retching or unconscious. Others failed and fell out of the sky with their passengers melted into bulkheads, decks, and one another. A number of ships inverted partway and then twisted into themselves and became plasma, part real and part imaginary, spewed across complex space. Some never made it at all, unable to invert at slow speeds. ESComm blasted them out of the skies like an exterminator fumigating insects.

Over two million people deluged the ports, shelters, and roads out of the city. In all that desperate mass, a black limo was swept along with the rest, caught in the panic. It arrived at Selei International with a million other people. Its sole conscious passenger was dragged out of the vehicle by frenetic officials even as he struggled and protested that his companions in the car needed help.

So it was that a Ruby Heir, third in line to the throne, was shoved into an aging, decrepit freighter with several hundred other people and launched off Parthonia.

Selei City had one of the densest mesh structures in Kyle space; more telops worked at that governmental seat than in any other. The attacks destroyed Kyle gate after Kyle gate. At the Assembly hall alone, several thousand nodes vanished when lasers destroyed the amphitheater. As the gates into the Kyle web collapsed, they ripped apart the meshes connected to them. The destruction propagated through Kyle space and brought down the nodes of delegates who had been attending the session through the mesh. The delegates were safe, light-years from Parthonia, but the failure of their nodes passed on the damage to other government and military webs.

Had either the Ruby Pharaoh or Imperator been available, the destruction could have been contained in a manner similar to the way backup generators alleviated power outages. But no one knew if the Ruby Pharaoh had survived, and the Imperator lay in a hospital on Diesha, deep in a coma. Just as the failure of backups in an overloaded energy grid could cause rolling blackouts, so the Kyle meshes suffered rolling failures. Most telops managed to protect their spacetime systems—the electro-optic, nanotech, picotech, and quantum meshes that net-worked Skolia—but they couldn't stop the Kyle space collapse.

Within minutes, ISC lost a substantial number of its Kyle links, and with those went a good portion of its ability to function as a cohesive military force on an interstellar scale.

The Traders had struck a crippling blow.

Eldrin squeezed into a mesh hammock designed to hold crates so they wouldn't bang around the cargo hold. He hinged his hand and clenched his four fingers in the mesh while refugees sandwiched in next to him and into other hammocks hanging from grips in the bulkheads. Others squeezed into the spaces between them on the deck and against the hull. No one would have protection against the g-forces of takeoff or landing; this hold had been meant to carry robotic components, not passengers. The crew had thrown their cargo onto the tarmac and packed in people, giving up their livelihoods to save lives.

Two children, a boy of about seven and a girl of about four, huddled together in a corner. They were obviously terrified, and it made Eldrin think of Taquinil. When the boy glanced his way, Eldrin motioned them over. The boy scrambled to his feet, drawing the little girl with him, and they squeezed through the crowd to Eldrin, their eyes wide, their faces scrunched up with fear. He wedged them in the hammock with him, one on each side, and put an arm around each. They shivered against him.

"Where are your parents?" he asked in Iotic. When they only stared at him, he tried Skolian Flag. "Are your parents here?"

The girl shook her head, her motions jerky.

"We were in school," the boy said.

"We'll find them," Eldrin assured them, using the same gentle tone that soothed Taquinil.

The engines muttered and then roared, bypassing the usual warm-up. With a great shudder and no preparation, the freighter launched. Eldrin grunted as acceleration shoved them against the bulkhead.

When they inverted, he almost threw up. He was dissolving, dissolving, dissolved . . .

Suddenly he was whole again. He gasped and sagged forward. Sweat covered his forehead. The distinctive growl of inversion engines vibrated through the hold. They had made it. Eldrin had no idea how long they would be on this freighter, but he doubted they would have medical help soon.

He needed phorine.

"Reestablish contact!" The Weapons officer of *Roca's Pride* hit the oval table in the conference room with her fist. She was facing off with Brigadier General Devon Majda, the ship's captain. A Fleet officer should have been in command of the cruiser during wartime, but it hadn't turned out that way. Soz had no doubt Devon could do this command, but the general had to convince her bridge crew, most of whom were present. They were all standing around the conference table with its gleaming holoscreens: the First Officer, who had experience herself commanding a Firestorm; Weapons, Intelligence, Communications, Navigation; and a few minor aides, including Soz.

"We're working to reform our Kyle nodes," Communications said. She had been crawling around inside the guts of consoles, jury-rigging gates from the cruiser into Kyle space. Every portal she had so far constructed had collapsed; right now, *Roca's Pride* and its attendant flotilla had no links with the rest of ISC.

"We might get several gates working within a few hours," she added. "If we put our best telops on the job."

Hours. Soz felt ill. They had just learned of the attack on Parthonia when they lost interstellar communications. That ESComm raid had to have been a suicide mission; an attacking force that small couldn't take out the entire Parthonia defenses. They were going after the Kyle web, determined to destroy it at any cost. Given the complex, multipronged nature of the attack and the extent of the intelligence ESComm had apparently amassed on ISC, they must have been planning this for years, even decades.

"Who are our best telops?" Devon asked.

"Raylor over in Control," Communications said. "Mak in Navigation."

Soz spoke quietly. "Permission to speak, Captain."

Devon nodded. "Go ahead, Cadet."

"I'm one of your best telops, ma'am." Soz tried to project a confidence she didn't feel. "I can bring Rhon power to the job."

That left the room silent. They all stared at her. Soz could almost feel them remembering the "other" identity of the lowly cadet among them.

"Can you reactivate our Kyle gateways?" Devon asked.

"At least one, maybe two or three." As a Ruby Heir, she had the training. But if this problem was more widespread, fixing a few gates here wasn't likely to help. ISC needed Dehya or Kurj for repairs that extensive. If Dehya reached Safelanding, she could use the Dyad Chair there, but the last Soz had heard, before they lost communications, no one knew what had happened to the pharaoh. Kurj was in no condition to save anything, including himself.

"We must regain communications," Intelligence said. "ES-Comm could be invading and we wouldn't know. We could arrive at Parthonia to find the battle over hours ago, even days, and all the time we were needed elsewhere."

"We aren't without communications," Weapons said. "We've sent ships to Parthonia, Diesha, Metropoli, and four other centers."

"But none have returned yet." Communications raked her hand through her close-cropped hair. "What if Kyle nodes everywhere are affected? If we get ours up, we can't talk to anyone unless theirs are also operational."

Navigations spoke. "Even if we get the interstellar comm working, who will coordinate our forces across space? We have no Rhon psion in the War Room on the Orbiter. Imperator Skolia is in a coma on Diesha."

"Councilor Roca is on the Orbiter," Intelligence said. "She can use the Dyad Chair there."

Soz glanced at Devon, and the general nodded. "Go ahead."

"My mother intended to return to Skyfall," Soz said. "She probably isn't on the Orbiter."

"And that was before the attempt on Imperator Skolia's life," Devon said. "Gods only know where ISC has her now. We're going to have to assume the worst and do our best with what we have." She spoke to Soz. "Work with the bridge team. Bring up any Kyle nodes you can manage."

"Aye, aye, ma'am," Soz said. But she suspected they needed to fix far more than a few nodes.

The Bard sat on the floor in Taquinil's room and rocked his grandson as the boy cried. The house had dimmed lights in response to the boy's anguish and played soft music, but nothing helped. Taquinil clung to him and sobbed, his young face wet with tears.

"It will be all right," Eldrinson murmured. He enveloped the boy in a cocoon of comforting emotions, but fear lurked at the edges of his mind. Taquinil was at the most sensitive limit of human empathy; any further along that continuum and the boy probably couldn't survive with his sanity intact. But Eldrinson was having trouble maintaining a mental shield for his grandson. His own mind was burning and he didn't know *why*.

"Grandhoshpa." Taquinil buried his head against Eldrinson's shoulder. "Make it stop."

Eldrinson layered comfort over his mind, trying, trying to protect him. He didn't know what Taquinil had picked up, but he felt the swirling terror around them.

Gradually his efforts took effect. Taquinil sagged in his arms and his crying trailed off. After another few moments Eldrinson realized the boy had fallen into a fitful sleep. Nothing eased his own fear, however. Something was *wrong*. The Kyle meshes that intertwined with his family were damaged. People he loved were in trouble. Everyone claimed Roca was fine, the Ruby Dynasty was fine, everything was fine. He wanted to believe them, but he couldn't shake his terror.

Shannon sat with the Eloria. His tribe. They arranged themselves around the campfire, which flickered in glasswood colors: red, blue, green. Clouds covered the sky, hiding the moons, and it was hard to tell how much of the night had passed. The Archers had lived in these shrouded mountains for thousands of years, and they seemed to know the meaning of every moment.

All his life, Shannon had gone into trance alone. It had never occurred to him it could be communal. The Eloria sang together, voices chiming, lilting, hypnotic:

> sing your heart.
> sing so high.
> sing high.
> sing low.
> sing forever.
> sing of endless seas.

the endless blue.
forever blue.
forever blue.

Shannon sailed with them, their thoughts spreading to encompass the dales, the forests, the mountains, the mist, the sky itself. They submerged into a collective mind. It wasn't telepathy, nothing as specific as shared thoughts or images. Nor was it empathy, exactly. Rather than emotions, they shared trance. They blended with its mind-drenched beauty. They were everywhere and nowhere, existing here and beyond, spread into another realm, one they had no name for except the *Otherplace* or *forever blue*.

He knew it by another name: Kyle space.

The Eloria created a Kyle gateway. Shannon's brothers had always wondered why he understood the physics so well when he seemed otherwise disconnected from their universe of science and technology. But the misty, fanciful universe of quantum theory had always felt right to him. The Eloria were Fourier transforms, except they transformed thoughts into the Kyle universe, a Hilbert space built out of an infinite, orthonormal set of Kyle eigenfunctions. The Archers knew none of the theories; they just went into trance.

Shannon had no idea how long they spent in that glorious spell, the ecstasy of dreaming, dreaming, dreaming forever . . . The Archers drifted and fell behind, growing vague as he went deeper into trance. He sensed structures. Nodes and meshes. He wasn't fully in Kyle space; he formed only blurred impressions. But it was there, the web, glistening, the ephemeral handiwork of the Dyad.

He became aware of light. It took him a while to realize dawn was spreading across the Blue Dale Mountains. Mist surrounded him, shades of blue, even white, a color rarely seen in the fog, except here in the highest mountains where the ubiquitous glitter thinned.

The Eloria stirred, looking at one another, a few murmurs, greetings of the morning, a sense of completion and satisfaction among them. Shannon nodded to Varielle, needing no words. They knew what they had shared. He had sensed the richness of the Kyle web, just a glimpse, and he couldn't interact with it here, but its beauty had saturated him.

Unlike the Eloria, however, he felt no contentment this morning, for he had learned more. The web was unraveling—with no one to stop its destruction.

He had to go back into the blue.

A shudder wracked Eldrin. Sweat plastered his shirt to his torso and darkened his blue trousers. The programmable cloth had disposed of the moisture at first, but he had gone beyond its capability to deal with him. He was on fire. Crammed into the hammock with the two children and a dock worker from the port, he was suffocating. He pressed the heels of his hands against his temples. Fever blazed in his head and body. No one else seemed to feel the heat; other refugees were shivering.

"Sir?" the boy at his side asked. "Are you sick?" His voice trembled.

Eldrin patted the boy's shoulder, and tried to smile at the girl, who sat between them and was watching with wide eyes. He was all they had right now, and he didn't want them to be afraid. "I'll be fine," he rasped and hoped he was right.

As Eldrin shivered, he realized the man in a hammock to his right was watching them. Everyone was crammed so close, the fellow literally rubbed elbows with him.

The man spoke with concern. "We might find a doctor onboard."

Sweat ran into Eldrin's eyes. "I doubt I could get through to look, if it's this crowded everywhere." He couldn't even stand up. The health alarms in his body were surely sending out signals, but he doubted anyone here had the equipment to receive them. The distribution of medical personnel during the evacuation seemed to have gone awry after ESComm fired on the city.

An older woman in the hammock beyond the man spoke to Eldrin. "Son, you're as pale as snow."

His attempt at a smile felt like a grimace. He resisted the delirious impulse to ask if she meant he was blue. Pain stabbed his temples, and white blots sparked around him like afterimages of too-bright lights. He wanted to assure her that he was all right. but he could only clench the cables holding up the hammock, He leaned his forehead against one, praying for the misery to stop, the fever to recede, any relief.

Words echoed around him. The man next to him was speaking to a young woman on the deck. Eldrin saw the man's lips move and heard his voice, but they seemed disconnected. Words leapt out. "Spread the question from person to person," the man said. "Any healer. I don't know what's wrong, but he's in trouble."

"Phorine," Eldrin rasped. "Ask if they have phorine."

"Phorine?" the older woman asked. "What is it?"

Eldrin couldn't reply; it had taken all his resources to get out those few words.

The man said, "I don't know. His medicine, I think."

Yes. Eldrin would have cried the word if he could have spoken. He wanted a drink so much, he burned. Combined with his voracious craving for phorine, it was unbearable.

He had to bear it. He had no other choice.

Blankness smothered Soz's mind. She ripped the exoskeleton off her body and ripped its prongs out of her sockets. As she shoved up her visor, the bridge snapped into focus.

"Good gods." She stared at Communications, who was floating by the console, holding a grip, with Devon on one side and Weapons on the other.

Devon looked from Soz to Communications. "What happened?"

Communications seemed bewildered. "According to my link with the console, Cadet Valdoria reformed its gate into Kyle space. Then the gate disintegrated."

"The web is unraveling." Soz took a breath to slow her racing pulse. "If I had stayed in contact with that gate, it would have taken my mind with it and possibly erased parts of my brain."

"Are you all right?" Devon asked.

"No damage, ma'am." Working on Kyle nodes felt strange to Soz because of her lack of experience, but it also felt natural.

Right, somehow. However, that only made her more aware of the danger. The unstable nodes could destabilize her own mind if she was working too closely with them when they failed.

"You're saying we can't link into Kyle space?" Devon asked. "That we are losing more than the gates?"

"It's all failing," Soz said. "If ISC doesn't start repairs soon, we'll lose the entire thing."

"We can't rebuild it!" Weapons said. "Only a member of the Dyad can do that."

"It's not gone yet," Soz said. "If we staunch the damage now, we could save part of it."

"How?" Communications had gone pale. "Kurj Skolia is in a coma and no one knows if Pharaoh Dyhianna is alive. We need the Dyad to stop a collapse."

"No," Soz murmured. "We don't."

Devon spoke firmly. "Cadet Valdoria, the answer is no."

Soz regarded her steadily. "Ma'am, if we don't risk it, the Kyle web *will* collapse. It could take years to rebuild. We don't have years. We're under attack."

"You can't risk it," Devon told her.

"I don't understand," Weapons said.

"The web requires a Dyad member to create and power it," Devon said. "They are also the best choices to support it, but any Rhon telop can do maintenance work."

Communications spoke dryly. "The web is already collapsing. It's a bit late for maintenance."

Devon glanced at Soz. "Cadet?"

"I can't rebuild what has already failed," Soz said. "But I can try to hold together what's left."

Communications went very still. "You're suggesting you go into the Dyad Chair."

"It would kill you!" Weapons said.

"She is Rhon," Devon said. "In theory, she can use it." She regarded Soz. "But you aren't ready."

Soz agreed. The idea scared the blazes out of her. She had no idea if she had the strength, and she knew she lacked the skill, but too much was at stake to let the risks dissuade her.

"I have to be ready," Soz said. "We have no choice."

Weapons shook her head. "The few non-Dyad telops who tried to use that Chair died."

"They weren't Rhon psions." Soz felt its presence even now, as if it were aware of their discussion.

Come to me, she thought.

No response.

Come, she coaxed.

The Chair's mind stirred.

Soz spoke to Devon. "Let me go now, before it's too late."

Devon looked around at the others. "Opinions?"

"We need the gates," Communications said. "Without them, we're blind."

Weapons spoke flatly. "We can't risk the Imperial Heir."

"This is why we *have* Dyad heirs," Intelligence said. "To step in if the Dyad becomes incapacitated."

"And if it kills her?" Navigation demanded.

Soz rubbed the muscles at the back of her neck, working at a kink that even her nanomeds couldn't ease. "If we can't keep the web, we're all dead anyway. Or worse, if the Traders capture us."

Devon let out a slow breath. "All right, Valdoria. Try."

The Chair waited, suspended in space, its lights glowing in subtle patterns. Soz *felt* its mind. It knew she was coming. It waited. It had yet to decide what it thought about her.

About halfway down the ladder, Soz paused and looked up. Tapperhaven was sitting in the hatch above, ready to start down. Rajindia and a group of officers were visible behind her, standing around the hatch.

"I need to go alone," Soz said.

"Are you sure?" Tapperhaven asked.

Soz nodded. "Otherwise I don't think the Chair will respond."

"If you are in too long, I'll have to send in medtechs to make sure you're properly nourished and monitored."

"I understand."

Tapperhaven nodded with obvious reluctance, then stood and spoke to an aide. "Close the hatch."

They secured the hatch, closing Soz into the bay.

Soz considered the Chair. **It's just you and me.**

It remained motionless.

She continued down the ladder, acutely aware of the stars and endless froth of nebulae all around, brilliant in fiery red, orange, blue, and white. Only dichromesh glass separated her from that gorgeous, cold void. Silhouetted against that vista, the Chair was a massive shadow. It waited, assessing this callow Ruby psion who would dare sit in a throne owned by no one and allowed only to the Dyad.

You need to make an exception, Soz thought. **Otherwise, the web will die.**

No response.

Soz stopped when she was level with the Chair. Hanging on the ladder, she gazed out at interstellar space. She thought of her parents, her siblings, of Kurj and Dehya, seeing each in her mind. She imagined sending them the affection she had so much trouble expressing in person. This could be her farewell.

Then she thought, **Come to me.**

A deep hum vibrated through the Chair. The throne swung closer and closer, until she feared it would crush her against the ladder. Just before it hit her legs, it stopped. Soz released the breath she had been holding. The Chair was designed from an ancient composite that contained granite, diamond, and synthetic components modern science had yet to reproduce. Its blocky seat was squared, the back rose in a meter-tall slab, and its armrests were half a meter wide. A visored helmet waited above its back and an exoskeleton lay on the seat. She laid her hand on its arm and energy pulsated through her.

Soz steeled herself and slid into the Chair. She expected it to be hard and unyielding, but it gave under her body. As she sat with her spine against its back, a web settled over her head and extended threads into her scalp, though she knew only because she sensed its intent, not because she felt anything. She laid her forearms on the armrests, and psiphon prongs clicked into her gauntlets. The visor lowered over her head and the exoskeleton folded around her body, plugging psiphons into her ankles and spine.

Her awareness of the bay receded. She existed in a universe of fog. It sparkled in a glitter of enigmatic moods.

Getting poetic, Sozoozala?

What the blazes? Soz peered into the mist. Only Jazar could get away with calling her that; she would deck anyone else. **Jaz?**

He formed out of the fog, his well-built body coalescing from silver and blue streamers. *Heya, Soz.*

How did you get here?

He smirked at her. *So you like my body?*

She felt herself flush. **Stop eavesdropping on my mind.**

He came to the Chair. Mist swirled around him, silver and blue. *I can't help it.*

You aren't really here. The Chair created you. This was nothing like her interactions with the fake Chair in practice runs at DMA.

Jazar's smile faded. *You forgot your mother's birthday.*

What?

Her birthday yesterday. You forgot. He seemed genuinely upset. *She forgot.*

How did he know her mother's birthday? Soz had never told him and it wasn't public knowledge. But he was right. It *had* been yesterday, ship's time. **What are you trying to tell me?**

Your mother forgot. He was fading away. *Althor forgot. He and your mother. Forgot . . .*

Jaz, wait! Tell me what you mean. She was on the edge of something obscured, something important, if she could just make it out.

Suddenly the fog cleared. She was in a room full of consoles, blue Luminex instead of the usual white. Secondary Tapperhaven was walking toward her, which made no sense, either, because the battle cruiser had no console room like this.

They are failing, Tapperhaven said.

The Kyle nodes?

The mesh.

We can fix it.

No . . . Tapperhaven blurred into the mist. *Need Dyad.*

Desperation tugged at Soz. **We must hold the web together.**

Tapperhaven had become blue light. *How?*

An idea came to Soz. So far the Chair had communicated using images she recognized. **Can you show me a mesh? Silver strings for the operational links. Gold for nodes. Black where the meshes are failing.**

A net appeared around her in every direction, a three-dimensional maze that went on and on, silver and gold, so thick with nodes that many blended together. Dark, empty patches showed everywhere, ragged holes that were growing even as she watched.

Soz gathered up the mesh and clenched the lines, determined to keep them from unraveling. She held only a tiny fraction of the web, and those few lines dragged her deeper into the mist. They strained to pull out of her grip or slingshot her into dark holes where the web had already ceased to exist. Planting her booted feet wide, with her arms outstretched to her sides, Soz gripped the lines in her fists.

Come, she called to portions beyond her grasp. **Come to me.**

More lines wrapped around her arms and hands. She clenched them hard, resisting their pull, and hung on, knowing if she eased her hold, the encroaching darkness would swallow what remained of this mesh. She couldn't stop the collapse, only slow its progress. But she was entangled in the web, and more and more lines were wrapping about her, seeking the stability of her Rhon mind.

Holding the lines, she finally, truly understood what it meant to wield the full power of the Dyad—because she didn't have it. She could stand here, yes, and slow the failure, but she also knew the inescapable truth: alone, without the power of the Dyad behind her, she could neither escape this snarled mesh nor prevent its final collapse.

When the web failed, it would drag her into oblivion.

14

Corridor of Ages

The Bard sat in the living room, his arms folded on the table in front of him, his head lying on his arms, his eyes closed. Taquinil had finally fallen asleep, and Eldrinson had put him to bed. He didn't know how much more his grandson could endure. Or himself.

He felt disoriented and too weary to move. He wasn't even sure how long he had been at the table. He was almost certain he had suffered a convulsion, but he remembered nothing, only a sense of blankness. It couldn't have been dramatic; he was still seated where he had been before. He hadn't fallen to the floor and no medics had come thundering through the door. But he felt as if he had been wrung through a press.

He had come to the Orbiter for treatment of his epilepsy. Why, then, had nothing improved? His doctors claimed they had made progress, but he was falling apart. Nightmares about Roca agonized him. He had never felt this sense of *absence* from her even when she was across the Imperialate. He dreamed he was running through tunnels calling her name, but she never appeared. Then once he saw her ahead, running, her nightgown torn and ragged. She turned a corner, and when he reached the junction, he found no sign of her. He woke up gasping, his sleep shirt drenched with sweat.

For Althor, he dreamed emptiness. *Brain dead.* His son breathed, took nourishment, slept, even woke, but without a conscious mind. Althor truly had become a machine. In other dreams, he saw Eldrin—not as an adult, but as a little boy reaching out to his father, his face lit with a smile. *Swing me, Hoshpa!* When the Bard reached for him, the boy ran away, his footsteps echoing in the halls of Windward, not the castle he loved, but an empty Windward with stone walls the color of snow, blue and icy.

A drop of water fell on the Bard's arm. Bewildered, he lifted his head. Another drop rolled down his cheek and hit the table. Its surface absorbed the moisture, but no magic technology would heal his grief or his fear. He rubbed his cheek with his palm, then slumped back in his chair. He couldn't seem to help anyone he loved. What could an archaic farmer do in this morass of interstellar hostilities? He knew they were at war. ISC could coddle him all they wanted, but they couldn't hide from his mind. He knew.

He also knew one other inescapable fact. The Kyle meshes were dying. It would leave ISC blind and crippled, as Raziquon had done to him—but on an interstellar scale. ISC had surely trained for this worst-case scenario. But unlike ESComm, they didn't have centuries of experience operating without the Kyle meshes. ESComm knew that weakness. When it came to managing with the more limited spacetime webs, they had the edge.

They were sinking in a quagmire. The Dyad had to save the web. It was their reason for existence. Kurj couldn't do it, so it had to be Dehya. But something had happened to her. Although no one would tell him, he picked up flashes even from the guarded minds of his Jagernauts. This much he had guessed; if Dehya didn't reach a Chair soon, ISC would put someone else into the Dyad. Roca was their only realistic choice, but her presence in the Dyad would kill one of the three people in the link. Given Kurj's condition, he would probably die, but it could be Dehya. To kill her own son or sister would destroy Roca—and if anything happened to her, the Bard thought he would surely go mad.

Eldrin screamed and his body arched up from the deck. He was spinning apart, exploding. No longer could he feel the press of humanity in the cargo hold. People had surrounded him before, when they laid him here, but they had withdrawn. Maybe they had died; he no longer knew anything except this unbearable agony. He couldn't control the pain in his head, couldn't stop the endless, bottomless *need* that consumed him. Wraiths, fire-bright and fire-harsh, flamed within him, and burned his mind into ashes.

Someone lifted his head and held a glass to his lips. He clutched it and spilled liquid over his shirt even as he gulped down the water. The cup shattered in his grip.

"Please." His voice was raw from screaming. He grabbed the man in front of him. "Please. My medicine."

"You have to tell us how to get it." The man sounded desperate. He was kneeling next to Eldrin, leaning over him, his face haggard, his hands on Eldrin's shoulders. "I've been a doctor for twenty years and I've never heard of phorine."

"It's for telops." He gave up talking. The craving was too great. His thoughts would fly into shreds and tear apart his mind. Ah gods, he couldn't bear this—

Eldrin screamed again, his body rigid. Then he convulsed on the deck. When the seizure eased, he heard someone sobbing, pleading for them to stop the agony, and he barely recognized it as his own voice.

"Gods, what do I do?" the man said. "I've never treated psions." He had an air syringe in his hand and he was frantically rotating its cuff. "Could phorine have another name?"

Eldrin rolled onto his side and curled into a fetal ball. "I don't . . . it's bliss . . . node-bliss."

"Ah, hell," the doctor whispered. "Bloody hell."

Eldrin clawed at him. "Help me."

The man took Eldrin's arm. "How strong of a psion are you?"

Eldrin tried to answer, but he couldn't form words. Anonymity was his only protection, but gods knew, if the truth would bring more bliss, and if he could speak, he would tell them.

Another man said, "Do you know what he meant?"

"I've heard the slang," the doctor said. "The effect of the drug depends on the strength of the empath. The greater his Kyle rating, the stronger the addiction."

Eldrin rolled onto his back, chilled, though moments ago a fever had blazed through him. He kept rolling, onto his other side, clutching at the deck. He couldn't stop shaking. How long had he been on this ship? A day? Longer? He didn't know. It was only an endless, fractured misery.

"Can't you give him *something*?" someone asked.

"I don't know the chemical composition of the drug or its other effects." The doctor sounded agonized. "If I give him the wrong medicine, it could kill him."

Eldrin doubted it mattered. He couldn't survive this agony.

Blue Dales. Blue mists. Blue snow. Blue Archers. In a blurry atmosphere saturated with glitter, the universe turned blue. Shannon's mind blended with mist and snow.

Blue.

Kyle Blue.

The Eloria touched the blue with their trance and lent him their strength while he searched for his family. The Kyle meshes were vanishing. Disintegrating. His family would disintegrate with them—followed by the Imperialate. ISC didn't know how to deal with it, not like this. They would fail his family because they couldn't walk the blue.

He searched for the answer, deep in trance.

Blue chaos encompassed Soz: threads, strings, cables, meshes, nodes—all crumbling. Tattered remains of the web billowed as if they were buffeted by the gales of an oncoming storm. She clenched the lines and braced herself against the destruction.

Memory fragments whipped around her: years ago, just after her sixth birthday, she had spent hours building a tower of bagger bubbles outside. Then the wind had knocked it over. She had wept terribly, hunched over her destroyed masterpiece. Her sister had known. Nine-year-old Chaniece had come out and held Soz in her arms, rocking her back and forth until her tears slowed and her loss didn't hurt so much.

Another memory: her brother Del, twin to Chaniece, had been sixteen when Soz was thirteen. He taunted her constantly about what he called "her silly business," training with a sword—until she trounced him in a practice bout. He had clenched his fists and stalked away. That night she had been wandering outside the castle when she had heard him composing one of his wild ballads. It was about his regret that he couldn't understand her. She had never told him that she overheard, but after that she hadn't resented his challenges as much.

Another memory: Kelric, her youngest sibling, when he had been seven and she sixteen. Strapping Kelric, with his gold skin, hair, and eyes, and his sweet-natured laugh. He would be as big as Kurj, and probably as dangerous if he chose the military as everyone expected. A metallic warlord. But to her he would always be her little brother with his hair sticking up in unruly curls, hooting as she tickled him with a bubble-reed until they collapsed in the reeds, out of breath from laughing.

And Aniece: her little sister, always wanting to follow Soz around. It had exasperated Soz no end during the throes of her adolescence, but right now she would have given anything to be home with Aniece tagging after her.

Memories swirled in Kyle space, this universe of thought. They brushed the mesh she held so desperately, and as the strands slipped, so did her memories, her thoughts, her essence. She was losing the web bit by excruciating bit, and with it herself. She had too little strength. But if she loosened her grip, these lines that crisscrossed Kyle space would snap away and cease to exist.

The web would cease. So Soz hung on.

The web, and her life, continued to dissolve.

The hand on his shoulder startled the Bard, and he jumped to his feet before he was fully awake. His hip hit the table and he stumbled, his bad leg giving out under him. Both legs were biomech, but the right one responded less to his brain than the left. Flailing for the table, he started to fall.

A strong hand caught his arm, and held him firm. Flustered, he looked up, *and up,* at a dark Abaj towering over him. Eldrinson only came to his shoulder and had about half the Abaj's mass. An insignia on the man's chest indicated he was a captain. His black hair, sleek and straight, was pulled into a warrior's knot at his neck and fell halfway down his back in a thick queue.

Eldrinson swallowed and looked around. More dark blurs

stood in the room. When the captain released his arm, Eldrinson felt nervously behind himself on the table until he
found his glasses. He fumbled them on and the scene came
into focus. Abaj filled his living room, all just as large as
this captain, with black hair, black eyes, black uniforms,
black boots, and the glittering black bulk of Jumblers on
their hips.

Gods. Eldrinson instinctively stepped back, then stumbled
and grabbed the table to steady himself. He didn't know what
to think about this plethora of giants. He felt like a wild animal caught by hunters, except they didn't regard him like
predators. Instead, he sensed—concern. They were solici-
tous.

The Jagernauts all bowed to Eldrinson from the waist.
Then the captain spoke in accented but otherwise flawless
Iotic. "Our honor at your presence, Your Majesty."

"What may I do for you?" Eldrinson asked in the careful
Iotic he had learned years ago from Roca.

"Imperator Majda requests your presence in the War
Room," the captain said. "And Prince Taquinil."

Eldrinson knew ISC well enough to interpret "request." It
was an order. In the past he might have bridled at such a summons, but now he could think only that Jazida Majda might
have news of his family.

He inclined his head. "I will get the boy."

As Eldrinson limped past the Abaj, they bowed again. It
unsettled him to receive such deference from these techno-
warriors who epitomized the power of his wife's people. He
thought of getting his cane, but he didn't want to appear any
more frail than he already looked. Self-conscious, he went
down to Taquinil's room. Its door rippled open, a molecular
airlock in the middle of a house. It seemed strange to have
airlocks here, but he understood it was another method ISC
used to guard his family. If the habitat suffered a major
breach or anyone succeeded in releasing poisons or other
dangers into the house, the airlocks could protect them. Then
he remembered Vitarex Raziquon. For all its astonishments,
the technology of his wife's people had limitations.

Taquinil's bedroom was dim. The boy had nestled under a
blue comforter and blue sheets, with stuffed animals tumbled

all around him. He was sleeping with his arms around a fluffy white one with large eyes and a long tail.

Eldrinson touched his cheek. "Taqui?"

His grandson burrowed deeper under the comforter.

Eldrinson nudged his shoulder. "You must wake up."

Taquinil opened his eyes, groggy, his gold irises shimmering even in the dim light. "Grandhoshpa?"

Eldrinson's heart melted. "My greetings, Sleepy-ears."

Taquinil's drowsy contentment washed over him. Apparently his mental shield was having an effect; the boy seemed free of the anguish that had tormented him these last few days. Hope stirred in Eldrinson. Perhaps his grandson felt better because the people they loved were better.

Taquinil sat up, yawning, and tugged at his shirt, which was patterned with smiling animals. "It doesn't feel like morning," he said, his voice softened by sleep.

"It isn't." They were in the middle of the fifteen-hour night on the Orbiter. "We have to go see General Majda."

Taquinil rubbed his eyes. "Why?"

"I'm not sure," Eldrinson said. "Many Jagernauts came for us."

"Oh." The boy seemed confused. Eldrinson sympathized. He felt the same way.

After Taquinil climbed out of bed, Eldrinson pulled out some clothes for him and helped his sleepy grandson dress. Then the boy padded toward the door, pushing his bangs out of his eyes. They went to the living room together. The Jagernauts were still there, eight of them filling the place with looming black.

Taquinil stopped and stared at the formidable company. Then he backed up against his grandfather. Eldrinson put his arm around the boy's shoulders. "It's all right," he murmured. "They're friends." He took Taquinil's small hand in his large one.

The Abaj bowed to Taquinil, eight giants making obeisance to a slender and not very tall seven-year-old boy. Taquinil tried to nod the way his parents would have done, but he looked more afraid than royal.

"Well." Eldrinson strove to project confidence. "Shall we go?"

The captain moved aside for them. Taquinil's grip tightened on Eldrinson's hand and he stayed close to his grandfather. As they walked forward, the Jagernauts closed around them, taking up formation, two in front, two in back, and two on either side.

Their bodyguards took them away from the house.

The web was losing stability. The lines had become ragged and frayed, but still they came to Soz and still she held them, her arms stretched. The meshes wound and tangled around her, all blue and gold and white—and shrinking as the darkness expanded.

I never flew a Jag starfighter. The thought was soft, just for herself here in the blue, not for the Chair. *I never visited Earth, the birthplace of my ancestors. I never loved a man.* Her life had only started. She had so much to do. She couldn't bear to die this way.

The darkness continued to expand. Black spaces were filling Kyle space. Holding the lines, she stood in an isolated bubble of light that slowly and inexorably contracted around her.

The War Room was located in the spherical hull that enclosed the Orbiter biosphere. Consoles and equipment filled its amphitheater, one of several ISC nerve centers scattered across the Imperialate. In the twenty-six years of his marriage to Roca, the Bard had come here only a few times. As he and Taquinil entered with their guards, he looked up and around. Far overhead, a command chair was suspended under a holodome like a great throne silhouetted against a star field. He knew the stars were only holos, but the panoramic view took his breath away. He felt insignificant here, in this nerve center of a military that went so far beyond the army he had commanded that he couldn't even encompass the idea of it with his mind.

People filled the amphitheater, officers working at consoles and pages hurrying on errands. Robot arms swung above the scene with console cups at their terminuses and telops working within the cups. At the far end of the amphitheater, a dais supported an oval table large enough to seat twenty people. Officers from the Pharaoh's Army, the Imperial Fleet, and the Advance Services Corps sat there, deep in conference.

Beyond the dais, the Lock Corridor reached to infinity.

The corridor began on the far edge of the dais, flush with the raised disk. Pillars rather than walls delineated it, each column constructed from a transparent but virtually indestructible composite, as was the archway that framed the entrance. Ancient mechanisms gleamed within the pillars, moving gears and levers that flashed with lights, yet were eerily silent. The corridor stretched away from the dais until it dwindled to a point, as if it went on forever. It was part of the original station that modern Skolians had found derelict in space, a relic of the ancient Ruby Empire that had survived for five thousand years while humanity struggled out of its Dark Age.

At the table on the dais, Jazida Majda, the acting Imperator, was standing up now with her top officers, all of them facing the archway where Eldrinson was entering with Taquinil. The Bard recognized none of them, but the insignia on their uniforms marked them as generals and admirals. He and Taquinil climbed the steps to the dais. As they reached the table, everyone bowed—twenty of the most powerful war leaders in an empire honoring an illiterate farmer and a frightened seven-year-old boy.

Eldrinson kept Taquinil's hand in his, as much for his own reassurance as for his grandson, and inclined his head to the intimidating array of brass. The boy watched him, then inclined his head to the officers in the exact same manner.

Majda spoke. "You honor us with your esteemed presence, Your Majesty and Your Highness."

A ripple of amusement came from Taquinil's mind. He found the titles funny. His grip on his grandfather's hand eased. Eldrinson shielded his mind and hoped his grandson wouldn't sense how much this terrified him. He had no idea why these war leaders had summoned them, but he doubted it was anything good.

One of the admirals stepped back, a tall man with black

hair and a blue uniform. He pulled out the two chairs closest to General Majda. Eldrinson nodded formally to him, then paused for Taquinil. In the convoluted hierarchies of Skolian nobility, Eldrinson was "Majesty" because they considered him a king in his own right, try though he might to tell them otherwise. Taquinil was a "Highness" because he was a prince rather than sovereign. However, the boy was heir to the Ruby Throne, the highest title in Skolia, so he outranked Eldrinson—and everyone else alive except the pharaoh. The First Councilor of the Assembly ruled Skolia, but even she bowed to Taquinil.

As soon as the boy sat in his chair, Eldrinson settled into the one next to him, with the boy between himself and Imperator Majda. The Imperator sat next, followed by the other officers. The Abaj took up positions around them like dark statues. Eldrinson's unease was building. What did these people want? He concentrated on Majda, but she had shielded her mind and face, and he could read neither her dark eyes nor her emotions.

"What has happened?" Eldrinson asked.

Majda answered with an eerie calm. "We have a problem."

Nausea surged within Eldrinson. "What kind of problem?"

"With the Kyle meshes." She glanced from him to Taquinil. "Can either of you sense it?"

"It is collapsing," Eldrinson said.

Taquinil spoke in a low voice. "Coming apart."

"I'm sorry." Majda sounded heavy. More lines creased her face than Eldrinson remembered, and her eyes had a parched look, as if she hadn't slept in days. "We have no functioning Kyle links here. We've sent racers to rendezvous with our forces, but communicating by starship is a slower process. We've only a diffuse sense of what is happening out there."

"Do you mean with the war?" Eldrinson asked.

A Fleet general with bronzed hair was sitting on Majda's other side. "How can you know?" he asked. "No one else does except the people on the world affected."

The *world*? Eldrinson rose out of his chair, his bad leg stiff under him. "ESComm attacked *Lyshriol*?"

"Not Lyshriol." Majda paused.

Eldrinson was suddenly aware of everyone watching him. He took a breath to calm himself. Then he sat down. "Where?"

She spoke grimly. "Parthonia."

"My Hoshpa!" Taquinil cried. "Hoshma!"

Eldrinson laid his hand on his grandson's arm, and Taquinil looked up at him, his eyes wide.

Majda spoke to the boy as if she were treading a field of plasma mines. "We've had no reports of any harm come to either Pharaoh Dyhianna or Prince Eldrin."

Her carefully chosen words didn't fool Taquinil. "Because you have no reports at all," he said.

She answered as gently as was possible for the iron-willed general. "We've an idea what is happening, but nothing specific. We isolated your mother before the Kyle space meshes started to disintegrate, and we hope the failure didn't affect her. We know her ship took off in time."

"And my father?" Taquinil's gold eyes seemed huge.

"We think he is all right," Majda said.

His voice quavered. "But you don't know. For either of them."

She spoke softly. "I'm sorry. Terribly sorry."

Eldrinson gripped the arms of his chair. "What about the Assembly? They were in session."

"We had enough warning to evacuate the amphitheater," Majda said. "Our forces have destroyed the ESComm ships and secured Selei City."

Taquinil spoke in a monotone. "But not before thousands died."

Majda said, "Your Highness—"

"It's true, isn't it?" His voice broke. "They died. The beams came from the sky and annihilated them."

Eldrinson wondered if the boy's phenomenal intelligence was as much a curse as a gift. Taquinil understood only too well the meaning of his nightmares and the fragments of thought his painfully sensitive mind picked up from the people around him.

He laid his palm on the boy's arm. "It will be all right."

"No, it won't," Taquinil whispered.

Eldrinson took his hand. "I'm here."

Taquinil looked up at him, his face drawn, his eyes haunted. He managed a nod.

"I'm sorry," Majda said. "I wish I had better news."

Eldrinson regarded her. "Is the attack over?"

"At Parthonia, yes." She set her palms on the table as if to brace herself. "Their force was small, which helped them infiltrate our defenses, but it also meant they were too few to survive. It was a suicide mission. They intended to cripple the Kyle web no matter what the cost." She leaned forward. "We believe they intend to launch a larger invasion. Without the web, we may not prevail. ESComm is stronger and harsher, and now they're faster, too."

Eldrinson didn't want to believe it. "Dehya can repair the meshes. She can use the Dyad Chair at Safelanding."

Majda started to speak, then glanced at Taquinil and stopped.

"What is it?" Taquinil asked.

The general answered with difficulty. "As far as we know, Pharaoh Dyhianna never arrived at Safelanding." She quickly added, "She might still make it. Or perhaps she is there but for some reason can't use the Dyad Chair."

"We must help her!" Taquinil said.

"Yes." Majda exhaled. "For some reason, the web is holding together. We don't know why, but we don't think it can last. We need to send a Dyad Key to fix the system, and we have to act now, while we still can. Otherwise, we will lose what remains." Grimly she added, "If that happens, we're dead."

Eldrinson understood immediately. "You need a new Key."

"Yes," Majda said. "I'm sorry."

He wasn't the one they needed to apologize to. They weren't asking him to kill his own son. "How does Roca feel about it?"

Silence. All the officers just looked at him and Taquinil.

"What?" Eldrinson asked.

Majda took a deep breath, as if steeling herself. "We can't put Councilor Roca into the Dyad."

The apprehension that had plagued Eldrinson for days surged. He felt clammy, then chilled inside. "Why not? She is the logical choice." The only choice.

"We believe it would kill Imperator Skolia."

That wasn't the reason. He saw it in the way they all averted their eyes, heard it in her drained voice, suspected it from the heavy shields guarding her mind. Yes, they feared Kurj would die. But in a choice between saving Kurj or the Imperialate, they would choose the Imperialate.

Somehow he kept his voice calm. "Tell me the truth."

Majda met his gaze with tired eyes. "We've lost touch with your wife's escort. They disappeared."

No. *No.* His nightmares couldn't be real. He had to deny the words. Refuse them. Banish them. "It can't be true."

"I'm sorry," Majda said.

Sorry. *Sorry?* He wanted to shout at her. Sorry didn't tell him what had happened. If the Traders had Roca, he would know. He would feel the tortures they inflicted on this woman who was the other half of his soul. If she had died, he would know. A ragged cavity would have opened in his heart.

But he felt . . . nothing. *Nothing.*

He couldn't voice his fears. They went too deep, too far. It would tear apart his precarious calm. Eldrin, Dehya, and Roca had vanished, Althor and Kurj existed in a living death, and his other children were on Lyshriol, vulnerable and alone.

He struggled for composure. "Who will you put in the Dyad?"

"Who?" Taquinil echoed.

Majda regarded the boy with a look of apology. "We have a—a less prepared candidate."

The Bard couldn't believe they meant Taquinil. Less prepared was an understatement. No seven-year-old, no matter how intelligent, could operate as an effective member of the Dyad.

Then he suddenly understood. They were training another candidate. "No! Soz is too young. Too much like Dehya." Putting her in the link would kill one of them. Dehya had decades more experience, but he suspected Soz had the stronger mind. He stopped, aware of Taquinil at his side, but he saw the knowledge reflected in the boy's face. He knew what it would mean if Soz entered the powerlink. No wonder Majda wanted to apologize to him.

"We cannot put Cadet Valdoria into the Dyad." Majda had

an odd expression, as if she were on a runaway maglev train hurtling off its rail. "The cruiser where she is assigned has no access to a Lock."

"Lock?" Eldrinson had never sorted out the differences among Locks, Keys, and Dyad Chairs. Dyad members were human beings known as Keys. They used one of the three Locks to join the Dyad, and they used the seven Dyad Chairs to work with the Kyle web. But he had no real sense of what that all meant.

The man with tawny hair spoke. "What we call a 'Lock' is an anomaly where a singularity in Kyle space pierces space-time."

"My wife has told me," Eldrinson said. "One used to orbit Parthonia."

"It still does," Majda said. "It was the first installation ES-Comm went after when they attacked. They didn't destroy the Lock, but they severely damaged its space station. We can't use that Lock until we repair the supporting structure."

Eldrinson saw their dilemma. "And the Lock on Raylicon is too far." It would take days to reach, far too long in this crisis. Given Roca's disappearance, it could also be dangerous right now to send Rhon psions anywhere.

He tilted his head toward the Lock corridor. "You must use this one."

"So you see." Majda glanced at Taquinil, then turned back to Eldrinson. "We don't have time to bring anyone else in your family here."

Yes, he saw. Eldrinson didn't want to, but it was clear. He put his arm around Taquinil's shoulders. "The boy is too young." Surely they realized that with Taquinil's mental sensitivity, he might not survive. And if Soz's mind was too much like Dehya's, what about *Taquinil*? Both he and his mother were geniuses with similar minds. Either Dehya would be responsible for her son's death or he would kill his own mother. No matter what happened, it would leave the survivor too shattered even to save themselves, let alone Skolia. Eldrinson shook his head. "You cannot put a child in a Dyad powerlink with his parent."

Majda's gaze never wavered. "We weren't thinking of the boy."

Her answer slid over him like water running off the table. His voice cracked. "You have no one else."

They all continued to watch him.

"No," Eldrinson rasped. *"I cannot."*

"We see no other choice." The general sounded exhausted. "I am sorry, truly sorry. We don't know if you will survive. But you have a better chance than Prince Taquinil."

His pulse was racing. "If I do this and live, it will kill Dehya or Kurj." He couldn't look at Taquinil. "That would destroy our family just as thoroughly as if the Lock killed me."

Majda spoke heavily. "Would that we had another choice. But either we do this or Skolia falls."

Eldrinson thought of the tension he and Kurj dealt with every time they faced each other, and of his difficulties with Dehya. He wanted peace with them, for Roca's sake as much as his own, but he had never found it. Would he cause the death of Roca's firstborn, the child she had loved first and longest? Or would he kill the sister who was a part of her? Roca would never forgive him. Eldrinson would give his life to protect his family. If Kurj or Dehya died, the backlash in their newly-formed Triad could leave him incapable of anything.

"What will adding me to the Dyad achieve?" he asked. "I have no idea what to do and no time to learn." He looked around at the other officers. "Can any of you tell me how to use a Dyad Chair?"

Silence answered him.

"None of us have worked in a Chair," Majda acknowledged. "We don't even know if the one here will accept you."

Eldrinson felt as if he were drowning. "This is insanity."

"Your Majesty, I implore you." For the first time in all the years Eldrinson had known her, Jazida Majda looked desperate. "If you can't help, Skolia will fall."

What could he say to that?

Taquinil laid his palm on Eldrinson's arm. It will work out.

Eldrinson thought of Dehya. **Our wanting to believe something won't make it so.**

You would never hurt my mother.

Not intentionally, no.

You have to try, Grandfather. If you don't, my parents could be hurt much worse. The Traders might get them.

Eldrinson knew he was right. They all were. The only reason the powers of Skolia accepted his marriage to Roca was because he was Rhon. Now they needed a Rhon psion. He had sworn to support them the day he married her, and implicit in that vow was an oath to the Dyad. But he had always assumed it would be his children who inherited the titles. Not him.

He took a shaky breath. "Tell me what to do."

Screams ripped his mind, his body, the ship, the universe, screaming, *screaming* . . .

Colors pummeled Eldrin. Jagged red. Green, sharp and acid. Blue so cold it froze. Black. Dark, empty black. He cried soundlessly, lost in this place of horror. Slices of violet hacked his body, but the bloody parts reformed, reattaching themselves so the colors of his terror could cut him apart again.

Smells assaulted him. Rotting meat. Death. He would have vomited, except he had nothing left. He heaved anyway, silent and dry. Another smell, the sickly stink of bagger-bubbles moldering on the stalk. He and Althor had harvested them in their youth. He had loved the job, but now he heaved with disgust.

A face wove into view above him, yellow, so bright it hurt his eyes. He tried to push it away. A claw folded around his hand and held his four fingers in a powerful grip, a hand with a *thumb,* a nightmare hand. The mouth opened and words echoed . . .

"I'm here," the face said. "I won't leave you."

The words rang around Eldrin, distorted, ricocheting back and forth. He wanted to shout his denial, make this madness stop; gods, he wanted it to stop, stop, *stop.* The words of comfort gave him an anchor, his only anchor, in this terror. He clutched the claw until his fingers ached.

I'm here. I won't leave you.

But the insanity grew worse.

Soz felt her brother's agony across the blue, across Kyle space, across universes.

Eldrin, she thought.

His anguish pierced her.

I'm here! she thought. Fraying mesh threads whipped through the darkening fog and wrapped around her arms—including threads from her brother with a ragged, heart-breaking beauty unmatched in the functional web around her. She held the threads of his consciousness and refused to let them unravel. Even from the depths of the agony that wracked his body and his mind, his incredible mental strength came through to her. He was dying, but he *refused* to die.

Memory fragments of Eldrin flowed around her. Of all her brothers, he was the only one she had never teased. It wasn't just that he was the eldest, the firstborn. He had a quality about him that set him apart from the rest of them, not through any intention of his own, but simply because he was different. Then he had gone to war with their father and come home a warrior. It had leeched his soul and darkened his life, and Soz had been too young to know how to offer comfort. That had hurt as much as his pain.

And he had sung.

Soz had no artistic talent. She could plan strategy, solve equations, and fire any number of deadly weapons, but she could never create beauty. Many of her siblings sang; their father was a Bard, after all, and had taught them. Shannon had an exquisite tenor, Del a compelling bass, Aniece a lilting soprano. But none came close to Eldrin. He had inherited their father's enhanced vocal cords. All Lyshrioli had them to some extent, but in certain genetic combinations, they created an unparalleled tool. Eldrin outstripped even their father's glorious voice. He thought nothing of sliding through his five octave range. His voice chimed like crystal on impossibly high notes and rumbled in his deepest range. He had an artistry unmatched by anyone else Soz had ever heard. When he sang, she cried.

Now he was screaming in agony.

Live! She thought. **Live and be well, my brother.** She didn't know what had happened, why he suffered such torment. She gave him as much strength and succor as she could manage, and she kept the threads of his mind on the outer layers of hers, so that when the web dragged her under, she could release her tenuous link with him.

She would die, but she wouldn't pull him down, too.

The Bard stood at the entrance of the Lock corridor. The floor beneath him glittered, steel and diamond. Columns delineated the walkway, and machinery within them caught his attention, gears and levers in three-dimensional tessellations. Lights spiraled within the pillars along the rotating gears. Like those gears, apprehension spun within him, intricate and complex—and also fascination. The corridor mesmerized him.

He turned to the table on the dais behind him. They were all on their feet, every officer, all the generals and admirals and Jagernauts, and Jazida Majda, acting Imperator, General of the Pharaoh's Army. Taquinil was standing by his chair a few steps away.

I do this for you, Eldrinson thought to him. **That you may live free.** He couldn't make the universe perfect for his grandchildren, but he could try to make it bearable.

Majda and her officers waited, motionless, as if they feared any movement on their part would send him fleeing. He *wanted* to leave. But he had given his word. He would do this. What, exactly, he would do, he didn't know. Walk the corridor. And then? They seemed to assume he and the Lock would understand each other. He hoped they were right.

Eldrinson settled his glasses more firmly on his nose. Then he lifted his hand and hinged his palm, folding it in half, a gesture of farewell among his people.

Majda lifted her hand, palm outward, a gesture that among Roca's people meant, "Until we speak again."

Taquinil was watching them. Yes, Grandhoshpa. Until then.

Eldrinson knew this might be his last chance to touch a member of his family. Once he did this, he couldn't turn back. His family would forever be wrenched onto a new path. He stretched his arm toward Taquinil, and the boy reached

out to him. They were too far away to touch; after a moment,
they each lowered their arms.

Then he turned and limped down the corridor.

It went on forever.

Surely this Lock corridor wasn't possible. It had to end.
The Bard knew he was inside a space station only four kilometers in diameter. But the corridor stretched out, straight
and true, to a white dot, an impossible point of infinite perspective.

They called it the Corridor of Ages. He walked, his boots
muffled on the diamond-bright floor. No sound existed. No
smells. No color except the gears in the columns: bronze,
copper, silver, gold, platinum, turning, turning, turning . . .

Echoes. Voices.

Eldrin.

His son was screaming. Terrified by the raw despair in
those cries, the Bard strained to find him with his mind. He
sent out strength, support, comfort. He lost his focus and the
cries faded.

"Eldrin, my son," he whispered. "Where are you?"

Tears wet his face. He knew he might kill Dehya when he
entered the Triad, if he didn't die himself. His eldest son—
Dehya's husband and Taquinil's father—was in mortal trou-
ble. What would happen to Taquinil if he lost both parents?
Eldrinson would care for him, bring him home to Lyshriol.
But how could Taquinil ever endure the man who killed his
mother? What if Eldrinson lost Roca? Soz? If he died in the
Lock, who would protect and care for the children of the
Ruby Dynasty? So much grief. It was too much. He couldn't
bear this.

Stop, he told himself. He refused to dwell on uncertain-
ties. For every one that brought pain, another held hope. A
fog of probabilities surrounded him, what Dehya called un-
collapsed quantum states. The mists of *what-could-be* enveloped him.

Suddenly the luminous point before him was no longer at
infinity. It expanded into an arch shaped like a tall octagon,

not Luminex, more like alabaster with an inner light. He stopped before it and white light bathed him. His mind whirled as if he were sweeping around the edges of a whirlpool.

WHO?

The question filled his mind. As ancient as the birth of stars and as deep as interstellar space, it came as a sense rather than a sound. He set his hand on the glowing edge of the octagonal arch. A small chamber lay beyond, filled with so much light, he could see nothing but its sparkle.

I am Eldrinson, he thought.

STRANGER.

Yes. He adjusted his spectacles and entered the chamber, a room with eight walls, an octagonal prism saturated with light.

Time slowed.

In the center of the chamber, a column of light rose up, radiant. It came out of an octagonal depression and vanished overhead in a haze of blurred reality.

The Lock. A Kyle singularity.

Eldrinson understood nothing of this column. He knew only that a Lock offered a portal into another reality. Only here did it exist in his universe. It rose out of a universe where space and time had no meaning. Overhead, it pierced the fabric of spacetime and vanished back into another reality. Yes, he had heard the words. They made no sense to him.

None of that mattered.

He had expected to feel pressure from the power coursing through this chamber. He had been certain it would overcome his weakened body and limited mind. He had lived with his flaws and lacks for so long, all these years, knowing how little he had to offer Roca. His inherent weakness would crush him.

Instead his mind soared.

Finally he knew the reason for the anomalies on Lyshriol, the differences in the people, world, and stars—the binary and octal forms of their existence, their Memories, their need to identify symbols by exact location and details. Their designers hadn't intended them to be illiterate; it was an unplanned side effect caused by millennia of undirected genetic drift. Here he felt the truth: their ancestors had designed them for Kyle space. And he was, in many ways, the ultimate result of that ancient experiment by a long dead people. He had been created for this.

The Bard limped to the column, his motions slowed in the turgid time of the chamber. He stared into its depths, enthralled by its terrible beauty.

Then he stepped into the singularity.

15

Key to the Web

the planters jumped high,
jumped high.
so high.
they sang their news,
sang their news.
sang so high.
they sang high.
they sang low.
they sang forever.
they sang of endless seas.
the endless seas of trance.
forever beautiful.
forever blue.
forever.

The endless blue stretched forever, as natural to the Bard as breath in his lungs, as thoughts in his mind, as natural as the love for his family, or the legendary music of the Blue Dale Archers that had almost vanished from the world.

The forever blue.

He had come home.

16

The Ocean of Elsewhere

The withdrawal was killing his patient.

Doctor Lane Kaywood had worked most of his career in rural areas surrounding Selei City. He had never encountered anything like this. The youth writhed in agonized seizures. He clutched Kaywood's arm, his four-fingered hands hinged like claws, his gaze lost to whatever hallucinations haunted him. Caught in his private hell, he had gone beyond any treatment they could give him here.

Suddenly the man gasped and his spasms released. He collapsed onto the deck, shaking. Kneeling at his side, Kaywood murmured comfort and brushed hair out of his patient's eyes. He felt so damn helpless. When the youth had been coherent, he had described a medicine dispensed to his wife, one he had taken without permission. Kaywood didn't understand how any doctor could have allowed him access to a drug that produced this horrendous withdrawal.

He had almost killed his patient earlier. Desperate to calm the youth's wildly palpitating heart, Kaywood had given him a tranquilizer. Although his pulse had slowed, his cries turned even more frantic. Then his body had stiffened in a generalized tonic-clonic seizure, a grand mal attack, an attack even worse than his others, one that kept going. For three excruciating minutes Kaywood had hovered over him, horrified he had killed the man.

Mercifully, the seizure had ended. After that, Kaywood dared no other medications. Now, finally, the youth slept, though he continued to twitch with whatever nightmares haunted his mind. Kaywood sat cross-legged next to him, his head hanging, his hands clasped in his lap. They had been confined in this slow-traveling freighter for more than three days, and the youth had been in withdrawal during all of it. For the first time since the trip began, Kaywood rested.

He was dozing when a hand touched his shoulder. Raising his head, he squinted at the elderly woman leaning over him. She was the one who had come in search of a doctor.

"Here." She pressed a hot mug into his hand. "Soup."

"Thank you." He raised the mug to his lips. The thick soup ran down his throat and spread warmth in his body.

She pushed gray hair away from her face. "Good, eh?"

Kaywood lowered the mug. "Very good. Do you have some for the boy? When he wakes?" He would save his food if they were short on supplies. His patient needed to eat; he had kept almost nothing down for several days.

The woman sat next to him, her work clothes loose on her gaunt build. "We've enough." She regarded the young man with concern. "Will he live?"

"I can't say." Kaywood didn't know much about "node-bliss," but in the few cases he had heard about, the patient died from the withdrawal. Phorine affected the Kyle centers of the brain. This young man was obviously in good physical shape, but to survive he would also need a phenomenal strength of will.

"I hadn't thought he would survive this long," he admitted. "But he is strong. Healthy."

She scowled. "Then why was he taking such medicine?"

"I've no idea." He didn't add what had undoubtedly occurred to everyone, that the youth might be an addict who claimed his fixes were "medicine." Kaywood didn't think so, though. Over the years of his practice, he had developed an intuition for people. His patient genuinely believed he had been taking medication. Gods knew, if he had suffered a hint of this withdrawal before, it was no wonder he thought he was ill.

With his limited resources here, Kaywood could do only a rudimentary analysis, but it was enough to tell him that phorine was an odd chemical. Its effect was neurological. He questioned whether the drug would even show up in a routine physical exam. To detect its effect, a doctor would have to compare the youth's neural discharges with his neural map when he wasn't affected. It would be an involved process, one they would need a reason to perform.

Kaywood took a swallow of his soup. He knew too little to treat his patient, but he could watch over him, provide food and water, and protect him from injury during the convulsions.

Whether that would help the young man survive, Kaywood didn't know.

The Bard limped down the Lock corridor toward the War Room. Light inundated him. Kyle space filled his mind.

They were here, in his mind. Dehya. Kurj. Alive—but in trouble. He felt Kurj's battle for life against the ravages he suffered in the assassination attempt. And Dehya. Something was wrong, very wrong, but he couldn't tell what. She was in pain yet not in pain; in anguish yet untouched. The essences that defined Kurj and Dehya floated in a great sea, one of light rather than water. He, Eldrinson, was the sea. He would hold them up on his swells. If he raised his arms, surely the universe would flood with that endless, exquisite radiance.

He reached the end of the corridor and stopped. Lights scintillated within the transparent columns that held up the archway there. What purpose to all those gears? They caught his mind like bright toys and whirled his thoughts around, around, around; so satisfying, so very, very *right*. The blue of Kyle space filled him, and his mind reached everywhere.

The corridor was flush with the dais, but he knew ISC could lower the dais if they wished, knew it as clearly as if he had taken that fact straight from their secured meshes. Perhaps he had. Imperator Majda and her officers were waiting at the table, standing by their chairs. Staring at him. Their faces had paled. Taquinil alone showed no fear. The boy understood. He felt the glorious power of the blue.

Someone had turned up the light in the War Room. Everyone on the dais was lit up brightly. The Bard looked up to see where the light came from. Robot arms were suspended above the amphitheater, each with a telop in the console cup.

The operators were watching him, their faces bathed in radiance. Everyone was staring at him, all the techs, officers, and pages, and all the many people in the rows of consoles beyond the dais. Everyone seemed stunned. Was it truly so startling he returned alive? Yes, it was that surprising. He, himself, had doubted it would happen.

Imperator Majda spoke. At least, her mouth formed words. An echo vibrated in his ears, unintelligible.

Then Taquinil said, "Grandfather?"

Eldrinson smiled at the boy. More than ever, he felt the luminous purity of his grandson's mind.

Taquinil stepped toward him. Before the boy could go any farther, Majda and the Abaj on Taquinil's other side grabbed the boy, each of them grasping one of his arms to hold him back.

"Let me go!" Taquinil protested.

"Prince Taquinil," Majda said quietly. "You must wait."

The boy looked up at her. "He won't hurt me."

Eldrinson didn't understand what was wrong. Of course they should let his grandson come to him. He had just spent several days looking after the boy.

"**Let him come,**" Eldrinson said—the words thundered in the amphitheater.

"Gods almighty," someone said.

Eldrinson froze. Why amplify his voice? And where *did* that light come from? He looked behind him. The corridor was brighter than before, with more lights flashing in the columns, but nothing to create the radiance that bathed the amphitheater. It had to originate from someplace near where he stood.

Eldrinson looked down.

It was *him*. He radiated the light.

Saints above. He thought he had spoken aloud, but the words echoed only within his mind.

Eldrinson realized Taquinil was watching him, unafraid. The Bard walked toward his grandson, and his light poured over the boy, the table, the officers. He was aware of Majda approaching, but it wasn't until she spoke that he realized she had stepped between him and his grandson.

"Your Majesty." She faced Eldrinson, flooded with his light, her face drawn. "You must not hurt Prince Taquinil."

"I would never harm him." His voice was quieter now, but it echoed with that powerful resonance.

"Not intentionally." Her face was pale but her gaze never wavered.

"You must trust me."

She stood unmoving. The Abaj guarding Taquinil had their hands on the Jumbler guns at their hips. Eldrinson waited.

Majda took a deep breath—and stepped aside. When the man holding Taquinil glanced at her, she nodded, giving him leave to release the boy.

As soon as they let him go, Taquinil walked over to Eldrinson. "You are very bright, Grandfather."

"So are you." Eldrinson pushed his glasses into place and took Taquinil's hands, bathing the boy in his light.

Majda had a strange look on her face. "So the gods wear spectacles," she murmured.

Eldrinson didn't know what she meant—or perhaps he didn't want to know. He was a man, neither as lacking nor as powerful as they alternately seemed to think.

With reluctance, he released his grandson's hands. He looked up, beyond the consoles above his head, into the holodome. At the end of a robot arm, a massive chair waited. He had thought this amphitheater had no Dyad Chair, only a command chair, an immensely powerful station built by modern technology, but just a machine, not an intelligence. Now, though, that command chair had vanished and a Dyad Chair waited, a throne five thousand years old. The War Room had gone shadowy around him, until he questioned whether he and the Dyad Chair were even fully present.

But no—this wasn't a Dyad Chair.

It was a Triad Chair.

I am your Key, he thought.

Its response came at a level below conscious thought, but with perfect clarity:

YES.

"Can you help us?" Majda asked Eldrinson, standing with him and Taquinil, close enough that she hadn't faded with the rest of the War Room.

He refocused on her. "I will do my best."

She bowed to him. Then she spoke into her gauntlet comm.

"Secondary Belldaughter, His Majesty will go to the Chair now."

A robot arm lowered to the dais, its engine growling. The sharp scent of lubricant tickled his nose. The arm terminated in a console cup big enough to hold several people. A woman in the black leathers of a Jagernaut stood within the cup, Belldaughter apparently.

The Jagernaut bowed to Eldrinson. *My honor at your presence, Your Majesty.* Her voice echoed in his mind.

He inclined his head, trying to recall why she was familiar. She brushed a panel on her console and a gate in the side of the cup opened. Eldrinson came forward and touched the Luminex. It thrummed with energy. Bemused, he stepped into the cup with Belldaughter, certain he should know her. He raised his hand to Taquinil, and the boy waved.

Belldaughter touched another panel and the cup closed into a smooth surface. With a surge in the hum of its engines, the arm rose into the air, carrying them upward. Eldrinson clutched the edge of the cup as the amphitheater receded below.

We're safe, Belldaughter said.

Have we met before? he asked her.

Her answer came with sadness. *I knew your son, Althor. I flew with Blackstar Squadron.*

His grief welled and he instinctually closed his mind. But no, that wasn't what he wanted, not with the last person who had ever spoken to Althor. She had been Tertiary Belldaughter then, instead of Secondary.

He eased down his mental barriers. **You brought my son home.**

I wish I could have done more. She had a kindness in her manner he had never associated with Jagernauts. *His last thought to me was this: Tell my family I love them.*

Moisture came into his eyes. **Thank you.**

They had reached the holodome. The Bard adjusted his spectacles and faced the Chair. The massive throne waited, close enough to touch, huge and silent.

Alive.

COME TO ME.

I come, he thought.

The cup stopped in front of the Chair and opened so his legs were at the level of its seat. Eldrinson stepped forward and slid onto the throne. As he settled into the blocky chair, the console cup with Belldaughter lowered back down to the War Room. She lifted her hand, palm out, and stood that way as she descended.

Eldrinson laid his forearms on the armrests. He was aware of Dehya and Kurj in the same way he sensed the Chair, even himself, as presences so inextricably wrapped up with Kyle space that they couldn't distinguish where their minds left off and it began. Neither had died, but he could feel them both on the edge. He didn't know how to help, or if he could do anything at all.

A spider mesh fitted to his head and an exoskeleton clicked psiphons into his ankles, wrists, and spine. He had never wanted biomech in his body, but he had wanted even less to be crippled and blind. Now he was grateful, for it would let him help his family.

A realization hit him. Despite the immense powers flooding his mind, he had suffered no seizures. None. For the first time in his life he was fully within his natural habitat. How truly strange. He closed his eyes as the visor lowered. Then he let his mind spread into the blue . . .

Blue . . .

Blue . . .

Blue . . .

His thoughts drifted as his trance deepened.

He opened his eyes. And blinked. For some reason the Chair had lowered to the dais. It faced the oval table across from the Lock corridor. Odd. He had felt no vibration of motors. Even stranger, Majda and her advisors had left. In fact, the entire War Room was empty. Why would they all go? He had never heard of such a thing.

But wait. A woman was walking toward him, coming out of the point of perspective within the Lock corridor.

Roca! Joy flowed from Eldrinson. Suddenly she was *here,* coming past the table. With every step, she became more radiant. Her golden hair drifted about her body.

She stopped at the side of the Chair. **My greetings, love.**

I thought you had disappeared. He wanted to reach

for her hand, but the exoskeleton held his arm to the arm-rest.

I am gone, she said.

Gone? Something was wrong here. The ISC brass claimed Roca had vanished, yet here she was. True, she could have showed up, safe and sound, even asked to be alone with him, but given Majda's desperation that he fix the web, it was hard to believe they would just leave him chatting with his wife.

This wasn't Roca. It was the Chair. **What are you trying to tell me?**

I would like my mind back.

Roca, don't talk in riddles. What must I do to help?

Find me. Take me home. Her body turned misty blue. *While I have a mind to bring home.*

Roca, wait! He strained to pull free, but the Chair wouldn't let him go.

His wife faded into nothing.

Roca!

Dehya suddenly appeared at his side. *My greetings, Eldri.*

What! Eldrinson would have jumped if the Chair would have let him move. **I thought you were going to Safe-landing.**

She folded her arms on the armrest. *You're in the wrong chair.*

I am?

This isn't a Dyad Chair.

Dehya was never this casual. The advent of a Triad would evoke a multitude of emotions in her, but nonchalance surely wasn't one of them. This couldn't be her.

I thought it was a Triad Chair, he thought.

Either way, it shouldn't be here. The War Room has only a command chair, powerful, yes, but without sentience.

Then why did Majda have Belldaughter take me up here?

She didn't. Dehya began to fade.

Dehya, you mustn't leave, Eldrinson thought. **Always you do this, saying abstruse, confusing things and then going off without explanations. Maybe you know what you mean, but no one else does.**

She faded into nothing.

The War Room was gone.

The universe was blue mist.

Eldrinson closed his eyes, fighting vertigo. He was no expert on telop chairs, but he had used them with Roca's help. This was like none other he had known. He was sure he was in the Triad Chair, not the War Room command chair. He didn't know how to interpret these scenes.

Another figure was walking through the mist. Eldrinson saw him even with his eyes shut. As the figure came closer, he took on more definition. A man. No, a youth.

Shannon? Eldrinson opened his eyes and peered into the blue. **Is that you?**

His son stopped ten paces away, partially obscured by mist. 𝔪𝔶 𝔤𝔯𝔢𝔢𝔱𝔦𝔫𝔤𝔰, 𝔣𝔞𝔱𝔥𝔢𝔯.

How are you here?

𝔦𝔫 𝔱𝔯𝔞𝔫𝔠𝔢.

Although Eldrinson had never fully understood what his son meant by trance, it felt right to him. He, too, had let his mind drift into meditation. But into Kyle space? Surely not. This felt different than what had happened with Roca and Dehya. They had been easy to hear, easy to see. He could barely make out Shannon. Yet this felt real. He had no doubt it was his son.

𝔣𝔞𝔱𝔥𝔢𝔯. Shannon's thought lilted. Behind him, many figures showed indistinctly. 𝔦𝔱 𝔦𝔰 𝔥𝔞𝔯𝔡 𝔱𝔬 𝔠𝔬𝔪𝔢 𝔥𝔢𝔯𝔢 𝔴𝔦𝔱𝔥𝔬𝔲𝔱 𝔥𝔢𝔩𝔭 𝔬𝔣 𝔱𝔥𝔢 𝔪𝔢𝔰𝔥𝔢𝔰.

How did a trance bring you? Eldrinson asked.

𝔴𝔦𝔱𝔥 𝔱𝔥𝔢 𝔅𝔩𝔲𝔢 𝔇𝔞𝔩𝔢 𝔄𝔯𝔠𝔥𝔢𝔯𝔰.

Into Kyle space?

𝔶𝔢𝔰. Shannon and the figures behind him faded.

Wait. Eldrinson doubted they could hold the link much longer. **Help me look for your mother. See if you can find her the way you found me. We must help her!**

𝔦 𝔴𝔦𝔩𝔩. Shannon paled until nothing remained but blue shadows.

Eldrinson wasn't certain what these visitations meant. He knew only that he had to accomplish what he had come here to do or his family would suffer, even die. He had to fix the webs. Well, fine, but *how*?

A memory came to him of toys his children had played

with in their youth, meshes that winked and glinted as they twisted into ever more complicated shapes. The Bard tried to imagine such a web in Kyle space. Then he envisioned his mind freeing its tangles and mending its rips. The blue lost its misty quality—

Suddenly an ocean stretched in every direction, all the way to the horizon. Blue! Sky arched overhead, blue instead of lavender. Blue everywhere. He *was* the ocean, rolling, swelling, deepening. There! In the water. A mesh floated, buoyed by the sea. Pieces of it were everywhere, damaged, torn and ragged. Huge sections had fallen apart. Raveling, disintegrating—

He saw the woman.

She stood on a crude raft, her boots planted wide. The web stretched from her arms in every direction, tangled in and above the water from here to the horizon. She was the only full node in the web, a desperate goddess holding together a universe, and he had no doubt that if she lost hold of those lines, the web would cease.

Her raft was disintegrating.

Even now, a portion crumbled under her boot. She stepped onto a more stable section, but it wouldn't last much longer. When it dissolved, she would plunge into the ocean and drown.

He thought her name.

Soz.

She looked toward him, though he was everywhere, no longer a man but an ocean. No, he was a man, too. A father. He thought of Soz, and then he was next to one of her out-stretched arms. He laid his hands over hers and tried to take frayed strands of the web. She stared at him with emerald eyes, her gaze hollow, unseeing, and she clenched the mesh, either unwilling or unable to let go.

Eldrinson felt her exhaustion. She must have been here since the mesh had begun to unravel, over three days ago. *She* was the reason it survived. He had known she was strong, having dealt with her tenacity all her life, but even he had never realized the extent of her indomitable will. He could answer Majda's question now, why the web continued to exist. Soz held it together, even knowing its final collapse would pull her down as well.

He tugged the lines. *Let me help.*

She regarded him with haunted eyes, and he sensed his son Eldrin's mind, too, somewhere distant, both buoyed by her and buoying her mind, all despite his own dying.

No! He would lose no more of his children. He folded both of his hands over hers. *I can help.*

Soz groaned. By the barest amount, she loosened her grip, just a twitch of her fingers, but enough that he could pull a few lines free. He handled them with care, and they coiled around his body. Then he eased the swell of the ocean under her precarious support. He wove it into glasswood and rebuilt her raft.

Her thought came to him, drained and ragged. **Hoshpa, how are you here?**

I made a Triad. He gathered more of the mesh from her hands. *ISC should take better care of these webs. They have many weak points.*

A Triad? Hoshpa! No, that cannot be. Do you know what that means? It is impossible!

Well, it must be possible, he thought. *I am here.*

Tears ran down her drawn face. **I am glad.**

I, too. Had he been speaking, his voice would have caught. But here it flowed around them in a healing mist.

He set about fixing the mesh, just as he had mended the ripped toys for his children when they were young.

It was so very easy.

Brigadier General Devon Majda didn't return to her quarters at the end of her shift. She stayed on the bridge of *Roca's Pride*, monitoring communications among her crew and the ships in her flotilla. Messenger vessels were regularly arriving and leaving now, carrying out news and bringing it back to the flotilla. Devon had sketchy details of the situation; ISC had repulsed the invaders at Parthonia but only after extensive damage to Selei City. No one knew how many ships had escaped. If the evacuation had foundered, hundreds of thousands could have died—including a significant fraction of the Assembly. Her flotilla was due to arrive at Parthonia in less than a day, but she felt certain ESComm intended to attack some other Imperialate center. They were needed elsewhere.

Where?

Devon touched a panel on the arm of her chair, and holos formed above it, updating her on Soz Valdoria's condition in the Dyad Chair. Nutrient lines nourished Valdoria, and medtechs kept close watch, but strain showed in all her medical signs. Devon had no idea what Soz was doing, but the web continued to exist beyond all expectations. She wrestled with her decision continually—let the Imperial Heir stay in the Chair and risk her death or bring her out and let the Kyle meshes fail.

The captain knew her duty; she had to leave Soz connected. But it was grinding her down. She had known the royal family all her life and had almost married Soz's brother. The young man had declined, freeing Devon to marry the man she loved, though it meant abdicating her title. The members of the House of Skolia lived by their hearts, with an intense and fierce loyalty to those they loved. Unlike many of the imperial court, they honored strength of character above wealth, heritage, or style. They had their flaws, but they didn't care a mudrat's ass that their titles gave them stature. They actually wanted to do what was right for their people, not what satisfied their egos. She would have put her life down for any of them, and she hated that instead she was killing Soz.

Her comm hummed. She touched a panel. "Majda here."

"General, this is Major Kolonta. A messenger has arrived from the Orbiter, a Captain Gerrat. I have him on channel four."

"Understood," Devon said. "Switching."

A man spoke. "Captain Majda, this is Major Gerrat on the ISC-IF Zephyr."

"Understood, Major. What message do you bring?"

"From Imperator Majda, ma'am. You're to proceed to Onyx Sector. They've had a report of ESComm ships. I'm sending the holodocs to your EI."

Devon touched another panel on her armrest. "Verify identity and authenticity of incoming documents."

"Verified." That came from Sigma Alpha, the central EI brain of the battle cruiser.

"Come onboard, Captain Gerrat," Devon said.

"Thank you, General."

It startled Devon to hear her army title; the crew here called her captain. A holo appeared above her comm, the blaring horn that indicated an urgent summons on six, the bridge channel.

Devon switched channels. "Majda, here."

Communications answered. "Ma'am, several bridge systems just activated."

Devon wondered why Communications thought she needed to report such routine information. "Is that a problem?"

"It's odd they would come online now."

"Which systems?"

"One feeds coolant to the neutrino transmitters. The other regulates the doors for docking bays."

Devon still didn't see the problem. "Probably they're on timed cycles." Communications ought to know that.

"They were, a few days ago. The cycles failed because the systems they control have links into the comm network. Ma'am, four more systems came on—what the hell? Make that five."

The voice of Weapons burst out. "Captain, our Annihilators are reactivating!"

"Long distance comm, too," Communications said. "This is incredible. We've had crews working on these for days, with no luck. How could so many come up so fast?"

No wonder they had contacted her. Every one of those systems had links to short- or long-distance comm, which meant they had faltered when the Kyle web began its collapse. Devon spoke to Sigma. "Put me through to Cadet Valdoria."

A new voice came on the comm, young, but resonant with power. "Valdoria here, Captain."

"Gods almighty," someone muttered on the bridge channel.

Communications inhaled sharply. "I didn't open a channel to the Dyad Chair, Captain."

Devon swallowed. Neither had she. "Cadet Valdoria," she said evenly. "How did you access my station?"

"I'm in all the systems, ma'am." Soz's voice remained strong, but Devon heard its underlying strain.

"How can you be in all of them?" Devon asked.

"I'm bringing them back up," Soz said.

Devon realized her crew was listening throughout the ship. Soz's voice was coming over all the channels, and other voices were murmuring on many lines. She didn't know what had happened, but power coursed through Soz's voice.

Devon rubbed her chin. "Valdoria, the systems you're fixing failed because they were linked into Kyle space."

"Aye, ma'am," Soz said. "We're fixing the nodes."

"I can confirm some of that," Weapons said. "Our missile systems are back in operation."

"Our gates into Kyle space are reforming at a rapid rate," Communications said. "Not just here on the *Pride,* but throughout our flotilla."

"Gods," Devon said. "Valdoria, did you manage all that with the Dyad Chair?"

"It's no longer a Dyad Chair, ma'am." Soz's voice had an odd sound, drained but exultant.

"What is it?" Devon asked.

"A Triad Chair."

The voices went silent on every channel. Devon stared at the comm. Either the impossible demands of her duties had pushed Soz over the edge—or history had just changed for the human race.

It was a good five seconds before Devon found her voice. "You joined the Dyad?" she asked.

"Ma'am, no! Not me. My father."

Her father. Devon had no way to fit her mind around this concept. Skolia had a new Key? The last time a Rhon psion had made the Dyad into a Triad, a Key had died. Kurj Skolia had killed his own grandfather. Who would die this time? The pharaoh? Imperator Skolia? Devon couldn't absorb the immensity of that disaster.

"What about the rest of the Triad?" Devon asked.

"For now, they're alive." Soz sounded subdued. Then she suddenly spoke more urgently. "Ma'am, Imperator Majda wishes to speak with you."

It took Devon a moment to switch mental gears. "My aunt?"

"Yes, ma'am."

"But she is on the Orbiter."

"Yes." Soz took an audible breath. "I'm in contact with the War Room."

Gods all-flaming-mighty. They had brought back the Kyle web. Devon took a breath. "Very well. Put her through."

A man spoke. "Imperator Majda coming online."

"Understood," Devon said. Protocol required she answer first, as the officer of lesser rank.

Jazida Majda spoke in a clipped voice. "Devon, forget about Onyx Sector. With the web coming up, we have new information. ESComm has launched an invasion ten times the size of the one that attacked Parthonia. Half a million ships. It's too large for them to hide with our sentry nodes coming back in-mesh." Then she said, "They're headed for Metropoli."

Devon swore. With ten billion people, Metropoli was the most heavily settled world in the Imperialate, with even more people than Earth's seven billion. "I'll need everything you have on it."

"We're transmitting now," Jazida said. She spoke quietly. "Gods' speed."

Devon swallowed. "We'll need it."

17

The Blue

Like great waves rolling across an ocean, power flooded Kyle space. It coursed through the blue and supported meshes everywhere in its undulating embrace. Nodes reformed. Lines knit together. A new web didn't need to be created; enough remained of the old to repair. Throughout Skolia, lights switched to green, probes sent reports, and telops reestablished links. The recovery surged across space.

With that resurgence came the news: an invasion fleet was sweeping through space, straight into the most heavily populated center of Skolia.

Soz sat in the War Room command chair.

She wasn't actually in the War Room; the Chair on *Roca's Pride* had created this simulation because her father believed he was in the War Room rather than the Triad Chamber on the Orbiter. It allowed him to center Soz's mind here. She was serving as a central node for ISC as it rewove its forces into a coherent defense. Soz had nothing resembling the experience needed to coordinate the War Room; however, she knew enough to ensure that the information Imperator Majda needed to command ISC was properly routed through to her.

Jazida Majda's voice came over her Kyle link. *Valdoria, do you have contact with Pharaoh Dyhianna?*

Nothing. It worried Soz. **If she has access to a Triad Chair, she isn't using it.**

Her father asked, **What about your mother?**

Nothing. Soz couldn't forget her first time in the Chair, when it had reminded her about her mother's birthday. The bizarre interaction preyed on her thoughts. **Something is wrong. We must find Mother. I don't think she can help herself. She may not even remember us.**

Majda's answer came with tension. *The Traders are using Kyle space to infiltrate our defenses. It connects to your family, but we don't know how. We cut our Kyle links with the non-military members of the Ruby Dynasty, but we didn't have a chance to warn your mother. She disappeared before we could tell her escort not to use the Kyle web.* Majda paused. *We didn't know, when we cut Pharaoh Dyhianna out of the web, that we would need a Key.*

Soz didn't see what difference it would have made. Either way, Dehya would have disappeared when her shuttle tried to invert. Soz wanted to search for her mother and her aunt, but messages were pouring into her mind from all over Skolia. Data about the invasion flooded the War Room, coordinated by Imperator Majda through Soz and the Chair, and

telops rerouted it to millions of ships, from the giant
Firestorms roaring through space to tugs lumbering among
asteroids.

The ESComm fleet was currently hidden in inversion. Unlike their ISC counterparts, however, they had limited communications during superluminal travel; the longer they
spent inverted, the more their ships were spread out in time
and position when they dropped into normal space. To remain a coherent force, they periodically had to reenter normal space and regroup, taking hours to gather their fleet. It
was their greatest vulnerability.

ISC saturated space with probes around the predicted
course of the ESComm fleet. Most returned nothing useful,
but a few were in the right place each time the invaders
dropped out of inversion. Although ISC could have attacked,
Majda held back. The Traders didn't know Skolia had regained the web, and ISC would have the element of surprise
only once. They had neither the personnel nor the resources
to match ESComm, but they could move faster and with more
precision.

It might be enough to prevail.

Maybe.

Eldrin slumped against the bulkhead, his legs stretched
across the deck. The freighter managed a low apparent gravity with its rotation, but it was uneven enough to create no-
ticeable Coriolis forces. He doubted that was what nauseated
him, though. He just plain felt like hell.

But he was alive.

Although the craving remained within him and his head
ached, he could bear it. His hallucinations had faded to visual
distortions and an unsettled sense that colors were too bright,
edges too sharp.

Refugees crammed the cargo hold. He had expected he
would disgust these people, who had witnessed his bone-
crushing weakness. As an empath, he would feel con-
demnation, especially with his mind so sensitized by the
withdrawal. And a few did condemn him. But most felt

sympathy. Many spared him an encouraging word or nod. His years in the elegantly cutthroat universe of the Imperial Court had jaded him; this reaffirmation of human kindness was a gift.

A slender man was making his way through the refugees, his gait awkward in the minimal gravity. Gripping a projection on a bulkhead, he stepped past a group of young people playing a game with sticks that floated lazily off the deck and settled again. He edged around a sleeping man strapped into a hammock and past an elderly couple chewing on the ship's dull rations. The man looked familiar to Eldrin, but it took him several moments to figure out why. It was Kaywood, the doctor who had stayed at his side during his ordeal—the man who had saved his sanity and his life.

Eldrin became aware of two children, a small girl dozing against the bulkhead and a boy who sat on her other side, also asleep, his cheek resting on her head. They had curly dark hair and similar features, probably brother and sister. He remembered; they had shared his hammock.

As Kaywood reached them, the girl opened her eyes, then closed them again. The doctor knelt next to Eldrin and spoke in Skolian Flag. "Good morning."

"Good morning." Eldrin's ruined voice grated. Gods only knew if he would ever sing again. It hurt too much to contemplate, that the phorine may have taken away the only other thing he loved besides his family.

Kaywood offered him a water tube and a stick of food. It was all Eldrin could do to accept the tube calmly rather than yanking it away. He fumbled with it, but he didn't have the patience to open it properly, so he tore off the top. He drank deeply, and water ran down his parched throat.

Kaywood had an odd expression, as if he wanted to rejoice, but wasn't certain yet if he should. He gave Eldrin the food stick.

"My thanks," Eldrin whispered.

"You seem better today," Kaywood said.

"You've a gift for understatement."

"It was rough for a while."

Softly, Eldrin said, "I am in your debt."

Kaywood sat cross-legged on the deck. "I felt like I wasn't helping at all."

"You were." Eldrin would never forget his words of comfort. They had been a lifeline for him. "More than you know."

"Well." Kaywood nodded self-consciously. "Good."

They sat for a while, chewing rations. Eldrin wasn't certain he could keep the food down, but he was too hungry to hold back.

Eventually Kaywood said, "I was wondering if I might ask you a question."

"What did you want to know?" Eldrin asked, wary.

"Sometimes your accent sounds Iotic. Other times I can't place it."

Eldrin hesitated. If Kaywood recognized an accent as rare as Iotic, he probably knew only royalty and the nobility spoke it as a first language. It didn't surprise him, given that the doctor worked on the outskirts of the Skolian capital.

"I learned Iotic in school," Eldrin said, which was true. His parents had also taught him, but he didn't want anyone to guess his identity, not only because it could endanger his life, but also because they would probably give him special consideration that he didn't deserve. Other people needed it more, and he had put these people through enough.

"What is your native language?" Kaywood asked. He seemed only curious; Eldrin had no sense that the doctor suspected who he had been treating.

"It's called Trillian," Eldrin said. "That is the accent you hear." Although the language had probably descended from ancient Iotic, it had changed over the millennia until it became a separate tongue. He had learned Trillian and Iotic together, but he used Trillian more and considered it his first language. "My parents wanted us to have a good education."

"They are wise."

"Yes." Eldrin's voice had lost its chime, and he feared it would never heal. So much destroyed in one day. He thought of his bodyguards, the Abaj in the limo, and prayed they had survived.

Kaywood spoke carefully. "I also wondered about the phorine."

Eldrin knew what the doctor wanted to know. He brushed back his hair, which had tangled over his collar. "I thought it would solve a neurological problem. I didn't know it was addictive."

Kaywood's gaze turned to steel. "I assume you will never again take it without supervision."

Eldrin shuddered. "Not even with."

"Good."

The girl stirred in her sleep. Relieved to avoid the doctor's stern gaze, Eldrin watched the children. The boy reminded him of Taquinil. Fear wrenched Eldrin. Were his wife and son safe? The Orbiter was always on the move, which could protect Taquinil and the Bard. Eldrin's hallucinations had included the agony of torture by the Traders, but he had no way to know if the withdrawal had caused it or something else. When he thought of his family, especially his parents, his worry spiked. But he didn't know *why*. Nor did he have any idea where Dehya had gone. He tried to sense her mind, but it felt diffuse, even . . . gone.

No. She couldn't be gone. She couldn't.

He should have been with Dehya in the Assembly, or with Taquinil on the Orbiter. Node-bliss. Better to call it node-misery. He had let it take him away from his family and his singing. His bodyguards had protected him even as he risked them all, insisting they delay while he searched for his damnable "medicine." If not for him, they might have reached the hospital in time to prevent whatever injured them. If not for his soul-killing need, he wouldn't have drained his life until he had nothing left but the empty Ruby Palace. If he had another chance, he would honor it. He would be a worthy Ruby Heir, a better husband, a better father.

A bell clanged, jarring Eldrin out of his haze. The captain's voice came over comm, as brusque as always. "Prepare to invert."

Eldrin glanced at Kaywood and saw his apprehension reflected in the doctor's face. They could come out into empty space—or among ESComm battleships.

"Have you heard anything about the situation?" Eldrin asked. People around them were murmuring similar questions to one another.

Kaywood shook his head, his face pale. "This ship apparently had only limited Kyle access to start with, and it lost those few links during the attack. People are saying the web collapsed."

"It didn't." Eldrin wasn't sure how he knew, but he was certain. For some reason Soz came to mind. Then he thought of his mother and his unease returned, magnified.

"I thought we were going to invert," a woman muttered.

"It was a warning," a man said dryly.

"Don't complain," another man said. "He's a good captain."

Eldrin agreed. The captain could have taken off to ensure his own safety, but instead he had stayed during the attack and given up his cargo so he could jam hundreds of people into his freighter. Eldrin intended to make sure he received recompense for his lost goods. He hadn't seen the captain, but then, he had seen little else but hallucinations for the past few days.

Another alarm sounded, the ten-second warning. They had no chairs or pads, nothing to ease the drop out of inversion. Eldrin just stayed against the bulkhead, his arm around the children. When the ship inverted, his nausea surged. Grotesque monsters with red eyes and shimmering black hair capered at the edges of his vision, hawks with the heads of Aristos. They were a dim nightmare, though, weak reminders of the terrors that had haunted him.

His sense of the universe abruptly righted itself, and the hallucinations faded. Grateful, he leaned his head against the bulkhead and closed his eyes.

The captain's voice came over comm. "Drop complete." Relief crept into his brisk tone. "Looks like we're clear, folks. We're coming up on Baylow Station, an outpost in Ivory Sector designated to accept evacuees."

Kaywood exhaled. "Thank the saints."

Eldrin opened his eyes and smiled wanly. "Also the EIs that ran the evacuation and this ship."

The doctor laughed, his voice uneven. "I guess sainthood is beyond their capabilities."

Eldrin had grown up immersed in Lyshriol culture, with its saints of the suns, moons, lands, reeds, bubbles, and more.

He knew, logically, that it was mythology, intricate and lovely, but only stories. His emotions believed, though. Right now he would thank them all for bringing him through to this place—and eventually back to his home, he hoped.

If he still had a home.

Shannon walked the Blue.

He no longer saw the Eloria in the mists. He had gone too far for them to follow. Their mental support, as nebulous as it had become, remained, allowing him to walk the strange edges of Kyle space. He searched for his mother. His father had tasked him to this deed and he would succeed no matter what it took. His fear for her drove him onward, searching, searching, searching.

mother, can you hear?

Gripping the web, Soz searched. **Mother, can you hear?**

The Bard called with the power of the Triad. **Roca, where are you?**

Slowly she opened her eyes. She was lying on her back under a silver sheet. Her arms were pulled above her head and bound at the wrists. Her ankles were strapped down.

A thought formed. Councilor?

Odd. She heard the word in her mind, it wasn't her own.

This is Arabesque, it thought. Your node.

Node. Spode. Code . . .

Councilor, I need your help.

Who is Councilor? she asked.

You.

Me . . . ?

Your name is Roca Valdoria Skolia. You are heir to the Ruby Throne and Councilor of Foreign Affairs in the Assembly.

The meaning of the titles eluded her. *What do you want?*

I have been dormant. Someone nudged me.

What?

People are searching for you. They cannot find you if your brain is off.

You are my brain.

No. I turned you off.

That made no sense. She pulled at her bonds, but her limbs were tightly fastened. *Free me. It hurts.*

I can't.

Fear sifted through her mind. *They want to hurt me.*

Yes. I am sorry.

Have they . . .

They stopped when you went into the coma. They are waiting for you to awake.

She stiffened, and pain shot through her wrists. *I am awake.*

Yes. Nor can I suppress your physiological responses much longer. I have infiltrated the meshes on this ship, but if I manipulate the systems, they may catch what I am doing. If I don't hide your vital signs, however, they will soon realize you are awake.

What is wrong with me? Bile rose in her throat. *Why can't I think?*

You have a great deal of brain damage.

Her anger sparked. *You did this to me.*

Yes. You commanded it.

Why would I give such a command?

To stop the torture. They cannot transcend if you are in a coma.

She remembered pain. *We must escape.*

Someone is searching. If we could just—Suddenly it thought, The EI for this medical bay just notified Commander Raziquon that you have come out of your coma.

A chill went through her. *Who is Commander Raziquon?*

The Aristo who abducted you. She and her brother.

What should I do?

Make contact with the people searching for you.

How?

I don't know.

A hiss came from across the bay. Footsteps entered, boots on the deck. A face appeared above her, a woman with eyes as brilliant and as red as rubies. Her hair hung to her shoulders and shimmered as if it were made from black gems. She was beautiful in an inhuman way. Her mind was a vortex pulling Roca into a nightmare place where no empathy or humanity existed.

She is an Aristo, Arabesque thought.

The word chilled. Roca instinctively tried to jerk away, but with her arms and legs bound, she couldn't move.

The woman smiled, like ice. "My greetings."

Roca regarded her blankly. "What?"

More footsteps entered the room. A man appeared next to the woman, a male version with the same cold eyes. His hair glittered.

"She seems confused," the woman said.

"Good," the man said.

Roca thought she should know these people.

The woman is Vitarex Raziquon's daughter, her node thought. The man is her brother Kryx. Raziquon's son.

The man spoke to the woman. "Will you stay?"

The woman inclined her head as if he offered a gracious invitation. "Thank you." She considered Roca the way someone might survey an expensive acquisition. Then she moved away. Her steps receded, followed by a squeak of furniture as she apparently sat down.

Kryx watched Roca with a pitiless gaze. He took the sheet between his thumb and forefinger and twitched it off her body. Heat spread in her face. She pulled her arms, trying to bring them down, to cover her nakedness.

A cruel smile touched his lips. "You don't like me looking at you? Good."

With growing panic, she struggled to free her arms.

Kryx reached under the table and removed a small cup and a brush. He swirled the brush in the cup, then showed it to her. Iridescent powder covered the bristles. "See this?"

"Yes." Roca couldn't see what he wanted, though.

"While you were in your little coma, we matched this to your DNA." He spread the sparkling powder across her shoulder. "So it will affect only you."

Affect her how? She felt nothing. "What is it?"

He swept the glitter onto her breast and rubbed the palm of his hand over her nipple. It made Roca ill. She struggled again, with no more success than before.

"It is seeded with nanobots," he said.

"What are those?" Her voice sounded slowed. Dull.

Kryx laughed coldly. "I had heard you were intelligent. More Skolian lies, eh?" He went to work on her abdomen. "Nanobots are molecular machines. Hooks on these will fasten to your skin. *Only* your skin." He spread glitter on her hip bones.

Roca thought she should understand. But she saw only that he wanted to cover her with sparkling dust. After coating her legs and arms, he set the cup and brush back under the table.

"What do you want?" Roca asked, her voice thick.

He watched her with undisguised contempt. "You have spent your life making offensive assumptions. You are a provider. A slave. The idea that the Ruby Dynasty should have authority is an abomination to all that is decent. You need to be controlled."

The hell with him. "By what? Glitter?"

"Oh, didn't I mention?" He poised his finger above a panel on his gauntlet. "The nanobots extend threads into your body that touch your nerve endings."

Then he tapped the panel.

Pain!

All over her body, nerves caught fire. She screamed, arching her back, but she had nowhere to go, no escape. *Unbearable—*

Suddenly the agony stopped. Roca gasped, sobbing, her throat raw. The Aristo watched her with a hateful ecstasy. Sweat broke out on her forehead. She had never experienced pain that intense.

"She is exquisite," Kryx murmured.

His sister's voice came from behind them. "Indeed she is." Dryly she added, "But loud. Fix that."

He took a sponge and a silvery roll out from under the table. To Roca he said, "Open up."

She stared at him with loathing. "What?"

As soon as she opened her mouth, he shoved in the sponge.

Before she could spit it out, he taped her mouth closed. Then he poised his finger above his gauntlet, deliberately letting her see.

No! Roca fought her panic. *Stop him! Help me!*

I can turn you off again, her node thought. You will feel nothing.

Kryx moved his finger a hair's breadth above his gauntlet.

Turn me off, Roca answered, frantic. *Fast!*

If I do, it will damage your brain so severely, I can never help again—

She didn't hear the rest. Kryx touched his guard and agony wracked her body. The gag muffled her screams but nothing stopped the pain. It went on and on, and encompassed the universe.

When it finally stopped, Roca shook with anguished, muffled sobs. *Turn me off. Now.*

Councilor, listen! her node thought. People are looking for you in Kyle space. If I stop your neural processes, they won't find you. You will never be free of this insanity. You will either die or be his provider forever. But if you hold out a little longer, the searchers may find you.

I can't bear it. She was crying inside as well as out. *Turn me off.*

It will destroy your only hope of escape.

A lifetime of this. Roca would rather die.

Can you bear staying conscious for even a few more minutes?

Tears rolled from her eyes. *I will try.*

Soz was tracking the ESComm invasion when the mental quake hit her. In the virtual simulation, she was in the War Room command chair; in reality, she sat in the Triad Chair on the cruiser. When the quake hit, the War Room simulation distorted. Vertigo rolled through Soz, and she felt as if she were going into shock.

"Cadet Valdoria!" Devon Majda's voice snapped over the comm in her ear. It echoed, but at least the Chair was giving her the transmission. Sometimes it either couldn't or wouldn't let her communicate with the cruiser.

"Your stats just jumped," Devon said. "Your pulse is too high and your brain waves went off the scale."

I'm all right. Soz thought her response, and the Chair sent it to Devon's station on the bridge as words. **Something happened in Kyle Space.**

"What was it?" Devon asked.

I don't know—Soz broke off as another quake rocked through her. Bile rose in her throat. It was all she could do to hold down the acid in her stomach.

Soshoni? the Bard asked.

Father, is that you? Are you all right? What happened?

The War Room wavered around her and disintegrated into blue mist. A figure took form, a man, but he seemed more slender than her father and not as tall.

Soz mentally stumbled in the mist. **Shannon?**

𝔰𝔥𝔢 𝔥𝔲𝔯𝔱𝔰. Shannon sounded agonized. 𝔴𝔢 𝔪𝔲𝔰𝔱 𝔥𝔢𝔩𝔭 𝔥𝔢𝔯.

Soz barely understood him. His "voice" came with even more chimes and lilt than native Trillian. He had an accent, one reminiscent of ancient ballads about the Blue Dales, a dialect that had died when the Blue Dale Archers vanished. Yet now it saturated his thoughts.

Who, Shannon? she asked. **Who hurts?**

Her father answered, frantic. Your mother! It is a sword slicing me to pieces.

Soz extended her mind further into the mist and tried to sense what they had found, but she couldn't shed her fatigue. She had spent too many days in the Chair, kept alive by a machine.

Another quake hit.

This time, with her attention focused, Soz *felt* it. Agony blazed as if her nerves were on fire. She gasped and went rigid. *Were they doing this to her mother?* Fury swept through her and turned the mist red. She hurtled her mind forward, through fog the color of an Aristo's eyes, straight to the epicenter of the quakes. Shannon flew at her side, shadowy, half formed, more thought than boy. Beyond him, almost invisible, more figures ran, many people, ethereal here in the red mists.

Red.

The color of rage.

Her father's rage.

It surrounded them, everywhere. That was why she hadn't seen him before. He *was* the mist. He was the Kyle. The blue had turned red with the wrath of a man who had known and loved one woman in his life, the mother of his ten children. His fury saturated the universe.

They converged on the epicenter. Mist whirled around this place of pain like a vortex. Another quake came, Roca's agony, and the Bard roared in fury.

Roca could take no more. Kryx inflicted the pain again and again, and each time it stopped, he fondled her body, until she thought she would choke with horror and disgust. His gaze seemed to expand until it filled her universe, turning everything red, nothing but carnelian shadows. He leaned over her, his eyes glazed with ecstasy—and hit the panel on his gauntlet.

Roca couldn't scream any more. Agony wracked her body and she thought she would shatter. *Make it stop!* she pleaded with her node. *I don't care if I die. Turn it off. End this.*

Mother! Soz's thought broke through the pain. **Mother, give me your hand! Reach for me.**

Roca knew then she had truly gone insane. The brain damage had destroyed her memories, intellect, personality, but nothing could make her forget her family. Except they couldn't be here.

Roca! The Bard's voice thundered. **Reach out with your mind!**

It was impossible. But Roca reached anyway.

Suddenly blue surrounded her in a mist, cradling her in its embrace. It filled the universe. She heard Kryx shouting, heard his fury, but it was receding. The pain, mercifully, had stopped.

A woman's authoritative voice spiked through the eerie fog. "Cadet Valdoria! This is Imperator Majda. You need to keep the comm lines active. We're losing your signal."

What the hell? Roca thought.

Soz answered. **I'm coordinating them, ma'am.**
"Are you having trouble?" Majda asked. "We're getting a ten-second delay in your responses."

Roca's thoughts spread over her daughter's like a glaze, and data from Soz's augmented brain flooded her mind: ISC and ESComm forces would engage each other as soon as their respective fleets dropped out of inversion. At relativistic speeds, ten seconds were an eternity. Entire battles could be won or lost in that time. Those seconds could mean the difference between triumph and defeat for the ISC forces defending Skolia.

We're freeing my mother from the Traders, Soz said, her thoughts accelerated. **I can't let her go. That's what is causing the delay.**

"Valdoria, concentrate!" Majda answered. "We get one chance, Cadet. *One.* If we come out in the wrong place or at the wrong time, we haven't a hope of defeating ESComm."

Hold her, Soz, the Bard said. **Hold your mother.**

Eldri? Roca asked. The blue mist curled around her. He was the mist, the ocean of fog, everywhere and everytime.

A chant drifted through the fog, eerie and distant, rich with chimes, lilting, hypnotic:

> sing your heart.
> sing so high.
> sing high.
> sing low.
> sing of endless seas.
> endless seas of blue.
> forever beautiful.
> forever blue.

"Valdoria, respond!" Majda said. "Link the damn ships!"
Father, Soz thought desperately. **Take Mother.**
The Bard's voice surrounded her. **Roca, come to me.**
Roca reached out—and she had nothing to grasp. She didn't remember this place, but from her daughter's mind, she knew it was impossible to move a physical body through Kyle space, a universe of thoughts. Mass, space, and time

didn't exist here. It was painfully clear to Soz: they would have to transform her body into a thought analog, like a Fourier transform took a time-dependent function into one dependent on energy. Even if it were possible, the energy required would be immense.

Eldri . . . Roca knew she was on the Trader ship, that her family was only shielding her mind so her brain couldn't register the pain. Her link to them slipped—

Roca, come back! Eldrinson cried.

Roca wanted to, but she couldn't. She was losing them—

A new thought formed around them.

It existed everywhere, filled with nuanced power and the knowledge gained from decades of operating in this universe. Where the rest of them were struggling to define themselves, this mind existed with ease—and a finessed power that had no equal.

No equal.

None other like it existed.

Hold her, the Ruby Pharaoh thought.

The mist took form and shape, resolving into a vivid sky and ocean, all with incredible detail. The mist coalesced onto Roca's body, covering her in a shift from shoulder to knee.

Dehya! Soz thought.

Gods almighty, Eldrinson thought.

The song of the Blue Dale archers swelled:

> sing of endless seas.
> endless seas of blue.
> forever blue.

Imperator Majda's voice thundered around them, not truly in Kyle space, but transmitted by the web. She spoke in real time rather than the accelerated mode used by Eldrinson, Soz, Shannon, and Roca in their enhanced link.

"Cadet Valdoria, respond!"

Soz never had a chance to answer her. Another voice spoke, overriding her in this place and resonating everywhere.

Five more seconds, Jazida, Dehya thought. *Give us five more seconds.* The Chair translated her response into words and transmitted them to Majda's comm on the Orbiter.

"Pharaoh Dyhianna!" Majda shouted. "You're alive!"

It would seem so.

"Where are you?"

In the Triad Chair at Safelanding, Dehya thought.

To her credit, Majda barely missed a heartbeat despite her shock. "Five seconds. No more. Any longer and we could lose our window of attack."

Take my wife home, Eldrinson thought to Shannon and the Archers. **We have only five seconds.**

Take my sister home, Dehya thought.

Take my mother home, Soz thought.

ꟺe ꜧaꟷen't tꜧe strengtꜧ, Shannon answered.

FOUR SECONDS, the Orbiter Triad Chair thought.

You must! Eldrinson thought. The sea churned and clouds massed.

**endless seas of blue.
foreꟷer blue.**

THREE SECONDS. That came from the Safelanding Chair.

Soz hung onto Roca, tears on her face, their minds blending. Roca felt her straining to do the impossible, to pull her out of the Trader ship. Eldrinson supported them with the ocean of his mind; Dehya gave the universe definition; Shannon and the Archers sang; and Roca tried to add her strength to theirs, though her mind was injured, perhaps beyond healing. Soz drew immense energies from the flotilla, but it wasn't enough. They had too little strength.

They were losing the link.

Good-bye. Grief wrenched through Roca's thoughts. **Remember that I love you.** She would never lose that knowledge no matter what happened to her ravaged brain. She would take it to her death. **Live and be well. All of you.**

Roca, no! the Bard screamed the words.

Mother, hold on! Soz cried. Shannon shouted her name.

Roca couldn't hold on. Her grip slipped.

In the distance, a bank of clouds swelled in the sky. Roca felt ill, knowing it would tear her away from her family and leave her with Raziquon. Forever. The Ruby Dynasty could never repeat this confluence of Rhon minds; through her link with them, she knew they had managed this time only because the newly recovered web had too little structure to define Kyle space. The more it gained, the less they could mold it to their minds.

TWO SECONDS.

The clouds rushed toward them. No natural storm moved that fast—no, it wasn't a storm. It was a swell in the sea, huge, gigantic, *monstrous*. It came on, relentless and unswerving, drawing up water from all around them. It lifted them high into the cloud-drenched sky, incredibly high. It had no nuance, no finesse, no subtlety—just sheer, implacable, inescapable *power.*

ONE SECOND.

A new voice thundered around them, one Roca had been certain she would never hear again—an impossible, incredible voice so full of strength that it infused the entire Kyle universe.

Take her home, Shannon, Kurj thought.

Blue Dale singing filled her mind. Kurj's wave rolled through the Kyle, a mental strength unlike any other ever known. It lifted the song, drenching it with power. The wave-song swept over and past them—

And took Roca.

TIME ENDED.

18

The Choice

Dehya thought, *Eldrinson, transfer web control to me.*

Kurj thought, **Soz, transfer War Room control to me.**

Their power deluged Soz's mind. With an exhale of relief that echoed throughout Kyle space, Soz released control of the meshes that coordinated ISC. Kurj took over with an expertise accumulated over decades of experience.

Welcome back, she thought. Those two words held a world of gratitude. In the backwash of his mind, Soz could only marvel at his strength. She sensed her father relinquishing his hold of the webs to Dehya, who took control with an ease that humbled Soz. Dehya and Kurj blended with a power that Soz had never understood until this moment.

The voice of Devon Majda crackled over her comm. "Cadet Valdoria, we're bringing you out of the Chair." She sounded stunned. In shock. "Imperator Skolia has informed us that he has control of the web."

He. She meant Kurj. Not Jazida. No wonder Devon was shocked. Incredibly, their commander had returned when they all feared he would die.

Yes, ma'am, Soz thought. As grateful as Soz was to have Kurj back, she had too little strength to rejoice aloud. That final effort for her mother had drained her resources.

RELEASED, the Chair thought.

Thank you, Soz answered.

The visor over her head lifted and she saw the observation bay lit by stars and nebulae. It was as if she were out in space, alone. For a moment she just sat. After more than four days in this Chair, she needed to readjust. She had to absorb that her father had become a member of the Dyad.

The Triad.

Soz began to free herself from the med lines. She rolled her shoulders and kneaded the back of her neck. The Chair looked hard, but its surfaces had flexed to keep her muscles from going into spasms from her sitting so long. Sometime earlier it had moved away from the ladder, and it now hung suspended in the center of the bay.

A grinding noise came from above. As she looked up, the hatchway opened. Medics descended into the bay, a trio on a hover platform and two others climbing down the ladder. The trio had an air stretcher, along with monitors and other equipment.

As Soz unfastened her exoskeleton, the platform reached her and hovered in front of the Chair. A medic stepped forward, a stocky woman with streaks of gray in her hair. She wore the green jumpsuit of a Fleet major with the silver insignia of a medic.

Soz saluted, extending her arms with wrists crossed and fists clenched. "Cadet Valdoria, reporting for duty." Her voice sounded rusty and her arms felt too heavy.

The major smiled. "Relax, Cadet. You're off duty."

"Thank you, ma'am." Soz wearily slid toward the platform, which was flush with the bottom of the Chair. She stood up on the hovering disk, then swayed as vertigo swept over her.

The major grasped her arm, offering support. "We have a stretcher."

"That won't be necessary," Soz said. "I'm fine." She felt drained, but she had no intention of letting them carry her out.

The three doctors scanned her with various objects and studied their monitors. No one tried to put Soz on the stretcher. Either they had verified she could manage on her own, or else they respected her pride and didn't insist.

As the platform rose through the starlit bay, Soz looked down at the Chair. **I'll be back.**

A light flickered on the throne, blue then gold. For a moment, Soz thought she sensed approval, but she couldn't be certain. She might be attributing human emotion to an entity that had none.

At the top of the bay, Soz climbed out under her own power. It surprised her to see Devon waiting with several aides. She had expected the general to remain on the bridge. Her presence here told Soz a great deal about the importance Devon attached to her work in the Chair. She had allowed Soz to draw immense amounts of energy from the battle cruiser.

Soz drew herself up and saluted.

Devon inclined her head. "Good work."

"Thank you, ma'am." Soz did her best to remain upright, though her head was swimming. "Is my mother all right?"

"Your mother?"

"We had to . . . pull her home."

"I'm afraid I don't know what you mean."

Soz wasn't sure herself. She was about to pass out.

"Cadet Valdoria." Devon was watching her closely. "Report for duty at thirty-two hours, ship's time. I will check into your mother's whereabouts in the meantime."

Node, how long is that from now? Soz asked.

Eleven hours.

Eleven merciful hours. Soz swallowed. "Thank you, ma'am."

Devon's voice gentled. "Go get some sleep."

"Yes, ma'am." Soz hoped she made it to her quarters before she collapsed. She didn't want them taking her to sick bay.

And when she awoke—she would go to war.

Roca became aware of hands holding her shoulders. Someone had wrapped a blanket around her. That blue—the mist, the ocean—it had been . . . Eldri. Soz and Shannon had been there. Dehya and Kurj, too? It had to have been an illusion. Dehya was lost and Kurj was dying.

Her mind felt dull. Strangers were crouched around her, slender people with silvery eyes and hair. They watched her with unwavering attention, and blue mist curled around them. The hands holding the blanket around her shoulders belonged to a young woman with a fey face. They were sitting in a forest with drifts of glitter all around and bubble trees above. Home?

A voice came softly at her side. "Mother."

Roca turned her head. A man was kneeling next to her, his face creased with concern. "Shani?" she asked. Shannon was a boy, and this was a man, but she felt sure they were one and the same.

His eyes filled with moisture. "You will be all right. I promise." He said it softly, with pain, as if she wasn't going to be all right at all.

"Where is this?" she whispered. Her voice was so hoarse from screaming, she could barely speak.

"The Blue Dale Mountains."

"The what?" The names meant nothing.

"It's all right." Tears slid down his face. "We'll take care of you. You're safe now."

"Thank you," she whispered.

But she would never feel safe again.

Nothing populated this volume of space but interstellar dust, cosmic radiation, and stray chunks of rock. There were no settlements, no habitats, nothing. No living entity recorded the moment when an ESComm probe dropped out of inversion into real space. Then a Starsprinter appeared, the fastest of the ESComm warships. Within seconds, hundreds of small ships were darting through the deserted region of space.

More ships appeared. Big ships.

The ESComm force came on, huge numbers of ships dropping into real space every second, vessels ranging in size from tiny booms all the way up to mammoth Starslammers and the indomitable battle cruisers. Solos accompanied the invasion force, as deadly and versatile as their Jag counterparts, but lacking the advantage of the Kyle meshes. The ships came on, a thousand, ten thousand, one hundred thousand. When they finished gathering, half a million ships spread across space in a giant wedge aimed straight into the heart of Skolia.

No Skolian had seen them appear.

No living Skolian.

One tiny ISC probe recorded their arrival.

The sleeping giant awoke.

Like a mythological leviathan stirring from a slumber of eons, Kurj Skolia slowly opened his eyes. As he sat up, monitors flashed lights, alarms blared, and frantic medics ran into the room.

He merely nodded.

Kurj ordered them to take him to the Chair. His doctors tried to refuse. Just a few moments earlier, they had believed he was near death. He ignored their protests. Being a military dictator had its advantages, even if officially he had less authority than the elected civilian body that governed Skolia. Few dared to refuse him. His civilization was, after all, called an Imperialate.

They soon left the hospital.

A full retinue accompanied him. His anxious doctors, his military aides, numerous web techs, and his Abaj bodyguards—they all came with him. A military Class One flyer took them to a vault secreted high in the Red Mountains. It had been there for five millennia, and would probably survive for another five.

Inside, the Triad Chair waited.

A sense of acknowledgment came from the Chair as Kurj walked into the vault, surrounded by his people. The web techs fastened him into the throne. He sat with his spine straight against its back, his face drawn, his skin sallow, his powerful body thinner than before. Holographic starlight from the dome overhead glinted on his metallic skin. Control panels surrounded him, and the doctors tended him with meds, lines, and monitors. The silver exoskeleton folded around his body and the visor hung poised above his head. He set his muscular arms on the armrests of the throne and looked out at the people attendant on his session.

Satisfaction showed in his gold metallic gaze.

The Military Key had returned.

An insistent alarm woke Soz. She peered blearily at the clock on her console, about a handspan from her bunk. She had slept four hours.

"Valdoria here," she said, trying to sound crisp instead of groggy, and failing miserably.

Devon responded. "Cadet Valdoria, this is Captain Majda. We've heard from Diesha. Imperator Skolia wants you back in the Triad Chair. He'll have orders for you."

Soz wanted to groan, but she kept quiet. If Kurj could be in command only four hours after coming out of a coma, she could damn well manage to wake up. "Right away, ma'am." She dragged herself out of bed and got dressed.

The Triad Chamber was well down the cylinder. Soz took the magrail and arrived within minutes. A group of techs waited for her, but she shook her head at them. The Chair just tolerated her presence; if she brought in too many people, it might rebuff her. When the techs protested, Soz remained firm, and they soon gave up trying to change her mind. Better to let her go alone than risk the Chair's refusal to help.

As Soz descended the ladder, she felt the Chair's awareness. The techs closed the hatch above, isolating her in the bay. Slowed by fatigue, she reached the massive throne and slid into it. The visor lowered and the exoskeleton folded around her.

ATTENDING.

It felt different. Deeper. More powerful. More like . . . Kurj.

Imperator Skolia requires my help. Soz thought. She tried to hide her fatigue, but with this close of a mental link, she doubted she succeeded.

LINKING.

Suddenly Soz was in the War Room on the Orbiter.

Soz. Kurj's acknowledgment rumbled in her mind.

Cadet Valdoria reporting for duty. Then she added, **It's good to see you back, sir.** That was, perhaps, the understatement of the century.

Good to be back. For all that Kurj seemed drained, his thoughts formed with clarity and strength. **I need your support for the communication meshes I'm creating among our defending forces.**

Yes, sir! Even under normal circumstances, it would have been difficult to maintain such an extensive set of links among so many ships. Normally Kurj could have managed it, but given his condition, it didn't surprise her that he wanted assistance.

She checked the status of *Roca's Pride* and its flotilla. Devon had over a thousand war craft under her command. Their orders: proceed to the Metropoli star system. It was the most heavily populated region in the Imperialate. The majority of the ISC forces would engage the invaders in a distant region of space, far from the settled areas, but if any invaders slipped past the defenses and penetrated this deep into Skolian territory, Devon's forces would be here to take them on.

Ready? Kurj asked.

Yes, sir, Soz answered.

Data flooded her mind from the ISC defense forces. Soz lost her awareness of the Chair and became a part of those distant ships. Among that deluge of information, she found data from a probe that had detected the invasion force.

Yes, Kurj thought. His next command didn't just go to her; he sent it out over all the meshes to the ISC defense forces ready to engage the invaders.

Kurj said, simply, **NOW.**

Four hundred thousand ISC ships dropped out of inversion at exactly the same moment—in the midst of half a million ESComm ships.

Waves of multiple independently targeted reentry vehicles, or MIRVs, preceded the ISC forces at relativistic speeds. The defenders hurtled among the invaders, firing Annihilators, antimatter beams that created brutal radiation and particle cascades. They used the relativistic exhaust from their ships as weapons. The tau missiles they released were miniature starships that relentlessly plotted and replotted courses as they hunted their targets.

The war was engaged.

Within four seconds, the ISC defenders had destroyed a fourth of the invasion force, cutting the ESComm numbers to 375 thousand ships while the ISC numbers only decreased to 350 thousand. But the element of surprise bought ISC little more than those four seconds. It took the invaders that long to recoup and marshal their resources.

A maelstrom of energies roiled through space as the combatants wielded forces that could have slagged entire moons. ESComm had more firepower and ships; ISC had more speed. Without the Kyle web, the defenders would have had no real chance; even as it was, a gambler would have been hard pressed to lay odds.

Soz monitored the combat from her Chair, holding the lines of communications among the ISC ships. The battle raced through space at close to the speed of light, no two craft at precisely the same velocity in either direction or speed. They fired beam weapons as if they were jousting. Time dilated, passing at different rates for different ships, depending on their relative speeds. Lengths appeared to contract as ships shot by each other; in three dimensions, they passed like giant coins flipping over. No unaugmented human brain could handle such combat; only the EI brains of the ships could respond fast enough to compensate for the relativistic effects.

Ships that survived the first wave of the ambush came around to try again. Many were drones controlled by EIs. They blanketed space with clouds of smart-dust. It corroded the enemy ships, but recognized friendly vessels by coded signals and left them alone. EI analysts in both fleets strove to break the codes for their opponent's dust and missiles, and turn them against the very military that had created them.

Vessels continually jumped in and out of quasis, or quantum stasis. A quasis field fixed the quantum wavefunction of the ship and everything in it, including any crew. The ship didn't freeze; its particles continued to vibrate, rotate, and otherwise behave as they had when the quasis began. But nothing could alter their quantum state. While quasis operated, a vessel became a rigid body that could neither deform nor explode. It also protected humans from the killing accelerations of combat. But ships could only endure so many hits before the quasis failed. Annihilators ate away at the field faster than missiles, compensating for the drawback of beam weapons, which unlike smart missiles, couldn't chase their targets.

Embedded in his Triad Chair, Kurj created and shaped the

links for those hundreds of thousands of ISC ships. Soz supported his work. The battle flashed by at phenomenal speeds and left an expanding cone of radiation and debris in its wake throughout a huge volume of space. Ions spiraled along the magnetic fields that shielded vessels against Annihilator fire. Ships exploded in geysers of debris, and space became a chaos of oscillating fields.

An ESComm Wasp drove its antimatter stinger into an ISC Thunderbolt—and detonated. Plasma tore the Thunderbolt apart from within, annihilating everything it touched, and gamma radiation ripped through the decks. Soz was connected to the ship through her mental links—and she *felt* the deaths of the crew. With a choked cry, she clutched the arms of the chair. Tendons stood out on her hands.

One minute after the battle had begun, ISC had lost over half its ships, down to 175 thousand. The ESComm numbers had dropped to 190 thousand. By that time, Soz was so sensitized to the mesh, she couldn't shield her mind. It hit her harder than other psions. They lost a Jagernaut when his fighter exploded—and Soz screamed as if she had died herself.

With sweat soaking her jumpsuit and her hands contorted into claws, Soz forced herself to keep going. She thought of Althor, who had been deep in a four-way link with the other members of his squadron during battle. Their deaths must have ripped apart his mind. Somehow he had kept going, and in doing so he had saved billions of lives. She prayed he hadn't suffered in those last moments before he died.

A memory jumped into her mind: the first time she had sat in this Chair, it had told her that her mother forgot her birthday. And Althor.

Why Althor?

Devon Majda's voice came over her ear comm. "Cadet Valdoria, I need you to work with this flotilla."

Disoriented, Soz focused on the meshes for *Roca's Pride* and its attendant ships. As soon as she stopped concentrating on the distant ISC defense fleet, her connections with them weakened. The mesh that coordinated their ships fluctuated, links vanishing and reforming by the millions every second.

She couldn't monitor all of that *and* keep track of the mesh here. It was too much.

Captain Majda, Soz thought. **If I switch to this flotilla, I'll start losing my links to the ISC defense fleet.**

"We're about to go into combat," Devon said.

Bloody hell! **Display flotilla and defense force stats,** Soz thought.

Two grids formed in her mindscape, one for the flotilla here and one for the much larger and more distant defense force wielded by ISC against the invasion. The grid for the flotilla was partially overlaid on the one for the defense force, but they had different textures, metallic for the flotilla and stone for the defenders. Each bar symbolized a ship's system. Many glowed yellow, warning of incipient collapses; others had already gone red for failed systems.

Show hostiles attacking *Roca's Pride,* Soz thought.

A display appeared in a corner of her mindscape; ES-Comm ships were racing out of inversion, headed for the flotilla in a solid angle that was fast expanding in space. Only a sliver of the invasion fleet had made it this far, about two thousand ships, but it was twice as many as Devon commanded. The invaders had no Kyle links; with the more limited information gleaned from their probes, they hadn't pinpointed the flotilla. They were coming out a full light-minute distant and in ragged formation, spread out over time and space.

As the two forces hurtled toward each other, Soz scanned the grid with a familiarity gained from her practices at DMA. She quickly located the most urgent problem; the environmental systems on this battle cruiser were having problems again, as when the Kyle nodes had collapsed. Environmental had little to do with communications, but the damn enviro systems were piggybacked on the comm systems because it saved energy. It was a perennial weak point in ISC engineering. When the cruiser began taking hits, environmental would be the first to slip.

The grid in her mindscape for the distant battle flickered and dimmed. Her links with the defenders were starting to fail.

Kurj's thought cut through Kyle space. **Cadet Valdoria, keep those links firm.**

Yes, sir. Soz refocused on the defense grid and fixed errors in the flow of communications. At the same time, she sent a message to Devon. **Captain, I can't maintain the web for this flotilla and my links to the defense fleet at the same time. I have to let one go.**

"We're compensating as best we can," Devon said. "But if you release our links, environmental units will fail. This cruiser will get damn cold and we may start losing breathable atmosphere."

"Understood." Soz directed a thought to Kurj. **Sir, we're under attack. If I don't work here, it could damage our flotilla.**

Fatal damage? he asked.

Not immediately.

If you withdraw my backup, I could lose Firestorm cruisers.

What to do? Soz thought of the exercise at DMA last year where she had needed to decide: fix local environmental systems or the SCAD defenses for more distant ships. She had chosen environmental and lost more people than Kurj, who had fixed the SCAD systems. But she had lost fewer than the other cadets who had chosen the SCAD. Had she lost more than Kurj because she lacked his experience or because his was the better choice? *Which one?*

More bars on both the flotilla and defense grids were turning red. She couldn't wait; she had to decide now.

Soz sent an accelerated thought to Kurj. **Sir, request permission to focus on flotilla.**

Explain, he thought curtly.

The environmental failures would affect the crew's ability to perform. We are the last substantial force before the invaders reach Metropoli. If we don't rebuff them, they will attack our most heavily populated civilian center.

He paused the barest fraction of a second. **Permission granted.**

Soz snapped her attention back to the flotilla. Data poured

erratically through her mindscape, and her node absorbed the reports. As she worked on strengthening links among the various systems, the data flow became less ragged. Within seconds, red bars were changing color: blue for systems under repair, gold for partial repairs, and green for fully operational systems.

Devon's voice came into her ear. "Good work, Valdoria."

Soz didn't answer. No words could compensate for the hideous decision she had just made. On the grid for the distant ISC defenders, more bars were turning red or vanishing altogether. For every bar she repaired in the flotilla grid, one went dark for the defense. She died inside, knowing what those bars meant. Lives were being lost because she had chosen to protect environmental units. She hadn't understood what Kurj had tried to tell her last year, after that DMA exercise. People hadn't died then.

Here it became real.

Only a few seconds had passed during her exchange with Kurj. Statistics streamed into her mindscape. The ESComm force had 2,036 warships; Devon had only 998.

Forty-six seconds after the invaders appeared, one of the leading ships engaged a Jag in the ISC flotilla. Within moments, the outer layers of the two fleets were in combat. With her mind boosted into accelerated mode, Soz coordinated thousands of messages every tenth of a second. She couldn't follow each one individually; she monitored the overall grid in her mind. When she fixed errors, the Chair translated her work into commands for the associated ships. Her DMA training barely scratched the surface of what she needed. She felt like someone who had only learned to multiply being asked to solve quantum field equations.

The battle moved through space in a cone of ships and debris expanding toward Metropoli. Drones jousted with beams; tau missiles and MIRVs hunted targets; and Annihilators ripped apart matter with antimatter plasmas. The battle skimmed along the edges of the star system, which consisted of a single hot yellow star with three gas giants, each shepherding an asteroid belt, and two small planets closer in— including Metropoli.

The grid in Soz's mindscape flexed and warped as the fighting raged. When an ESComm missile detonated against an ISC Cobra, it registered as a flare of red light along one bar. The Cobra's quasis had weakened to almost nothing. Soz sent a repair tug to the damaged ship and linked the Cobra's EI to those of several other ships that could offer aid as it repaired itself. The red light on the bar turned yellow; the Cobra would survive.

All over the grid, other red flares were erupting. Sometimes she could get them back to yellow or even green; other times the bar vanished altogether. When that bar represented a crewed ship, Soz groaned as their deaths pounded her mind, and she reeled as ship after ship detonated.

After two minutes of fighting, only 436 ships remained in Devon's flotilla. They had lost more than half their vessels. The invaders had fared even worse, with about seven hundred ships left, a third of their initial force. Gritting her teeth, Soz kept her focus on the links among the ISC forces, repairing breaks, straightening distortions, doing everything within her power—and the Chair's—to save lives.

Soz had no links to the ESComm ships, so she couldn't input much about their forces into her mindscape. She had a grid representing them, but it was blurred and sketchy, no more than a vague sense of their meshes.

She turned her focus to the Chair. **Can you break into the ESComm mesh systems?**

A sense of pause answered her, but nothing else. Either she hadn't asked the right question or she hadn't asked in the right way.

She tried a different tack. **Scramble enemy grid.**

Nothing.

Soz felt the sweat on her forehead despite the visor and the medical lines monitoring her. She imagined the ESComm grid bending and melting, but nothing changed. She had no idea if the Chair could even reach the meshes of the invading force. The two forces continued to decrease, the flotilla down to 374 and the invaders at about 650. The attrition of ESComm ships was faster than for ISC—but it wasn't enough. At this rate, the invaders would destroy the Metropoli defenses before all of their ships were gone. It would leave Metropoli vulnerable. The planet and its star system had called up their defenses to join the combat, and the sides were closely matched, but from Soz's reading of the grids and the projections she calculated, ESComm would prevail.

Metropoli would fall.

Help us, she thought to the Chair.

An indistinct sense of strain came to her: the Chair couldn't connect well with her mind. Whether it was because she wasn't in the Triad or because she was just too different, Soz had no idea. But this wasn't working. It couldn't *fit* with her. She needed more memory; or not more, but memory of the right kind.

Soz thought of the red-robed women known as Memories on her home world. Although rare in the general population, they were a familiar presence at her father's castle. The Bard was a historian and a judge; as such, he worked closely with them. The Lyshrioli could neither read nor write; the Memories used their holographic minds to store knowledge. Soz's ISC doctors believed Soz had inherited the genes that produced a Memory. It wasn't as useful a trait for her as for people on Lyshriol; everyone in her life as a cadet could read and write just fine. The illiteracy of the Lyshrioli didn't seem deliberate, though. Scholars believed Soz's people had been designed to mimic an ancient computer. Maybe they were only partially right. Perhaps the intent had been to increase their ability to work with the ancient Ruby machines.

She tried again. **I am your Memory.**

Nothing changed in her link to the Chair.

Soz concentrated on the image of a Memory she knew, Shaliece, an elderly woman, one of her father's advisors at Castle Windward. While the battle between Devon's forces and ESComm raged in microsecond pulses, Soz strove to calm her mind into the clarity she had always sensed from Shaliece. The Memory wouldn't have said, *Help me.* She would have said, *Show me how to help myself.*

Soz thought, **Show me what I can do.**

BEHOLD, the Chair thought.

Soz diligently tried to behold something. Nothing changed.

Well, almost nothing. Her view of the grids sharpened. The Chair had improved the resolution of her mindscape. No, that wasn't it. It had accessed the extra memory in her node.

Whispers tugged at her awareness like a conversation half overheard. After a fraction of a second, she realized the Chair had extended her capacity to link to the ISC flotilla ships. It hadn't managed to link her to any ESComm meshes, but it had improved her ability to work with her own forces. She became aware of smaller anomalies in the grid, finer shadings of color. Taking a deep breath, she went deeper into her mindscape and redoubled her efforts to optimize the ISC forces.

Her heightened awareness didn't manifest in any dramatic manner. She didn't explode the remaining ESComm forces or rip apart their communications. No spectacular displays of energy suddenly appeared. She managed nothing more than a slightly improved sensing capability for the ISC ships. They became a shade faster at evading weapons fire and a shade better at hitting their targets. It was a small change—

But it was enough.

The rate of loss decreased for the ISC flotilla and increased for the invaders. The ISC forces dropped to 321 ships and ESComm to about 530.

Then a Jag exploded—and Soz screamed. She was more closely connected to the telepaths, especially with the Chair expanding her awareness. She wanted to curl up into a fetal ball and quit. But she couldn't or many more would die. She forced herself to keep going, holding links within the flotilla together much as she had held together the Kyle web before. A shiver tingled through her mind, a whisper of precognition, perhaps real, perhaps false: someday she would do this on a much greater scale. She pushed the distracting thought aside and focused on the flotilla mesh.

ISC 288 ships: ESComm 453.

Soz dimly heard sirens, and a large bar on her grid erupted in red. She concentrated on the rupture, and data poured into her mind. The quasis that protected the battle cruiser was weakening. Deck thirty-five had taken a severe Annihilator hit. Soz threw her support into the systems directing resources and repairs for the damaged area. She sped up the summons racing through the cruiser's mesh, calling medics to the injured.

ISC 253: ESComm 386.

Another alarm was going off, this one closer. A psicon in a corner of Soz's mindscape warned that the medical systems watching her had recorded a dangerously high blood pressure and pulse. It urgently advised her to report to the nearest medical station. Soz just gritted her teeth.

ISC 239: ESComm 298.

An ESComm Asp fired a tau missile at an ISC Jack-knife. The Jack's quasis failed and the missile tore it apart from within. In desperation, the ISC crew rammed the dying Jack straight into the Asp. The two ships detonated—and a hundred deaths wrenched through Soz's mind. She cried in agony, in shock, in grief. This battle had taken everything she had, even resources she hadn't known she possessed, and it wasn't enough. Their people kept dying and nothing she did would stop it. Never again would she see military strategy as only a puzzle to solve. Warfare had taken on a crushingly human aspect.

ISC 214: ESComm 213.

ISC 199: ESComm 118.

ISC 182: ESComm 43.

As the ESComm numbers plummeted, a sob escaped Soz. The flotilla was going to make it. This sliver of the invasion would fail to reach Metropoli. Had it succeeded, it could have committed an unprecedented massacre. That bloodbath was averted by the barest margin.

ISC 180: ESComm 12.

ISC 179: ESComm 0.

The remains of the flotilla limped into Metropoli, 178 ships and the cruiser. Soz heard voices over her comm, some excited, some weary, all relieved. She couldn't join their celebration. She didn't know—and never would—whether or not her decision to withdraw support from Kurj's force had made the difference in achieving that hard-fought victory.

Soz returned her attention to the distant struggle between the main invasion and defense fleets, the battle Kurj was directing from his Triad Chair. She resumed her work for Kurj, and she sent reports to Devon Majda, who transmitted updates to the flotilla and Metropoli. So it was that they all heard—and cheered—when the news came:

ESComm was in retreat.

The rest of it came more slowly, and silenced the cheers. ISC had taken gruesome losses, a third of a million ships.

Reeling with grief, Soz remembered Kurj's words from last year: *The problem, Soz, is that to lead well you have to know how to lose. You can't always win. You can't always be right.* She had thought she knew what he was telling her, but she had been so very wrong. She would have to live with a bitter knowledge for the rest of her life, that in defending the flotilla and Metropoli, she had condemned an untold number of men and women to die.

The worst of it was, she would never know if she had made the right choice.

19

Baylow Station

Eldrin stood in one of ten long queues formed by the refugees outside the starport, leading to a row of outdoor gates. People were crowding off the many ships putting into Baylow and coming here, thousands of them, with heat beating on their backs.

Sweat plastered Eldrin's shirt to his skin. The air smelled strange, too sweet. This world had been terraformed, so the air should be breathable, but it made him nauseous. Nor did the gravity help. He felt too light. After his ordeal on the ship, he was queasy, weak, lightheaded. His exhaustion went deep. Although bearable now, his craving for phorine remained. He would live with the miserable specter of its power over him for the rest of his life.

He had the two children with him, and he stood holding the girl's hand. The boy stood next to her, trying to be brave but obviously scared. About seven, he was old enough to have a better understanding of their situation. He reminded Eldrin of Taquinil, with his dark hair and alert gaze. What if something had happened to Taquinil? Or Dehya? He had to believe they were all right.

He spoke to the children in Flag, as he had many times today. "I'm Eldrin." He touched the boy's shoulder. "And you?"

The boy regarded him with solemn eyes and the girl clutched his hand. Neither had spoken in days.

"Ah, well," Eldrin murmured. "I would be afraid, too."

The girl moved closer to him. He laid an arm on her shoulders and wished he could find their guardians.

The line moved forward. Restless with the wait, Eldrin thought, **Allegro, do you have any data about this place?**

His node answered. I have a summary from the EI on the freighter. It accessed visual centers of his brain, and a translucent display appeared in the air. Baylow orbited a yellow sun, which orbited a bigger, cooler star. The yellow sun appeared white from the planet, and the distant star was like a brass stud, smaller in the sky despite its large size because it was so far away. Allegro estimated that "day" here lasted tens, even hundreds of hours.

Right now, both suns were up. The sky had a blue-green tinge, which bothered Eldrin. Sweat dripped down his neck, and he tugged at his collar. He had on a white shirt and gray slacks, all self-cleaning. The captain of the freighter had also let his passengers break open soap-bots from the ship's mess, and Kaywood had tended Eldrin with them during the four-day ride. The doctor seemed to think this was a small thing, but it had made an immense difference to his patient.

A woman in front of Eldrin pulled up her hair and fanned her neck. The girl with Eldrin fidgeted with her brother's shirt, which hung out of his trousers, and he glared at her. They moved another few steps toward the gate. The official there was a member of the Imperial Relief Allocation Service, a civilian group run by the government. The blue and white circle of the IRAS insignia gleamed on the shoulders of her khaki jumpsuit.

The closer they came to the gate, the more ill-at-ease Eldrin felt. He never spoke to anyone outside the Imperial court. It was one of the few things his family, the Assembly, and ISC agreed on; the less time the Ruby Consort spent in public, the better. He valued his privacy, and ISC liked it because it made him easier to protect. On Lyshriol he hadn't been guarded night and day, but he had just been a farm boy, far less a target for abduction or assassination. Here, without bodyguards, he felt uncertain. Anonymity was his shield.

He also wished his bodyguards were here for another reason; it would mean they were all right. He was responsible for their absence. He spent a great deal of time with the taciturn giant. He liked and respected them. He prayed someone at the port had seen to their needs better than he in the tumult of the evacuation.

No one here was likely to recognize him, though, given how rarely he appeared in public. Discretion seemed his best course. If he revealed himself, they would give him attention and resources other people needed. He had caused enough trouble for the refugees crammed in that cargo hold, forced to spend days with him while he screamed his throat raw. That was done with. The limited resources here should go to others.

The IRAS officer at the gate was dark-haired and tall like most Skolians, though nowhere near as imposing as the Abaj. She waved the woman ahead of them through the gate and beckoned to Eldrin.

This was it. As he went to the gate, he told himself he had no reason to be nervous. She looked him over, including his disheveled hair and wrinkled clothes. Even with top-notch nanos in the cloth, his shirt and trousers couldn't erase the effects of the past four days. He didn't know how he appeared, but he doubted it was good.

She spoke curtly in Flag. "Are these your children?" Her harsh tone startled him, and for the first time he realized they might take away the boy and girl. Given how scared they were, he doubted it would be a good idea, but he had no claim to them.

"Well?" the officer demanded.

"They were separated from their parents." He answered in Flag, his voice thick from his strained vocal cords. "I'm taking care of them."

She studied him with an appraising gaze. "Any injuries? We have doctors available."

He had seen how the officials here rushed Kaywood through processing because they needed doctors to treat the injured. Eldrin saw no reason to take up any medic's valuable time. His head felt as if it had been through a rock crusher, but he was fine now. Or maybe not fine, but well enough.

The officer frowned at him. "Can't you speak?"

He jerked at her hostile tone. Instinctively, he dropped his mental barriers and probed her mood. She wasn't an empath, so he only gleaned an impression, but it was enough to make him flush. She was sexually attracted to him and feared reprimands if she slipped up and let it show. So she was overcompensating.

"All right," she muttered to herself. "He won't talk. I'll deal with it." She flicked her finger through an icon above her holoboard and a new page appeared on its display.

"I'm sorry," Eldrin said. "I'm a little shaky."

Her posture relaxed. "It's not surprising, after all this." She unclipped the light stylus from her board. "Name?"

"Eldrin Jarac Valdoria." He omitted his fourth name. Skolia. Only one family in the Skolian Imperialate could claim it. His other names weren't likely to identify him, but his ID would trigger a flag in her system and spur a discreet notification to ISC.

She marked the form with her stylus. "Home?"

"Parthonia." He gave her the address of the mansion where he and Dehya sometimes stayed in Selei City. The Sunrise Palace in the hills had no address.

She directed her light stylus toward him. "This will scan your retinas, for your ID. If family or friends are searching for you, they can locate this record in our databases after the Kyle web comes back up."

He squinted as light played over his eyes. "The web is down?"

"Parts of it." Her voice was losing its edge. "Or it might be us. We've had problems, having to set up this station too fast. We don't know what is happening out there."

Eldrin hoped the problems came from here rather than the Dyad. His certainty that they had been in trouble, in *agony,* could have come from the horror of his withdrawal, but he feared it was real.

"Do you have medical training?" she asked. "Engineering or communications? We're short on personnel."

"No. Nothing." Eldrin wished he had more to offer. Since his marriage to Dehya, he had spent most of his time caring for his son or creating his music. Even if he had been able to sing, which he no longer could, it had about as much utility here as mud.

The officer peered at the children. "What are your names?"

They hung back, the girl halfway behind Eldrin and the boy close at his side.

"I'm going to shine a light on your eyes," the woman told them. "It won't hurt." She scanned them with the stylus and recorded the results. Then she spoke to Eldrin. "You can go on through."

He inclined his head. "Thank you."

She gave him an odd look. He wasn't certain why. All he could tell from her mood was that most people didn't nod in such a formal manner. He didn't know what else to do; he had no referent for Skolian customs except the protocols of the Imperial Court that he and Dehya entertained at the palace.

Eldrin led the children through the gate and onto a casecrete plaza. Its brilliant white surface reflected the sunlight. Many people were crossing it, and most looked as dazed as he felt. Beyond the plaza, meadows of stubbly grass spread out with the synthetic look of plants engineered for durability. IRAS workers were helping refugees set up tents and medical stations. People poured into the camp; by the time the deluge ended, the population here could be in the tens of thousands. He hoped it was that high. Over three million people lived in Selei City and its outlying areas. If the attack had continued as it began, few would survive who didn't go underground or offworld.

Eldrin wandered with the children, unsure what to do. Surrounded by so many people, he intensified his mental barriers, but their bewildered dismay still pressed against him. Some were in pain, injured in the attack or the rush to flee the city. He felt their distress like mental blows.

He stopped and gazed across the camp. Everywhere, people were sitting, toiling, staring. He caught sight of a familiar figure, Lane Kaywood, working in a makeshift infirmary. Patients surrounded the physician. A sudden thought came to Eldrin; he *did* have something to offer, a way he could be of some small use.

He smiled at the children. "Shall we go see the doctor?"

They looked up at him, silent. The boy nodded gravely.

The infirmary consisted of little more than a table strewn with equipment and tarps held up by poles. Patients lay on blankets. Kaywood was kneeling next to an elderly man in a bloodstained shirt.

Eldrin stopped a short distance away and spoke to the children. "You two sit here, so we don't disturb them."

The girl clutched his hand, her gray eyes wide.

"It's all right," Eldrin said. "I'm not going away." He put her hand in the boy's. "This big fellow can look after you."

The boy pulled himself up straighter, and the girl eyed him with a skepticism that made Eldrin want to laugh, it reminded him so much of Soz. They sat on the tarp and regarded him with a trust that astonished Eldrin, given what they had seen him go through on the freighter.

As Eldrin turned toward Kaywood, the doctor's elderly patient groaned. Kaywood knelt and pressed an air syringe against his neck. Eldrin hesitated, reluctant to intrude. Listening to them, he gathered that several of the man's ribs had broken and he had sustained internal injuries when his hover car crashed during the evacuation.

Eldrin went over and knelt next to them. "I can help."

Kaywood glanced up with a start. Strain showed around his eyes, even more than on the ship. "Do you have training as a medic?" Hope surged in his voice.

"Not exactly," Eldrin said. "I've biofeedback training."

"Ah." Kaywood seemed to sag again. "Yes, it can help you."

Eldrin spoke self-consciously. "I'm a psion. I feel and send emotions, sometimes even thoughts. It works with biofeedback, too. I can affect others as well as myself." As a Rhon heir, he had trained all his life to develop his abilities.

Kaywood blinked. "What can you do?"

"Ease pain. Aid healing."

The elderly man regarded him with bleared eyes. "What is your name, son?"

"Eldrin." He ached from the man's discomfort. "And yours, sir?"

"Rory Canterman Willham."

"My pleasure at your company, Gentlesir Willham." Eldrin used the formal cadences of the Imperial Court.

Willham gave him an approving look. "Nice to see our youth showing some manners."

"Do you need anything special to work?" Kaywood asked Eldrin.

"No. You can continue treating him." Eldrin indicated the children. The boy was watching him and the girl had laid down, curled next to her brother. "I won't be able to look after them, though."

"I'll see they aren't left unattended." Kaywood's expression was carefully neutral. Eldrin had a sense the doctor didn't really believe a psion could help, but was willing to try anything at this point.

As Kaywood cut away his patient's bloodied shirt, Eldrin sat cross-legged on the other side of Willham, who studied him with faded blue eyes. Although Willham made no sound, Eldrin felt the pain splintering through the man's body. The medicine Kaywood had administered either hadn't worked or wasn't enough. Unfortunately, medical supplies were limited.

Eldrin bent his head and closed his eyes. He imagined blue mist spreading through his mind until his sense of place and time blurred. He linked his internal node with the picoweb produced by the nanomeds within his body, augmenting his natural abilities with his technological enhancements. The meds were depleted after laboring so hard during his withdrawal, but he had enough left to establish a weak link. Then he turned his concentration outward, similar to the way he would send thoughts to another person. He shut out the creaks and clatter of camp and focused on Willham.

Eldrin sank into a universe of muscles and blood vessels. He knew only damaged tissues, ripped arteries and veins, the sharp edges of broken ribs. He went deeper, to where molecular catalysts aided repairs and carriers ferried nutrients or hauled away cellular debris. He submerged into the chemicals striving to heal, those molecules the body naturally carried and those Kaywood had injected. He followed threads of pain to Willham's brain and damped the neurological centers that registered them. He helped ragged membranes knit together. He supported energy cycles that provided strength. Wilhelm's full recovery would take more than Eldrin could give, but he could aid the natural healing processes.

After a while Eldrin tired and his concentration lagged. Surfacing from his trance, he opened his eyes to find the light had become dimmer, as if a thin layer of clouds covered the sky. Willham was asleep, his torso bandaged, his hair damp and smelling of soap. A medical monitor hummed by his head.

Disoriented, Eldrin rubbed his eyes. When had all that happened? Although no clouds covered the sky, it had darkened into a deeper shade of aqua. Only one sun was up, a small disk in the sky. The camp had become a city of tents. People talked in quiet voices or sat staring at nothing, as if they couldn't yet take in what had happened. The children were sleeping under a blanket. Packages of food lay next to them and a hologame that glimmered with starships.

"Welcome back," a voice said behind him.

Eldrin turned as Kaywood crouched next to him. The doctor set his hand on Willham's forehead. "No fever. I was worried his wounds were infected. But he seems all right."

"That's good." Eldrin tried to sharpen his fuzzy mind. "What happened to the other sun?" His voice was thick, and he slipped into his natural speech patterns, both his Trillian burr and Iotic accent.

Kaywood squinted at him. "Say again?"

Eldrin spoke more carefully. "The sun is gone."

"Ah. Yes. The yellow one set."

Bewildered, Eldrin said, "It couldn't have crossed the sky that fast."

"It took about eight hours."

Eldrin gaped at him. He had been in a trance for *eight hours*? No wonder he was worn out. "It hardly felt like any time at all."

"Maybe it's a lingering effect of the phorine."

"Perhaps." Sometimes after he had taken it, he had spent hours staring at a work of holoart or swirls in a glass of wine. Phorine. Node-bliss. Never again would he know its ecstasy. He would crave it forever, but he was done with that lie. It had turned his days into heaven and left him in hell.

Kaywood was watching Eldrin with an odd look. "It's amazing how fast Willham is healing."

Eldrin wondered at his strange expression. Kaywood seemed more reticent with him than on the freighter. Eldrin had dropped his mental barriers to help Willham, and it left him more open to the doctor. Although Kaywood was trying to guard his mind, he had little experience with psions. He also had natural empathy, as did many healers, and his mood came through clearly. Awe.

"What you did," Kaywood said. "It was incredible."

His reaction disconcerted Eldrin. "It isn't much. I'm just glad I could help."

Kaywood started to speak, then stopped.

"Yes?" Eldrin asked.

"If you feel up to it—" He indicated the people sleeping on tarps in the infirmary. "I've more patients."

Eldrin felt the haze of their minds. He wasn't close enough to distinguish any one person clearly, but he sensed their need. "I will do what I can." Self-conscious, he added, "I need a meal first. And rest." He had lost everything he ate on the freighter.

"Yes, certainly," Kaywood said. "It must take a lot out of you to do such healing."

"I—it's not something I talk about." How it felt to be an empath, that vulnerable sense of living without a skin, had always been intensely personal. He wasn't comfortable discussing it even with Dehya, let alone someone he hardly knew.

Kaywood didn't push. Instead he ushered Eldrin to a spare corner of a tarp. The children were awake now, sitting side by side, watching him with uncertain gazes. When Eldrin beckoned, they scrambled to their feet and ran over. They hugged him, and he put his arms around their shoulders.

Kaywood smiled. "Your children are charming."

"They aren't actually mine," Eldrin said. "I shared my hammock with them on the freighter."

"I had wondered. They didn't seem to know you that well. But they stayed with you during the entire trip."

Eldrin couldn't fathom why they gravitated toward someone they had seen in the throes of agony. His withdrawal must have been terrifying. He looked down at them, one under each of his arms. "Why me?" he murmured.

They watched him with that inexplicable trust.

"From what people told me, you were kind to them," Kaywood said. "Even after you were ill." He smiled at the girl. "I sometimes think children have an innate ability to recognize goodness."

Eldrin spoke quietly. "Thank you." It meant a great deal to him that someone he respected saw him in a positive light, all the more so because the doctor gave it genuinely, with no idea he was speaking to a Ruby Heir.

After Eldrin ate dinner, he tried to sleep, but his thoughts went around and around, keeping him awake. He had spent the last six years confused. At times he was happier than he would have thought possible; other times he couldn't cope with his life. He was lonely. He had gone from a big, close-knit family to living in an empty palace with a wife who was gone for days on end. His marriage to Dehya was wrong, forbidden, maybe illegal, but he would die before he gave her up. For all that they shouldn't have had a child, he loved Taquinil more than life. The Assembly and Imperial Court saw him as deficient and inferior, and he often feared they were right. The alcohol and the phorine had made it easier to forget why he loathed himself.

He was too young for Dehya, too inexperienced, too closely related, too slow, too unpolished, and too confused, but somehow, incredibly, she loved him anyway. And she had given him Taquinil. Seeing these children look at him with the same trust as his son, he swore he would make himself better, that he would become a person his son could admire, even someone he could admire himself.

White light.

The Bard became aware of a diffuse glow. Squinting, he made out the blurred outlines of a circular chamber with metallic struts around its perimeter. He was . . . in a chair. But this was the wrong place. How had he come to this Dyad Chamber? Techs were unfastening his exoskeleton, taking out lines that fed him, reading monitors, clustering around. He rubbed his eyes. He distinctly remembered sitting in the command chair in the War Room. Yet here he was in the Dyad Chair.

No. Not Dyad. Triad.

Eldrinson didn't claim to understand the ramifications of forming a three-way powerlink; he knew only that in becoming a Key, he had come home. Scenes from his experience with the Chair swirled in his mind: Soz, holding the web; Shannon, half in the blue; Dehya, brilliance and clarity; Kurj, immense power.

Roca.

Roca! The memory hit like a blow. He tried to lunge out of the Chair, though he was attached to lines and monitors.

"Your Majesty, please." A tech laid her palm on his arm. "If you pull out too fast, you can injure yourself."

"Where is my wife?" he demanded.

"I'm sorry. I don't know."

His pulse beat hard. "Who would know?"

"General Majda. We notified her that you were coming out." She clasped a ring around his upper arm and it flickered with lights. Then it beeped.

"Is Majda coming here?" he asked, scowling at the ring.

"Right away," the tech assured him.

Eldrinson forced himself to stay put while she examined him. He sifted through his memories: Soz, Shannon, Dehya, Kurj—they had combined their minds to help Roca. Where had they gone? He looked around the chamber. "How did I get here?"

The woman glanced up from reading a monitor. "You came with a group of ISC officers."

"But I was in the War Room. I rode up its command chair with Belldaughter." He would never forget; she was the last surviving member of his son's squadron.

The woman took the ring off his arm. "Pharaoh Dyhianna once told me that sometimes the Chair creates virtual scenes that seem real." She hooked the ring onto her belt. "Perhaps it did that for you."

He supposed it wasn't any less plausible than anything else that had happened today. "Do you know when Jazida Majda will be here?"

A throaty voice came from beyond the techs. "Now, Your Majesty."

Eldrinson looked up. Jazida stood a few paces away with Taquinil at her side. Four Abaj waited with them like obsidian statues.

Eldrinson spoke formally, always self-conscious with these officers who looked female but acted male. "My greetings, Imperator Majda." His gaze shifted to his grandson and his smile warmed. "And to you, Taqui."

The boy smiled wanly. His face was pale and dark circles showed under his eyes.

Majda said, "My honor at your presence, Your Majesty." In her shadowed voice she added, "I am Imperator no longer."

"Then it is true? Kurj lives?" He had no wish to see his stepson die, not because he had any abiding love for Kurj, but because it would upset Roca.

"Yes." Majda came forward, her dark eyes intent. "When you formed the Triad, it brought him out of his coma."

And he had feared he would kill Kurj. He wanted to know more, but not now. He had a more urgent question. "My wife?"

Majda hesitated. "She is on Lyshriol."

The relief that flooded him was so intense, he couldn't speak. She was *home*. His rage flared as he thought of the Aristos who had tortured her. He wanted them to die. Slowly.

Excruciatingly. But their ship was undoubtedly in ESComm territory. They would go free—for now. Someday he would find them.

Someday they would pay.

He recovered his voice. "Do you know who captured her?"

Majda answered quietly. "The heirs of Lord Vitarex."

Eldrinson felt as if an iron fist hit him. Vitarex was the Aristo who had crippled and blinded him. They were probably furious Roca had escaped. Acutely aware of Taquinil, he strove to shield his anger from his grandson.

"So Vitarex had children," he said.

"Two." Majda wore that strange look they all had with him now: half fear, half awe. "You and your children pulled Councilor Roca out of their ship."

"But how?" Even having helped, Eldrinson didn't understand.

"We aren't sure," Majda admitted. "Somehow you transformed her into Kyle space and then transformed her back to Lyshriol. Your daughter Soz drew energy from the battle cruiser and shunted it through her Triad Chair."

"But that is impossible," Eldrinson said.

"Yes. It is." Wryly Majda added, "Nevertheless, you seem to have done it."

No wonder they were all watching him as if he had grown two heads. "Is Roca all right?"

Majda hesitated.

"Tell me," he said.

After a pause that lasted too long, the general said, "She has brain damage. A few memories remain of her family, but she has lost everything else."

"Surely you can help her." He had to believe that. They had helped him see and walk again.

"Her node claims to have stored her brain," Majda said. "It wishes to 'commence download.' But we don't know what that would do to her."

Eldrinson usually avoided thinking about the technological marvels his wife carried in her head, for fear it would make her seem less human, but he would do anything to have her back again. "Will you let it try?"

"Councilor Roca wishes to. But we need your permission."
It sobered him to think Roca could no longer act on her
own behalf. "Is it safe?"

"We don't know," Majda said. "We're investigating."

He spoke slowly. "If she wishes it, I would be inclined to
say yes. But I would know the results of your investigations
first. I don't want her hurt any more."

Majda inclined her head. "We will keep you informed."

"When can I see her?"

"We have a ship for you." Majda glanced at Taquinil, and
he met her gaze, his face uncertain. To Eldrinson, she said,
"But can you stay here until Prince Taquinil's parents return?"

"Yes. Certainly." As much as Eldrinson wanted to get
home to Roca and his children, he didn't want his grandson
to feel deserted. He smiled at the boy. "Gladly."

My hoshpa and hoshma will be back soon, Taquinil thought.
They will.

I'm sure they will, Eldrinson thought. To Majda, he
said, "Where is Eldrin?"

Her expression shuttered. "We are searching every possible ID database."

"Why?" Eldrinson asked, baffled.

Taquinil answered, and his voice trembled. "He was in Selei City during the attack."

He stared at the boy, then at Majda. "My son is *missing?*"

Majda answered quickly. "Chances are he is fine."

"Chances?" Eldrinson gave her an incredulous look. "How
the holy blazes could you lose my son?"

"Grandhoshpa." Taquinil came over to him, and the techs
moved aside for him. It impressed Eldrinson. Taquinil was
one of the few people alive who felt no fear walking up to a
Chair. The boy looked up at him. "Hoshpa is all right. He was
hurting. But he's getting better."

Eldrinson laid a hand on the boy's shoulder. "Do you know
what happened?"

Taquinil shook his head. "I think he's all by himself."

Eldrinson glanced at Majda. "Where are Eldrin's bodyguards?"

"On Parthonia," Majda said. "They were caught by the sabotage when the Traders tried to deactivate the Jagernauts." She met his gaze. "We will find your son. I swear it."

First Althor, then Roca, now Eldrin. He knew it would help nothing if he lost his calm, but gods, it took a concentrated effort to keep from demanding they let him join the search. They were better equipped to find Eldrin, and he would only be in the way, but his instincts drove him to seek and protect his son no matter what the cost.

He spoke stiffly. "Please inform me when you know more."

"Immediately," Majda said.

"If I can help in the meshes . . ." He could offer an aid none of their machines could match: the mind of a Rhon psion.

"Thank you," she said. "We may ask."

"What about my Hoshma?" Taquinil asked.

"Her Majesty had to travel in a shuttle," Majda said. "It isn't designed for more than short trips, so it took longer than expected." She had an oddly cautious tone. "But they reached Safelanding."

"I am glad," Eldrinson said. That barely touched the surface of his gratitude. His presence in the Triad had affected it differently than anyone expected. He couldn't explain it in the mathematical terms Roca's people used, but he knew at an intuitive level that his mind occupied a different part of Kyle space than Dehya or Kurj. He was different from them. The same qualities he had that inspired such condescension among Roca's people also made it possible for him to form the Triad without killing any of its members.

"Is Dehya all right?" he asked.

Majda hesitated too long. "Yes."

"She was sick," Taquinil said. "They don't want to say it in front of me."

Majda seemed ready to deny the boy's words. Then she exhaled. "The pharaoh suffered the symptoms of a severe withdrawal. We don't know why; the medics at Safelanding found no sign of chemical dependency."

"My father was sick," Taquinil said. "I had . . . dreams."

"Has your mother experienced his illnesses before?" Majda asked.

"All the time," Taquinil said. "We all share like that. But it's never strong." In a subdued voice, he added, "Unless the sickness is really bad."

"Did you feel anything?" she asked.

"Some," Taquinil said. "But Grandfather was protecting me."

"I'm sorry I can't tell you more," Majda said.

"He'll be all right." Taquinil sounded as if he were convincing himself more than them.

"I'm sure he will," the Bard said, and hoped it were true. He remembered his son Eldrin at this age; the boy had always wanted to run outdoors. Taquinil was a quieter child, studious instead of athletic. He loved math and logic; Eldrin had taken to swordplay and archery. Taquinil would probably become a scholar; Eldrin was a singer. But for all that, the father and son were much alike. Each had a luminous quality to his spirit, as if an inner light filled him. It was why people liked to be around them so much, but it also made them seem so very vulnerable.

Taquinil tried to smile at him. "You're body is normal again, Grandfather. You glowed in the War Room."

"You remember that?" Eldrinson asked. He wasn't certain what had been real and what an illusion.

The boy nodded. "Yes. And your voice echoed."

Eldrinson regarded him curiously. "What did I do after you and I talked?"

"You don't remember?"

"I'm afraid not."

"You spoke to the Chair. In your mind."

Majda said, "We brought you here, Your Majesty."

Eldrinson glanced at her. "The Chair wanted me to think I was in the War Room."

"Because of Uncle Kurj," Taquinil said.

Eldrinson stiffened. "Why Kurj?"

"Maybe so you could know him better," Taquinil said. "So you wouldn't always be angry at each other. You have to be a Triad."

Eldrinson wished he could hide his dislike of Kurj better. He didn't want to alienate Taquinil from his uncle. Eldrinson would have liked a good relationship with his stepson, but it wasn't likely to happen.

Majda spoke thoughtfully. "Imperator Skolia uses the War Room far more than this Chamber. Maybe the Chair sought to reach him through you."

"Perhaps," Eldrinson said. The techs had finally finished poking him. Now they were brushing his hair and smoothing out wrinkles in his clothes. He glared at a woman with curly red hair. "You can stop that," he said. "I am fine."

She bowed to him. "Yes, Your Majesty." She and the others stepped back.

Eldrinson retrieved his glasses from his shirt pocket and put them on. Then he slid out of the Chair. The techs were watching with that careful attention everyone had with him today. He stood up and winced at the aches in his legs. He had sat in one position too long.

Taquinil took his hand, and Eldrinson hinged his palm around the boy's fingers. Then he took several steps. He limped more than usual, but he managed. The techs hovered about, looking much too worried. He waved his hand at them, and they backed off. At least they didn't patronize him like some of his doctors: *We understand your confusion, you needn't worry, we will take care of it, just do what we say,* as if he were too mentally slow to be treated like an adult.

Today no one said anything. Instead they all bowed. Including Majda. Usually she seemed so stratospherically far above him, he wondered that she didn't asphyxiate from lack of air. Bewildered, he inclined his head.

The general indicated an exit beyond the graceful scaffolding that buttressed the chamber. "Shall we go?"

"Certainly." He didn't know where, but they couldn't loiter here all day.

They walked through the scaffolding and left the Chamber through an archway at the back. Too many people came with them: aides, medtechs, the Abaj. Outside, they followed a gold and bronze hall with tessellations engraved at waist height. Graceful light rods bordered the ceiling, an effect Eldrinson liked better than Luminex, though he still preferred the stone and glasswood of his home.

The elegant corridor ended in a circular room with gold

walls graced by panels of holoart that glowed like stained-glass windows. The ceiling curved in a dome with a gold Luminex ball at its apex.

"This is beautiful," Eldrinson said.

"It is the foyer for the royal reception hall," Majda said.

"Isn't that where Dehya makes speeches?" Considering how diligently she avoided public appearances and how rarely he visited the Orbiter, it didn't surprise Eldrinson he had never been here before.

"Yes," Majda said. "She speaks here. Also the Imperator." She paused. "And you."

He adjusted his spectacles. "Me?"

"The Triad."

The impact of his situation finally hit Eldrinson. Until this moment, he had unconsciously assumed his presence in the Triad was temporary, a desperate act ISC would undo after he completed his duty. But that was wrong. A Key couldn't leave the powerlink. Pulling out his mind would disrupt so many neural connections, it would kill him. In the past, that explanation had seemed abstract, but now he sensed it within himself. He was one of three primary nodes. He could no more leave than he could stop his heart from beating.

"The Heart of the Web," Taquinil said.

Eldrinson focused on the boy. "What did you say?"

"They call Hoshma the Mind of the Web and Uncle Kurj its Fist," Taquinil told him. "You can be the Heart."

Eldrinson smiled. "My thanks."

"You do need a title," Majda said. "Pharaoh Dyhianna is the Assembly Key. Imperator Skolia is the Military Key."

"I've no idea what would be appropriate." He motioned at the chamber around them, though his gesture included far more, all the nebulous meshes he sensed with his mind. "But I do know this place you call the Kyle. I feel as if I was born to it."

"Perhaps you were," Majda said. "We've been trying to unravel why your people differ from other humans. The original Lyshrioli colonists may have been genetically engineered to use Kyle space."

He thought of the Blue Dale Archers, indistinct and elusive, and of Shannon, his uncanny son. The boy was mists and blue rain, part of a nomadic life that called to Eldrinson, too, though it would never truly suit him. The Archers touched him on a primal level. That heredity had remained dormant in his line for generations, until he bequeathed it to his son.

Eldrinson had learned enough genetics to realize that more went into making him than the whims of saints in Lyshriol mythology. His differences set him apart from Kurj and Dehya enough so that they had formed a Triad without destroying one another. Dehya knew the Assembly. Kurj knew ISC. They both needed the web, but they struggled to carry the responsibility for its existence on top of their other duties. For him, the web was simple. A game. His genetics ideally suited him for Kyle space. He would tend it while Dehya tended the government and Kurj tended the military.

"I am the Web Key," he said.

Majda inclined her head in acknowledgment. Then she indicated the far side of the chamber. "Shall we?"

"I don't know." Eldrinson smiled. "Shall we what?"

She paused, again showing this strange new side, as if she no longer knew how to deal with him. In truth, she had never seemed certain. Half the time she treated him as she would a prince of her House, a man to be secluded and hidden; the other half she seemed as if she were straining to accept his nature, which by her standards was primitive and role-reversed. She usually solved her quandary by avoiding him; when they did interact, she maintained an aloof courtesy.

"Your people will wish to see you," she said. "You needn't give a speech, but you should make an appearance."

"My people?" Eldrinson asked. "You mean here on the Orbiter?"

"Yes. Also the broadcasters."

"Broadcasters?" He didn't know if he liked that. They made holos and sent them to other places. "Why?"

"So everyone can see you," Taquinil said.

"Everyone who?" Eldrinson asked.

Majda regarded him steadily. "Everyone alive."

Eldrinson felt the blood drain from his face. No wonder the techs had fussed over him in the Triad Chamber. "You want me to go out there and address the entire *Imperialate*?"

"Let them see you," Majda said. "They need to know the Triad is strong."

"I can't go out there," Eldrinson said, panicked.

"Your Majesty." Strain showed on Majda's face. "We need you to do this. Your people need you."

His perception changed like the shift of an optical illusion. On Lyshriol, he had responsibilities as a Bard. The people of the Dalvador Plains needed him to act as a judge, to lead their army during the war, and to sing. This was something similar.

Eldrinson spoke self-consciously. "Very well."

Relief washed across Majda's face. "Thank you."

He looked at Taquinil. "Do your parents let you appear in broadcasts?" He had never seen the boy in any, but he hadn't watched every appearance of every member in his extended family.

"Sometimes," Taquinil said. "Not often."

Majda spoke to Taquinil. "If Your Highness would agree, I believe this would be a good time. Your people will want to see the Ruby Heir alive and healthy."

Eldrinson agreed. His people had rejoiced when Roca gave him heirs, especially at the birth of Eldrin, their first child. It reassured them. After all the attacks on the Ruby Dynasty, the people of Skolia needed to know Taquinil thrived.

He spoke to his grandson in a confidential tone. "You must come with me. Such a handsome fellow as yourself will distract everyone from my homely face."

Taquinil laughed. "I'm not. And you're not."

Eldrinson smiled at him. "Let us go, then."

Majda escorted them across the chamber. When she touched a panel, an area of the wall shimmered and vanished. The general went through the archway, followed by an aide, two medtechs, and two of the royal bodyguards. Eldrinson's pulse ratcheted up, though he had done nothing yet but watch a door open.

The Abaj captain remained at his side. When Eldrinson looked up at him, the captain said, "We will follow you in, Your Majesty."

"Ah. Yes." Normally sweat would have gathered on Eldrinson's forehead, but it seemed the techs had done something to stop that from happening.

Taquinil moved closer to him. When Eldrinson reached for his hand, the boy shook his head. I don't want them to think I'm too little to walk on my own.

Eldrinson gave him a look of approval, adult to adult. All will see how brave you are.

Taquinil straightened up. Together they walked out onto a stage with a Luminex rail bordering its edge. Majda stood at the rail with officers on either side of her and the medtechs and Abaj behind. A rumble of voices came from beyond, but Eldrinson could see nothing from here. He and Taquinil continued forward, and the others stepped aside for them. He joined Majda, watching only her, afraid to look anywhere else. She inclined her head and he nodded, aware of the diverse moods out there: curiosity, relief, joy, apprehension, awe, desire, fascination, and too many other emotions to distinguish.

He turned and gazed out.

People. Many people. A huge bay lay below, hundreds of meters long and wide—and filled with *people*. They thronged the bay and pressed around the columns that supported the ceiling. More stood on ledges around the walls or in balconies, and others rode above the crowd in cup-consoles at the end of robot arms. Everywhere he looked, he saw people.

Eldrinson froze like a wild animal caught in the glare of a flame. He was aware of Taquinil at his side. He glanced down without moving his head and saw that the boy had gripped the rail so hard his knuckles turned white.

Majda spoke to the people. "I present to you His Majesty, Eldrinson Althor Valdoria Skolia." Her voice carried throughout the bay, husky and dark. "The Key to the Web."

Silence.

Sweat finally did gather on Eldrinson's forehead as he looked at the crowd. They were staring at him, all of them, several thousand citizens. No, more than that. Those people in the robot arms held holovid cameras. They were feeding this moment live to all the worlds and habitats in the Imperialate, possibly among the Allieds and Eubians as well. This broadcast would go to millions of settlements, billions of cities, trillions of people.

Grandfather, I'm afraid, Taquinil thought.

Eldrinson couldn't move. So am I.

Then the throng shifted.

The people directly below Eldrinson moved first—and went down on one knee. They bowed their heads and rested one elbow on their bent knee. Those behind them followed suit, and the people behind them, and more, until the gesture spread like a wave across the bay. They were all kneeling, a gesture of fealty as old as the Ruby Empire, one of the few customs both Skolia and Eube had retained from that ancient era. Very few Skolians used it in this age where egalitarian concepts held sway and leaders won power through election. Yet now, of their own volition, the people knelt, tens, hundreds, then thousands, going down on one knee to an illiterate farmer.

Eldrinson suddenly remembered the day Althor had knelt to him, two years ago. Bursting with pride for his magnificent son, he had drawn his sword for the Ritual of the Blade, to accept the offered fealty. The gold curl had floated down from his son's head, glinting in the sunlight. But this bay had thousands of people. He couldn't very well cut a lock of hair off every one.

So he spoke simply, in Iotic. "I thank you."

Whatever process had amplified Majda's voice also sent his out over the bay, resonant and deep, with a baritone vibrato. He was acutely aware of Taquinil, of the boy's acceptance that these people should kneel to his grandfather, these powers of Skolia, these nobles and technocrats. For twenty-five years Eldrinson had lived in their shadow, unable to comprehend so much of what mattered to them, painfully aware of his lacks in their estimation of the universe.

Now they knelt to him.

20

Ballad of Sunrise

Eldrin's first sight, when he awoke, was blue-green sky. The dimmer sun was on the horizon and the gold one hadn't yet risen. The children were playing hologames nearby, watched over by a young woman. He stretched and sat up, rolling his head to work out kinks in his neck.

Clock, he thought.

His node created the image of a digital clock in front of him. It claimed he had slept for eighteen hours.

End display, he thought. As it disappeared, he muttered, "Too much sleep."

"You needed it," a familiar voice said. Kaywood came around and knelt at his side. "How are you doing?"

"Not bad, actually," Eldrin said. His nausea had faded, and his throat didn't hurt nearly as much as before.

"I'm glad." Kaywood seemed genuinely pleased. "I've been getting ID confirmations on my patients."

"Good." For some reason, his statement seemed odd. Then Eldrin realized it wasn't wrong, but right.

"The web!" The words burst past his usual restraint. "It must be up, if you're doing confirmations."

Kaywood rubbed the small of his back. "Parts of it, anyway."

"That means the Ruby Pharaoh is all right." It was a leap in faith; the meshes could operate without Dehya. But he could hope.

Kaywood settled cross-legged on the tarp. "It is odd to think how much of our lives, our freedom, everything we value depends on only a few people. What would we do if the Ruby Pharaoh died?" His expression turned thoughtful. "Survive, probably. She isn't the only Rhon psion."

Eldrin gave him a dour look. Up until this moment, he had

liked the doctor, but now he felt an urge to deck the fellow. Ruby Pharaoh die, indeed. "One should speak with respect of our pharaoh."

Kaywood laughed amiably. "If you could incinerate a person with a look, I do believe I would be ashes right now. I meant no disrespect." In a confidential tone, he added, "The Ruby Dynasty is our mythology, eh? Our gods and goddesses. It makes you wonder how they act among themselves."

Eldrin's face flamed. "I imagine like anyone else."

Kaywood stretched his arms. "What do you say? Think they are as beautiful as everyone claims?"

The woman watching the children snorted. "I doubt it. I'll bet they doctor the holos."

"I've a theory," a man said. He was sitting near the woman and leaning back on his hands. "They hide so we won't see they're like the rest of us."

"You think they hide?" Eldrin asked. He avoided appearances because he valued his privacy and felt foolish before the public. He supposed that was, in a way, what the fellow was saying.

"When was the last time you saw one of them?" the man asked, as if that proved his point.

Eldrin decided that question was better left unanswered.

"I wish we knew what was happening," the woman said.

Kaywood grimaced. "The last I saw, Selei City was in flames."

"I'm worried about my wife and son," Eldrin said.

"My son works at Selei International," the man said. "Maybe someone in charge can tell us about them." He squinted at the headquarters across the camp. "Except for that blasted queue."

Eldrin saw what he meant. A line of people wound around the building. It would be a long time before they had news.

Eldrin spent the morning with Kaywood, helping patients. He felt steadier, less affected by remnants of phorine in his system. He took care not to lose himself in the trance and tried to come out of it after thirty or forty minutes, before it drained him too much. Kaywood gave him a drink that helped his throat.

Later he went with the doctor on rounds. While Kaywood treated patients, Eldrin tried to ease pain and speed healing. Once, when he surfaced from his trance, Kaywood was still splinting the leg of his patient, an older woman. So Eldrin sang softly to her, and she seemed to like it. His voice hurt and had a flat quality, but it felt better after he warmed up.

As Eldrin let his song fade, the woman patted his hand. "That was lovely." To Kaywood, she said, "You're a godsend."

The doctor grinned. "My wife would tell you not to give me a swelled head." His smile faded. "If she were here."

"You'll see her soon," the woman assured him.

"Yes." He made a visible effort to sound confident. "I will."

When Kaywood and Eldrin were walking back to the infirmary, the doctor spoke quietly. "She probably wasn't in Selei City."

"Your wife?" Eldrin asked.

"Yes. She was planning to visit a friend out of town." He paused. "And yours?"

Eldrin looked out at the horizon. "She was in the City Center."

"Ah, gods." Kaywood started to say more, but Eldrin shook his head. He couldn't talk about it. The fear went too deep.

Up ahead, a group of young people were sitting in a circle, talking and drinking wine. Eldrin wondered where they got such a luxury item. Maybe from their ship. Watching them, he wanted a drink so much, it felt like pain. No, he didn't want a drink. He wanted the damn phorine. He hated his need for it, but the craving didn't go away.

As they reached the infirmary, Kaywood said, "I could use help putting up shelters, if you're not too tired."

"Not at all." Manual labor might take his mind off his worries. He had always liked working on his father's farm, toiling in the plains under the endless lavender sky.

They spent several hours setting up poles with tarps stretched across them as canopies. By the time they finished, Eldrin was exhausted. He washed up and flopped down with Kaywood and the children on a tarp crowded with other people. Closing his eyes, he leaned gratefully against a pole.

"The healing takes a lot out of you," Kaywood said.

Eldrin opened his eyes. "I wish I could do more."

"You've already done so much. I could use empaths like you at the hospital in Selei City." Kaywood offered him a tray with a sandwich and vegetables. "Lunch."

As Eldrin crunched on the stalk of some plant, he noticed eight armed IRAS officers approaching the infirmary. Two of them flanked a civilian woman with a cap of dark curls. She wore no uniform, only pale trousers and a blouse. The group had a tension about it that made the hair prickle on his neck.

The boy glanced up idly, a flat-cake halfway to his mouth—and froze. Then he shouted, "Hoshma!" He sprang to his feet and his sister scrambled after him. As they ran to the woman, she knelt with her arms extended. The children barreled into her, and she gathered them into her arms, hugging them hard.

Eldrin stood up with Kaywood, grateful to see the children reunited with their parent, but aching also, wishing he could do the same with Dehya and Taquinil.

The woman straightened up, holding the children's hands. She started toward the doctor, but the IRAS officers stopped her. Eldrin frowned, hoping they would see that the people disapproved of their keeping her away. It actually seemed to work; the officers released the woman. Although they let her come forward, they seemed tense enough to snap in two. He recognized their behavior. She probably held a high position and they feared Kaywood posed her a danger. It was absurd, but from his own experience he knew that guards never took chances.

It wasn't the doctor she sought, though. Accompanied by the IRAS officers, she came to Eldrin with tears glistening in her eyes. "My children told me how you took care of them, even when you were sick." Her voice caught. "I cannot thank you enough."

"They're lovely children," Eldrin said. His mood dimmed. "I hope to find my family soon, too."

One of the IRAS officers, a husky man, spoke with deference. "We may be able to help, Your Majesty."

Ai! Eldrin flushed, suddenly aware of everyone around them. He hadn't noticed the constant murmur of conversation until it stopped. He had become so used to the words *Your Majesty*, he had never realized until this moment the impact they could have outside the confines of his restricted life.

None of that mattered, though, when he realized the officers might have the answers he wanted. "My wife?" he asked. "Is she all right? My son? The rest of my family?"

Another officer answered, a tall woman. "Pharaoh Dyhianna is safe. Your son is with your father." Quietly she added, "Your father is now a Key."

Eldrin was certain he misheard. "What did you say?"

"Your father joined the Dyad." She sounded subdued.

His father? She couldn't mean what she had said. It was impossible. Then the rest of it hit him: a third Key would be a death sentence to one of the Triad. "What about Dehya? And Kurj! What happened to them?"

"Dehya?" the female IRAS officer asked. "Who is that?" At the same time, the male officer said, "Do you mean Imperator Skolia?"

"Yes. The Imperator. And my wife." Eldrin couldn't bear to lose them, not Dehya, not his father, not the half-brother who had treated him with a familial love Kurj showed few others. "The powerlink can't support three people."

"All three live," the man said. "The Triad is stable."

Eldrin's mind whirled. *Triad.* "This is—unexpected." It was probably the greatest understatement he had ever made. No one disputed his comment.

"Gods," Kaywood muttered.

Eldrin turned to him. "Lane—" He didn't want the doctor to treat him any differently.

Kaywood spoke numbly. "You are the Ruby Consort."

Eldrin could only say, "Yes."

"You worked with me for hours," Kaywood said, incredulous. "You never complained. You never asked for a single privilege. *Nothing.* You kept on going when you were exhausted. You gave your rations to the children and took my orders as if you were a medtech."

Eldrin winced. "I'm afraid I would be a lousy medtech."

"Are you a king?" the boy asked.

Eldrin smiled, relieved to hear him speak. "Just a bard. I compose ballads."

The girl clapped her small hands. "Oh, sing!"

Their mother, who had been staring at Eldrin with undisguised shock, finally recovered. "Honey, hush!"

"It's all right." Eldrin knelt in front of the children. "What songs do you like?"

"Pretty ones," the girl said.

The boy answered shyly. "Adventures."

Eldrin chose a ballad he had written about how the suns of Lyshriol hung above the plains at dusk, with floating bubbles silhouetted against them. His mother had taken him on a trip when he had been small, and he remembered that lovely sunrise as their ship took off. He began in his deepest voice, singing in Trillian:

> The sky curved wide
> It curved wide and long
> Curved wide above the suns
> Wide above my heart.

His voice didn't have its full resonance, but it was returning. He rose into his baritone range and his voice swelled with the excitement he had felt that day:

> The sky ship flew
> It flew long and high
> Flew clear above the suns
> Clear within my heart.

He soared into the tenor section and even managed the high notes he had worked for so many years to perfect:

> The sky turned vast
> It turned vast and deep

Turned with bright stars
Graceful in my heart.

As he let the last note fade, his eyes closed, and he felt the song within him.

Silence.

Eldrin opened his eyes. Many people had gathered to listen. It felt strange; he never sang in public, only in virtual concerts over the meshes. He was about to stand up when the girl put her pudgy arms around him.

"Pretty song," she said, her cheek against his.

Eldrin hugged her. "Thank you."

"That was incredible," her mother murmured.

He rose to his feet, relieved they liked his offering. The boy put his arms around Eldrin's waist, and Eldrin bent his head, his hands resting on the children's shoulders. He would miss them. When he lifted his head, the mother bowed and spoke in formal tones, using the correct protocol for a Ruby heir, even the arcane phrasing specific to the Pharaoh's consort. "I thank you for the grace of your time, Your Majesty."

Eldrin inclined his head, automatically lapsing into court protocol. "It is our pleasure."

The woman held out her hands to her children. "Come, you must let him go now. He has important matters to attend."

Eldrin couldn't think of anything more important than ensuring the future of the Imperialate was well cared for in the person of its children. As one of the IRAS officers took them away, Eldrin murmured, "Gods speed."

He said his farewells to Kaywood. Then he went with the IRAS officers to face his future.

21

Gaps

Soz felt strange coming home. A gold and black shuttle ferried her down from the battle cruiser *Ascendant*, and she walked to the village. A breeze whispered across her uniform, the black leathers of a Jagernaut, but without arm rings to indicate rank. The lavender sky, blue clouds, and silvery plains—nothing had changed. She had lived here all her life. It should feel the same as always. But it wasn't, nor would it ever be again. The universe had turned inside out. ISC had just barely rebuffed ESComm, and they would have to live with the specter of the war's possible return.

Althor should have been here. Never again would he bring his Jag down in that spectacular flare of exhaust. It was all gone in the strike of an unseen enemy. Nor was it only Althor. Her father's message had arrived on *Roca's Pride: Come see your mother before it is too late.*

Soz reached the top of the hill where her family's house stood, a small castle actually, though these days it served an aesthetic rather than defensive purpose. She simply walked through the open gateway. No one had posted a gatekeeper. Her family had no real enemies in Dalvador, besides which, an orbital defense system monitored them, even more stringently after what had happened with Vitarex. Nor did anyone have reason to expect the return of the prodigal daughter. She had sent no messages. She had feared if she let them know, her father might change his mind and tell her not to come home after all.

Inside the house, Soz wandered into the Hearth Room. No one lounged there today, nor did flames lick the glasswood logs in the hearth. Lamps stood in corners, elegant gold poles with stained-glass shades. A staircase swept up to her right and curved out of sight. She stopped and searched with her mind. Her father and some of her siblings were here somewhere, but she couldn't find her mother.

The next two rooms she checked were empty. Frustrated, she went to the Solar Chamber. It had many tall windows, which filled the room with sunlight this late in the day. Panels of yellow glasswood brightened the walls, and cabinets displayed vases in swirls of color. The place was full of light and warmth.

Here she found her mother.

Roca sat across the room, in an armchair by a window, gazing at the plains. Her hair poured over her body in a glistening fall of golden curls, with tendrils curling around her face. Her gold skin, eyes, and eyelashes glimmered. Relief flooded Soz. Her mother looked fine, as healthy as always.

Soz paused just inside the entrance. "My greetings, Mother."

Roca continued to stare out the window. Then, slowly, she turned her head. "Soshoni?"

Soz crossed through the gilded light, and Roca watched her with an oddly placid expression. Soz had never realized what a mobile face her mother had, or how much her intelligence showed in her alert manner, until it was gone. Today her face was *too* beautiful, soullessly perfect, all character lines smoothed away.

"Mother?" Soz sat on the windowsill by Roca's chair. "Are you all right?"

"Yes, of course." Her voice was soft. "How are you?"

"Fine." Soz felt adrift. She had expected more reaction.

"You look tired," Roca said. "Are you sleeping enough?"

"Probably not." Soz shifted her weight. "Don't you know where I've been?"

Roca frowned. "Did you forget your homework?"

A sinking sensation came over Soz. "Mother, I've been in combat."

Roca's eyes filled with tears. "Soshoni, you mustn't go where you might be hurt."

"It's all right," Soz said, bewildered. "I'm fine."

A man's voice came from the doorway. "*Soz?* Is that you?"

Soz jumped off the sill. For an instant she didn't recognize the man in the arched entrance. Then it hit her; this was *Denric*, her little brother. Seventeen now, he was taller than when she had left home, his shoulders broadened, his face matured.

"Deni!" Soz strode to him, and they collided in the middle of the room. She grabbed him in a hug and was startled to discover the top of her head only came to his ear.

"Soz—" His voice sounded strained. "I can't breathe."

Mortified, she let him go. "Sorry! I forget about all that hardware in my body." Adapting to her enhanced strength was an ongoing process.

He grinned, a yellow curl falling in his eyes. "You can be my bodyguard."

She glared at him. "I most certainly did not spend all that time learning to be a Jagernaut so I could stand around watching you read books."

Laughing, he pushed back his hair. "But they're so good."

"Deni." Roca spoke behind them. "Did you bring my book?"

As Soz turned, Denric spoke gently to their mother. "I brought it earlier. Don't you remember?"

A shadow crossed Roca's face. "No." She turned back to the window. Sunlight made her skin glimmer. It disoriented Soz to see her look so well, because something was obviously very wrong.

It is killing Father, Denric thought, guarding his mind.

How much has she lost? Soz asked. She and Denric had often done this in their youth, shrouding their minds so they could talk without being "overheard" by siblings or parents. It worked only if they were close together.

She doesn't even remember she is an Assembly Councilor.

Can anything be done?

He glanced at their mother, who was either ignoring them or had forgotten they were in the room. *Father is talking to the biomech doctors. Apparently Arabesque, her node, recorded her neural patterns. It already knew many of them, since it had been part of her brain for so many decades.*

How would it bring them back?
Use the bioelectrodes in her neurons to reestablish firing patterns.

Soz didn't like the sound of it. **That could cause more damage.**

That is what they fear. But it could also return part of what she's lost.

Does she understand the risks?
Not really. The doctors say Father must decide.

This had to be agonizing for him. **Does she remember what happened on the Aristo ship?**

Some. Denric shuddered. I would wish for her to lose those memories.

Soz watched her mother. **I also.**

Roca sat in the sunlight, oblivious to them.

The Bard waited in the chamber at the top of the Blue Tower. The circular room fit his mood: smooth and empty, polished bluestone, with a blueglass door and domed ceiling, no furniture, only a few engravings, nothing else. Echoing. Like his heart.

He stood at the window and gazed at the village and silvery green plains he had known all his life. He didn't see today's landscape; instead, he remembered lying with Roca far out in that waving sea of reeds, shimmerflies and bubbles floating above, just the two of them and no one else. Several of their children had been conceived under that vast sky. He remembered Roca laughing, Roca glowering, Roca orating in the Assembly. Roca touching him. He wanted her back. The doctors had healed her wounds, but the woman in the Solar Room was a lovely shell, an empty place where his wife belonged.

He had told the doctors to go ahead.

Arabesque claimed it could kick-start her brain. It might bring her back, but a good chance existed it would fry her neurons and take away what little she had left, leaving her incapable of even minimal care for herself. He clenched his fists and pressed them against the window that had been part of Roca's wedding present to him; glass panes in all his houses. He *had* to try. She had never given up on him during his long recovery, even when he pushed her away. But if he made a mistake, if he condemned her to a living death, nothing he could do would heal it. He would care for her the rest of their lives and die each time he saw what he had done to his wife.

A knock came at the door. Eldrinson turned, afraid to answer lest someone had come with news. *I'm sorry, the procedure failed.* Perhaps it was too soon to tell. She needed time to adapt, as he had needed for his legs and sight.

He went to the door and found his son outside. Shannon had always been the smallest of his boys, the youngest except for strapping Kelric. Eldrinson was used to thinking of him as a child, but a man faced him, nearly as tall as Eldrinson, almost two octets old, an Archer with his own life far off in the Blue Dales.

"My greetings, Father," Shannon said.

"My greetings." Their formality troubled Eldrinson. It had been this way since he returned home. Once he and Shannon had been close. The boy had often run with him in the plains. But it had been years since then, two years since they had even spent time together. First he had let his convalescence separate him from his family; then he and Roca had gone offworld. He longed to take back that time. Nothing would fix his mistakes with Althor, but he had a chance with Shannon.

"I am glad to see you." Eldrinson stepped away from the door. "Come in."

Shannon entered. "I can't stop worrying about her."

Eldrinson knew he meant Roca. "I also."

A mental knock came at Eldrinson's barriers. He lowered his defenses and Shannon's thought came to him: 𝔦 𝔨𝔢𝔢𝔭 𝔰𝔢𝔢𝔦𝔫𝔤 𝔥𝔢𝔯 𝔞𝔰 𝔰𝔥𝔢 𝔴𝔞𝔰 𝔞𝔣𝔱𝔢𝔯 𝔴𝔢 𝔭𝔲𝔩𝔩𝔢𝔡 𝔥𝔢𝔯 𝔣𝔯𝔬𝔪 𝔱𝔥𝔢 𝔱𝔯𝔞𝔡𝔢𝔯 𝔰𝔥𝔦𝔭 𝔦𝔫𝔱𝔬 𝔱𝔥𝔢 𝔞𝔯𝔠𝔥𝔢𝔯 𝔠𝔞𝔪𝔭.

𝔖𝔥𝔬𝔴 𝔪𝔢.

Shannon relaxed his barriers and let him see . . .

Roca slowly took form out of the blue fog, coalescing out of the mist, a gold woman with haunted eyes. A lovely young female Archer held a blanket around Roca's shoulders, and

Shannon stayed at his mother's side, kneeling in drifts of glitter. Nothing took away the terror in Roca's eyes, that blankness where strength and a keen intellect had existed. She recognized Shannon at first, but then her awareness seemed to die.

"Mother?" Shannon asked. "Don't you know me?"

"Who are you?" she whispered.

"Your son." He used the edge of the blanket to clean tears off her face. "It's all right. We will take care of you."

Her voice shook. "No more hurting."

"No more," he swore. "Never again. I promise."

The scene faded into blue haze. Once again Eldrinson was standing with Shannon in the tower. Rage shuddered through him. The Traders had done this to his wife. He would take them apart, one by one, if only he could. He wouldn't forget.

nor will i, Shannon thought. Another memory came, vivid and clear: the Bard, broken and blind in the tent of Vitarex.

Eldrinson took a deep breath. Vengeance had cost them their chance to question Vitarex. **Remember it as a reason to protect what we love. Not for revenge.** He spoke as much to himself as his son.

mother knows how escomm broke the defense codes here.

She does? Although ISC had figured out how ESComm sabotaged the Jagernauts, they still didn't know how the Traders had infiltrated the ISC defenses on Lyshriol.

it was in her mind when we pulled her off the trader ship.

Eldrinson didn't see how Roca could know. **Have you told ISC?**

no. i thought you should choose whether or not to speak to outsiders.

It was the way of the Blue Dale Archers, to put the tribe first. However, they had to inform ISC. **I will talk with them.**

Shannon nodded, his silver eyes pale from lack of sleep. Neither of them would acknowledge that they might never speak with her again if the procedure failed. Instead they talked about Shannon's life with the Archers. A name came up often. Varielle. She was the young woman in Shannon's memory. Charmed by his son's shy interest, Eldrinson wanted to ask about her. He held back, though, knowing the boy would tell him in his own time.

A tap came at the entrance. Taza Rajindia, the biomech adept who had treated both Althor and Soz, stood in the archway.

Eldrinson tensed. "You are finished?"

Rajindia nodded with a neutral expression. "We thought you might like to be there when we wake her."

Roca opened her eyes.

A ceiling curved above her. Pale colors. Pretty patterns. A face appeared, a woman with dark eyes. Her mouth moved and sounds came out. She went away. A man appeared. He made sounds. He seemed upset. Then he went away.

Councilor Roca?

Where did that come from?

From your node. Arabesque.

Where? . . .

In your brain.

Oh.

Don't you remember?

No.

The man reappeared. "Roca?"

She would have answered, except she had nothing to say. He made more upset sounds and went away again.

Councilor, Arabesque thought. You should have regained your memories.

Go away. Roca closed her eyes and faded into a forever blue trance.

Soz pressed her hand against the closed door. The room beyond had been a nursery years ago, then a family room after Kelric had his own bedroom. Now it was an infirmary for their mother. The door moved and Soz jumped back. A medtech came out, a short man with light brown hair. Soz didn't know how she looked, but as soon as he saw her, sympathy softened his face.

"How is she?" Soz asked.

"It's too soon to know."

It didn't take genius to interpret his answer. Soz felt as if her stomach dropped. "I have to talk to the biomech adept."

"Rajindia is working with your mother." He went to a wall niche with a bluestone fountain and filled a cup with blue water.

"Look at me," Soz said.

He quit avoiding her gaze. "I can't let you in."

She struggled for calm. "Can you give Rajindia a message?"

"All right." He gulped his water.

"She needs to have the node use extra memory in my mother's mind. Like mine does. I don't know if my mother has as much, but she's Rhon." Soz wanted to stride into the room, grab Rajindia, and tell the adept herself.

"I will tell her." He went to the door, then paused with his hand on the antique doorknob. "Quaternary Valdoria, I'm sorry I don't have better news."

She spoke awkwardly. "I'm no Quaternary. I haven't graduated."

He nodded. Then he went inside and closed the door.

The Bard sat by Roca's bed, grieving. She responded to no one, did nothing more than open her eyes. The doctors knew. The worst had happened. He would have picked that up from them even if he hadn't possessed a shred of empathic ability.

Rajindia and a medtech were conferring in low voices. Eldrinson watched listlessly. Then he turned to Roca and hinged his hand around hers, his four big fingers holding her slender five. So soft. So precious. So empty.

Rajindia joined him. "Your Majesty?"

Eldrinson regarded her dully. "Yes?"

"We would like to try one more procedure."

He wanted to shout at her to leave his wife alone, get away, spare her any more indignities. But he was the one who had asked them to try. How did you cure a deadened mind? He had no answer. So he said, "What procedure?"

"We may be able to expand the memory used by her node."

It sounded as arcane as everything else they said. "What would that do?"

She brushed a strand of hair off Roca's mouth, then took a cloth and dried the spittle on Roca's lips. "Your daughter thinks Arabesque doesn't have enough memory to reactivate your wife's brain."

Bile rose in his throat; they turned the people he loved into machines. He forced down his nausea. He would do whatever it took. Nothing mattered but filling this husk that had been Roca. "Could it make her worse?"

"Probably not." Softly she added, "But it isn't likely to help."

His voice caught. "Try."

Roca opened her eyes.

The ceiling arched in vaults, patterned with stained-glass mosaics. A face came into view, a woman with dark eyes.

"Councilor?" the woman said.

Roca tried to respond, but her voice wouldn't work.

"Did she answer?" a man said, out of sight.

Roca wet her lips and tried again. "Yes?"

"Do you recognize me?" the woman asked.

"No," Roca answered. "Should I?"

"I'm Taza Rajindia, a biomech adept."

The man spoke again. "At least she understands words."

Roca lifted her head and frowned at the medtech who had spoken, a young man she didn't recognize. "And why," she inquired sweetly, but with an undeniable edge, "would that be a surprise?"

"Gods above!" a familiar voice said. "That's *her.*" A man strode past the medtech, up to her bedside.

Eldri.

His eyes were full of tears. "Roca? It is you?"

"Of course it's me. Why are you crying?" She tried to sit up and discovered she was attached to all sorts of lines, tubes, and monitors. Confused, she lay down and glared at Rajindia. "What is all this stuff?"

The biomech's eyes turned glossy as if she, too, had been

hit by an urge to shed tears. Odd. She didn't seem the weepy type.

"Welcome back, Councilor," Rajindia said.

Their responses bewildered her. "Back?"

Then her memories stirred.

They came slowly, like a wave rolling up a beach. Another wave of recollections came after them and soaked her mind. A larger wave followed, then another, even bigger. The memories flooded her, one after another, each deeper and more turbulent. They piled up, then curled over and crashed down, pounding her mind. More breakers came, huge, towering, thundering. Behind them, bigger waves loomed, higher, too high, *she would drown—*

Roca gasped. Alarms blared and red lights flashed.

"Knock her out!" Rajindia yelled.

Roca had no idea what they put in what intravenous line, but almost immediately she felt woozy. Lethargy spread over her and the waves withdrew, becoming smaller and choppy, until they settled into rolling swells. She closed her eyes and drifted like flotsam, grateful the onslaught had stopped.

For some time she stayed that way. When she opened her eyes, she realized she was in the old family room, though someone had transformed it into an infirmary. Her memories still inundated her, but they were bearable. Gods. That blue universe had been real. Somehow, incredibly, her family had pulled her through Kyle space to the Blue Dale Mountains.

Eldrinson sat on the bed. He looked like hell, his hair uncombed, his clothes wrinkled, his eyes dark—and she had never seen such a welcome sight. She squeezed his hand, too woozy to speak.

"Do you remember me?" he asked.

She raised her eyebrows. *It would be rather difficult to forget you, given how long we've been married.*

Ah, Roca. A tear ran down his face. He brushed it away and blushed until it hid the freckles on his nose.

She smiled. He truly was a mess. *You look lovely.*

He glared at her. **Men are not lovely, Roca. They are handsome.**

You're truly a handsome sight. She laughed softly. *But you are also a mess, love.*

Rajindia was watching with a puzzled expression. That tended to happen when someone saw telepaths going through the facial expressions of a conversation. It was why Roca rarely had mental discussions in front of people who weren't psions.

The Bard slanted a look at the doctor. "The operation must have worked. My wife is insulting me."

"I am glad," Rajindia said. When he glowered at her, she laughed. "I meant that Councilor Roca is recovering."

Judging from her mood, Roca suspected "glad" was a far too mild a description of Rajindia's response. The adept withdrew, leaving them as much privacy as they could manage with so many people in the room. Roca's memories continued to roll in slowly. She wished she had lost those of the Aristos, but they remained.

Your memories are intertwined, Arabesque thought. *If I erase the brutal ones, others will go as well. Do you wish me to delete them anyway?*

No. Let them stay. Roca would rather endure the bad than give up the good. *Is it true?* she asked Eldrinson. *Did you make a Triad?*

It is true.

Good. She felt a fierce satisfaction. All the nobles who had condescended to her husband, the Assembly delegates who plotted to dissolve her marriage, the ones who tried to deny him status as a free citizen so they could study him in a lab— now they had to bow to him. Every last one.

He smiled. *You look ferocious.*

Just gratified.

He lifted her hand and pressed her knuckles against his cheek. *This feels like a miracle.*

Warmth spread through her. But the "miracle" had flaws. *I have holes in my mind. It hurts.*

You must not retreat to Windward and refuse to see anyone.

She smirked. *I must stay here. Otherwise, who would bedevil you?*

He laughed and pulled her into his arms, lines, sheets, equipment, and all. **I am here. Remember that. I *will.*** She had a long recovery ahead, but with her family around her, she could manage anything.

"It isn't absurd!" Soz crossed her arms and faced off with Rajindia and Colonel Corey Majda, commander of the Lyshriol orbital defense system. They were standing outside the infirmary with Soz's father.

"The Chair tried to tell me," Soz said. "It showed me Jaz."

"Jaz?" Eldrinson asked. "What is that?"

"Not what," Soz said. "Who. He was one of my roommates last year."

"*He?*" Her father's face turned thunderous. "You had a *male* roommate?"

"Oh, Hoshpa." Soz didn't want to argue. "The Chair showed me an illusion of him. Jaz told me that Mother had forgotten her birthday."

"This has significance?" Rajindia asked.

"She *forgot.*" Soz wished she could express herself better. "That was about the time Arabesque closed down her mind. The Chair was saying she needed help."

Colonel Majda considered her. Dark-eyed and dark-haired, the Majda Matriarch resembled her sister, Devon, but she was younger and less austere. "Soz, don't you think that's far-fetched?"

At least she hadn't said, *That's crazy.* "I can't give you proof," Soz said. "But the Chair protects us. The Ruby Dynasty. That includes Althor. It told me that *he* forgot. Like Mother."

"The Chair couldn't have known," Rajindia said.

"How do you know?" Soz demanded, painfully aware of her father listening. She would hate herself if she gave him false hope, but she couldn't let this go, not if any chance of success existed. "Althor had his node for less time than Mother, but it's a more advanced model by decades."

"Your mother lost knowledge," Rajindia said. "Your brother's brain is dead. It isn't the same."

Soz knew they believed she was in denial. Maybe they were right. But this went beyond her resistance to accepting his condition. "Yes, he died. His ship revived him."

Rajindia spoke with the sympathy of someone who often dealt with bereaved families. "It revived his body. By that time, the brain damage was too extensive. He had almost no neural activity left in his cerebral cortex."

"Neither did Mother," Soz said.

"A great deal more than Althor," Rajindia said.

Soz made herself stay calm, though she wanted to shake someone. "The first attempt to revive her didn't succeed because after storing her neural patterns, her node had too little memory to activate her bioelectrodes. But you gave it more, right? You augmented it with her Rhon brain cells."

Corey Majda spoke. "You think Althor's node is holding his mind, but it doesn't have enough memory to fire the bioelectrodes in his neurons?"

"Yes," Soz said.

"It sounds to me like a surefire way to destroy his brain," Corey said.

"It's a risk," Soz admitted. "But Mother survived it."

"Althor's node had no time to store his mind," Rajindia said. "They were in combat."

Her father finally spoke. "Soz, are you sure this isn't just wishful hopes on your part?"

"I can't be certain." It was true, though she struggled to admit it. "But we'll never know unless we try." She forced out the truth she had denied for so long. "It isn't as if he has any other chance."

Rajindia glanced at Eldrinson. "It is your decision."

He answered quietly. "Try."

22

The Viewing Chamber

The Bard particularly disliked hospitals at night. Death waited in the halls, at home in the dark hours. Nor had he ever liked the world Diesha, with its red hills, red mountains, and red air. Such a harsh place. Even after his visits during his last trip here, this ISC hospital felt strange and unwelcoming. He slouched on the sofa in the viewing room, half asleep, hungry but unable to eat. His legs ached.

"Would you like some kava? I'm going for some."

He opened his eyes and fumbled on the sofa for his glasses. When he put them on, the blur standing in front of him resolved into Soz, dimly lit by a lamp across the room. Denric was sprawled in an armchair near the door, his head back and his eyes closed. They were the only family members who had accompanied him to Diesha. Del and Chaniece had stayed home to look after Dalvador and the younger children. He wished the doctors would let Roca travel, but they hadn't, so he would deal with this all himself.

He sat up straight, as tired as when he had first tried to go to sleep. "Yes, kava would be good. Thank you."

Denric yawned and opened his eyes. "I'll go with you," he told Soz. "Take a look around." He stretched his arms and cracked his knuckles. Despite the curl of hair that stuck up over his ear, he no longer looked like a boy. It bemused Eldrinson that yet another of his sons had turned into a man, this one a scholar who planned to attend the university on Parthonia if no more wars intervened.

"Not much to see at the canteen," Soz said.

"This is my first trip offworld in years," Denric said. "I want to see everything."

Soz squinted at him. "In the middle of the night?"

"Maybe not now," he allowed. "But at least the kava place. I've never been to a canteen."

"Well, hell," Soz said. "Why not?"

Eldrinson scowled at her. "Sauscony, watch your language." He knew she was a soldier and probably said worse when he wasn't around, but his instinctive parental reaction came out anyway.

"Sorry, Hoshpa." She didn't glare the way she would have in her earlier teen years. She wasn't a child anymore, either. His little girl had grown into a formidable woman.

As Denric stood up, Eldrinson rolled his shoulders, working out the stiffness. The viewing window across the room was dark and opaque. The doctors, Callie Irzon and Tine Loriez, were in there. They could have worked on Althor in a biomech lab, but they didn't consider it necessary. They weren't operating, only trying to communicate with his node. They had been cloistered with him for such a long time. Hours.

Soz followed his gaze. "We didn't hear anything while you were sleeping. We checked at the doctor's station outside."

Denric came over to her. "It's taking too long."

"He's been in a coma for months," Soz said. "Even if this helps, it won't happen immediately." She didn't sound convinced by her own words.

"Yes." Eldrinson rubbed the muscles in his neck, which felt like cords. He wondered if they would ever relax again.

"Want to come with us?" Denric asked him.

He had seen plenty of canteens in his travels with Roca. He found them about as interesting as an inert log. "I should wait here, in case anyone comes with a report."

After the children left, Eldrinson stretched out his legs, crossed his arms, and closed his eyes. His attempts to sleep had so far been futile, but he tried anyway.

Eventually the door opened again. Footsteps entered, only Denric's heavier tread. Eldrinson yawned. "Did Soz stay in the canteen?" He opened his eyes—and froze.

"*Shannon?*" Eldrinson stood up with alacrity. "What the blazes are you doing here?" The doctors had been adamant; Shannon wasn't to leave Lyshriol until they understood if travel would adversely affect his remarkable brain. Eldrinson spoke sternly. "Does Rajindia know?"

Shannon's face was hard to read in the dim light. Then he spoke in cultured Skolian Flag. "I'm sorry. I don't understand you."

Saints almighty. Eldrinson had never heard that voice in his life. Nor did he sense Shannon's mind. He was facing a stranger, a man in his twenties, perhaps, though it was hard to tell with Skolians, who could cheat the aging process. Now that he looked more closely, he realized this man had a stronger jaw than Shannon and more classic features, with blue eyes instead of gray. In fact, he looked like one of those infernal holovid actors women liked so much. His yellow hair hung straight and thick to his collar. He took better care of it than Shannon, who let his hair grow in a shaggy mane until someone coerced him into trimming it.

Although Eldrinson was fluent in several Skolian languages, he rarely used any but Iotic. He answered in stumbling Flag. "My sorry. I think you are other person."

"You're the second person I've met here who reacted that way to me." The man lifted his hand, palm up in a traditional Skolia greeting. "My pleasure at your acquaintance, sir. I am Chad."

"You doctor Althor?" No, that wasn't right. Eldrinson tried again. "You treat my son?"

The man paled, going so white that Eldrinson saw the change despite the dim light. Chad responded in heavily accented Iotic. "You are Althor's father?"

"Yes. I am."

The young man bowed deeply. "My honor at your presence, Your Majesty."

Well, hell. Eldrinson was too tired for bowing and titles. He wanted to tell this Chad to stop, but his family kept insisting he learn to accept Skolian protocols.

"Thank you," Eldrinson said, which wasn't really the right response, but would do. "Have you news about Althor?"

"I'm not a doctor. I'm a—a friend of Althor's."

Eldrinson didn't recall hearing about a Chad. Then again, he knew so little about Althor's life, almost nothing of the last two years. He inclined his head. "I am glad to meet you."

"You are?" Chad immediately looked as if he wished he could take back his words.

"Shouldn't I be?" Eldrinson asked.

Chad pushed back his hair, moving with unusual grace, another reason Eldrinson thought he might be a performer. "I mean no offense, sir," he said. "Sire?" He seemed bewildered.

"Eldrinson."

"Your Majesty?"

"Call me Eldrinson. Please."

"Yes, Sire. I mean, Eldrinson."

"It is kind of you to visit Althor." His son and this fellow must have been good friends, for Chad to come even when the doctors gave no hope. "It is so late."

Chad seemed relieved to change the subject. "We had two shows tonight. We just got out."

"Are you an actor?"

"Yes, I am." Chad's face relaxed. "We're doing *Harvest of Light.*"

"*Harvest of Light,*" Eldrinson mused. "That is the story about the two brothers, yes? They find a teacher for their village. The older brother falls in love with her, and the younger one gets upset. Then a sandstorm destroys the village."

Chad's expression lit up. "Yes! That's right. I play the younger brother."

"It's a good role." It pleased Eldrinson that they had this in common. "Years ago, my wife danced the teacher in a ballet based on the story." It was a gift to say those words without the pain that had weighed on him since his nightmares about her capture. She might never regain all her memories, and she had to relearn a great deal, but she was Roca again, the woman he loved.

"You must have enjoyed the performance," Chad said.

"Yes, I did."

The conversation ground to a halt.

"Well." Eldrinson tried to think of more to say.

Chad motioned toward the window. "Have you seen Althor?"

"Not yet. They haven't finished." He hesitated. "Or maybe they are done, but they aren't getting any results."

"Finished?" Chad went rigid. "What happened?"

Eldrinson wanted to kick himself. Of course Chad didn't

know. With care, he explained what they were doing. "His doctors aren't optimistic," he concluded, fearing to express his own hope. "But they were willing to try."

Chad started toward the window, then stopped and turned back. "You mean he might wake up?"

Eldrinson went over to him. "Son, don't get your hopes up. Even if he does revive, he will probably have severe brain damage."

Chad twisted the sleeve of his sweater. He seemed in shock.

"Are you all right?" Eldrinson asked.

"I just—I can't believe even a tiny chance exists that I—I might see him again. Talk to him. Touch him."

Eldrinson felt the same way, though he couldn't say it aloud, especially to a stranger. In fact, Althor's friends never talked this way. They tended to be laconic and military in bearing. They certainly never showed their emotions. Well, Chad was an actor. He was supposed to emote. Odd, though, that he and Althor were friends. How did they meet? And "touch him"? What did that mean?

Hell and damnation. Chad wasn't a *friend* friend. He was a "friend" of the type Eldrinson had tried very hard not to think of when it came to Althor. Eldrinson stepped back and banged into the sofa. He stumbled to the side and bumped his shin on the end table. Jerking back, he straightened up, crossed his arms, and stared at Chad.

The actor hesitated. "Eldrinson—"

"Your Majesty," he said sharply.

Chad flushed. "My apologies, Your Majesty."

Eldrinson didn't know what to do. He had managed to forget his son might have a "friend." The harder he tried to block the thought, the more he thought about it. Did they hold hands? Did they—no, he couldn't think about that.

"Father?" A perplexed voice came from the entrance. "What's wrong?"

Eldrinson almost jumped. Denric was standing in the doorway holding a large mug patterned with holos of the Red Mountains. Steam curled up from it and around his face. He glanced at Chad, then at his father, his forehead furrowed.

"Deni, come on. Move." Soz's grouchy voice came from

behind him. "I'm so tired I'm going to fall over if I don't sit down."

Denric looked over his shoulder and grinned at her. "Gods forbid." But he did come into the room. Soz stalked in behind him, holding two mugs. She hesitated when she saw Chad, but then she said, "My greetings, Chad," as if he were the most natural sight in the world.

Eldrinson recrossed his arms and remained by the end table.

Soz glanced at him. "You can relax, Father. We aren't under attack, you know."

"What's going on?" Denric continued to look confused, standing in the middle of the room with his steaming kava. Chad glanced from Denric to Soz to Eldrinson as if he didn't know what to do.

Eldrinson spoke stiffly to his daughter. "You have the acquaintance of this man?"

"Oh, Father." She sounded exasperated. " 'This man' is Chad. And yes, I have his acquaintance."

Denric scowled at them. "Well, I don't."

Soz motioned at Denric with one of her mugs. "Chad, this is my brother Denric. Please don't call him 'Your Highness.' It makes him terribly cocky. Denric, this is Chad. He's an actor."

"My greetings, Chad," Denric said. Then he glared at Soz. " 'Terribly cocky?' You're in a mood."

Soz set one of her mugs on the table in front of where Eldrinson had been sitting. "This is for you," she told her father. She went to an armchair at the other end of the couch, dropped into it, and put her booted feet up on the table. She took a swallow of her kava, then lowered the mug and let out a satisfied breath. "I needed that."

Chad had turned red. "Perhaps I should leave."

Eldrinson thought it an excellent idea, but before he could agree, Soz spoke firmly. "Absolutely not, Chad." She motioned at the sofa. "Here. Sit. Stay with us."

Eldrinson scowled at her. "If the boy wants to leave, you shouldn't push him around."

"Oh, for flaming sakes." She glared at him, then spoke more quietly to Chad. "Stay. Please."

When Chad continued to hesitate, Eldrinson decided it

would behoove him to quit acting as if this harmless actor were threatening him. He didn't want to deal with Chad, but if he had tried earlier to deal with all this, perhaps he wouldn't be estranged from his son. Lowering his arms, he said, "You needn't leave."

Soz looked relieved. "Yes."

Chad nodded awkwardly. With his eyes downcast, he sat on the couch near Soz's chair, which was the farthest he could get from Eldrinson.

Soz fixed Denric with a stare. "You, too."

Denric cleared his throat. "Well. Sure." He sat in his armchair, his hands folded around his mug. He glanced at his father and sent a mental knock, but Eldrinson kept his barriers up. Although he had no idea how much Denric knew about Althor, it was hard to keep secrets in a family of empaths. Denric had probably guessed about Chad. It wouldn't surprise Eldrinson if everyone had known except him; he seemed slower than his children in picking up these things. Sensing moods didn't mean he understood the reasons for them.

The tension in the room was so heavy, Eldrinson wondered that no one creaked under its weight. Surely Chad felt it; Althor wouldn't have liked someone who wasn't an empath. Or maybe he would have, if his interest had been purely physical. Eldrinson couldn't handle that thought, so he decided to stop thinking. He pushed back his spectacles. His head throbbed.

"So," Soz said. Then she ran out of words. She took another swallow of kava.

"So." Denric said, his tone a perfect replica of hers. He smirked and she glowered at him.

Eldrinson limped to the couch and sat on the other end, as far from Chad as he could manage. Everyone tried not to stare at anyone—except Soz, of course, who fixed her father with her indomitable gaze.

"Chad comes to see Althor every day," Soz said. "Even when he gets off work late."

"Oh." Eldrinson wished he could have done the same for his son. He nodded stiffly to Chad. "We appreciate your loyalty to Prince Althor."

"You better not call us princes," Denric said. "Soz thinks it gives us swelled heads."

Soz laughed, her strain easing. "You never call me Princess Soz."

Denric stared at her in horror. "That's because I value my life."

Hearing their banter, Eldrinson began to relax. He picked up his mug of kava and took a swallow. Even knowing their bodyguards would have tested it in the canteen, he felt strange drinking kava after the assassination attempt against Kurj.

"Well." Soz spoke to Chad. "How is *Harvest of Light*?"

"Better." He shifted his weight. The cushions kept adjusting under him, trying to ease his tension, their motion almost invisible, but Eldrinson could tell because his side of the couch was doing the same thing.

"Are the performances pulling in more people?" Soz asked.

Chad's expression warmed. "Yes, actually. We had a full house tonight for both shows."

"Good." Soz looked as if she wanted to say more, but she had apparently run out of words. It made Eldrinson smile; she had never known how to make small talk.

Obviously, though, she knew this fellow, who apparently came often, even thinking Althor would never recover. It was a notable loyalty on Chad's part. More than loyalty, but that edged into the areas Eldrinson was trying not to think about. He didn't want to like Chad. He wanted to believe that if Althor would just find the right girl, he would settle down, marry, and make babies. The Assembly wanted him to wed Corey Majda, the Majda Matriarch. They hadn't pushed the union, though. Eldrinson had assumed it was because their attempt to marry Vyrl to Devon Majda had been such a disaster, but now he wondered if they had other reasons. They had dossiers on all his children, which undoubtedly included whatever they knew about Althor's private life. Not that a lack of sexual compatibility had ever stopped the powers of Skolia from trying to force a politically advantageous marriage.

Eldrinson frowned. People didn't respect arranged marriages anymore. In his day, you married who your parents told you to marry. Well, in theory, anyway. He and Roca had married against everyone's wishes. But that was different. His parents had been dead, and regardless of how the Assembly viewed the Ruby Dynasty, that governing body had no right to control their lives.

"We're certainly a talkative group," Soz said.

He couldn't help but laugh. "Ah, Soshoni. You are ever the soul of graceful converse."

She glared at him, but behind her frown he sensed gratitude that he hadn't outright rejected Althor's friend. She seemed to like the fellow.

Denric slid down in his chair, his eyelids drooping. His head nodded to his chest and he jerked it up again, shaking his mug. He swore as hot kava splashed his arm. Then he set the mug on a table and closed his eyes. The cloth of his shirt began cleaning itself.

Soz yawned and squinted at her kava. "This isn't helping."

"Why don't you sleep?" Chad said. "We'll wake you if any news comes."

Eldrinson wished the young man would quit being so kind. Chad was making it difficult to dislike him.

"I suppose." Soz set her drink on the table.

With no warning, the door next to the opaque window opened. Soz was facing away from it, but Eldrinson saw clearly from his seat. A woman stood in the opening, Callie Irzon, one of Althor's doctors.

She said, simply, "It's done."

Soz jumped, twisting around, and Denric's eyes snapped open. Eldrinson slowly rose to his feet, suddenly aware of his breathing, of his heartbeat, of the muted silence in a hospital late at night. It all seemed acutely detailed, with a clarity that hurt.

"Did anything happen?" he asked. His voice was too quiet.

When Callie didn't answer, Eldrinson knew his heart would break. He had tried not to hope, but despite his efforts, he had let himself imagine the impossible. Seeing Irzon's face, he felt as if he were dying inside.

"You must not be angry," Irzon said.

"Angry?" Eldrinson felt only grief. The anger would come later, at himself for hoping, at the universe for taking his son.

"Please," she said. "It is important. This is a time to let go of the past."

He wasn't certain what she meant. "I'm not angry at you."

She spoke gently. "I didn't refer to myself."

"Then who?"

"Prince Althor." And then she said, "He is asking to see you."

23

Sunrise Eyes

E ldrinson had never tried to avoid the highs and lows of his life, but neither had he sought emotional swings. They simply came. He tried never to dwell on the lows. Instead he remembered the highs: the day he met Roca; that afternoon he saw Eldrin, his son, for the first time; the births of his other children—

And today.

Althor was sitting up in the hospital bed. His shirt hung on his emaciated body, and his bones made sharp angles under the cloth. Nutrient lines fed his arms. His face was gaunt, his eyes hollowed. He looked terrible—and he was a sight to treasure, for his expression crackled with intelligence.

Eldrinson wanted to shed tears, and he might have if the medics hadn't been present. Holos of Althor's body and brain floated above panels arrayed on either side of the bed, and Doctor Loriez and two medtechs were studying them. Statistics flowed across their screens too fast to follow. Maybe they had augmentation that allowed them to process data faster. Lately it seemed to Eldrinson that he was always grateful to the unfeeling technology that made humans into partial machines.

This time, it had given him back his son.

He walked to the bed with Callie Irzon. Loriez and the

medtechs kept working, but Eldrinson knew they were discreetly watching him. *Let the past go.* Could he?

Somehow he found his voice. "My greetings, son."

Althor's response was barely more than a whisper. "My greetings, Father."

"I am glad to see you." That barely touched what he felt.

Althor tried to smile. "And I, you."

"How do you feel?"

"Tired." After a pause, Althor said, "Confused."

Callie spoke quietly. "Your node is doing neurological repairs and reestablishing firing patterns. It will take some time for you to reintegrate any memories it recovers."

Eldrinson wondered if Althor recalled how he had left home. Perhaps he no longer—

I remember. Althor's thought came unevenly, but without hesitation.

Eldrinson hadn't realized he had relaxed his mental defenses. Over the past year, he had often imagined what he would say to Althor if he were ever given this chance. He had never expected it to happen, yet now it had come and all his carefully considered apologies fled from his mind.

So he simply said, **I'm sorry for what I said to you.**

Althor became very still. **Does that mean I can come home?**

Always. Anytime. Awkwardly Eldrinson added, **Even if you don't want to bring a wife.**

"Thank you," Althor whispered.

Callie answered, apparently assuming he was responding to her comments. "The thanks go to your node. Ever since a conversation it had with you over a year ago, it's been backing up your mind."

"Conversation?" Althor asked.

"With your sister, when you and Colonel Tahota took her to Diesha in your Jag. Apparently it told you it was going to do backups."

"I thought it was joking," Althor said.

Loriez glanced up. "You remember the conversation?"

Althor nodded, but he didn't try to speak.

"Can all nodes do this?" Eldrinson asked Callie.

"The newer models, yes," she said. "Including yours."

He wasn't certain how he felt about that, but he could live with it. He knew what he had to do next, though every part of him resisted. But it had to be done. Although he doubted he could ever speak the words his son wanted to hear, he could at least try to accept Althor's life choices.

"Your friend is here," Eldrinson said. "Waiting to see you."

"You mean Grell?" Althor asked.

"Who?" Eldrinson asked.

"Grell. She was one of Soz's roommates last year."

She? Eldrinson's hope surged. "Is Grell your girlfriend?"

"She's . . . a friend."

Unfortunately, Eldrinson could tell that "friend" this time meant just that. So he made himself say, "Not Grell. It's Chad. He's come every day."

That evoked a reaction. Althor's mood surged in a confused meld of hope, elation, disbelief, and yes, desire. Eldrinson barricaded his mind, but not before he had no doubt that Grell wouldn't be replacing Chad.

"He's come *every* day?" Althor asked.

"Yes." Eldrinson squinted at him. "He's an actor."

"I know."

"Ah." Eldrinson cleared his throat. "Yes, I suppose you do."

Althor spoke in a careful voice. "Will you bring him in?" He waited for his father's response with a sense of stillness. Eldrinson wanted to say no, to entreat his son to see this Grell or Corey Majda or *anyone* female. But it wasn't going to happen. He had hoped for years Althor would change, and he suspected Althor had tried just to please him. It was time he accepted his son.

Eldrinson spoke some of the most difficult words he had ever given to one of his children. "Yes. I will bring him in."

Soz had expected her brother to be asleep, but the panels in his hospital room were lit even at this late hour. He sat sprawled in a chair by his bed, dressed in sleep trousers and shirt, his long legs propped up on a cushioned stool, his gauntlets black and silver against his sleeves, lights blinking.

He was reading a holoboard. Although his face was paler than normal, his metallic skin had a healthier cast.

Standing in the doorway, Soz put her hands on her hips. "For flaming sake, Kurj. Don't you ever sleep? It's the middle of the night."

The Imperator looked up, his irises large and black from medication. "Heya, Soz." He grinned, a rare sight. "Don't you?"

She scowled at him. "Only when my brothers aren't putting me through an emotional wringer, dead then alive again."

He laughed, low and rumbling. "Glad to see you, too."

He was never like this, so relaxed with his emotions. Perhaps almost dying did that to a person. Or maybe it was the drugs. "Can I come in?"

He motioned at a nearby chair. "Be my guest."

She settled into the chair, and its cushions diligently tried to ease her tension. "All my brothers are up and about tonight."

Kurj set down his holoboard. "Callie Irzon told me about Althor." His normally impassive mind held no secrets tonight; he hid neither his astonishment nor his joy. Seeing Kurj genuinely happy was a rare occasion. He even added, "It's incredible," which for him was a remarkable display of emotion.

"It is." Soz was no better at expressing herself. Perhaps that was why she got along with Kurj. He could be articulate when discussing military strategy, security, or troop movements; but for him, as for Soz, emotions were a far more difficult matter.

"They only let Father and Chad see him this evening," she said. "The rest of us can go in tomorrow."

"Chad?"

"His boyfriend."

Kurj raised an eyebrow. "And your father didn't have heart failure?"

"Actually, no."

"That's a surprise."

She smiled slightly. "Yes."

They sat in silence, companionably inarticulate. Soz finally said, "You work too hard. You were practically dead last week. What are you doing up, anyway? You should rest."

"I am," Kurj said.

"This is rest?"

"For me." He handed her the holoboard. "We're unraveling how those ESComm energy spikes worked."

She wondered how Kurj concentrated so late at night, especially in his depleted condition. Perhaps the rumors were true, that he had augmented his body so much, he didn't need sleep. He just recharged. Although he seemed subdued, he was otherwise well into his recovery. Unlike Althor or Roca, he had suffered no brain damage, only a severe form of an antiquated disease called pneumonia, with complications from the invading meds, which had attacked his biomech and internal organs.

Soz studied the report on the holoboard. Although her mind was mush, she took in the gist of it. "The effect of that spike passed from Jagernaut to Jagernaut like a contagion? That makes no sense. Energy fluctuations aren't viruses."

"Not the spikes," Kurj said. "The invading nanomeds spread the virus."

"What invading nanomeds?"

"The ones that almost killed me." He cracked his knuckles and his biceps flexed. "The spikes were artifacts of the signal that sabotaged bioelectrodes in the Jagernauts."

Soz frowned. "How could those little spikes carry enough information to sabotage a Jagernaut's biomech web?"

"They didn't. They just damaged it enough to leave it undefended."

"And the nanomeds?"

"They rewrote parts of the biomech. Corrupted the system."

Soz found it hard to believe. "How could ESComm design such effective meds against us? They would have to know the structure and coding of our biomech. Surely our security can't be that bad. Even if it was, they didn't have access to our Jagernauts."

Kurj's inner eyelids came down and his eyes became an unbroken expanse of gold.

Soz scowled at him. "Don't do that."

"Do what?"

"Hide behind your eyelids when you get uncomfortable."

A corner of his mouth quirked up. He raised his inner lids and let her see his eyes. "Happy?"

"What is it you don't want to tell me? Surely I have a need to know. I was one of the damn Jagernauts affected."

It was a moment before he responded. But he did answer. "The Ruby Dynasty spread the infection."

Soz was certain she had misheard. "Say again?"

"*We* carried it. The meds targeted our DNA." He rubbed his eyes, then dropped his hand onto the arm of his chair. "Vitarex infected everyone in his camp. He knew it would spread. Shannon must have picked it up there. He infected your family on Lyshriol. Mother infected me, Eldrin, and Dehya. You and Althor probably got it from Eldrin when he visited Diesha last year. You two took it into DMA. I spread it to my officers. Dehya and Roca carried it into the Assembly. Among the group of us, we exposed just about every major government and military institution in the Imperialate."

She stared at him. "That's nuts."

"Apparently not."

"How could ESComm know how to infect the Ruby Dynasty?"

"They have our DNA from Grandmother."

"It's diluted by two generations."

Kurj shrugged. "We carry one fourth of her genes. Mother and Dehya carry half." He sounded as if he were tiring. "Anyone can catch the virus. In dormant form, it hides in a sheath of programmable matter. It activates when it hits its target DNA."

"Ours."

"Yes."

The idea was maliciously clever. The traits of a psion arose from Kyle genes and manifested only if someone received a pair of every one of the genes, one from each parent. Most psions had only a few paired, but the Rhon had them all. Their DNA was unique.

"So no matter how many people carried the virus," she said, "it didn't activate until it reached us."

"Yes. Or until an ESComm signal triggered it."

"That blasted energy spike!" Soz hit the arm of her chair with her fist. "ESComm had two signals, right? The first weakened our biomech defenses, and the second activated the virus. Individually, the signals couldn't do much, but the first made it possible for the second to work. The second activated the nanomeds. Once they were loose, they wreaked havoc."

"That about sums it up," Kurj said. "Mother helped us figure out how the signals penetrated our defenses."

The last time Soz had seen their mother, Roca had been barely able to get out of bed. "How?"

Kurj picked up a holosheet from the table by his chair and handed it to her. "While she was on Raziquon's ship, her node infiltrated its systems."

Soz studied the sheet. Apparently an ESComm ship would drop into Skolian space, send the signal, and invert out in seconds.

She looked up at Kurj. "We should have detected the ships."

"For normal spacecraft, yes. These were shrouded."

"All ships have shrouds. It doesn't make them invisible." She waved the holosheet. "If ESComm racers were popping in and out of our space, we should have picked them up from their exhaust or from spacetime ripples when they rotated through complex space."

He smiled dryly. "You've read your security manuals."

Soz grimaced. "Thrilling reading."

To her surprise, he laughed. "They're boring as all hell."

"Well, yes. But I wasn't going to tell the Imperator that."

He motioned at the sheet she held. "ESComm has a new shroud. It uses programmable matter similar to the material that changes the opacity of a one-way mirror, like in Althor's hospital room. But they've taken it much further."

Soz cycled through several menus on the holosheet and brought up the entry on the programmable matter. It described *quantum dots,* also called McCarthy matter, tiny sandwiches of superconducting p-n-p junctions. Applying a potential to the dots created a quantum wavefunction similar to that for the electrons in an atom. However, the dot contained no electrons.

It was a simulated atom. Tuning the field simulated different atoms, including ones that corresponded to no known element. Fake matter.

The racers altered their hulls when they dropped into Skolian space. They simulated matter that matched no natural material. With careful tuning, they could evade detection, at least for a second or two.

"We can use this technology," Soz said.

"We've started work on it." He leaned his head against the tall back of his chair. "We checked Vitarex's camp on Lyshriol. Knowing what to look for, we found several programmable shrouds. They were keyed to his biomech, so they deactivated when he died. That's what made them hard to find. He even had programmable matter designed into his skin."

"So ISC didn't detect him." It sounded horrific to Soz. What if something had gone wrong and his body simulated the wrong stuff?

"He also had more conventional shrouds with extensive reach," Kurj said. "It's why no one could find Shannon. The shrouds hid him."

Soz considered that. Had they found Shannon, he wouldn't have killed Vitarex, which meant ISC might have known this sooner. But Shannon wouldn't have rescued their father. Could they have found the Bard in time to save his life? They would never know, just as Soz would never know if she had made the best choice when she withdrew her support from Kurj's forces. It would always haunt her. It also made her think that she should be nicer to her brothers, let them know she liked them, that indeed, she loved them. One never knew when she might not have them to growl at anymore.

She didn't know how to start, though, so she just said, "I don't see how Vitarex got into Lyshriol. Regardless of how well he disguised his matter, it's still matter. ISC should have detected him."

"He came in on one of our own ships."

"An *Aristo*?" She refrained from questioning his sanity. He was her CO, after all, not to mention dictator of the universe, if one listened to the more melodramatic broadcasts.

Kurj smiled. "You should see your face. And yes, it is incredible."

"I can't imagine any technology that would allow an Aristo to ride an ISC ship to Lyshriol." Gods. What a macabre thought.

"I'm afraid it involved a much older method. He was a spy." Kurj pushed his hand over his short hair. "ESComm has been planning this mission for decades, ever since your mother married your father. They understood what it meant, two Rhon psions forming a union. Rhon children. Heirs for the Dyad. It was too much of a threat."

"They trained him for twenty years?" How many other agents were hiding among her people, aimed like a spear to strike her family?

"Longer," Kurj said. "He trained from birth to pass as both Skolian and Rillian. They built his cover as an impoverished youth from Sandstorm. He enlisted in our army and worked his way through the ranks." His fist clenched on the arm of his chair. "Finally he won the posting he had sought for decades. Lyshriol."

"Didn't ISC notice he disappeared?"

"Supposedly he died. Incinerated in a flash fire accident."

"Then how did he plan on leaving Lyshriol?"

"We think it was a suicide mission."

"That isn't what he told Father."

Kurj exhaled. "Raziquon may have believed he could go home. Maybe ESComm claimed they could extract him. We don't think they could have, especially if he tried to take any of your family."

It chilled Soz. "There could be more like him."

"Then we will find them."

"We should put ISC agents into ESComm."

His eyes glinted. "So we should."

She recognized his look; it meant ISC already had such agents. "What about the Ruby Palace? The nanobots that turned the place off and contaminated your kava couldn't have been the ones that infected the rest of us."

"They were, actually," he said. "When the meds interacted with my DNA, their sheaths dissolved and they activated, attacking security meshes, disabling systems, and releasing their poison."

It still didn't make sense. "The rest of us were fine. If it was supposed to react with our DNA, why would it affect only you?"

He gave her a rueful smile. "It's all that glitter."

She doubted he meant glamour, given the lack most of them had in that department. Her family might seem glitzy to the public, but most of them preferred a quiet night by the hearth to the starjet lifestyle of celebrities. "What glitter?"

"On Lyshriol," Kurj said. "It's everywhere. The dust it creates is mostly invisible, but it saturates the biosphere."

"Oh. You mean the stuff that turns the water blue."

He nodded. "It's in everything: air, plants, clouds, lakes, rivers. The Lyshrioli have carried those meds for thousands of years. Your father passed them to your mother through, ah—" He cleared his throat.

Soz's face heated. "I get the idea."

"She gave them to you and your siblings in the womb. Eldrin gave them to Dehya." He shrugged. "They not only neutralize the glitter, they also neutralize the ESComm species. It kept the invasion meds from fully activating in your bodies."

Good gods. "Well, I'll take a ride on Rillia's arrow."

He laughed. "Whose?"

"Rillia. He shot the Lyshriol moons into the sky." Another thought came to her. "Eldrin got sick from the kava you and he drank."

"That's because the meds had already activated in my body. From me, they got into the palace. They're vicious little things. They spread everywhere. His kava had the toxic version."

"But not toxic to him."

"He didn't drink much and he had his blue dye meds." Kurj's voice was slowing. "In any case, we're developing a counter series, like an antidote."

"Well, that's good to know." Soz watched him with concern. "You sound tired."

"Maybe I do need to rest." He let out a breath. "It's been a long night."

She spoke quietly. "But we're coming out of it now."

Epilogues

An ISC racer returned Eldrin to his home on the Orbiter. Over the years, he had arrived in this dock many times, back from travels—sometimes relieved, other times tired, most often tense after the Imperial Court, which consisted of nobles who thought him inferior and Assembly delegates who never much liked the aristocracy. Today was different. He had never been so glad to come home. Two reasons waited for him.

As Eldrin left his ship, he saw those reasons high on a metal-mesh platform that overhung the bay. They were standing at its rail, two raven-haired figures peering down at the main airlock of the ship rather than the smaller one where he had disembarked. His pleasure at seeing them hit him with an intensity that made his eyes fill, which would have been embarrassing in front of his temporary bodyguards, except he managed to hold back the tears.

Eldrin and his Abaj walked to a lift that would carry him up to the platform. Taquinil grabbed his mother's arm and pointed excitedly toward Eldrin. As Dehya turned, her face lit with a smile. They both waved and Eldrin lifted his hand.

He felt as if he had gained new senses. The bustle of crews, the corrugated deck, the tang of machinery and oil—it was all so vivid. Before, lost in his drugged euphoria, he hadn't realized how much it blunted his perception of the world. Now he saw its sharp, intense beauty. Never again would he lose that in a haze of alcohol or "aids" he thought he needed to deal with life. What he had to lose—Dehya and Taquinil—was too precious to risk.

For the past seven years, he had struggled with the conflicts of a life he had thought demanded more than he knew how to give. Perhaps too much had been asked of him at too young an age and he had made mistakes, but he was done with dwelling on his past. It was time to become the man that his family, his heredity, and his sense of self asked of him.

As he stepped onto the lift with his bodyguards, the captain glanced at him and smiled. It startled Eldrin. The Abaj were ciphers, never talking, always alert in their deadly, augmented efficiency. The smile was at odds with the captain's severe face and long warrior's queue.

"It is good to be back," the Abaj said, his voice a deep counterpoint to the creaks, clanks, and hisses of the bay.

"Yes. It is." Eldrin hesitated. "I was wondering—"

"Sire?" The Abaj closed the bar on the lift. He touched a panel on the rail and the lift rose up from the deck.

"I heard that my bodyguards from Selei City have recovered," Eldrin said. "I wish them commended for their efforts." He wanted there to be no question that they had acted with honor.

"I can inform the proper authority," the captain said. "They will contact your AI secretary."

"Thank you, Captain."

The lift reached the platform where Dehya and Taquinil waited. As Eldrin stepped onto the metal mesh, Taquinil ran over and flung his arms around his father. Eldrin held him close, bending his head. A hand touched his shoulder. He lifted his head to meet Dehya's gaze, her eyes a deep green overlaid by a translucent film of gold and rose, sunrise colors, luminous with tears. He pulled her into the curve of his arm, and held his wife and his son.

Taquinil spoke beside him. "I'm glad you're home, Hoshpa."

"I also," Dehya murmured. "Dryni—the medical report—gods, *phorine*—"

"I'm all right," he whispered.

"The doctors don't know how you survived."

"It's over." It wasn't true; it would never be over. He would be an addict even if he never touched phorine or alcohol again. He had no illusions about the difficulties he faced in readjusting without them. But he was home, finally home.

Moisture overflowed his eyes despite his determination not to cry in front of the Abaj. Except somehow it was all right.

He held his family, reunited.

In the highest reaches of the Blue Dale Mountains, in a hidden dell overhung by stained-glass trees, a waterfall sparkled, catching the last rays of fading sunlight. Its muted roar muffled other sounds, and the fragrance of high-peak bubbles scented the air, clear and faintly sweet. Shannon and Varielle stood facing each other on a ledge behind the falls. A great sheet of water cascaded down from a cliff above and poured into the pool below.

Shannon hinged his hand around her cheek. She turned her head and pressed her lips into his palm. Then she drew him close and he finally embraced her, what he had longed to do since they first met. They held each other, her arms around his waist, his cheek against the top of her head. Her small size made him feel large. He might be the slightest of the Ruby princes, but among the Archers he was tall and strong. With Varielle, he could be anything.

She lifted her head, and he brushed her lips with his. As he deepened the kiss, spray from the waterfall wafted across them, warmed by underground springs. They undressed slowly, shy with each other. Untutored but unafraid, they explored, their hands sliding on the curves and planes of their bodies.

Slowly they moved closer to the waterfall. They paused at the sheet of water, and mist sifted over them, thinned to a veil with specks of glitter. Shannon put his hand in the waterfall and huge, blue drops sprayed over it. Then they dove through the curtain of water, pounded by its force, and sliced into the pool below. They plunged in deep, then came up and broke the water with great splashes. Together they swam under the Blue and Lavender Moons. Ferns overhung the water, their fronds tipped by glimmering bubbles. Trees and underbrush filled the dell; beyond it, mountains rose into the darkened sky. Shannon and Varielle played in the moonlight as they swam.

Later they lay under the whispering ferns, bare skin

against bare skin, their arms and legs entangled. That night, a prince of the stars joined with a Blue Dale Archer, a woman born to the dreaming, misty blue of another universe.

On a breezy day that blew red dust across the sky, the three-hundred-and-sixteenth class of cadets graduated from the Dieshan Military Academy and received commissions as Jagernaut Quaternaries.

Sixteen of the graduates had spent four years advancing to this moment; the seventeenth had taken two. Sixteen had racked up no more than the usual number of demerits; the seventeenth had broken the record. Four graduates received honors, twelve didn't, and the seventeenth would have, except her probation forbade that distinction.

Sixteen had trained in battle simulations.

The seventeenth had fought in combat.

Sixteen had trained to use the Kyle web.

The seventeenth had halted its collapse—and in doing so, saved an interstellar empire from defeat.

So it was that the Dieshan Military Academy graduated the smartest, most versatile, and worst-behaved cadet in its history.

Soz sat with the other seniors in a quadrangle bordered by a colonnade of arches. The white flagstones under their chairs glinted with mica and a mosaic of the J-Force insignia, a soaring Jag. A stage faced the audience and their families and friends sat in risers around the plaza. The officers on the stage were impressive in black and gold Jagernaut dress uniforms—Fleet blue, Army green, ASC khaki—all the instructors who had trained the cadets. Commandant Blackmoor sat at the front, with Secondary Tapperhaven on one side and Lt. Colonel Dayamar Stone on the other.

One man drew attention above all others.

His imposing size and metallic coloring caught the eye, but the reason he riveted every gaze was because his people had feared he would die. Kurj Skolia, Imperator of the Skolian Imperialate, sat in a high-backed Academy chair and looked out over the cadets. In the harsh sunlight, his gold inner eyelids glinted like shields over his eyes.

The Ruby Pharaoh was sitting next to him. The edges of

her body rippled, the only clue she was attending as a holo, a creation of light sent through the webs. The Assembly and ISC concurred: the Imperator and Pharaoh should never be together in one place, even on a world as prodigiously well defended as Diesha. Kurj was on Diesha, so Dehya stayed on the Orbiter. She wore her hair swept into an elegant roll, and her dark jumpsuit had no adornment save the Imperialate insignia on her shoulder.

A new insignia.

In the past, the Imperialate symbol had shown a sun exploding out of a circle. Now the sun burst out of a triangle inscribed within the circle.

Triangle.

Triad.

ISC allowed only three other members of the Ruby Dynasty to attend: Eldrinson, Roca, and Denric. They sat under the colonnade, separated from the rest of the audience. Abaj Jagernauts surrounded them. Althor was in the hospital and ISC had forbidden the rest of the family to travel, but they would watch through the web. They could have appeared as simulacrums, but Soz didn't ask. To see them as only light, untouchable, made their absence harder. It was enough to know they watched.

Secondary Foxer gave a speech, followed by Tapperhaven. By the time Commandant Blackmoor launched into his address, Soz was sleepy. The oration wound on and on until her head nodded forward. When her chin hit her chest, she jerked upright, embarrassed. It would hardly be fitting to snore on the august occasion of their graduation.

Mercifully, Blackmoor finished his words of wisdom quickly and introduced Kurj. Soz's attention picked up; this would be the first time her brother had spoken in public since the assassination attempt. He went to the podium, his tread measured. She thought he was moving slower than normal, but she doubted anyone noticed except their mother. To most, Kurj surely appeared as huge and imposing as ever. His presence would inspire the millions watching via the web. Although DMA ran every graduation live, most years hardly anyone linked in except families and friends of the graduates. Today was different; after the invasion and the attacks on the

Ruby Dynasty, people wanted to see the Imperator, to assure themselves he lived and commanded as always.

Kurj's deep voice rolled through the air. "In a few moments, you will each become a Jagernaut. One of an elite, or so you've been told. I could promise you a career of glory and honor." He paused, his eyes hidden behind their molten gold shields. Then he said, "I won't."

He looked out over the assembled cadets. "We task you with a duty. Protect our people. Our future. When glory turns into nightmare and honor stretches thin, remember this: without you and those who fight with you, our freedom will die." His voice rumbled. "You have chosen an unforgiving path, one that will take your mind, your spirit, even your soul into battle. And there *will* be battles. When the day comes that you question your sanity for this life you have chosen, remember: your sacrifices are the reason our people endure against such formidable odds."

Soz stared at him. Not only was this the longest speech she had ever heard him make, it was also the darkest. She had expected uplifting words, proclamations for their future, the sort of things Foxer, Tapperhaven, and Blackmoor had said. On this day, when they celebrated their journey from cadet to Quaternary, none wanted to hear the truth. But Soz knew another truth; when she flew in a squadron, it was Kurj's words she would remember. He had given them a reality to hang onto when the glossy veneer of being a Jag pilot wore thin.

Kurj began the roll of graduates. One at a time, the seniors went to the stage to receive their diploma and the armbands that signified their rank. Soz settled in to wait; regardless of whether he called her Valdoria or Skolia, she would be toward the end. The roll wound on, until the fellow next to her stood and went up. There were only seventeen of them, but it took a while for each one.

Then Kurj said, "Sauscony Lahaylia Valdoria Skolia."

The murmurs throughout the plaza went silent. Soz stood, aware of everyone staring. Kurj's use of her dynastic name meant everyone knew a Ruby Dynasty heir graduated today. She made her way down the row of seated graduates until she reached the aisle that ran down the center of the seats. Gusts of wind tried to tug her curls out of their queue, but today she had taken control of them. She walked past graduates on the right and left, and she felt their gazes. Gods only knew what they thought, if she met their expectations for an Imperial heir or fell short. She was only one of two heirs now, and she wouldn't have had it any other way.

When Soz reached the stage, she walked to the podium where Blackmoor waited. Kurj stood with him, his face unreadable, the shields of his eyes lowered. Soz wondered if he had questioned whether or not this day would come. She certainly had.

Soz stopped before Kurj and looked up at him.

He spoke quietly. "Congratulations, Quaternary Valdoria." Breezes blew across Soz's face. "Thank you, sir."

Blackmoor handed her a scroll. It felt good and solid, an anachronism from an age when diplomas were written documents instead of entries in a mesh, a parchment done in glimmering ink by an artist, with seals of DMA, the J-Forces, and the Skolian Imperialate.

The Commandant took a box from under the podium. He opened the lid to reveal eight gold armbands. Soz's breath caught. This was it. Most Jagernauts wore uniforms with cloth bands as part of the sleeves, but the true mark of their rank were these gold rings, four thin ones on each upper arm for a Quaternary, three wider for Tertiary, two for Secondary, and one large band for Primary.

Soz stood motionless while he slid the bands onto her left arm. She wanted to twist the scroll, but she controlled the impulse, merely passing it to her left hand so he could slide the bands up her right arm. When he had put on all eight, he nodded to her. It was done. She had become a Jagernaut.

Instead of indicating she could leave, though, Kurj continued to watch her. They stood that way, facing each other. Then his inner lids rolled up to show the gold pupils and black irises of his eyes. He laid a hand on her shoulder, a gesture technically against regulations, though no one was going to say that to the Imperator.

He spoke in a low voice. "Good work."

She wondered if he would ever know how much it meant to hear his approval, and to know he was willing to give it like this, for all to see.

"I won't disappoint you," she said.

"I never doubted it."

He lowered his arm and nodded, giving her leave to go. As she continued across the stage, she caught sight of her family up in the tiers. Soz grinned and lifted her diploma over her head, despite the strictures of DMA protocol, which required new Quaternaries to behave with decorum. She didn't feel decorous. She wanted to hoot in triumph.

As she descended the stage, Kurj called the next cadet. Soz strode back to her chair, past the marshals at each row, all of them honors cadets spiffy in their dress uniforms. She looked around for friends, but she didn't know many seniors. So she scanned the risers. There, at the top row—yes, that was Grell and Jazar. She waved, then dropped her arm when a marshal scowled. Soz went to her seat and sat with the other new Jagernauts. She winked at the fellow who had gone just before her, and he laughed silently, then discreetly saluted her with his diploma.

As the ceremony finished, the new Jagernauts rose in unison and saluted the Imperator, every one extending their arms straight out with fists clenched and wrists crossed. It was all very impressive, but what Soz really wanted to do was throw her diploma in the air and shout. She restrained herself; one could only push protocol so far.

Finally the graduation was done. As the Quaternaries mingled with the audience, Soz went looking for her family. They were standing with their Abaj Jagernauts under the colonnade, separated from everyone. Her father's spectacles glinted and her mother looked so thin. Denric was with them, his blond curls tousled. Soz met with them beyond the swirling crowd. Abaj surrounded them, deadly weapons themselves. They were a bulwark that separated her family from everyone else. Soz threw her arms around her father and mother, and then Denric, too, in keeping with her resolution to be nice to her brothers. Half the fun of having so many brothers was tormenting them, but she would be good for as long as she could manage.

"Well," her father said. He sounded pleased and bewildered.

"I'm glad you could come," Soz said. That was an under-

statement on the order of *I'm glad the Trader invasion failed.*
She slanted a look at Denric. "You, too."

Her brother laughed. "I don't know if I can deal with this
new you, Soz. You have to glower at me every now and then."
She gave him a wicked grin. "Don't worry."

Roca spoke in a quiet voice. "You've done well."

"I spent most of the time cleaning mechbots," Soz said.
Denric smirked. "Why am I not surprised?"

Before Soz could make a suitable reply, something involv-
ing Denric and spamoozala hell, her father burst out laughing. "Soshoni," he said. "You will be a force to reckon with,
eh? I am so proud of you."

Her eyes grew hot. "Thank you."

Roca glanced past her. "I think your friends are here."

Soz turned to see Grell and Jazar hanging back, out of the
way of the seven-foot-tall Abaj. Grell had on dress-leathers,
but since they were off duty, Jazar had worn civilian clothes,
a sweater and slacks that accented his physique. His trousers
fit his long legs snugly and reminded Soz why he had been
such a distracting roommate. He wasn't as big or as muscular
as many cadets, nor did he have the flamboyance that gave
Jagernauts a devilish reputation, but she liked him exactly the
way he was. His chocolate-brown hair had grown out until it
brushed his ears, which would have violated regulations if he
had been in uniform. His face reminded her of the holovid
actors who played rugged types wandering in the remote
mountains of absurdly mysterious planets. Silly movies, but
worth seeing for the sexy mountain men. Jazar was like that.

"Heya, Soz," Grell said, laughing. "You done staring at
us?"

Soz flushed and hoped no one had realized she was ogling
Jazar. She went over and grabbed each of them by the arm.
"Come meet my parents."

"Your mother already met me," Jazar protested. Grell
looked similarly alarmed.

Soz pushed her friends forward. "Mother, Father, may I
present Jazar Orand of Humberland Space Station and Grell
del-Glynn from Parthonia." To Grell and Jazar, she said, "My
parents, Roca Skolia and Eldrinson Valdoria." She hooked
her thumb at Denric. "This is my brother." Remembering her

vow, she resisted the temptation to add commentary and just said, "Denric Valdoria."

"She's being nice to me today," Denric said. "I don't know if I can handle it." When Soz glared at him, he grinned, daring her to make a comeback. Grell tried to hide her smile by putting her hand up to scratch her chin. Jazar looked confused.

Roca spoke with elegant courtesy. "We are pleased to meet you, Jazar and Grell." Imperial protocol let her use their first names, but not the reverse for them, unless she gave permission.

The Bard spoke in a baritone, with the lilt of his Lyshriol accent. "Yes, very pleased."

The ensuing small talk was strained and stiff, given the abject terror Soz's family seemed to evoke in her friends. But her parents chatted with that gracious style they did so well, and soon Grell and Jazar relaxed. Soz wished she knew how her parents managed that.

The plaza emptied out as people headed to various celebrations. Glancing beyond Soz, Grell stiffened. Jazar followed her gaze and froze as if he had turned into marble. Puzzled, Soz turned around. She saw nothing unusual, just Kurj walking toward them. Then again, that could explain terror in two second-year cadets.

"Kurj! Good." Roca waved, the only one of them who was perfectly relaxed in his presence.

"My greetings, Mother." As Kurj joined them, he spoke stiffly to Soz's father. "Eldrinson."

"Kurj." Eldrinson's voice was flat, without its usual chime. But he met his stepson's gaze. The Bard was a Key now, with a rank equal in the Triad to the Imperator.

Kurj inclined his head, acknowledging his stepfather's rank. It was painfully formal, but at least they were being civil.

When Kurj glanced at Grell and Jazar, they started to salute. He lifted his hand. "At ease, cadets. Right now I'm just your friend's brother."

They blinked at the concept of the Imperator being "just" anyone's brother, but they did lower their arms.

Kurj smiled at Soz, and his inner eyelids retracted. "Are you coming up to the palace later?"

"You bet," she told him.

"We promised her food," Roca said. "I can't believe this girl eats so much."

"I need fuel," Soz said. "It's all that biomech."

Kurj's smile quirked. "What, your microfusion reactor doesn't supply enough?"

"No taste," Soz said.

He actually laughed. "You better get yourself to Hazard's, then."

"We're all going." Soz waved at Grell and Jazar, who looked dazed. It was a tradition as old as DMA that new graduates got drunk at Hazard's after the ceremony.

"Hazard's?" Roca asked. "You mean the pub?"

"Everyone will be there," Soz said.

Roca scowled at her. "Not you."

"Why not?"

"You're underage."

Ah, hell. Her mother would remember that; at eighteen, Soz had two years left before she reached legal age. It was annoying, because Lyshriol had no drinking age. The other seniors were twenty-one or twenty-two. Grell and Jazar were twenty. Although Soz doubted anyone would deny her the tradition, she wasn't about to argue with her mother in front of her friends and Kurj. Flustered, she said, "Oh, well, I'll have a virgin drink."

Grell spluttered a laugh. Jazar turned red and suddenly became interested in straightening his sleeve.

Denric sent Soz a shielded thought. You'd certainly know about that drink.

For flaming sakes. Soz decided her resolution to be nice to him was premature. So she had more talent at shooting Annihilators than wooing men. Who had time to think about romance? She glared. **Some brothers would beat up anyone who dared besmirch their sister's fine name.**

You would beat them up first, he thought.

He was probably right. She supposed if she tried a gentler approach, she might have more success with men, but she doubted she could keep it up long enough to make a difference.

Even so, he added. I would defend your fine name always. He even sounded like he meant it. He was still grinning, but she could be benign today.

They talked a while longer, and Soz arranged to meet her parents and Denric at the Ruby Palace for dinner. Althor would join the family as well, if his doctors agreed. His recovery had progressed enough that he would soon move into the palace.

Soz respected Grell and Jazar for their guts, because it wasn't until after her family left, along with their Abaj escort, that a group of other cadets migrated over, including Rex Blackstone, the first-year student she had met after she ran the Echo, the one who had challenged her to command the toughest, smartest, most notorious squadron in the J-Force. Several female cadets were looking in his direction. Soz didn't blame them. With his dark hair, chiseled features, and tall, muscled physique, the man was undeniably gorgeous.

As they headed out to the pub, Rex fell into step with her. "Two years," he said.

"Two years?" she asked.

"Never heard of anyone going through DMA that fast."

Soz smiled. "They wanted to get rid of me. I give them a headache."

His answering laugh was a throaty rumble. Gods. The man was devastating. "You remember what I told you?" he asked.

"I'm already making plans for my squadron."

"Good. I'm your Secondary."

"You've got to be a Quaternary and Tertiary first."

"No problem."

"What problem?" Jazar dropped back to walk with them. He wasn't smiling.

"Rex here is going to be the meanest Jagernaut pilot ever," Soz said.

Jazar gave Rex the once-over. "Lot of people say that."

Rex met the challenge in his stare. "You a cadet?"

Ouch. Soz suspected Rex knew perfectly well Jazar was in the class ahead of him, regardless of Jazar's clothes.

"You should recognize me," Jazar told him. "My team whipped your sorry first-year butts in the last track meet."

Soz held back her smile. She had never heard Jazar come on so strong.

"We took pity on you," Rex said.

Soz couldn't help but laugh. "Second-year always whips

first-year. You remember, Jaz? We got our posteriors kicked last year."

"Posteriors?" His mouth curved upward. "You're getting verbose in your old age."

"Old age, pah."

"That's right." He maneuvered closer, insinuating himself between her and Rex. "Pretty soon you'll need medical help."

Soz gave him a quelling look. "Only after you."

He didn't look the least bit quelled. "That's all right, Soz. I'll take it at your speed." He slowed down.

She whacked him across the shoulder. "You just wait!"

"Ah, no." He raised his hands. "I surrender." His grin flashed. "Do whatever you want to me."

"Oh, Jaz." They had fallen behind the others. Rex drifted away with the other cadets, taking a hint Soz hadn't even realized she had given. Dusk was settling over the academy and only a line of red remained on the horizon. A few stars glittered in the indigo sky.

"How does it feel to be a Jagernaut?" Jazar asked.

"Same as before." That wasn't true, though. She spread her arms wide. "It feels great." She knew ISC would face ES-Comm again, someday, but at least now they were better prepared. "It's frightening and exhilarating."

Jazar drew her to a stop. "Soz." The dusk shadowed his face.

She hesitated, puzzled. He was shielding both his mind and expression. "Yes?"

"When the invasion came and I knew you were out there, I—" He shook his head.

"What?"

"I kept thinking of one thing."

"You going to tell me what it is?"

"No."

She crossed her arms. "What, I'm supposed to guess?"

"No." Softly, he said, "I'm going to show you." He grasped her elbows and pulled down her arms.

"What are you doing?"

"This." Drawing her into his arms, he bent his head. Then he kissed her.

"Oh," Soz said. It came out like "Oomph."

Jaz lifted his head with a frustrated noise. "I swear, you have the romantic instincts of a rock."

"I'm in uniform. No public displays of affection." Her pulse was doing odd things, acting up even more than when she had gone into the Dyad Chair. "Ah, hell," she said. She pulled him down again and kissed him good and hard.

They stood that way for a while, on a path hidden in a maze of buildings. After a while, Jaz moved his lips to her ear. "I looked it up in the manual. After you graduate, it's no longer fraternization."

"When we're out of uniform."

His voice turned wicked. "I can take care of that."

"Heya, Jaz. Behave." When he laughed, she pulled back to look at him. "Will you come to the palace with me later, for dinner with my family?"

"Are you sure?" He spoke awkwardly. "I'm not any nobleman, Soz. I'm just a tech's son. I don't want to embarrass you."

She touched her fingertips to his face. Maybe this was the real reason she had never dated. She wanted Jazar. She couldn't have him until she graduated, so she had waited, grumbling and lonely, but patient.

"My family will like you just as much as I do." She thought of how the noble Houses had treated her father. "My father, especially."

He brushed his lips across hers. "In that case, Quaternary Valdoria, I would be honored to accompany you tonight."

"Good." She put her arms around his neck. "But let's not go anywhere with people right now. No pub, no palace, no nothing. Let's just walk for a while."

"I would like that."

Soz went and changed her clothes. Then they strolled through the academy grounds, enjoying simple moments they had never had the time or permission to enjoy before. It was a good night. Soz didn't fool herself that they faced an easy future, but it also held promise. She had seen what her people could do. She had no doubt they would endure.

Family Tree: RUBY DYNASTY

Boldface names refer to members of the Rhon. The Selei name
denotes the direct line of the Ruby Pharaoh. All children of Roca and
Eldrinson take Valdoria as their third name. All members of the Rhon
within the Ruby Dynasty have the right to use Skolia as their last
name. "Del" in front of a name means "in honor of."

= marriage   + children by

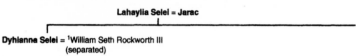

Lahaylia Selei = Jarac

Dyhianna Selei = [1]William Seth Rockworth III
                    (separated)

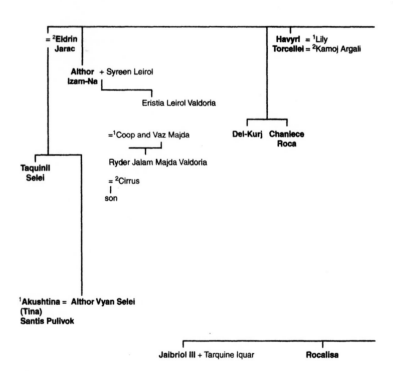

= [2]**Eldrin**
  Jarac

Althor + Syreen Leirol
Izam-Na

Eristia Leirol Valdoria

Havyrl = [1]Lily
Torcellel = [2]Kamoj Argali

=[1]Coop and Vaz Majda

Ryder Jalam Majda Valdoria

Del-Kurj Chanlece
            Roca

= [2]Cirrus
   |
   son

Taquinii
Selei

[1]**Akushtina** = **Althor Vyan Selei**
(Tina)
Santis Pulivok

Jaibriol III + Tarquine Iquar   **Rocalisa**

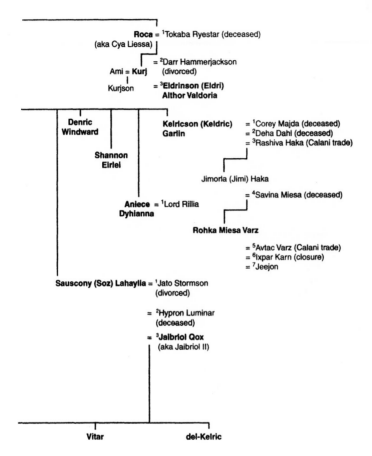

Roca = [1]Tokaba Ryestar (deceased)
(aka Cya Liessa)

Ami = **Kurj**　　= [2]Darr Hammerjackson
　　|　　　　　　(divorced)
Kurjson　　　= [3]**Eldrinson (Eldri)**
　　　　　　　　Althor Valdoria

Denric　　　　　　**Keiricson (Keldric)**　　= [1]Corey Majda (deceased)
Windward　　　　　**Garlin**　　　　　　　　= [2]Deha Dahl (deceased)
　　　　　　　　　　　　　　　　　　　　　= [3]Rashiva Haka (Calani trade)

Shannon
Eirlei
　　　　　　　　　　　　　　　Jimorla (Jimi) Haka

　　　　　　　　　　　　　　　　　　= [4]Savina Miesa (deceased)
Aniece = [1]Lord Rillia
Dyhianna
　　　　　　　　　　　　Rohka Miesa Varz

　　　　　　　　　　　　　= [5]Avtac Varz (Calani trade)
　　　　　　　　　　　　　= [6]Ixpar Karn (closure)
　　　　　　　　　　　　　= [7]Jeejon

Sauscony (Soz) Lahaylia = [1]Jato Stormson
　　　　　　　　　　　　　　(divorced)

　　　　　　　　= [2]Hypron Luminar
　　　　　　　　　(deceased)

　　　　　　　= [3]**Jaibriol Qox**
　　　　　　　　　(aka Jaibriol II)

Vitar　　　　　　**del-Keiric**

*Genetically, Kurj carries Jarac's DNA

Characters and Family History

Boldface names refer to Ruby psions, also known as the "Rhon." All Rhon psions who are members of the Ruby Dynasty use **Skolia** as their last name (the Skolian Imperialate was named after their family). The **Selei** name indicates the direct line of the Ruby Pharaoh. Children of **Roca** and **Eldrinson** take Valdoria as a third name. The "del" prefix means "in honor of," and is capitalized if the person honored was a Triad member. Most names are based on worldbuilding systems drawn from Mayan, North African, and Indian cultures.

= marriage

Lahaylia Selei (Ruby Pharaoh) = **Jarac** (Imperator)

Lahaylia and **Jarac** founded the modern-day Ruby Dynasty.

Lahaylia was created in the Rhon genetic project. Her lineage traces back to the ancient Ruby Dynasty that founded the Ruby Empire. **Lahaylia** and **Jarac** have two daughters, **Dyhianna Selei** and **Roca**.

Dyhianna (Dehya) Selei = (1) William Seth Rockworth III
    (separated)
                = (2) **Eldrin Jarac Valdoria**

Dehya becomes the Ruby Pharaoh after Lahaylia. She married William Seth Rockworth III as part of the Iceland Treaty between the Skolian Imperialate and Allied Worlds of Earth. They have no children and later separate. The dissolution of their marriage would negate the treaty, so neither the Allieds nor the Imperialate recognize Seth's divorce. Both Seth and Dehya eventually remarry anyway. *Spherical Harmonic* tells the story of what happens to **Dehya** after the Radiance War. She and **Eldrin** have two children, **Taquinil Selei** and **Althor Vyan Selei.**

Althor Vyan Selei = 'Akushtina (Tina) Santis Pulivok

The story of **Althor** and **Tina** appears in *Catch the Lightning*. **Althor Vyan Selei** was named after his uncle/cousin, **Althor Izam-Na Valdoria.** Tina also appears in the story "Ave de Paso" in the anthologies *Redshift*, edited by Al Sarrantonio, and *Fantasy: The Year's Best*, 2001, edited by Robert Silverberg and Karen Haber.

Roca = (1) Tokaba Ryestar (deceased)
= (2) Darr Hammerjackson (divorced)
= (3) **Eldrinson (Eldri) Althor Valdoria**

Roca and Tokaba had one child, **Kurj** (Imperator and former Jagernaut). Kurj marries Ami when he is about a century old, in *The Radiant Seas*. Kurj and Ami have a son named Kurjson.

Although no records exist of **Eldrinson**'s lineage, it is believed he descends from the ancient Ruby Dynasty. *Skyfall* tells the story of how he and **Roca** meet. They have ten children.

Eldrin (Dryni) Jarac (bard, Ruby consort, warrior)
Althor Izam-Na (engineer, Jagernaut, Imperial Heir)
Del-Kurj (Del) (singer, warrior, twin to *Chaniece*)
Chaniece Roca (runs Valdoria family household, twin to **Del-Kurj**)
Havyrl (Vyrl) Torcellei (farmer, doctorate in agriculture)
Sauscony (Soz) Lahaylia (military scientist, Jagernaut, Imperator)
Denric Windward (teacher, doctorate in literature)
Shannon Eirlei (Blue Dale Archer)

Aniece Dyhianna (accountant, Rillian queen)
Kelricson (Kelric) Garlin (mathematician, Jagernaut, Imperator)
Eldrin appears in *The Final Key, The Radiant Seas,* and *Spherical Harmonic.* See Dehya

Althor Izam-Na = (1) Coop and Vaz Majda
= (2) Cirrus (former provider for Trader emperor)

Althor has a daughter, Eristia Leirol Valdoria, with Syreen Leirol, an actress turned linguist. Coop and Vaz have a son, Ryder Jalam Majda Valdoria, with **Althor** as co-father. **Althor** and Coop appear in *The Radiant Seas.* The novelette, "Soul of Light" (Circlet Press, anthology *Sextopia*), tells the story of how **Althor** and Vaz met Coop. Vaz and Coop also appear in *Spherical Harmonic.* **Althor** and Cirrus also have a son.

Havyrl (Vyrl) Torcellei = Liliara (Lily) (deceased in 2266)
= Kamoj Quanta Argali

Havyrl and Lily marry in 2223. Their story appears in "Stained Glass Heart," a novella in the anthology *Irresistible Forces,* edited by Catherine Asaro, February 2004. The story of **Havyrl** and Kamoj appears in *The Quantum Rose,* which won the 2001 Nebula Award. An early version of the first half was serialized in *Analog,* May 1999-July/August 1999.

Sauscony (Soz) Lahaylia = (1) Jato Stormson (divorced)
= (2) Hypron Luminar (deceased)
= (3) **Jaibriol Qox (aka Jaibriol II)**

Soz's experiences as a cadet at the Dieshan Military Academy appear in *Schism* and *The Final Key.*

The story of how **Soz** and Jato met appears in the novella, "Aurora in Four Voices" (*Analog,* December 1998). **Soz** and **Jaibriol**'s stories appear in *Primary Inversion* and *The Radiant Seas.* They have four children, all of whom use Qox-Skolia as their last name: **Jaibriol III, Rocalisa, Vitar,** and

del-Kelric. The story of how **Jaibriol III** became the emperor of Eube appears in *The Moon's Shadow*. **Jaibriol III** married Tarquine Iquar, the Finance Minister of Eube.

Denric's story of his harrowing introduction to the world Sandstorm, where he teaches after graduation, appears in "The Edges of Never-Haven" in the anthology *Flights of Fantasy*, edited by Al Sarrantonio.

Aniece = Lord Rillia

Lord Rillia rules Rillia, which consists of the extensive Rillian Vales, the Dalvador Plains, the Backbone Mountains, and the Stained Glass Forest.

Kelricson (Kelric) Garlin = (1) Corey Majda (deceased)
= (2) Deha Dahl (deceased)
= (3) Rashiva Haka (Calani trade)
= (4) Savina Miesa (deceased)
= (5) Avtac Varz (Calani trade)
= (6) Ixpar Karn (closure)
= (7) Jeejon

Kelric's stories are told in *The Ruby Dice* (novella, *Baen's Universe*, 2006; novel to appear in 2007). *The Last Hawk, Ascendant Sun, The Moon's Shadow*, the novella "A Roll of the Dice" (*Analog*, July/August 2000), and the novelette "Light and Shadow" (*Analog*, April 1994). **Kelric** and Rashiva have one son, Jimorla (Jimi) Haka, who becomes a renowned Calani. **Kelric** and Savina have one daughter, **Rohka Miesa Varz,** who becomes the Ministry Successor in line to rule the Twelve Estates on Coba.

The novella "Walk in Silence" (*Analog*, April 2003) tells the story of Jess Fernandez, an Allied starship captain from Earth who deals with the genetically engineered humans on the Skolian colony of Icelos. The story of Dayj Majda, the Prince who was betrothed to Roca in *Skyfall*, appears in the novella "The City of Cries" in the anthology *Down These*

Dark Spaceways, edited by Mike Resnick. "The Shadowed Heart" tells the story of Primary Harrick, a Jagernaut traumatized by the Radiance War. It appears in the anthology *The Journey Home,* edited by Mary Kirk.

Time Line

circa 4000 BC	Group of humans moved from Earth to Raylicon
circa 3600 BC	Ruby Dynasty begins
circa 3100 BC	Raylicans launch first interstellar flights; rise of Ruby Empire
circa 2900 BC	Ruby Empire declines
circa 2800 BC	Last interstellar flights; Ruby Empire collapses
circa AD 1300	Raylicans begin to regain lost knowledge
1843	Raylicans regain interstellar flight
1871	Aristos found Eubian Concord (aka Trader Empire)
1881	Lahaylia Selei born
1904	Lahaylia Selei founds Skolian Imperialate
2005	Jarac born
2111	Lahaylia Selei marries Jarac
2119	Dyhianna Selei born
2122	Earth achieves interstellar flight
2132	Allied Worlds of Earth formed
2144	Roca born
2169	Kurj born
2203	Roca marries Eldrinson Althor Valdoria (*Skyfall*)
2204	Eldrin Jarac Valdoria born
2205	Prince Dayj Majda runs away ("The City of Cries")
2206	Althor Izam-Na Valdoria born
2209	Havyrl (Vyrl) Torcellei Valdoria born
2210	Sauscony (Soz) Lahaylia Valdoria born
2211	Denric Windward Valdoria born
2219	Kelricson (Kelric) Garlin Valdoria born
2223	Vyrl marries Lily ("Stained Glass Heart")

2227	Soz goes to Jagernaut military academy (*Schism*)
2235	Denric trapped on Sandstorm ("The Edge of Never-Haven")
2237	Jaibriol II born
2240	Soz meets Jato Stormson ("Aurora in Four Voices")
2241	Kelric marries Admiral Corey Majda
2243	Corey assassinated ("Light and Shadow")
2258	Kelric crashes on Coba (*The Last Hawk*)
early 2259	Soz meets Jaibriol (*Primary Inversion*)
late 2259	Soz and Jaibriol go into exile (*The Radiant Seas*)
2260	Jaibriol III born (aka Jaibriol Qox Skolia) (*The Radiant Seas*)
2263	Rocalisa Qox Skolia born; Althor Izam-Na Valdoria meets Coop ("Soul of Light")
2266	Lily dies
2268	Vitar Qox Skolia born
2273	del-Kelric Qox Skolia born
2274	Radiance War begins (also called Domino War) (*The Radiant Seas*)
2276	Traders capture Eldrin. Radiance War ends; Jason Harrick crashes on the planet Thrice Named ("The Shadowed Heart")
2277–8	Kelric returns home (*Ascendant Sun*); Dehya coalesces (*Spherical Harmonic*); Kamoj and Vyrl meet (*The Quantum Rose*); Jaibriol III becomes emperor of Eube (*The Moon's Shadow*)
2279	Althor Vyan Selei born
2287	Jeremiah Coltman trapped on Coba ("A Roll of the Dice"); Kelric deals with Coba and Jaibriol III (*The Ruby Dice*).
2298	Jess Fernandez goes to Icelos ("Walk in Silence")
2326	Tina Pulivok and her cousin Manuel go to the desert ("Ave de Paso")
2328	Althor Vyan Selei meets Tina Santis Pulivok (*Catch the Lightning*)

About the Author

Catherine Asaro grew up near Berkeley, California. She earned her Ph.D. in Chemical Physics and her M.A. in Physics, both from Harvard, and a B.S. with Highest Honors in Chemistry from UCLA. Among the places she has done research are the University of Toronto, the Max Planck Institut für Astrophysik in Germany, and the Harvard-Smithsonian Center for Astrophysics. A former ballet and jazz dancer, she founded the Mainly Jazz dance program at Harvard, and was a principal dancer for and artistic director of Mainly Jazz and the Harvard University Ballet. Her husband is John Kendall Cannizzo, the proverbial rocket scientist. They have one daughter, a ballet dancer and mathematics enthusiast.

In addition to the Skolian Saga, Catherine has also written *The Veiled Web, The Phoenix Code, Sunrise Alley,* and *Alpha,* near future science fiction; and the fantasy novels *The Charmed Sphere, The Misted Cliffs,* and *The Dawn Star.* Her work has won numerous awards, including the Nebula for *The Quantum Rose.* To receive e-mail updates on Catherine's releases, join groups.yahoo.com/group/asaro-announce/. To discuss Catherine's books with other readers, join groups.yahoo.com/group/asaro/.